The
Heart
of
Desire

John Klawitter

E-book versions of this book are available in all popular
e-book formats from http://www.double-dragon-ebooks.com

Double Spin

To Lynnie, always you, Lynnie.
Life is short, but love is forever.
How much love?
How about ten billion bushel baskets
Just for a start.
After all, you have to start somewhere

Introduction

Please allow me to introduce myself, as Mick sings in that lovely Rolling Stones song of yours; I'm your fondest dream, and your worst nightmare. And I've been around a long, long time. No, not a devil, you poor, sad little spirit! Why does it always have to be about you and your eternal rewards? I'll tell you a secret. We don't know anything more than you do about your heaven, your hell, your green pastures of endless joy, or your ever-burning cell in hopeless damnation...

See, there you've done it again! You people! There are times you get to every single one of us, you with your oh so very big and special dreams stuck in your miserable little mayfly lives. In that way, you are incredible! So much hope, so much ambition, all wrapped up in such a brief little fireball! It's enough to take my breath away, that is, if I relied on air and the suction of it was a matter of any significance.

Who am I? Or, better said, who are we? From your point of view, we are gods. True enough, with that caveat, *from your point of view.* Closer to the nut: from the little you can see, we are like demigods, at least. But then, with your limited senses, you can't see all that much of the wonder, anyway. Okay then, how can I best fill in the relevant blanks? Okay, sketch the beast, as they say: There aren't a lot of us, a few thousand, more or less. We really need room to roam, and we don't like each other all that much, so before the Great Adhesive Treaty we went about killing each other off with a distressing degree of regularity. Not anymore. We have rules against it. You live by rules; we live by rules. You can understand that.

What else? Well, relative to you, given our natural span, we live a long, long time. I know a few of us who have seen the dinosaurs roam. Yes, actual Tyrannosaurus Rex, stupid beasts thundering about, top of the food chain and not a care in the world. You'd know something about that, wouldn't you?

For all practical purposes in our relationship, yours and ours, such as it is, you might say we're eternal.

Okay, just a little more sketching and then we'll begin: We have all those powers you marvel at but can only begin to understand. Legendary powers. Comic book stuff. Red eyes on demand, of course. You want it, you've got it. There may be only a few thousand of us spread across the splendor, and yet we've inspired the image of some of your best gods. You really have good imaginations—though nothing beats the real thing, baby, as your high-voiced maidens sing over and over in the selling jingles.

That said, there are actually a few important similarities between us. On certain levels, our brain patterns are somewhat alike; that means we often think in similar ways, though we're far less governed by our emotions, if we actually have any at all. This very question is debated by our greatest theologians, and, believe me, over the eons they haven't gotten very far with it. *Do we really feel or do we just think we feel?* Oh, go figure that one.

What are we like? I'm not allowed to say very much, but I can tell you this: Living the relatively long spans we do, our lives are often boring. *Oh, let's take another spin out to Orion; Oh, let's go sun-spume surfing; Hum-hum, let's see if that species is evolving in the sum-sume quad, yadda yadda.*

What do we like? We like intoxication of any kind, including making love to earthlings. (Though supposedly it's forbidden, I've never heard of anyone vaporized for it). And we love anything that goes fast relative to its surroundings. We enjoy lectures and books on cosmology, country-western ballads and rock-and-roll music, and gambling.

Gambling? What's that all about, then? Why gambling? None of us really knows, but here's why, as best I can figure it out: Events and happenings like the expansion of the universe, the orbital swing of comets, the birth and death of stars, the suck of a black hole—these things are all so goddamn predictable. You humans introduce the rare element of chance into our sometimes drab and dreary lives. We love you for it, actually—or, at least, are, in our own way, fond of you.

I can tell you with a great deal of precision and detail when, where and how any two galaxies are going to collide.

But whether Jane is going to kill Jim with that shiny little nickel-plated revolver she bought at the sporting goods store because he fooled around with Joan or Joy...well, we'd have to bet on that. And because we'll pretty much bet on anything, we've had to come up with rules, mostly so we don't interfere too much with the outcomes. We call it The Game, and, believe me, the most interesting stories in our known universe come from your participation. Who would have thought?—an insignificant race of semi-sentient beings whose lives are nothing more than brief comet flashes against the backdrop of the eternal wonder! And yet, you say and do amazing things! We never know what's going to happen next!

I'll tell you one we've got running now. I'm known as somewhat of a storyteller, and I've always wanted to be an author, and there's no rule against it, so, if you've got the time (a little joke there) here goes. It's about a human person a very few of you know as "The Man With The Scar". He's alive now, running around the little mud ball, as one might say. It seems that, about forty of your earth spins ago, as a very young person, The Man With The Scar was dissatisfied with his very ordinary life. We really, really like people like that...you know, "be careful what you ask for"...He caught the attention of one of our recruiters, and we agreed he could trade that ordinary life of his in for a more interesting one.

What's the bet? Well, he doesn't know the specifics, but, straight up, it's simply how long he can survive. So far he's outlived anybody's expectations; fortunes have been won and lost, and he's become something of a legend in our circles. He's even earned a little extension or two (though I was against it, being against the entire idea of extensions as an obvious intrusion, and will vote against it, if and when it comes up again). By way of the perfect example of why extensions are entirely bogus, The Man With The Scar now suspects that, in that long-ago fly-wisp of time when he signed up for his new life, it wasn't a hallucination or a wild, drunken dream. And he's even got it at the back of his mind to change his path. Good luck with that one.

That would be impossible. Nothing he does can really change his deal with us, or affect us in any way, no more than your dog or cat pooping on the floor is going to change your life, your job, your marriage, who you are or what you do. But it is interesting. We endlessly debate what he's going to do next—and, of course, we bet on it.

Why do you even try, oh foolish mortal man? The heart of desire is an ever-opening blossom that can be neither sated nor consumed.
 - Immortal Samajani Kapek, Lessons 13:33

1

He was falling through air, weightless. The icy wind roared in his ears, whipped past the hairs on his naked body in a screaming flow. No, that long primal wail was coming from him as he plunged like a wingless angel, a broken-winged bird, a missile twisting on itself and gone awry. A few hundred feet now. A matter of seconds and he would wink out into blank nothingness. The bleak and frosty landscape below rushed up to greet him and...and...and...

He crashed through a brilliantly colorful stained glass skylight, all reds and greens and golds, still without a stitch of clothing on his bruised body, crashing down through the heavy tobacco and perfume scented air of an Asian casino. He had time to think the word *Macao* as his arms and legs flailed. His skin was scratched and cut, and his torso heavily bruised in a dozen places, tokens from earlier things he'd fallen through. He had a flash impression of Asian men in top hats and formalwear, their ladies in bustle-narrow waists and ornate gowns. They looked up at him in stunned amazement as his battered body impacted hard on the green felt baccarat table and...and...and...

He crashed through the green cloth as if it were thin ice and he was falling through air, past skyscrapers, on his way down while people stared and pointed from the windows. He glimpsed short hair and beaded dresses, city girls looking up from their lunches, all black early Detroit motorcars and horse drawn beer carts and carriages. "Early 1900's," he thought as his left shoulder and one side of his face impacted on the cobblestone street and...and...and...

He crashed through the asphalt like a clumsy walrus diving through a sticky film of coagulated oil on seawater and he was tumbling down, caught in the wake of a sinking steamship, down, down, down past the blue to the deep blue to the blue-black to the blackest black water crushing him from every side and...and...and...

He woke in a fit, shuddering and shaking with bruises and scratches and aches all over his body. He was alone in a small, cramped place on the deck of a boat. He waited while his thudding heart slowed. He listened to the low throbbing of the twin diesel engines from the engine room below. He took a shallow, hesitant breath. No more falling, no more falling...it was his own whisper, a quietly begging prayer for release from the crushing reality of his fright.   Even as he watched, he thought he saw the skin on his naked body healing and stretching itself over his wounds. The crushed bones on his left shoulder plumped, rounded and mended themselves. The bruises began to disappear. The aches were fading into near memory. No, that couldn't be. Nothing more than his imagination. No one else ever saw him actually mending, or if they did, they never mentioned it. True, there were times when his friend, the Old One-Eyed Mexican, seemed as if he was about to say something. But then he would only purse his thin wrinkled lips and shake his head.

The pain subsided, the injustice to his flesh mended flawlessly until just one old scar remained, a long, thin scar that began on the right side of his forehead and ran straight down his body to a puncture on the arch of his right foot. He felt the raised line on his cheek and smiled in sad recognition.

He was back. He was awake...or was he still dreaming?

You have an adventuresome mind, don't you? You're not afraid to go into dark corners. You love life; you want to see it all. You're interested in studying the dark and shadowy alley lurkers as well as the gay dancers happily flitting across the sun-dappled meadows. Something in you is probably also drawn to mummies and tombs, curses, vampires, and worse...yes, there are worse things, unimagined things sitting on the rim of your awareness.

You see, humans actually only sense a small fraction of everything that is. It's somewhere around 5%, I think. Of course you knew that; at least, you suspected it. Maybe you read it somewhere? No matter; you see, that tingle down your spine and the hairs raised in alarm on your arms do mean something, after all.

Some of the old hands at this business of living say it isn't wise to look for trouble, and you've heard many times that it's better to be safe than sorry...but don't we all take the same journey? I mean, yours is a lot shorter than mine, but that's not the point. The question is, do you really want to walk your little way with your hands over your eyes?

Not me. I'd prefer knowing where the vile scratchy spiders, the red-eyed snakelike spitting things and the mean-smelling flesh bugs are, just as much as I want to be sure to get my fill of the pretty brooks, the gentle purple leaves, the rolling fire hills of home. That's me personally, and probably a bit of you, too. That is why you're here, isn't it?

Still, a story like this...well, it's going to stretch your mind a bit. It probably should never have been written. The Game Masters are already saying there should be rules against it, and in a few more years, there probably will be.

Why? No real reason; it's just getting to be that there are rules for everything. You've noticed that, too, in your own world, haven't you?

In strictly human terms, you can't defend this story. In the first place, it's about impossible things. A pattern so against the law of averages is just not possible. Such odd patterns of events absolutely cannot be. Come on, now...danger and death at every corner. Violence and mayhem at every breath. Things happening all the time. And even more specifically, the strangely foreign beings, the demigods obliquely alluded to herein do not—cannot—exist.

On the other hand, suppose, by the very act of writing and reading about such things, we cause them to come to pass? Now there's a reason to pass a law!

Mea culpa, mea culpa, mea maxima culpa! Oops, I think that was the wrong Latin; I was thinking of an old Roman saying about innocence and out pops some old altar boy stuff about confessing. Oh well, maybe nobody will notice. After all, I don't have anything to confess, unless perhaps there is something to those old beliefs. You know, original sin. After all, we are monkeying around with you people and your so-called puny destinies. Ahh, I was pure once. But trailing clouds of glory do we come/ From God, who is our home. Milton? No, Wordsworth. Little matter; you won't have to know the poets to follow along here.

The final word on this one—and you have to believe me—I'm definitely not human and so I don't really know how important any of this could possibly be to you. And it's your fault you're hanging around here. You should be getting your kicks with far more sensitive creatures, mystics *gebornen* with spiritual talents, paranormally enlightened entertainers or perhaps hooded ones safely embalmed in their own prayers who can perhaps let you crouch under the lip of their ponchos and get into the sacred place when you die. Some people say, *Beware the storyteller.* But isn't that a bit like shooting the messenger?

This whole ramble reminds me of *Rosencrantz and Guildenstern*, the two men walking along the seashore; the one flipping a coin and it always comes up heads, heads, and heads. Remember them, after Shakespeare? *For God's sake, what does it mean?* The one asks the other, saying something like that. Well, R&G, maybe it doesn't mean anything. Maybe it is just entertainment. Nothing dark about a coin that always comes up heads, is there? Nothing hinting at deeper meanings, unseen forces, alien claws or flesh-burning suckers in the apple pie.

Not to change the subject, but if you'll indulge me for just a moment, don't you think talking about the world's greatest beer is a little like trying to discuss Hollywood's top intellectuals? It's not as if the young, sexy, in-the-know actors in the beer commercials can actually keg it and stay in the trim. Face the facts, friend; slurping up the suds makes you sleepy and sloppy. Drink beer and you belch, fart and grow fat. And yet the six-pack, the long neck, the wide-mouth and the kegger are celebrated the world over, probably because the noble brew numbs the brain—as if you all weren't already in a stupor. Don't get mad; all of us are, more or less.

Well, let's scramble past that uncomfortable business for now, and move on to the beer. There is one little-known beer that was popular in South Vietnam during that political body called The United States of America's fierce decade of participation in the wars there that had been going on for centuries before catching their attention. That beer is called *Ba Muoi Ba*, Vietnamese for the number Thirty-three. I'm told there's something to the smoldering formaldehyde taste of 33 that reminds old Nam vets of the days when the world was young and there was thunder in their veins.

Which brings us to our hero, the fellow with the falling-through-realities dream. Otherwise known as The Man With The Scar. While he wasn't a numerologist, he was a Vietnam vet, and at the moment we begin this complicated tale of lust, greed and violence, he is mulling over the fact that it had been 33 years since he'd been in Saigon. And this simple thought had him in a defeatist, even suicidal, state of mind.

The Terrible Thing had happened to him in Vietnam over three decades before. It was something strange and difficult to understand, and yet it had changed his life forever...and for no earthly reason that he could think of. He wondered, had he been carefully chosen? Selected for some spiritual virtue or genetic weakness? Picked at random? How could any of that be? To his mind, there wasn't anybody more ordinary than he had been on that fateful night...or is anybody really ordinary?

The Man With The Scar felt the cool sea breeze on his face. He watched the last of his scratches and bruises fade. He concentrated on the substance of his surroundings, as if doing so would keep this reality from fading away. He was on a sport fishing boat, returning to the southern tip of Baja, Mexico. His boat wasn't more than a couple miles out from their berth in Cabo San Lucas harbor. Their progress had been all too slow for his liking, and he had long since stopped looking ahead and had fallen asleep, and that had started those wicked dreams.

Now he sat up and stared numbly to the side, where the boat, a sturdy craft named the Southern Seas, was slipping past the gaunt flanks of the small islands known to local mariners as The Fingers. He was attracted to the desperate stretch of frothy surf where the jagged gray-and-beige tumble of uninhabited rocks slipped into the churning blue-gray sea. For the briefest of moments, he found himself wishing that he had the courage to leap over the railing and sink into the cold, dark water.

The day itself was predominantly gray colored, with the late afternoon sun little more than an annoying red orb hanging in a thick, foggy haze common in that part of the world at that time of year. There was no horizon, and the light was wavering, diffuse and somewhat confusing, like reddish lamplight through milky glass, dim reflections that had begun to lose their way in the thickening knots of fog.

You will now see for yourself the first example of how things conspire against The Man With The Scar. Realizing he wasn't going to have the willpower to test his fortune on the waves, he went below to the small bunk area he called his own.

At the same time, in the steering cabin of the Southern Seas, a scraggly-bearded young mate yawned behind the wheel. It was actually this young mate who first spotted the colorfully attired extremist kayaker paddling in the water near the barnacle-encrusted rocks of Land's End.

"Look at that stupid Yea-hoo!" the young mate said to nobody in particular.

A bored chummer, a young fellow of a certain limited intelligence (but related by marriage to Captain Griggs, master of the vessel), was at that same time fiddling with the electronic fish finder, pushing buttons with a certain idle curiosity.

"Those things tip right over," the chummer said, referring to the distant slim cigar shape of the kayak.

"Huh," the young mate, with two fingers on the wheel, said; and as he spoke, he made a small, precise adjustment, swinging his big charge a bit closer to the kayak.

"Careful, you might swamp it..." the chummer said, not really caring or paying much attention. "How come I can't see him on the fish finder?"

"He has to be under water, stupid. *Fish* finder, get it?" And with that, the young mate gave the Southern Seas another nudge closer to the little banana boat.

The extremist kayaker, a novice weekender, looked up in fright as the huge sports fishing boat veered toward him. From his point of view, it looked huge as a freighter. The kayaker began to paddle frantically toward what he figured was the relative safety of the nearby jagged rocky fingers.

At the same moment, confidently in charge at the helm, the young mate reached for a can of Diet Dr. Pepper. Unfortunately, his foot slipped off the console on which he had rested it, and he started to slide off his chair. He regained his balance by grabbing the wheel. At his unintended command, the big boat lurched even closer to the kayak. The young mate recovered in an instant, but now the Southern Seas was racing far too close to the rocks and with a bit of a yaw that was quickly narrowing the distance. Is this a coincidence, or do you see any fated intent in all this? Well let's continue; perhaps it's too soon for you to be making judgments.

The chummer, no longer bored, stared at the young mate, the doomed kayaker and the rocks.

"Oh, wow..." he said in awe.

The Southern Seas, now swallowing up the horizon, slapped the kayak aside as if it was a matchstick and careened into the slime-coated rocky fingers that raked it from stem to stern.

So you see, The Man With The Scar wasn't even on duty, and when the unfortunate accident happened he was actually below, lying on his bunk and trying to read an odd book by Jack London about a jailbird trapped in a straitjacket who learns to sort of travel using the power of his mind...an ability, by the way, that you all have, but rarely, if ever, use.

When the boat scraped the rocks, The Man With The Scar dropped the paperback and rolled off his bed, instantly alert. His bleached strawberry blond hair was white at the temples, and there were streaks of white in his long, droopy moustache and beard, which over the last decade had been getting on with more salt than pepper. On close inspection, he looked closer to sixty than forty, but he was extremely nimble for a man of any age. He sized things up quickly, rolling athletically to a sitting position on the end of his bunk and pulling on his pants.

The scar that ran like a line down the right side of his face was clearly visible. As he grabbed his socks, he ignored the continuing scar line that ran on down his chest, his thigh and lower leg, finally ending in a dramatic star on the top of his right foot.

"Where is he?" Captain Griggs's rage, muffled but still clear as to intent, could be heard from on deck up above. "Where is my bloody albatross?"

The Man With The Scar sighed. He bounced to his feet like a much younger man. He decided to do without shoes. He pulled on a sweater and moved swiftly to the steps that led up to the rear deck.

It was clear that, technically, he had absolutely nothing to do with whatever had happened; but he knew that dispenser of blame, Captain Griggs, would want to know *precisely where everybody was when.* The conversation would assume the tones of an inquisition, and life would turn more unpleasant before it got better.

By the time The Man With The Scar scrambled up the steps and arrived on deck, the bored chummer—trying to be extremely helpful—had gaffed the drowning kayaker and was pulling him onboard with help from several sports fishermen. Others looked on, attempting to appear industrious and interested, or failing that, hoping for a cloak of invisibility. Unfortunately, that is not a common human power.

Captain Griggs stalked about, glaring his menace at whatever fell to his gaze. He was a gruff and grizzled man who secretly believed he was the reincarnated spirit of Horatio Hornblower, Long John Silver or The Green Hornet. Never mind that somebody once told him Hornblower was a figment of some writer's imagination. Like most humans, there was no talking reason to him; Griggs simply knew what he knew. He puffed out his chest and pulled his left ear, obviously feeling in the Long John mode. He spotted The Man With The Scar the moment he showed up on deck.

"Rhett! Clay Rhett! Get over here and fix this man!" The Captain continued talking under his breath, "Miserable rotten Satan-cursed miscreant...I rue the day I ever let you onboard, oh, yes, rue the day!"

"It's not my fault. Nothing I can do," The Man With The Scar muttered over and over again like a grim mantra, "Not my fault. Nothing I can do."

Still, in his heavy heart, he knew neither assertion was quite true.

His gaze slipped back to the lonely stone bones of the fingers, which were now sliding away into the gray dusky twilight. He tried to sort out his thoughts. The unlucky extremist kayaker would live or he would die. It wasn't for any mortal to say. The Man With The Scar knew the paddler's life was in the hands of the invisible watchers, the red-eyed ones, the howlers and the chess players, the demigods of fate. Whoever and whatever they were. Oh, yes...I've already told you; his hard suspicion is that we're more than fantasy.

"Rhett," Captain Griggs shouted from the stern where the kayaker lay while inept crewmen took turns pounding at him, "For God's sake, man! Take a turn at the CPR."

"I don't know CPR," The Man With The Scar muttered, shaking his head. "And anybody who dresses like that might be better off dead."

He spoke loud enough so Griggs could hear and perhaps not push the point. He wasn't going anywhere near the errant extremist. *Give the poor soggy bastard a little distance*, he thought.

It was a predicament. On the one hand, the fool shouldn't have been out where he was in a kayak—but he didn't deserve to be run over by Goliath. Leaving the scene of his recovery was a small gesture, but The Man With The Scar felt it was the only thing he could do to help.

But then, bone-tired of the way his life was going, he changed his mind. Maybe if he helped out it would make a difference. *Who knew? Who ever knew?* He walked quickly to the scene and pushed the others out of the way. He gave the paddler CPR for a scant few minutes when the man barfed greenish Gatorade all over his shirt.

"Great. Just my luck."

In another three or four minutes, the paddler had staggered to his feet and was taking in great gulps of air and spitting bile and water over the side of the boat. Griggs watched as The Man With The Scar shook his head grimly and went below.

Some time later, the paddler wanted to meet the man who had saved him, but The Man With The Scar had retired to his cabin, and would not answer, even when they recruited the old man with one eye and sent him below to pound on the door to his closet-sized cabin.

"Just as well," the Captain muttered to nobody in particular. "Goddamn rotten albatross that he is."

"Unlucky for you, maybe..." the now revived paddler said, staring in the direction from which The Man With The Scar would not return.

The Captain's frown deepened. "No, son. Don't push the Lady. You got a break, but luck's a bitch; she'll turn on you any time."

2

He was not a homely man or even unpleasant to look at, although he did have that deep scar that extended vertically down his face, a straight old up-and-down mark which split the right side of his face as neatly as if a chalk line had been drawn down from the hairline, through the eyebrow, picking up on the cheekbone and running on down the rest of its cruel path. No one ever mistook him for someone else. *How could they?* Because of his humble station on the fishing boat and his quiet way, people rarely felt they needed to know more. When anyone remembered him for any reason, he was simply The Man With The Scar.

The paddler had lived. They had docked the Southern Seas without running over anybody else, though they did hit the wharf with enough force to send a shudder through the wooden pilings and cause the captain to look wildly about, wondering where his albatross was. They cleaned the boat, scraped combs through their hair and turned a garden hose on their best boots, and then they each headed for their favorite bar or house of fine ladies. The Man With The Scar did his chores; then went below and packed his few belongings in a duffel bag while the old one-eyed Mexican looked on.

"You cannot leave this boat, amigo," the old Mexican finally said. "You must wait until we return to San Diego."

"No, my friend. I'm off here."

"But *Capitain* Griggs will not pay you."

"I'm not so sure he would anyway."

"What about the fifty dollars you owe me for the cards?"

"You deal from the bottom of the deck."

"Oh. That hurts me, amigo."

The Man With The Scar raised one skeptical eyebrow.

"Of course," the old Mexican continued, "if you agree to go on my nephew's radio show, I might be willing to forgive your debt."

The Man With The Scar shook his head, but the one-eyed Mexican smiled. "You already promised, señor. That night you got into my tequila."

The Man With The Scar shook his head again, but the steam seemed to be out of the gesture. The old Mexican's smile broadened, "It will make you famous, señor."

The Man With The Scar threw his duffel bag over his shoulder and walked a half block away from the pier where he rented a simple room in a cheap motel where he knew the sheets were always threadbare but fairly clean. That night he slept the sleep of the damned, fizzed like a burned-out lightbulb until the first dawn light disturbed the gauzy curtains on the grimy windows.

He woke instantly, tense and ready to leap in any direction. After a moment, his heartbeat slowed, and he thought again about the desolate finger rocks at the lip of the land's end. Peaceful. They seemed so stark, and yet so at peace. *They were themselves, nothing more, nothing less. Could he say the same for himself? Certainly not. What was he? A wanderer. Or, closer to the heart of the matter, what had he become? A cursed albatross. He had become the man to whom things happened.*

He sat on the edge of the bed and stretched, hearing his muscles crack and snap in protest. He stood and went through his Military 12, a series of simple stretching exercises he'd picked up in the army. Nothing fancy, but by the time he finished fifty push-ups, he could hear himself breathing loud and clear in the humid air.

He opened his duffel bag and separated his clothing into two piles. *One for the dry and one for the wet.* He put the dry set, those he wore when hiking around the country, back in the bag. He left his seafaring clothing in a pile by the foot of the bed. The cleaning lady would no doubt find a use for them, as rags if nothing else.

The shower was hot for a while, and then the water started to chill. He stood under the weak spatter long after it retreated from tepid to icy. He wanted to be rid of the sight, the sound, and the smell of the sea. He was certain of one thing: when Griggs left Cabo on his next jaunt, the captain's unlucky albatross would not be onboard.

The Man With The Scar selected a tan polo shirt and a pair of hiking shorts with baggy pockets. It was late morning. He'd have time to pick up his mail and maybe pay for a short visit to the lovely dark-eyed Jolita before he had to be at the radio station. He'd learned never to expect anything ordinary, and as the hours progressed he was surprised that the day went by without incident.

There was a small happening when, in the middle of their throes of passion, Jolita's square old bed crashed to the floor. The lady started screaming; after all, he had a history with her. There was the time when the bed had caught on fire, and the funky 1930's fire truck had crashed through the cantina downstairs. And the time of the rabid dog, and the time of the mistaken but jealous gangster.

Now, once The Man With The Scar was sure the heavy bed frame wasn't going to continue a plunge through the somewhat flimsy floor to the cantina below, he gingerly rose from the mattress and reached for his pants.

"Calmness, Jolita," he ordered. "It was just the fire of your passion."

"But it was an antique, this bed!"

"No, my sweet. I'm the antique."

He found his wallet and fingered out enough money to put an end to it right there.

"I've got to run, sweet love," he said.

"What? So soon you go?" She managed a pout as she deftly counted the money.

"Yes. I'm going to be a star, and stardom waits for no one." He smiled sadly.

"What?" Her pout became a puzzled look.

"Radio. I'm going to be on the airwaves."

"Oh, yes! I heard! That is tonight? I'm coming to see this!"

She grabbed a sheet and dashed for the shower.

"I'll wait for you downstairs in the cantina," he said.

"You can wait here..."

"No, I don't think so. I don't want your shower to rain frogs."

"Noooo..." She laughed, but it was an uncertain sound. "Frogs? Could such a thing...?"

"Downstairs," he repeated. He gave a little wave and made his exit.

Talking about himself was against The Man With The Scar's personal rules, which were on the side of privacy. His fate was his, and his alone. On the other hand, a bet was a bet, and he'd lost one to the old Mexican with one eye. So now he would show up for a guest appearance on the little known and, in his circles, much derided Buddy Lucas "Talkin' America" radio show.

The Man With The Scar and old One-eye had been at sea together for six months. They had chased albacore, yellow fin tuna and the snappy fighting dorado from onboard their 110-foot sport fisherman's boat. The Southern Seas was an old PT boat with powerful engines, and it had converted nicely to its new mission. Captain Griggs ran it with limited patience and even less intelligence, but The Man With The Scar hadn't had many options when he signed on. He served as the grill chef and part-time bait boy. The Man With One Eye was too old to do much of anything but shout encouragement during those madcap moments when somebody yelled *Hookup!* and the big ones came storming, boiling up around the boat like the powerful predators of the sea that they were.

The rest of the time, The Man With One Eye slept, except on the long night hauls when he found sleep impossible. Then he and The Man With The Scar would sit in the dark on the forward deck and play cards or swap old lies while the billions of stars turned in, for a human, seemingly eternally slow circles overhead.

For just over 190 days the two men's lives had been fairly predictable; they would head out into the Pacific for two weeks and then back in to Cabo for one night to take on new fishermen and wash their laundry. An occasional trip to their home port in San Diego and back. And then Cabo and back out to sea again. The regularity of it all—in spite of a string of incidents like the sudden unseasonable typhoon, the near drowning of the captain, the ship's kitchen catching on fire, hitting the dead whale's floating body, nearly running into a 49-foot sport fisher named the Coyote, and that time the starboard diesel motor froze up on them off Santa Maria Island with a stiff onshore pushing them towards the reddish black volcanic rocks, and, of course, running over the fool paddler—in spite of these and other things, the regular in-and-out of their common routine had been so unusual for The Man With The Scar that he had found a faint ray of hope that perhaps his life was finally turning around.

Buddy's radio station was tawdry digs, run-down and smelling of stale beer and old fish tacos. A Carta Blanca beer commercial played as The Man With The Scar and his party entered. Lola, middle-aged and world-weary, sat behind the controls, glaring at the other people crowding into her small area.

There were: the old one-eyed Mexican, Jolita the young hooker and the one-eyed Mexican's nephew, Juan. Juan wore a colorful Hawaiian shirt unbuttoned down the front, and a loincloth. The shirt was unbuttoned because it had no buttons; they had been eaten by the large green-and-red parrot that endlessly walked from Juan's left shoulder to his right, and back again.

Lola gave Juan a dirty look. "If that damn green chicken craps on my control board, I'll cut his throat."

"He's worth more than you are," the nephew protested.

"Cut his throat! Cut his throat!" the parrot squawked in approval.

"Nephew, I told you not to bring that killer bird!"

At this, Lola gave the parrot a wary glance. "He's a killer?"

"He is my friend," Juan said proudly.

"The world's only attack parrot," the old one-eyed Mexican confided proudly to Lola.

"I trained him myself," the nephew added, the unmistakable note of pride in his voice.

Lola ground her teeth.

"Keep him away from me," she said.

Buddy Lucas was short and obese, with a glittery, fearful smile. The Man With The Scar instinctively took a step back, thinking Buddy's smile revealed too many of his too large yellow teeth.

Buddy liked to think of his show, "Talkin' America", as *pirate radio*; he thought of himself as a border outlaw, driven from the homeland by injustice, a scofflaw in the tradition of the legendary Wolfman, who had beamed radio from the other side of the Mexican border into the U.S.

Actually, "Talkin' America" wasn't much of a pirate radio show. Its signal was broadcast from the most distant southern tip of Baja and only capable of reaching the United States under the most rare of meteorological conditions. As such, the show was more likely to irk the scrawny band of dirt bike riding revolutionaries armed with their homemade zip guns and old M-1 rifles who lurked in the local low-lying hills than to be actually heard (much less taken seriously) by anyone in the States. San Diego was over a thousand miles away. Even El Paso, Texas, which was a few hundred miles closer than Los Angeles, was still hidden behind the spine of the Mexican Sierra Nevada mountains, and they tended to block 100% of the potential listenership in the Texan direction for "Talkin' America".

The Man With The Scar had pushed through the double doors into Buddy's inner sanctum. He held his hand out to Buddy, who ignored his gesture.

"You're late," Buddy said. "I thought you wasn't coming."

The Man With The Scar shrugged and grinned, giving a thumbs-up to the old one-eyed Mexican.

"Fastest fifty bucks I ever made," he said, turning to leave.

"No. Wait. Where you think you're going?" Buddy pointed to the stool on the other side of the mike. "Sit down."

- The dank little studio's air conditioning was acting up again, and Buddy could feel the beginnings of a foul mood moving in him like a storm off the gulf. He felt hot and sweaty as he played a 60-second Dos Equis commercial back-to-back in both Spanish and English. He tried to shake off the uneasy feeling he had about this scar-faced guest. *He was Buddy Lucas, Galahad of the air, and knight of the spoken word.* Once the Dos Equis button rang off, he cued Lola to slide a bar up and down the food-sticky soundboard in front of her, and the hoarse and pirated signature cut of Bruce Springsteen's "Born in the U.S.A." came up. *Hoarse* because that was the way Bruce was, and *pirated* because it was against Buddy's personal code of ethics and light-years out of range of his show budget to ever pay music royalties for anything. If the greedy lawyers of ASCAP wanted anything of him, they could jolly damn well come down to Cabo and get it. Let 'em try! Talk about squeezing lemons!

-

- He was going to have to stay. The Man With The Scar tried to hide his disappointment. He looked around. The host of "Talkin' America", for all his powerful vocal delivery, was barely over five feet tall, and had the general shape of a squatty pear with stout, stubby twigs for legs. Running down and broadening swiftly from his smallish, hairy chest, his sagging bottom put a heavy strain on the lower part of his faded Ralph Lauren polo shirt where it almost but not quite met the tightly stretched waistband of his cheap no-name XXX sweatpants.

He wore palm-twisted go-aheads on his tiny, unwashed feet, and there was a small, braided pigtail sticking out from the back of his oily, jet-black hair. A high, thin pompadour was rigidly frozen over the bald top of his head.

In the adjoining room, Lola dialed the phone.

"Taos, New Mexico, *por favor...*T-A-0-S," she added sarcastically, spelling out the word.

- Jolita petulantly hit Juan on the arm. The parrot flapped his wings and looked frightened, scrambling over to the nephew's far shoulder.

"Shhhhh!" Jolita hissed, "It's starting!"

Lola dialed "Born in the U.S.A." down with her free hand and pointed through the glass.

"Good Evening, Fellow Exiles," Buddy crooned, "It's Buddy Lucas, expatriate American, your Galahad of the Air, your Knight of the Spoken Word."

There was a muffled noise from somewhere in the studio. Buddy turned, momentarily annoyed, but he had a show to put on. He didn't stop to run over and take a peek in the gritty rest room adjoining his studio. If he had, he would have discovered two scruffy guerrillas wiring old dynamite to a Dusty alarm clock to make a primitive bomb. A third guerrilla, who had made the noise when he tumbled through an open window into the rest room, stood up and brushed off his clothes.

"*Aie, chiwawa...*" the newly arrived terrorist wailed, looking at his soiled pants.

"Lightly, lightly," his comrade warned.

"Put it in the bowl," the third man advised, pointing to the bundle of dark red dynamite sticks and then to the toilet.

Back in the business end of the studio, Buddy glared at Lola, who shrugged and pointed at him one more time.

Buddy cleared his throat, "Hmmm, yes...Tonight we've got a real treat for you. His name is Clay Rhett. He's a fellow American, one of the most decorated American soldiers in the Vietnam War."

Buddy took courage from his own voice, a voice that resonated in a deep, oily and yet somehow intimate bass.

The Man With The Scar frowned and glanced over at the old Mexican with one eye. He was obviously unhappy with the opening topic.

The old Mexican shrugged and confided to Jolita, "He talks in his sleep."

Actually, it had been during one of their drinking contests that the old man had dragged some details about the Nam War from his American friend, bits of information that he had no doubt passed on to their host for a small stipend.

"Yes," The Man With The Scar reluctantly replied to Buddy's probe, but not before shooting a dirty look at the old *vaquero*. "I enlisted and did three tours in Nam."

This was the kind of guest into whom Buddy felt he ought to be able to sink his canines. Buddy knew the sentiments of most of his ex-patriot audience ran highly in favor of the war. He loved to get poor patriotic vets on the air and poke their vague and silly balloons. *When in the course of human events a man becomes so screwed up that he actually volunteers to get his ass shot off, then he deserves to be harpooned on the Buddy Lucas Show.*

- "Is it true you enlisted right out of high school?" Buddy asked.

"No, I was in Grad School at UCLA, studying for my—"

Buddy, not liking the sound of that, cut him off, "Don't you think anybody who signed up for our disgraceful little cow pie in Southeast Asia should have had the decency to die for the cause...? Hmmm?"

His guest gave him a slight shrug, which wasn't of much use, this being radio. The talk show host's wide face flushed red.

That shrug from his guest gave Buddy a little shiver of what he thought of as *rightful rage.* He hadn't quite yet figured out how to get the needle into this guy. The quiet ones, they could be a problem. But give him time; he just needed a little time. He had a 100% success rate cracking open Nam vets. Digging into Southeast Asia freaks was one of his specialties, like spoofing runaway nuns about their careless pregnancies and sandpapering political correcties who had somehow drifted far enough from the safety of their cozy suburban nests in the good old U.S. of A.

Buddy eyed his poor victim over a cup of cool coffee laced with Wild Turkey. His guest, who he saw as silly and more than a little stupid, was really a sight to behold, with his sun-bleached mustachio and his receding hair cut at the shoulders in a pageboy style not popular since Ben Franklin— or maybe since that brief love-and-beads nonsense in the 1960's.

At that moment, The Man With The Scar was thinking Buddy had the look of someone related to greatness in an unfortunate way; in appearance if not in fact, Orson Welles' sweaty tub-thumper of a little brother. He felt a sad little tug for the man, sitting there all knotted up and sweaty in his investigative reporter role.

Like so many of you people, Buddy had all the cards of happiness in his hand. He could be living the life of royalty in Cabo. He could be the local personality, the great Buddy Lucas. But he didn't seem able to visualize it, to grasp what was within his reach. He wasn't happy with his own cards and wanted some other hand.

Buddy saw he was going to have to dig a little deeper. "Why are guys like you still around?" he asked.

"What do you mean, 'guys like me'?" The Man With The Scar gave him tit for tat. His voice was spookily quiet, and its calmness bespoke worlds of unwelcome moral judgment.

Buddy went for it like a bull at the red cape. "You know," he sneered openly, "Pretending you know more about it and somehow have a better moral compass than other people."

"What other people?"

"You know. People who didn't go."

"You mean draft dodgers?"

Buddy blinked his wide eyes and opened his mouth, but no words came out. It was a moment before he could shift his attack.

"I *mean*...what the hell was you thinking, man? Going over there like that?" he asked belligerently.

"Well, that's a good question," The Man With The Scar said, seemingly still not upset by Buddy's little *demo of attitude*.

27

"I was in grad school at UCLA. This was in 1961, and I was hearing a lot of propaganda both ways, and I wanted to see it for myself."

"Bullcrap!" Buddy snorted, "There weren't any real demonstrations until 1965!"

"Well," The Man With The Scar smiled, "I attended a pretty big one in the square in front of Royce Hall in the fall of 1961."

Buddy was about to accuse his guest of blatant revisionism when Lola caught his attention. She was waving and pointing to the telephone.

The "Talkin' America" Show put serious effort into tracking down old girlfriends, digging up hometown police records, and scanning local back-home newspapers to embarrass its unfortunate guests. At the heart of Buddy's nightly production was an attempt to prove that anybody who made his or her way to Cabo had dark secrets in their underpants, dirty little stuff that was worth sifting through and holding up to the light of day. This was certainly true in his case; it had to be true of just about everybody.

"Well, we're going to get to more of your boy-hero-in-the-jungle stuff," Buddy intoned, "but first, we've got a blast from the past on the line, all the way from New Mexico, somebody that you're going to really want to talk to."

The Man With The Scar's face seemed to pale under his heavy tan, but he said nothing.

There was a glint from the big zirconium ring on Buddy's little pinky as he flipped a switch with his chubby forefinger. Almost immediately, the hesitant voice of a young man said, "Hello? Hello?"

"Hello, there...America! This is Buddy Lucas, calling direct to you from the 'Talkin' America' Show."

"Never heard of it," the young man said. There was a strain to his voice, as if he found the call annoying. "Is this one of those local disk jockey gags or something where you try to be funny by making a person look silly?"

The Man With The Scar gave a brief nod of approval, but said nothing.

Buddy saw he was going to have to carry the load by himself. "Come on, man!" he growled into the mike, "This is Buddy Lucas, broadcasting with ten billion gigawatts from the tip of Baja."

"From where?"

"Baja, Mexico, you idiot."

"Hey, no need to get rude. Just a minute, my mom will be right here."

Buddy oozed a triumphant grin in his guest's direction. He pointed to the mike. "Do you recognize that voice?"

"That's my son, Hector." The Man With The Scar did not seem pleased.

Seeing his guest's reaction, Buddy's grin widened and he gloated, "Hector, is it? Hector Protector, Son of Erector. Why on earth did you saddle the kid with a moniker like that?"

"That was his mother's—"

"Well then, what was your wife thinking?"

"She's not my wife. We were never—"

"I don't think we have to know that," Buddy quickly intercepted. Actually, he loved his audience to know every intimate detail, but he would have preferred them revealed in another way. He was Mr. Pirate Radio and Mr. Pirate didn't like surprises.

Unfortunately, this interview, which had seemed like a nice idea for a slow weekday show, wasn't going well. Buddy couldn't get a handle on it, but he had the vague feeling that they were inexorably headed for a crash and burn, like the fab shots of that old kraut dirigible hitting the runway with all the people running and screaming like cooked ants. Only he, Buddy Lucas, was beginning to suspect that he himself might be one of the ants.

Buddy wrinkled his fat nose, thinking about the old man who had lined up his guest. It was a pity, and a surprise, too; when he wasn't in the jungles or the mountains or out on a fishing boat, the old one-eyed Mexican had always been one of his best scouts, foraging at the hotels for interesting people who had scooted down from north of the border for one dark reason or another.

But this guest wasn't an easy talker; there were issues they probably should have worked out beforehand, and Buddy could feel the little rivers of sweat starting down his back. He wiped his forehead with an already soaked kitchen paper towel and turned back to the phone speaker as a woman's voice came on the line.

"Hello?" The woman's nasal western twang, compressed over the telephone, was as strained as the young man's had been.

"Hi, there, ma'am. This is Buddy Lucas on the 'Talkin' America' Show."

"Never heard of it." The reply, tight-lipped and suspicious, was the last thing Buddy wanted to hear.

"Oh, come off it, lady. Everybody's heard of Buddy Lucas and the—"

"Just stay on the line for another 30 seconds, Mr. Dirty Mouth Pervert," she said grimly. "We've got a tracking service for crank calls. I think we can have you in jail before sunrise."

"Now wait, I'm not a—not anything like that," Buddy said, suddenly off the scale on the defensive end.

The Man With The Scar nodded sympathetically. "Joanie can do that to you."

"This is the 'Talkin' America' Show, coming your way—"

At that moment, The Man With The Scar wasn't concerned about Buddy's ratings; he was thinking that somebody was going to pay for going through his private codebook to get Joanie's phone number. He glared again through the glass window at his friend, the old Mexican with one eye. The old man grinned back and waved happily.

"Joanie doesn't want to talk to me," The Man With The Scar interrupted, not realizing he was on an open mike, or maybe, Buddy thought angrily, not really caring one way or another.

"Who is that?" Joanie asked from Taos, New Mexico, her voice rising on the static-loaded phone line. "I heard another voice. I heard him before, and I heard him just then! *Who is that*?"

The sharp edge of her attitude hinted at disaster, the prow of the Titanic just scraping the tip of its fated iceberg; but

Buddy, now running on inertia, had no choice other than to plunge ahead. "We've got somebody here, an old friend of yours, you're really going to want to talk to."

"Not in this life," the woman said, her words yapping over the long-distance carrier line in a shrill series of barks, the sound of an out-of-control Yorkshire terrier going after an interloping squirrel on a backyard telephone line.

There was a dull click as she hung up, and a frustrated Buddy found himself listening to the buzz from the long-distance line.

"Well, back to Vietnam," he said, with a hacking little cough to clear the phlegm and fury building in his throat. "Tell us how you became the most decorated man in Southeast Asia."

"One of the more decorated," The Man With The Scar corrected him. "And I didn't do anything to earn it. I mean it came about through no doing of my own."

"What do you mean?" Buddy screwed up his lips. "That sounds like pure bullshit to me."

"Can you say that on the air?"

"I just did. This is Mexico, son. What the hell are you trying to tell me with this Nam stuff? How many curve balls you got in your pockets, anyhow? You did it or you didn't do it. It's that simple."

"Not quite that simple," The Man With The Scar replied. "In a particular way, I can only describe my...adventures, if you will, by saying *they happened to me*."

"Come on, don't be so fricking modest, man; you must have done something to get the shiny little medals. Purple Hearts. Bronze Stars. Special Clusters. You got the whole medal factory here. What was it? You went in there and showed invader-gangster muscle, sprayed the jungle, raped the women, and killed a few babies along the way—right?"

"No," the man said, "none of those things. It's more like, it's my fate..."

"What-the-hell-are-you-talking-about?" Buddy asked through clenched teeth.

"I am always in the place where things happen, always in the center of the action. Always."

"My bullshit detector is off the end of the scale here," Buddy said cheerfully, pressing a little special sound effects button that gave out a weird *boing!* sound.

"Well, I don't care if you believe me or not. And it really doesn't matter whether I attract fate or not, does it?"

"You mean 'whether you did'," Buddy corrected like a prim sixth-grade teacher. "Past tense. We're talking about Vietnam here."

The Man With The Scar figured, *What the hell, let it all hang out. He was just another crazy old Nam vet, crazy as a coot from the blood and the slime and the leeches. Throw him on the pile with the other crazies who came back from every war we'd ever fought and forgotten. Nobody from here to Marble Mountain was going to believe him anyway except Toomley, and Toomley had been among the missing for several years now.*

"No. The war, as you say, is long over, but it's still the same. If something exciting and horrible is going to happen, chances are, I'll be there."

Buddy raised both hands, palms up like the old Catholic picture of the Sacred Heart of Jesus giving a blessing, in a gesture that perfectly represented the way he had neatly and perfectly trapped his nut-ball guest. "Well, nothing's happened here, and you're sitting right there, in that chair across the mike from me."

"Give it a little time. Something will."

"Oh, sure. You're saying that, wherever you go, disaster strikes?"

"Adventure strikes," the man replied in a voice that was barely above a whisper. "I said *adventure.*"

Buddy realized he'd been neatly counter-lectured, *Ka Bing, Ka Bang, Ka Boom, just like that*! *Jesus, what do you do with a nut-ball?* he asked himself. He snorted, the anger and disbelief obvious in his tone, "Come on, that's stupid. It's just not possible. Take the last big earthquake in Mexico City—"

"I was there."

"*Jesu Christi Morris!* What kind of a freak do I have on my show? What did you bring me, here?" He waved his fist and shouted directly at the plate glass window, behind which

32

the old man with one eye gave a small, sad shrug, realizing his fees for digging up show guests were almost certainly a thing of the past.

Buddy took a heavy swig from his cold coffee mug; he was finding this new direction even more frustrating than the aborted family interview.

"Look, this is the 'Talkin' America' Show, here. People take us seriously; that means no voodoo, flying saucers or crystal light people."

"We were talking about Mexico City," his guest said helpfully. "The earthquake."

"Okay," Buddy replied through clenched lips. "Score one for you. But so were six million other people. How about that big hurricane that swept over Hawaii a couple of years ago? Come on, you going to tell me you were there, too?"

"No, I missed that one. But I was on an Aloha Airlines 737 on April 28 in 1988 when the top of the fuselage blew at 24,000 feet, somewhere between Hilo and Honolulu."

"Okay, but—"

"And I was at Clark Air Force Base when the big volcano blew. You remember, Pinatubo...? And at Mt. Saint Helens—"

"Yeah, sure...Alright, I'll give you a couple eruptions; you know, *Into every life, a little volcanic ash must fall*, but—"

Buddy never got to finish his sentence. He opened his mouth, but whatever was going to come out next was interrupted by a tremendous explosion that tumbled him off his chair. The walls buckled, and dust and bricks flew through the air.

The Man With The Scar instinctively opened his mouth to save his eardrums. He didn't think, from his split-second analysis of sound and flash and the general look of the flying debris, that anybody would be killed.

His luck, or fate, or whatever Buddy might have called it, had held again. The rebel militants had chosen that moment to detonate eleven old sticks of dynamite in the bathroom next to Buddy's broadcast booth. That hated symbol of *gringo* interference in Latin affairs, the "Talkin' America" Show, was off the air.

The three triumphant guerrillas shook their fists through the big hole in the wall of the studio.

"Yip, yip, yippee!"

"Death to Talking Americans!"

"Buddy Lucas sucks!"

And with that, they hopped on their tinny old motorbikes and roared away.

No one was seriously hurt, but the broadcast booth, which was in the middle of a row of swank little shops in the lobby of the Hotel Mar de Cortez, was a shambles.

The Man With The Scar rose to his feet, dusted his pants and examined a small scratch on his wrist. He gave Buddy a shrug and a look that somehow managed to be sad and triumphant at the same time. His ears were ringing, but he was used to that. He helped the dazed Buddy to his feet.

"I don't have to say 'I told you so.'"

"We're off the air anyway, a-hole," Buddy snarled. "What did you do, blow up my studio to make your crazy point?"

"No, but that's not a bad idea."

"Who's going to pay for all this?"

"You mean the 'Talkin' America' Show doesn't have comprehensive insurance?"

"You got to be kidding."

"Too bad. I think I'm having fainting spells. My lawyer will be in touch."

The Man With The Scar gathered up Jolita, Carlos and the Mexican with one eye and headed for the front door, which was hanging by one hinge.

"Hey, where you goin'?" Buddy yelled after him.

"Over to the hotel bar. You don't think they've cancelled Happy Hour because of a bomb scare or something stupid like that, do you?"

He knew he was going to have to ply the old man with one eye with Dos Equis and tequila shooters to find out how much he knew. That codebook had secrets worth an almost unimaginable fortune. Old One-Eye was admittedly a self-taught reader, and he garnered his knowledge by trailing a slow finger down the newspaper page, and moved his lips while he read.

The Man With The Scar's codes were all reversals with plucked vowels placed at the beginning or end of the string. Chances were, it was all gibberish to the old Mexican. Still, he had gotten the uncoded phone numbers. The Man With The Scar would have to get some idea of just how much the old man had figured out.

3

It was a rainy afternoon in Oakland. Dusty was sitting in the sparse little office of Dusty's Car Repair, a deserted Shell station he'd bought and fixed up as his own legitimate enterprise.

Dusty was chilling out, honking over the times with a few of the brothers who hung around the place when the plump white grandma with the blue-rinse hair marched in, all in a huffy rage with her list of things which should have but hadn't been fixed on her spiffy little Plymouth Neon.

Dusty played two characters most of his life, running either cold or hot, depending on how he read the circumstances. Now he automatically put away Flame Boy and brought out Ice Man. Ice Man stood at attention and respectfully *Yes, Ma'am'd* his way through the long, woeful recital. Ice Man had all the cool of the world. Ice Man endured.

"Dusty, you should be ashamed," the old woman lectured like a schoolteacher. She was a schoolteacher. Indeed, she had been his second year high school English teacher, back at Oakland High before he went on to San Jose State. All that, but she couldn't melt Ice Man...and she didn't even know it.

"I'm sorry, Mrs. Rudimaker. I just can't seem to get good help here." Ice Man gave her the hangdog penitent shopkeeper's look, hands wringing, eyes wide and innocent and shoulders hunched in near despair.

Behind him, the bros who were hanging out gave a low chorus of sotto voce *Whoa's.* A flush came to Dusty's light yellow-beige features and the little alarm bell deep inside him muttered, *Somebody is going to have to pay.* That was Flame Boy stirring. *Later, Flame-ster, later,* one part of his brain said to the other—*just give me another moment here with the white mamma.* Ice Man continued without further interruption, "I'm going to make this right for you, Mrs. Rudimaker. And what's more, no charge for you. In fact, I'm going to tear up the check you gave us this morning, for the work we did not do right."

Another, even louder *Whoa* erupted behind him. The mask of civility slipped a bit from Dusty's calm features, like cheap makeup that was starting to crack or ooze with sweat. Ice Man didn't like interruptions when he was in the middle of serious business; Dusty silently vowed somebody was going to get himself or herself seriously dead over this.

"Well, you don't have to..." the old schoolteacher said in her high, tight voice. But she was retired on a fixed income; the sharpness of her moral vision was ground down by the constant economic pressures of her life, and her protest wasn't very strong.

"No, Mrs. Rudimaker. I wouldn't feel right doing it any other way." He went to the cash register, rang it open and fished under the money tray for her. In a grand gesture, he tore her check and tossed the pieces in the air.

"I don't know what to say..."

- "Oh, no," he said, gathering up the torn bits of the check and pressing them into her hand, "it is I who should apologize. You taught me so much of how to Do and Be in our society. Please trust me to make things right for you." Ice Man gave her a little half bow and accepted the keys from her. Mrs. Rudimaker's car keys were on a pink plastic poodle key chain with her house keys and probably the key to her safe deposit box as well. Ironically, they were entirely safe with both Ice Man and Flame Boy. People like Mrs. Rudimaker had to be protected; they were the solid-gold alibi for the things he did in his other world.

"I'll have that little white car of yours ready by three this afternoon, ma'am. And it will be 100% perfect, or I will personally know the reason why."

Mrs. Rudimaker left Dusty's office in a fluster of happy small talk. She hoped he would come to some of the football games, and he promised he would bring his girl to the homecoming dance if she could get away from her volunteer job at the hospital.

Dusty stood silently and watched as she got into her dim-eyed son's faded blue Ford pickup and was driven away. He was already feeling Flame Boy begin the hot bubble-and-rush through his veins.

Dusty was a complicated piece of work, and far more than the sum of his visible parts. He thought and spoke in a range of dialects, easily slipping from a literate highbrow to the slurred patois of the streets. Now, his mood slipped past gang violence towards the hot and dark reaches of his personal alter-psyche. Ignoring the smirking brothers in the office, Flame Boy marched quietly into the back service area where four or five mechanics were standing around, arguing the Raiders' chances and wasn't Al Davis truly the *dumbest* goddamn owner in the entire goddamn NFL to actually come back to Oakland after they'd let him off the hook the first time?

Dusty shuffled through the pile of work orders on the desk until he came to the one for Mrs. Rudimaker's white Neon. *Once again, Georgie Porgie!* The white-hot thought served to stoke his fury. *Always Georgie Porgie Pudding Pie!* Without a second thought, he picked up a heavy ratchet wrench and swung a vicious blow to the head of a big white kid wearing greasy mechanic's clothes with the name George stitched on them. Georgie Porgie sighed and dropped like a stone, and Flame Boy began working on his back in the general area of his kidneys. He punctuated his words with vicious kicks while the other mechanics scattered like flies to the farthest corner of the service bay where they buzzed at each other about what the fuck was going on.

"How-many-times-do I-have to-tell you?" Flame Boy shouted from between clenched teeth.

"Oh, man," one of the mechanics said, "Oh man."

Flame Boy spun around and reared back like he was going to attack the person who had spoken. Instead, he threw the wrench at George. The killing blow missed George's head by inches and the heavy chrome plated hunk of metal scuttled across the grease-blackened floor.

Dusty addressed them all in a voice that hissed and sprayed in the open bay like chunks of molten metal. "You want to get ahead. You want to learn a profession. Okay by me. But you got to do the work. This is a place of business, *do-you-hear-me*?"

There was an eager chorus of "Yes, boss, yes sir, boss!"

"Okay, then. Now get him out of here before I take a drill to his eyes. I don't never want to see his sorry white ass around my place again. Not ever, do you hear me?" They had to give him the *Yes, Boss!* chorus again before Flame Boy was appeased enough so that Dusty could turn from them and stalk back to his office.

Evening came to the southern tip of Baja. The Man With The Scar through his right eyebrow sat at a table at his favorite bar, sorting carefully through a small stack of first class letters and a larger, irregular and multi-colored pile of junk mail. The letters were largely junk mail, too, but the only way to make sure was to open them.

He was relieved to see none of the thin, official white letters that indicated a bank closure or a move of safe deposit box location that would have called for a response on his part. There were no personal letters.

He opened a chartreuse envelope from Chicago Heights, Illinois. He'd gone to high school there an impossibly long time in the past. The envelope contained a simple flier, also on chartreuse paper. Even though you couldn't call it personal, it was signed by (or at least stamped with the signatures of) three of his old high school classmates. The flier fluttered from his fingers and he had to retrieve it from the floor.

As he did so, he was suddenly conscious of the distance of his years, of being halfway around the world from the innocence of his youth. The three were inviting him to attend his 40th high school reunion. The faint and jumbled memories of his high school time tried to make a run on his present, but they couldn't break through the hard shell built up over the years. All that felt very long ago and very far away, as if those things belonged in another childhood lived by someone else. Still, he mused as he took a sip from the brown bottle of Carta Blanca on the table in front of him, the brutal reality of the matter was that things always were in every way connected to the things which occurred before them. If one were to string all the events leading to where he was at this place and time, they would inexorably lead back to those earlier, purer moments when all was Algebra, English Lit and embarrassing woodies caused by the barest glimpse of the perky breasts of the girl in the fuzzy pink sweater who sat in front of him and one aisle over in Mr. Lawrence's homeroom.

He bent over the wooden cantina table, nearly overcome by a sweeping sense of loss and nostalgia. *Now I'm little more than a weepy old man,* he thought to himself with little comfort. Tears briefly sprang to his eyes. He rubbed them away with the back of one deeply tanned hand. He remained motionless for a long time while the distant red-golden tropical sunset spilled from the veranda where he sat, light dancing across the shining sweep of the Sea of Cortez. He sat hunched over on the tiled veranda and the walls behind him were heavy with splashes of climbing purple and fuchsia bougainvillea.

His thoughts were years away, and he didn't notice as the fiery sun slipped down behind the distant ocean bay horizon. The guests were in from a blistering day on the hotel golf course or back from their day run after sailfish and swordfish, and a little Mariachi band was already courageously bleating its way through a weak and off-key version of "Tequilaville".

He visualized again the bleak rocks at land's end outside the marina, and wondered if a cold gray landscape was all that was left to his life. Perhaps his fate was to be worn down by constant adventuring until nothing at all was left. Perhaps the scar had been a warning, and he would be shot and blown to pieces, bit by bit.

The Man With The Scar remained for a long time on the picturesque patio at the southern tip of Baja, and the row of brown bottles grew on the table in front of him. He shuffled back and forth through his letters, but he already knew what was there, and each time he came back to the bright green one announcing his high school reunion. He couldn't say for sure why, but he was half-tempted to go.

He thought back to the day he'd hired on as short-order cook on the Southern Seas, the gig that had lasted for almost seven months. That had been one of the boat's rare two-day stopovers, and he was running from a young Lois Lane who was convinced he had to be a pyromaniac as he'd been camping in the local mountain parks when several wildfires lit up the San Diego skyline. After that, his life at sea hadn't been bad, and he hadn't been planning any changes. He could bear Captain Griggs's foul temper, in return for the relatively mild series of mishaps that had befallen the sport fishing boat since he had arrived onboard. His plan, back before they'd run over the goofy fool kayaker, had been to pick up his mail, do some laundry, have a few beers and then sleep it off in his bunk on the boat as they headed out to sea with a new load of eager sportsmen.

But the fool paddler had proven to be the last straw after all, and when they pulled into Cabo, The Man With The Scar realized he'd had enough of Captain Griggs's whining, needling command. It was an unfortunate moment to leave the boat, and more unfortunate that he had at the last minute informed the captain of his intentions. On the one hand, Griggs suspected he was the source of the bad luck that had plagued the Southern Seas, but on the other, the captain was always shorthanded. There had been a brief, nasty scene, and The Man With The Scar was dismissed without being paid.

The waitress came by with another set of beers. The Man With The Scar's attention was back on the Reunion letter.

The envelope announced that it was from Gwen. He'd convinced himself that he remembered the pretty sloe-eyed Gwen, with her lovely almond shaped face, her fresh white skin and lovely limbs. What had it been, forty years ago? *Yeah, forty years.* They'd both been just kids then. Was her name really Gwen? Just when he was sure it was, the memories fuzzed and slipped away and he couldn't remember for sure. There were a lot of things he couldn't keep exactly straight anymore. It didn't bother him much. He thought of it as clever disassociation, *having a senior moment,* in the few times he thought of it at all.

His eyes were expressionless as he stared out to sea. After a time, the dusky-skinned waitress flounced her cotton dress with the bright flower print on her return to the bar. Her passage knocked the empty envelope to the sawdust-covered floor. His hand trembled slightly as he reached down to the uneven faded red paver tiles. He turned his feelings over in his mind, trying to figure out why he found the letter so important. And in that moment he realized that he really would be going back.

Several thousand miles to the north, a steady rain settled in over the cold and inhospitable waters of the bay, and night brought an uncomfortable October chill to Oakland. It was late, time to close up in Dusty's Car Repair. The repair bays were almost empty and there was nothing to do but watch the steady sheet of rain pounding down on the asphalt. Ice Man and Flame Boy were at rest, at least for the moment. Dusty sat in his office with his gang of amigos, playing Mister Cool while he impatiently waited for two of the brothers to finish polishing his jet-black BMW 840ci out under the overhang where the pumps used to be when the place was a gas station.

"Hey, hurry it along," he complained.

"You say you want it perfect," one of the polishers shot back at him.

"Perfect mean *fast,* too."

Flame Boy yawned, wondering if he should wake up. Dusty had learned a lot of things in his thirty-odd years, but patience hadn't been one of them. His motto was, *The man who waits for things is a dead man,* or maybe, *Everything bothers me.*

From where he sat he could see the service bays were empty, except for one on the end, where he was letting Randy tinker with an old VW bus the kid had inherited when his father died. Randy was a little-white-boy-lost, a straw-haired honky yuppie who liked to hang out with the down-home boys after his daytime job as a flunky at one of the big stockbroker firms across the bay. He'd developed a little dope habit until Dusty had taken him aside and talked at him like a stern older brother. Dusty knew Randy was still sniffing a little on the side when he could get it, but the lad seemed to have it under control, so he didn't say anything more. To Dusty, you were an employee or a client; it was all the same to him.

The two brothers in the office with him were employees. They were just a couple of black kids from Amarillo, straight out of high school where their budding football careers had kept them from pursuits which would have landed them in jail, until high school ended and they took to scoring on local convenience stores and liquor stores. They were two more lost souls, 100% crack heads on the lookout for the next big score, and Dusty knew they would do anything for him.

"I need a clean face," he said so quietly he was almost talking to himself.

"What for?" Leon asked eagerly. Leon was only 5' 9", but wide across the shoulders, with ropy arms good for wrapping up a football or beating the manager of a Winchell's Donut Shop senseless with a tire iron, the latter the reason he'd hotfooted it out of Texas with his quiet sidekick, Bopo, in tow. Bopo, dubbed "Bopo the Blob-Man" could have been Leon's double, except that he was even bigger across the shoulders, and he moved twice as slow. He'd played offensive line, clearing the way for the nifty runs that had made Leon Texas High School All-Conference and given him visions of carrying the ball for the Dallas Cowboys. That was back before they realized their constant failing grades weren't going to earn them the high school diploma necessary to get into college ball, that necessary stepping-stone to the NFL.

Dusty sighed, "Bro, I need a messenger to go down to Mexico an' pick up something that belongs to me and bring it back to right here."

"We could do that, boss," Leon said, making it sound simple as picking up a loaf of bread for his mamma.

Dusty yawned more deeply and wondered out loud why his simple wax job was taking so long.

"We could, boss, we could," Leon repeated.

"I don't think so," Dusty said.

"Oh, man, give us a shot," Leon pleaded.

"You just think about it for a minute. Two lunkhead niggers, black as crows and dressed in fancy duds, driving a big, red truck full of frozen fish across the border. Now tell me, what is wrong with this picture?"

"Everybody know black folk likes to do fishin'," Leon stubbornly insisted even while he saw the vision of the thousand dollars or so that such a mission would be worth begin to dissolve in front of his eyes.

"Catfishing, maybe..."

"Yes sir, boss. Catfishing on the Mississippi!"

"Which ain't nowhere near Mexico...When they ask, what you going to say you was doing south of the border, nigger-boy? Looking for day labor? Deep sea fishing? Porking the Tijuana mules in the alley behind the Blue Fox?"

Leon didn't take offense; when spoken black-to-black, the word *nigger* has many shades and nuances unknown to or ignored by the current mania for correctness in communications.

"You look wrong for the job. First thing you know, the gentlemen at the border is going to want to have a closer look at your cargo, my friends. And those fish ain't going to stand close inspection."

"Well, I bet me an' Bopo could do it, anyways..." Leon's voice trailed off, like he'd run out of mental gas. He was tanked on ambition but exhausted on imagination.

"Maybe...just maybe..." Dusty was speaking to himself again. Leon unhappily followed Dusty's gaze to the end service bay where Randy was industriously hammering away at the disconnected muffler on his VW bus.

Leon was understandably miffed. "Oh, we don't get the deal, but you going to let that yuppie airhead make a run for you?"

Flame Boy stirred in his sleep. "Goddam it, I'm just thinking out loud, Leon. Just thinking to myself out loud."

Leon, who knew the signs, backed off right away.

Right about then, the two novices popped the last rag and were done with his car, and, looking at the way it shone and glistened in the night with the rain beading on its flawless black surface, Dusty decided it had been worth the wait after all. He peeled two fifties from his ready roll and handed the money across to the kids.

"Throw the white dude out and close up, would you?" he said to Leon. And without waiting for a reply, Ice Man slipped behind the wheel and drove off into the night. The Bolshoi was in town, and, if he pushed it a little, he could still pick up Baby Doll and get across the bridge in time for the opening curtain.

4

When I say "we", remember I mean "you". With that caveat, shall we begin?

Did anything at all happen exactly the way we remember it? Aren't we always taller, stronger, more handsome, and certainly far more heroic in our personal adventures, the second time around? And if this is so, wouldn't it be better to fling ourselves full throttle into life the first time, so that we could actually experience the actual thrill of adventure, rather than just remember it?

Still, isn't that the very definition of the word *impetuous*? Why can't we be both impulsive and measured at the same time? Assuming the impossibility implicit in the definitions of those two ways of being, what are the lives of the headstrong and the daring really like? The common belief is that such lives are necessarily brief, flaring like golden comets across the sky, one brilliant mark against the night and then gone forever.

There are people thrown into the center of the dusty pit of life who can't ever seem to claw their way to the relative quiet of the sidelines. While it isn't quite that simple, The Man With The Scar is one of these. But, at least for the moment, a truce with his fate seems to be in session. And this is as good a time as any for our Hemingway tribute. You'll know when it starts. Everything will become simple and yet significant.

The Man With The Scar sighed as the fat violin player with the greasy iron-gray hair came over to his table and took a sip from the closest of the row of beers lined on his table.

"Get your own beer, Carlos," he said.

"You are sad, *señor*?"

"Yes, Carlos. I am thinking of a time long ago and far away."

"Ahh, it is a woman, then?"

"Yes."

"Tell me of her, *señor*." Carlos put down his violin and slid into the chair across the heavily varnished table from The Man With The Scar. The violinist was very fat, and there wasn't much room, and so several of the empty bottles fell from the table.

"Gwen. And Beverly. And Karen."

"Three women?! Try to love three woman, ees like a ball and chain."

"Two women." The Man With The Scar had long been aware that most of Carlos's wisdom came from the Nashville balladeers.

"What?" Carlos gave him a blank look.

"Two women, Carlos. It's a country western song. 'Trying to love two women is like a ball and chain. Sometimes the pleasure ain't worth the strain. It's a long old grind, and it tires your mind.'"

"Well, then, *señor*. Three women, ees even *mucho* more worser grind than that."

"Yes, I suppose it is."

He signaled the waitress. "*Dos Carta Blancas, señorita*."

"Thank you," Carlos said, reaching for his bottle when the girl with the tray was still halfway across the room.

"Don't thank me. It's the only way I can keep you from drinking out of my bottles, which is not hygienically sane for either of us."

"You are saying my breath is bad, *señor*?"

"That too, Carlos. That too."

The beers came and they were silent for a while.

"The tuna are running again," Carlos said.

"Yes, I know. Late for this time of year. Do you go out with the boats?"

"No, *señor*." Carlos laughed as if that were a funny joke. "My son, Pablo. He takes the boats."

"Ahh, yes. Pablo."

"And you, *señor*?"

The man fingered the scar above his eye, remembering another boat and then the red roar of the claymore mine, the people flopping about like bloody, broken fish on the deck of the My Canh floating restaurant anchored on the bank of the wide and muddy Saigon River. That was over thirty years ago, just another memorable night in the Mekong Delta. Not his most memorable, but enough for now.

"No. I do not take the boat. Not anymore."

"What is this sadness of the three women?"

"It is a story of another time and another place. A time when the world was young and innocent and happy."

"I would like to hear it," Carlos said politely, "but not now. I must return to my band." Carlos finished off his beer in a few quick swallows and rose, again knocking some of the empty bottles from the table.

"Perhaps you should be more careful," The Man With The Scar admonished.

"Perhaps you should drink less," Carlos replied. "Then the bottles would not be in my way. *Vaya con Dios, señor.*"

"Vaya con diablos, señor."

The little band strummed and plunked and tooted a bit before swinging into a sour and offbeat version of "Achy Breaky Heart". The Man With The Scar turned his attention back to his letter. He was hearing another song, a chant, actually. *We're from Bloom, Couldn't be prouder, If you can't hear us, We'll yell a little louder.*

He wondered if the young couples still walked in the fresh green of the spring woods in May and June, loitering along the roundabout shortcut from the school to the football field. Odd, he hadn't thought about that forest path in years, the trail that led to his first lessons in love. *Blue and White, Fight, Fight; Blue and White, Fight, Fight!* He remembered light brown hair falling in tangled, perfumed piles about a young girl's bare shoulders as she lay back on a bed of spring grass by the mossy, rock-strewn creek. *Who was it, that first time, that first time, that first time?*

"You are unhappy, *amigo*?" The husky voice had the barest hint of accent.

"Nostalgic, Jolita."

"Shall we walk along the beach?"

"Not tonight. Tonight I think of home. Or, at least, of a home that once was."

Jolita slid into the chair vacated by Carlos. She was short and thin, but for a moment her dark, luminous eyes seemed to hold the hope and laughter of the world.

"Was the money enough to buy you a new bed?"

"Yes. Very much enough."

"At least no one was hurt."

"What make you so sad tonight?"

"I don't know. I received this letter." He handed it across to her.

"This ees not sad; ees funny. I like the airplane. See him? See the funny man flying there." Gwen or Beverly or Karen had used a computer drawing of a man in a chunky biplane towing a sign on which was typed "Bloom Township High School Class of 1956 40th Reunion."

"Yes," he agreed. "The airplane is funny."

She set the letter on the table and gave him a last look, her large, dark eyes imploring, her ruby red lips pouting.

"No," he said firmly. "Some other night. I've broken enough beds for the week."

He was thinking what it might be like to hitchhike back to Chicago, and that started him thinking of his favorite boyhood book, "On The Road". Crazy Jack K. racing his vintage Hudson with the thundering V-8 engine back and forth across '50s America. After reading that book, he, himself had thumbed it across the country dozens of times, riding the rails, camping out and living the beatnik times. The golden days after college and before the Vietnam thing.

Forty years had passed by already, and it felt like pages turning on yesterday. He remembered standing in the icy October rain outside a bus stop in Southern Ohio, knowing all he had to do was take a bus north and west around the udder of Lake Michigan and he'd be home to Steger, Illinois, in less than a day. Home was everything he knew: the Inland Steel mill, St. Liborius Church, pretty, plump Grace Ann, the gritty-brick and peeled-paint wooden apartments of South Chicago Heights, the old Lincoln Theater and the KarmelKorn shop with its big white-and-black sign out front, the old family homestead on Chicago Road where there was probably a blueberry pie baking at that very moment, or maybe some warm cookies sticky with melted chocolate chips.

But home was safe, and if he went back, he knew what he'd become. At least, forward, he didn't know. After a while the rain didn't stop but an old faded green farm pickup did. He had thrown his small suitcase in back and crawled up after it. It wasn't bad, scuttled forward so the rain missed most of him. Ten more local rides from southern to northern Ohio, and then the freeway in a one-shot to New Jersey. And that wandering road of his youth had eventually led to the army, to a special place in Saigon called *Coeur Desir*, and to the one special night that had led to everything that followed after, that had dictated everything he had endured. That night when, as a naive young man, he'd been tricked into signing the strange parchment and his life had become a serial adventure, an unpredictable comic book that went on and on, new chapters following the old in an endless stream of adrenaline pumping happenings. And thus ends our Hemingway tribute. Come on, you can't keep doing a thing like that forever. Why do you think the guy shot himself?

West across the bay from Oakland, Magnificent Millicent Abernathy—Millie, for short—came back to the big neo-Victorian mansion on the family estate in Palo Alto to announce to her parents the fantastic and incredible good news that she was pregnant, the somewhat less joyful news that her boyfriend Randy didn't want to get married, and the total bummer that she was probably going to keep the baby, anyway. The parents, not wanting the priceless china broken again, agreed to meet her in downtown Palo Alto.

Millie stood on an agreed upon street corner, and at the prescribed time a long black limo pulled up. It had the words Abernathy Industries painted discretely on the side. The door didn't open, but the window rolled down, halfway, and Millie soon found herself in an argument. As her mental processes were somewhat unique due to an overcharge of young adult hormones and a mild case of Tourette Syndrome, she was at somewhat of a disadvantage.

"What-what-what-what?" she shouted, oblivious to the attention she was garnering from passersby. "What do you care? You've never cared!" Here, her commentary drifted into something of a rap impersonation, "C-c-c-c-care-care-care. D-d-d-d-dare-dare-dare." Millie would never be accused of stuttering. Her repetitive phraseology was more of a verbal tic, almost painful in its delivery and certainly distressing to watch.

"Millie, get in the car." Her father sounded tired and bored. She knew him well enough to know it wasn't boredom; appearances meant everything to him and he was dreading another public scene. It was the Internet age; another few minutes and they'd be flooded with paparazzi. While he was wealthy but not famous, he had social and perhaps even political ambitions, and both publicly and privately his daughter was a constant prick in the big red balloon of his self-image.

"Oh, George," her mother said, "She just likes to make a scene."

"I announce I'm p-p-pregnant, and I'm making a s-s-scene?" Millie's voice suddenly changed to that of an officious doctor, "Why yes, Mrs. Abernathy, your daughter is in fact pregnant. Hem, obviously with child." And again, her mental cogs slipped into a cross between modern poetry and gangbanger hip hop, "Just my luck, fuck a ducka nucka chucka bing bang, nucka nucka chuck..."

"Congratulations." Her father's sarcastic voice drifted out the window.

"No doubt," Millie replied, snapping back to the harsh realities of life. "How about 'here's $5,000 to get rid of the s-s-sweet little love child?!'"

"Don't be ridiculous," Mrs. Abernathy said. "George, give her $2,000."

"Oh, two. Oh, two." Millie counted on her fingers; then switched gears again with lightning speed, this time to an attitude of ridicule and scorn, "Soooo, you think you can buy me off with your sordid funny money?"

By this time they knew Millie like an old show. The fact that she'd made up most or all of what she said from remembered scraps of movies, talk show conversations and old family arguments did not escape them. They were nearly positive she'd made the pregnancy up, the way she fabricated nearly everything else in what she saw as her pathetic and worthless life. Her Grandpapa Abernathy, now thirty years under a big marble slab, had helped the Stanfords to establish the university that bore their name. Millie's parents were on a fast track of high society, political influence and time-consuming jet-setting events. They had little time for Millie, and as she had now reached the age of adulthood (if not reason), she was operating under circumstances that could be described as *last chance.* In fact, were it not for the small but vital block of voting stock in the company that Gramps had left her, Millie would have been long gone from their lives. And good riddance, that.

But things being what they were, her father handed a check out the window.

Millie snatched it quickly. "You won't be seeing me again, s-s-so kiss me goodbye, darlings!"

"Never would be too soon," Mr. Abernathy said.

"Oh, if wishes were horses..." her mother's bored voice drifted from the luxurious interior. As the limo pulled away, she gave a casual wave out the window.

Millie pushed a credit card into a nearby ATM, oblivious of the stares of passersby as she chanted to herself, "If wishes were horses, beggars would ride. If turnips were watches, I'd wear one by my side...and if this was my own credit card I wouldn't be having so much f-f-fun. Fun-run-cun...no, that's 'cunt'...Punt-runt-funt. Huh, funt. That's not even a word."

Millie was extracting $300 from the machine when Randy pulled up behind her in his classic '74 Volkswagen Van.

"Thank you, Mummy," she said. "You shouldn't leave your purse lying around the house. Never know what scum might be about."

Randy brought her back to the present, shouting to make himself heard. "Millie! *Millie!* What did they say?"

"Putzer! Putzer-boy futzer! Love me tender, love me, do!"

Millie took the money from the machine and jumped in the van. She gave Randy a familiar smooch and her brightest smile, and settled into the front passenger seat, and her mood switched like lightning to one of grim determination.

"Daddy says he'll have you killed unless you pop $5,000 for the abortion."

Randy looked at the check he'd taken from his shirt pocket, "But I've already agreed to $2,500."

Millie snatched the check from his hand. "You sweet g-g-g-gerbil-dick. Just scribble a similar for the difference."

"But..."

"Don't be stupid, cupid. Daddy would love to have you killed. He kills for s-s-sport. He could do it for 500 beanos. Five hundred little chill-pills and you're a slab on the morgue..."

She thought about it for a moment; then corrected herself. "No, that's more correctly you'd be *on* a slab *in* the morgue...hey, do you think morgues still have slabs? Just what is a slab *for,* anyway?"

She stashed Randy's check and the little wad of bills from the ATM in the back pocket of her jeans.

He gave her a vexed look and reached in his briefcase for his checkbook.

"Make it $3,000 even," she said. "I'm going to need airfare."

He wrote the check without saying another word. "Will that be all?" he asked coldly as he handed it across.

"I really do need a ride," she said.

He slipped the car in gear, and they pulled away from the curb. For the first time, she saw the pile of baggage in the center part of the van. The middle seat was missing, replaced with an assortment of duffel bags.

"W-w-wait, w-wonderful Wee Willie. What's going down, Randy-Dandy?" she asked.

He gave her an evasive glance, pretending to be busy with his driving. "Oh, I might take a little trip."

"*Just where* are you going, Mandy-Pandy-Smandy?" Millie asked.

"South of the border."

"Oh, sure—let's slip-slip-slip, just a little trip. And what about little old preggie me? Left all alone with ba-bee, maybe? Come clean futzer-Putzer."

"Now Millie, this is business..."

"Schmizness, flizness. So is the two thou big ones you owe me, slick dick. No, you don't cream out of my sight, muster-fuster-luster-buster-boy".

"Millie, I swear..."

But then as only she could, she shifted smoothly into nice. She leaned over and blew softly in his ear. A vacation sounded nice; anything to get out of town. Randy ignored her, still playing the cold potato, but she knew she could thaw him with a little friendly persuasion. The Putzer had always been putty in her hands.

It was another of his Baja evenings and The Man With The Scar was sitting on the patio with the thorned purple bougainvilleas, drinking Mexican beers and thinking of the days gone by. The band swung into a local favorite, "The Loco Cabo Man", and he ordered another round of Carta Blancas and a shot of tequila. The waitress gestured and he indicated she should leave the bottle.

He should have left already, if he was going to get to the reunion in time. He didn't know why he was hesitating. When he hitchhiked, he meandered the back roads of America like an old stream looping through green lowlands. He raised the double shot glass and saluted Gwen and Beverly and Karen.

"*Saludos, Amigas,*" he muttered.

"So, drinking alone again, eh *Gringo*?"

It was the old, one-eyed man who had chosen to leave Griggs and the Southern Seas at the same time as The Man With The Scar, for a return to his career selling jungle birds with his teenaged nephew. The man was attracted to tequila like a Baja devil moth to flame.

"Yes, of course I drink. Drink is the writer's curse. It enables us to see too much of ourselves. And I drink alone because I'm feeling sorry for myself."

"That ees so much of literary crap, my friend. You write nothing, and I question if you ever did. And you drink because you like it." The old man slid into the seat opposite him. "In fact, you do everything because you like it."

"Well, that may be true," The Man With The Scar said, "but I'm not going back to the Southern Seas. I've cooked my last bacon-and-egg sandwich on a tilting grill while gulls crap on your head and barbed heavy metal flies in every direction."

"You know, *amigo*, Meester Big Shot Buddy Lucas has the local police looking for you."

"I heard. He thinks I dynamited his show."

"Somebody should have done it long ago."

"Where are your exotic jungle birds tonight?"

The old man shrugged and gave a negligent wave of his hand in the direction of the street as if his precious birds were only of the slightest importance.

"May I, *gringo*?" He reached for the bottle.

The Man With The Scar nodded. "Why not? You will anyway."

"The birds, they take care of themselves."

"You're not afraid some invader-gangster colonialist from Connecticut is going to run off with them?"

"That is about all I am afraid of. I am a dangerous man, *gringo*. I was in the war, you know."

"Yes, you told me."

"I did?"

"Yes. Actually, many times."

The old, one-eyed man poured himself a double shot and picked up the reunion letter, which The Man With The

Scar had allowed to slip to the floor. He squinted carefully at it, running his finger down the page. He was a very old one-eyed man; his wrinkled hands shook, and some tequila spilled from the glass, which he'd filled to the brim. It ran across the page, forming a small puddle at the bottom where the bold words read **DETACH AND RETURN WITH PAYMENT BEFORE**—and the rest was torn off.

"Thees Contempo Restaurant, it ees a very good place?"

"You would like it, old man."

"Will they have a mariachi band?"

"Perhaps not. Perhaps a band to play the old favorites."

"Ahh. I would guess, a piano, and drums with a cymbal and those brushes to make the swishing sound..." The one-eyed man nodded in approval.

Another fight had started in the bar, but it was a place noted for its many brawls, and the two men ignored the flying bottles and assortment of sailors, fishermen and tourists who were tumbling, wrestling and smashing at each other.

"Yes. Or an accordion," The Man With The Scar said, ducking as a potted cactus flew in his direction.

"What sort of favorites will they play?"

"Perhaps 'Old Cape Cod', or 'Good Night, Irene'."

"Ahh, yes." The old man seemed lost in reverie for a moment, and then he began to sing in a surprising tenor voice, "Going to spend an evening een the Salt Sea Air/ Quaint Little Villages, here and there...You're sure to fall een love...een Old Cape Cod..."

"Yes, that's the song. But do not sing it anymore. It makes me very sad."

"This makes to be a special gathering, *jefe*," the old man said. "And you must leave town, in the first place, for your implication in the dynamiting of Buddy's show." He grinned at The Man With The Scar and then squinted at the page until his single eye was almost closed. The Man With The Scar couldn't tell whether he was reading or laughing. He decided not to worry anymore about whether the old man had deciphered his codes.

"You shouldn't read in this candlelight, old man," he said.

They had shipped together as crew members, the old man leaving his birds with a young man who wore a gray loincloth and coming onboard at Cabo, and The Man With The Scar shipping out directly from San Diego, the two of them trading their lives on the land to cook, swab decks and chum bait for small-hearted Captain Griggs.

"I am proud that I can read."

"Of course, you would be." The Man With The Scar wanted to say something else, but the tequila was a shining fire in his brain and he wasn't quick enough. Now he would have to hear the story of how his friend had learned to read. When you've been to sea for several months, you hear certain stories not once, but many times.

"I learned to read the newspapers which I picked up in the streets as a boy. First the Spanish, and only later the tongue of the *gringos*."

"Yes, but it is not good to read in the dim light. It will make you blind."

"No, only *la masturbacion* will make you blind."

"Who told you that?"

"Father Filipo at the Church of the Madonna. But now that I am old, I do not have the urge very often, anyway."

"Oh. Well, he must know."

"What do you mean?"

"I have seen Father Filipo. He does have very thick lenses."

"He is a very holy man."

"The lenses of his glasses are thick as coke bottles."

There was a long silence between them. The man hadn't wanted to insult the old man's religion. He had to admit he was very tired. Perhaps he should not have made the decision to leave the Southern Seas. The ocean life was wonderful, at least after the first two dog days of seasickness. He thought about the endless rocking of the seas, the billion stars scattered overhead at night, the way the boat would arrive at small islands after being out of sight of land, and thought about how all this made him forget the endless sea of

57

troubles he had traveled since that one fateful night in Saigon when he had unwittingly signed his life away.

Now, for no reason but the letter he'd received which informed him of his high school reunion, he remembered sitting in Mr. Lawrence's homeroom in the seat in front of his cousin Robert. Class was over but he was suffering a hard-on big as a baseball bat for Kathleen Johnson, the sugar-sweet girl two desks up and one row over to the right.

"Come on, ding-a-ling," Robert had said. He had a flippant, churlish way. Robert would say things like that so the gang of bums he hung around with wouldn't suspect how smart he was. The Man With The Scar remembered that while he himself had always scored high on those stupid, prying tests, Robert was always stratospheric, off the charts.

He'd pinched himself hard on the thigh, harder and harder until the pain mounted and his woodie softened enough so he could stand without causing himself pain. Then, using his bookbinder as a shield, he limped out of the room after Robert.

Forty years later, looking out through the open arch of the covered patio, The Man With The Scar could see the evening swallows flitting against the last orange light of the swiftly fading sunset. *How had he made such a mess of things, run through all his luck, to end up here at the southern tip of Baja with maybe enough of his own change in his pockets to last out the year?* He held the end of the letter up to the tip of the candle in the center of the table in front of him. The chartreuse colored paper caught fire, but the flame fizzled out when it reached the damp part where the old, one-eyed man had spilled the tequila.

"Ahh, fate," the old man with one eye cackled.

"What? No, it's just that you spilled booze all over that end of the paper."

"No, *Meester Gringo.* Eees your Lady Luck, decided here. You must go to zee Contempo."

"Don't talk to me about fate. With the money in my pockets I don't think I could make it to L.A." Technically, at least, that was true. The Man With The Scar never talked about the nearly billion dollars at his disposal in various banks around the country and offshore accounts around the world. He always thought of it as *Toomley's Money*; if he were to use it, the last frayed cord that somehow held him aloof from a fate worse than death would be severed. Bad enough that it was there, he thought, dismissing the idea of that blood money lying on a broken pallet at the bottom of a mineshaft, the top quarter of it squirreled away at Toomley's request into deposit boxes all across the face of America, into lovely little white-pillared banks in Kansas, brick-faced banks in Georgia, shabby storefront banks in urban areas on the East Coast and great savings and loan institutions in California and Florida, New York and Illinois.

He had so many boxes stuffed full of tight packets of fifty and one hundred dollar bills that he had codebooks in five special deposit boxes, where he also kept the keys for the rest of them. And then there was offshore, so much money it became more than the sum of what it could buy; like he imagined it might be with drug money, the sheer bulk of it, the logistics of moving it around, had become a major problem. With increasing regularity, bank mergers and closures had forced him to travel across the country to relocate the contents of a savings box before the safe was drilled and its contents removed. So far, he hadn't lost anything, but he figured it was only a matter of time.

Not that the money was dirty; it wasn't exactly legitimate, but as far as that went, it was clean as a whistle. Still, let one safe deposit box be drilled, and the rumors that had floated around the country would be validated, and an old and dormant investigation would be renewed with great vigor and enthusiasm. Never mind that he had five solid identities, including passports and social security numbers, in his main boxes. The computer age had built webs unthinkable only twenty years ago, and he fully believed it would be the beginning of the end for him.

"Nonetheless," old one-eye was saying. In the flickering candlelight, the old man's one clear eye assumed a look of great and ancient wisdom. "Captain Griggs will have to pay you the six months he owes if you go back to San Diego.

Do this first and then you will have the money to go see
Contempo. Your path is clearly written for you."

But The Man With The Scar wasn't listening. He had
slid from his chair and was lying under the table with the wood
shavings and shards of broken brown bottle glass. The
double shot of tequila on top of a long afternoon of beers had
been too much for him. Under the table, he stirred restlessly,
and a soft moan came from his lips.

The old man with one eye squinted down at him for a
moment, and then reached for the bottle of pale gold liquor.
He could see the little worm floating around at the bottom of
the bottle. He wondered if he could get down to the worm
before the bartender came by to retrieve the bottle.

The old man sighed, and pushed the bottle away. He
waved to Carlos, signaling him to come on over. If their
advanced warning had been accurate, it would be nearly
midnight before the police came looking for The Man With The
Scar; and, if luck held, the old man with one eye and Carlos
would have their friend safely tucked out of harm's way by
then.

Clay Rhett was dreaming the Nam dream again. It was
almost the only one he ever had, except for the scary
adventure ones. It returned to him over and over again,
several times a year, and he invariably woke in a sweaty
panic, looking feverishly about for the contract paper he had
signed. Of course, it was never there.

This recurring dream was based on the actual event
that had taken place in his younger days. At the time, he was
a lowly enlisted soldier, working as a linguist-cryptographer for
the U.S. Army Security Agency in Southeast Asia. He and his
friend Dave Toomley had heard about a fabulous old French
whorehouse named *Coeur Desir*, which was supposedly in the
Da Cao suburb district of Saigon. He and Toomley had gone
to Language School together in Monterey, and now Toomley
was a sergeant attached to the CIA, while he was stationed at
the 3rd Radio Research Unit, at Saigon's Tan Son Nhut Air
Base. More to the point, Toomley's single abiding love in life
was money and he thought he'd found a way to make a big

pile of it. It wasn't that he needed money; he was already doing quite well with his various ventures. It was only three days until payday, and Toomley had once again stretched his sticky web, giving three for five up to a hundred dollars or 10,000 piasters to any G.I. who wanted it. That meant anybody who borrowed three dollars from him would owe him five in just a few days. He was feeling both profitable and itchy for more.

But he wasn't really honest and open with his friend. And The Man With The Scar only found out something of the roots of their adventure years later. At the time, Toomley only said that he'd heard from the lips of a tortured and dying urban Viet Cong sympathizer that the *Coeur Desir* was for sale.

The young man who was about to get his scar also had a Top Secret security clearance. But he was in electronic intelligence, a branch of far less glamour and renown than the CIA, which at that time and in that place was into fomenting riots, assassinations, and destabilizing and overturning local governments, whenever and wherever they could muster the energy.

Young Clay Rhett had been assigned to the White Shack, a Saigon outpost of the Army Security Agency, to work as editor for a small group of cryptographers and translators busily decoding covert Viet Cong messages. The war was heating up at that time, and everyone at the Puzzle Palace considered him dinky dao (a G.I. corruption of the popular Vietnamese street expression *dien cai dao*, which means "bats in the belfry") because he had lobbied long and hard for Vietnam duty.

The long and short of it was that ex-beatnik U.S. Army Specialist 5th Class Clay Rhett was fed up with his cushy Washington D.C. assignment. Just as he'd cruised the two-lane blacktops and railways of America, he next wanted to see the man's world of Hemingway and Crane and Conrad. He longed for excitement and adventure. He wanted to meet russet-colored Mars, the mad god of war and take his measure.

Now, over thirty years later, The Man With The Scar tossed and turned fitfully as he lay under the table in the Cabo San Lucas bar and dreamed about that pivotal time in the Nam. In his detailed and involved dream, Toomley and he were dressed in civvies, just leaving the Brinks B.O.Q. exactly the same as they had on that muggy and fateful night so many years before in real life. They hailed a *Xe Hoi Taxi*, a battered old blue-and-cream Renault, and soon were zooming across town with their driver honking and wheeling furiously through the late evening traffic. Although the immediacy and realism of his dream always stunned The Man With The Scar into a shocked awareness (even though he hadn't woken up and was still in his dream), it never really surprised him that he should dream of this time and this place over and over again. The night they went to the *Coeur Desir* was, after all, the night that changed his life, the night he got his scar.

5

There are all sorts of farewells, and The Man With The Scar's midnight leave-taking from Cabo was fairly quiet and uneventful by his standards. He was still hungover and grumpy when Carlos and the old man with one eye shoved him from the taxi and threw his knapsack after him.

"Watch out for *la masturbacion*!" the old Mexican with one eye cackled from inside the taxi.

"Eet will make you blind!" Jolita added, her hearty laugh seeming to echo in the empty hills as they prepared to drive off without him.

The taxi did a rude U-turn and disappeared into the distance. The night air was chill, and so he started walking along the rutted and bumpy two-lane blacktop that led north from La Paz. After a time, he paused on the gravel by the side of the road, munching on a Nestlé Crunch bar. He preferred dark chocolate, but he knew the few black, red and gold wrapped Toblerone bars he still had would last better in hot weather, so the Crunch bar would do fine for the moment.

He was lean and angular, and of medium height. He was in decent shape for a man his age, that is, closer to sixty than seventy. He was not worried, or impatient, or happy, or sad. If anything could be said of his mood or inclination, it was that he was glad to be in motion again, in an odd way looking forward to the next events of his life. The open road had a way of emptying the mind, and he looked forward to the journey, perhaps more eager to be on his way than he had been in years.

He had only two liters of water in his knapsack. In spite of the fact that Baja was little more than one long desert, he figured his supply should be enough. And if it wasn't, what loss was there? No little old lady waited in some warm living room for him, watching *Must See TV night* until he returned from bowling or a field trip to K-Mart. No one left the light on down the hall, or the latch off the door. No one even burned a candle for him at St. Liborius, not since his sainted mother had died.

His tan shirt and khaki pants were threadbare, but they were clean. His salt-and-pepper beard was full, his mustachio flared in the wind like an old Hell's Angel's, and his receding hair, bleached blond by his months at sea, was, if not short, at least clean and neat.

He wore a plain, wash-rumpled tan hiker's hat with the short brim turned down all around and dark aviator sunglasses which hid the upper two-thirds of the scar on the right side of his face, and on his feet were a pair of purple-and-black Gortex hiking boots which he'd gotten on sale at Price Costco and had barely worn because they logged water easily and didn't work as well at sea as ordinary rubber thongs.

While dawn was still a sliver of light over the black bulk of the craggy hills to the east, the wavering headlights of an oncoming car outlined him from the back in a rim of whitish-yellow light. He turned and threw out his thumb. The car, which turned out to be a Volkswagen bus of moderate vintage, slowed and then stopped next to him, the air-cooled motor choofing and coughing up carbon as it idled in the chill early morning air.

He slung his half-filled dark-blue backpack over one shoulder and jogged up to the waiting bus. As he approached, the side door slid open.

"Get in, Pops!" a voice said.

"Vy does ve schtoppen, o noble gerbil-dick?" a woman's voice complained in a bad imitation of Eastern European accented English. "It remains yet some thousand miles to ze border." The voice shifted to that of English nobility, a lady of fame and fortune, above the fray, "Is it some sort of trick, oh man-of-a-thousand-gerbils? Perhaps some fancy persuasion meant to persuade me to drop my knickers? Oh, sad, delusionary presence, quintessentially gerbilesque..."

The middle seat was missing, so The Man With The Scar tossed his backpack on the raised flat panel behind the rear seat and climbed in after it, pulling the door shut behind him. In doing so, he nearly stepped on a young woman who was sitting cross-legged on the floor of the bus in front of the parts of an old U.S. Army issue M-14 which she had spread on a greasy bath towel.

"Gerbil-Fuck," she mumbled to nobody in particular. "Double trouble, boil an' bubble. I swear, what we gots here is your typical purple, dick-nipping, flea-buggering, rat-fart dog-pooper monkey-humping geek-popping goose-mooning farker-napping logan-lumping horse-pucky dork-licking sixty-nine muff-diving nuns..."

"You weren't supposed to take it apart, Millie," Randy reminded her from the front seat.

"Putzer, I could shoot an apple off your butt. Or your butt out from under an apple. Either way, night or day, slingshot olay. Daddy taught me how."

"Why don't I believe you?"

"Go ahead, Putzer," she snorted. "Stick it up there if you dare. Be fair, pubic hair, devil's lair, in the air, if you dare."

"Hi," the male voice drifted over the high back of the driver's seat to The Man With The Scar. "I'm Randy. This is Millie, only she's not in a particularly good frame of mind right now, seeing as how she's trying to assemble a weapon she knows absolutely nothing about on a jolting bus in the middle of the night."

"Don't start me up, Putzer," Millie warned, the sharp edge on her voice leaving little room for conversation.

The Man With The Scar nimbly shifted his weight to avoid stepping on any of the gun parts and moved to the bench seat in back. The frayed ends of what had been seatbelts told him he didn't have to buckle up. He slid onto the bench seat, feeling grateful for the ride. Randy, he estimated, was thirty-something. Millie was maybe six or seven years younger, with curly blond hair and a chubby sexuality that, twenty years earlier, would have driven him wild.

"Is this a '73?" he asked over the sound of the engine as Randy steadily wound the bus up through the gears.

"'74. The one with the Porsche engine. She's only got a little over one hundred thou on her. Probably go another hundred, easy." Randy grinned and slapped the seat back. "They don't make them like they used to."

"Yeah. I hear they go a long way," the man agreed.

"Gerbil-fuck," Millie said petulantly, sweeping the various disassembled rifle parts with the back of her hand. "Now this is a job for a logan-lumping, horse-pucky, dork-licking, sixty-nine, muff-diving, lousy-loving *weapons assembler,* not a sweet Missy Muffjob like me..."

The Man With The Scar knew all about the M-14 because he'd been assigned one in his basic training at Fort Ord. The weapon was a short-lived heir to the World War II bolt-action M-1. Military suppliers had somehow convinced the army to switch over to the M-14 in the early 1960's. Back then there was a debate raging between the sharpshooters and the sprayers. The sharpshooters relied on the traditions of the Kentucky riflemen, the age-old belief that a good shooter could produce more death than a blast-away boy who just held down the trigger. The advocates of single shot offense won this argument, largely because the M-14 could hold more rounds and could be fired single-shot or automatic fire. Unfortunately their victory was short-lived; the M-14 had proven overweight, awkward and unreliable, and was swiftly replaced by the lightweight AR-15.

"I can help with that," he said before Randy could warn him not to.

She glared at him. "More of your chauvinistic crap, Mister Dorfeldinger? Where, I ask you, on God's Green Earth, can a woman find a little respect? Tina Turner knew where. Tina knew. Tina stomp the wienah, oh yeah. That'll make 'em cry."

"No crap. Just that I can do it."

"Okay-dokay, Smokey. F-f-ine."

She shook her yellow curls like Little Orphan Annie, slammed the wooden stock down on the rubber floor mat and scrambled to the front passenger seat. The heavy stock bounced and slid to one corner of the compartment. The Man With The Scar picked it up and assumed her cross-legged position on the floor. He was out of practice and it took a few minutes, but the weapon was finally reassembled.

Randy, who had been watching through the rearview, said, "Put the clip in."

"You have a place to store this antique? The locals don't take kindly to tourist militants."

"Very funny...but true enough." Randy paused a moment, making up his mind. "Yeah. Show him, Millie."

"No! Randy, we just—"

"Show him."

Millie did a midsized huff, but she got up from the front seat, and, hunching over, came through the walkway between the seats and back to the man's side. She took the M-14 from him and slammed the clip home.

"If Daddy taught me one thing, it was to shoot," she said. "I can hit a duck's ass at 200 yards."

"Not so good for the duck," The Man With The Scar said.

"D-d-damn straight, put you in a crate, s-s-seal your fate. See ya later, agitator."

An imitation leather pad on the panel across from the sliding door was neatly held with snaps. She pulled this pad away from the side panel, revealing a shotgun and two or three handguns supported by hand-welded racks that were padded with black foam rubber. The M-14 slipped neatly into its own rack, and she secured it with two retaining straps and then snapped the panel back in place.

"I have never liked the idea of traveling unarmed through Mexico," Randy said. "I've heard too many things."

"People do disappear," The Man With The Scar agreed.

"There you go! You know how it is. You never know what you're going to meet."

"Yeah," The Man With The Scar calmly agreed, as if they were talking about the price of skinned chicken breasts or the merits of Ben & Jerry's Cherry Garcia ice cream. The silence grew between them. Finally he asked the question foremost on all hitchhikers' minds.

"How far are you going?"

"We got to make one stop, but after that, we're all the way to San Diego."

Randy's eyes were on him, watching for his reaction. The Man With The Scar said calmly, "That would be great, if..."

"Sure. No prob, Pops."

The Man With The Scar hated to be called Pops. But you let a lot of things pass when you were a hiker.

"I'll help pay for gas," he said.

"No need. Consider yourself our guest."

"Gerbil-fuck," Millie said, in a disgusted tone that clearly said Randy was too generous. "You should have to pay, f-f-freeloader. Oh, no...free ride, let it slide." In the faint light from the instrument panel, The Man With The Scar could see the dim outline of Millie's hair. She was looking back at him over the seat.

"Hey, frumpy freeloader." And here her voice shifted to cowpoke, "How'd ya git thet scar, Louie?" she asked. "Was yer ridin' tew close to a longhorn?"

"This?" he said, fingering the deep ridge through his eyebrow where the bullet had forced its way before cutting a line through the skin on his chest and his right thigh and burying itself in the asphalt pavement between his feet. He was tired, and when he brought up the way it really happened, it always involved a long session with endless rounds of questions about what it was *really like*. "I fell down a set of stairs when I was a kid," he said. "I actually landed on the cement floor on my head."

"No, s-s-serious," she said. "Don't fruss me up."

The Man With The Scar gave her a sharper look, deciding that somewhere in this strange girl was a spark of something he could relate to.

"Clay, not Louie," he said. "It was at the Coeur Desir, thirty years ago."

"Coeur Desir," she interrupted. "Gimme a beer. Bet your rear. Hot dog's near." She stared at him. "What's Coeur Desir?"

"It means 'Heart's Desire' in French."

"No, I mean, *what*?"

"Oh. It was a whorehouse in Da Cao."

"A house o' whore. Oh, tell me more. Galore, galore, so piss an' roar, 'til I hit the f-f-floor..."

The silence lengthened between them until she finally said in a small, relatively normal voice, "Where's Da Cow?"

"A suburb just outside of Saigon."

It was too dark to pick up any expression on her face. It didn't matter anyway. As far as he was concerned, for her own good, the less she knew about it, the better. If they could just get through the next day or so without any adventures, she would never know just how lucky she was. The Man With The Scar hunched on the seat in the corner away from the hidden gun rack and tried to drift off to sleep, using his knapsack for a pillow. The steady roar of the engine in the compartment behind him made him drowsy. His mind wandered for a while; he was thinking he was back on the Southern Seas with her mighty twin diesels thrumming, one hundred miles out and waiting for the excited cry of "Hook Up!"

After a while, he did fall asleep. He dreamed a strange dream of Karen and Beverly and Gwen. They were all wearing prom dresses, red, white and blue, but each stood at attention with a fishing rod like a rifle at her side. When the wild cry *Hook Up, Hook Up!* finally came, they grabbed their rods and ran to the back of the boat to bait up. He saw they were using minnows, good fresh ones, so he figured they had to be only a day or two away from the bait tanks at Point Loma. Gwen was having trouble so he grabbed a fast, green-green one and gill-hooked it for her. The Southern Seas was smack in the middle of a feisty little pot of albacore boiling up all around her sides. Karen and Beverly had already hooked up; the early morning light glistened on the little jeweled crowns set in their perfect hair as they shouted and muscled their fish in toward the boat, but Gwen was just staring over the side.

"Cast, for God's Sake! Get your line out there!"

But then the dream cleverly shifted him back to the Nam. As Gwen turned to him, her facial features shrank and withered, and she turned into the oldest woman he'd ever known. The Southern Seas was gone as if it had never existed, and he and Toomley, leaving their *Xe Hoi Taxi,* had walked a few blocks through the semi-lit streets, breathing in the sour and muggy night air until they found the *Coeur Desir.* It had rained earlier that evening, and the worn brick-and-asphalt streets were slick and steamy with mist. Their destination proved to be oddly out of place, a run-down little European cottage-inn set back from the road by an overgrown weed patch that had once been an ornamental garden. Now it was littered with beer bottles and plastic garbage bags. The establishment itself seemed to be doing a thriving business, with groups of G.I.s coming and going, a loud hi-fi blasting, and people happily shouting over the music. The tilted blue neon script in one window read *Coeur Desi,* the 'r', the last letter of *'desir'* having been lost to the ravages of time. *Coeur Desir.* Clay recognized the words were French for something that, loosely translated, meant 'the heart of desire'. But French was a tricky language, and what else it might mean, he had little idea. He stood in the middle of the wet street, shifting his weight impatiently from one foot to the other.

"Okay, Dave. What are we doing here?" Clay asked. He knew Toomley never paid for anything, much less sex, which in the big T*hanh Pho,* the tattered pearl of the orient, was cheaper than Saigon Tea.

- "Honest injun, fellah. We're here to meet a guy about a deal. It's all set up. They're expecting us." Toomley rubbed his hands together and his eyes shone.

"*You*, you mean. They're expecting *you*."

"Whatever," Toomley said, pushing in through the grimy leaded glass front doors.

"Monsieur, Monsieur!" Clay looked up to see a man approaching them with a sense of some urgency. He quickly

led them back through the room, "I was beginning to think you would not attend."

"You must be mistaken," Clay said.

"No mistake, *monsieur! Non. Certainement.* Come! Come!"

Clay estimated the Frenchman was in his late 50s.

Toomley whispered, "Only $10,000 *Américain* for the entire establishment—the cottage with its battered old bar and small dark backroom office downstairs, ten little bedrooms upstairs, and nearly thirty girls."

"I don't think you can own property in Vietnam," Clay warned. "There's a law against it."

"Ahh, m*onsieur*," the Frenchman said quickly, "Zis ees so. Zat is why you have a partner *d' silence*." He gestured to an ancient, wrinkled native woman who was sitting at a smallish and battered marble-inlaid table next to the bar. She was so old it seemed as if she was made of some soft and ancient cloth, and he wondered for a moment if she was of this world, if her heart beat, if she still breathed. Laughter, shouts of rage and singing went on around her, but she sat in her own isolated shell, drifting along as if the glass and chairs flying through the air and breaking against the walls had no meaning and could do her absolutely no harm.

"He is not like the others," the old woman said in a voice whispery as old paper.

"What do you think, Clay?" Toomley asked.

The young man, who at that time did not yet have his scar, simply shrugged.

"I don't know. Why are you asking me, Dave?" He looked around at the bare stud walls with the plaster hanging in chunks and ribbons, at the dirty cracked-tile floors, at the groups of young Americans gathered in bunches around the bar as they sipped *Ba Muoi Ba* beers and eyed the girls, who in turn sat in demure or bawdy, raucous groups at tables near the waiting stairway.

It seemed to Clay that the Frenchman had an air of decayed expectancy as he led the two young Americans to the table next to the old Vietnamese woman, almost as if he had been through the motions many times before and he didn't believe this meeting was finally happening. He held out a chair for Toomley and then scooted to another table and retrieved one for Toomley's friend. On closer inspection, Clay saw the Frenchman wasn't as old as he'd thought; although nearly bald, the man had a bulbous, red-veined nose, and heavily veined cheeks caused his flushed appearance.

The Frenchie was nothing if not eager to serve. He retreated behind the bar, and after fumbling around for a few moments in a cabinet which he had to unlock, he returned carrying in one hand a dark bottle that had several glasses stacked upside down on the neck of the bottle, and a thin briefcase in his other hand. He sat and carefully poured Toomley and Clay a drink.

Toomley said, "Down the hatch," and knocked his down in one gulp.

Clay sipped a little from the top of his glass, which was full to the brim. The amber liquid was very strong; he wasn't used to hard liquor, and this particular concoction made him dizzy and sent a swarm of odd thoughts buzzing around and cutting through his normally calm composure. *And how are you, Mister Whiteskin? And how are you today? What have you come to buy from us? And what are you going to pay?*

Opening the thin suitcase, the Frenchman carefully unwrapped several layers of waxed or oiled leather to reveal what looked like an ancient yellow parchment. Clay had the odd feeling that it wasn't a legal real estate document at all; it was a genuine ancient artifact, centuries old and looking like it had been unearthed from a monastery or some Middle Eastern monk's cave. But what was it was doing here, in a feisty little whorehouse on the suburban outskirts of Saigon? He couldn't even begin to imagine.

But, if young Clay Rhett had his misgivings, his pal Toomley, the great and infamous CIA instigator, had no doubts at all. Toomley knew what he wanted. He didn't even bother to inspect the rooms upstairs; he saw the real estate deal memo (if that was what it really was) and he immediately began pulling rubber-banded piles of crumpled U.S. dollars from his pockets.

"You're going to do this here and now?" Clay asked nervously.

"No time like the present, buddy-boy. Move over, Red Rover, I'm going to get me a piece of the pie!"

The old woman stirred. Her heavily lidded eyes opened slightly, revealing whites that were yellowed with age. "Is zat what you want?" she asked Toomley in a voice that was little more than a husky whisper. She, too, spoke in heavily French-accented English.

The man who would soon have his scar examined her more closely. She had to be the oldest woman he had ever seen. She was wrinkled and frail, and looked as timeless as time itself, with the pulse showing from a network of blue veins on her high forehead below the thin and scattered white straw of her scarecrow hair. She still had most of her teeth, but they were blackened from chewing betel nut, and the bright orange juice limed her teeth and dribbled from one corner of her ancient, cracked lips.

"Beg pardon?" Toomley hadn't caught her soft remark.

"I believe she wants to know if your goal is to make a lot of money," Clay said.

"Jesus H. Christ! Of course it is!"

The old woman nodded, apparently satisfied, and stared at the empty glass on the table in front of her.

"Would you like a drink?" Clay offered, looking at her more closely.

"I dare not," the woman said quietly, but she eyed his drink with the sharp stare of a bird. The Frenchman frowned and pulled the bottle into the crook of his arm.

"Here, have some of mine," Clay said, pouring half his drink into her glass.

Before the frowning Frenchman could stop her, her ancient hands circled her glass and she drained it in one quick motion.

"Sign here, right here." The Frenchman shoved the parchment in front of Toomley's face.

"Tooms—aren't you even going to read that?"

"How could I? It's in French."

"You must drink with us," the ancient woman said to Clay. The man who was soon to have his scar looked at the glasses, and it was true, the other glasses were dry as if they'd never held a drop. His was the last drink remaining on the table, still nearly half full. He gingerly lifted the double shot glass to his lips and took a tiny sip.

"*Uong, Uong ruou*", the old woman urged. "Drink, drink the wine."

"Salud!" the Frenchman shouted, his merry eyes twinkling.

"Come on, Rhett, don't be a party pooper," Toomley said.

He sensed something wasn't right, but with great reluctance, he tilted back his head and tossed down the fiery brew. The strong liquor burned his throat and brought tears to his eyes.

"*Chet roi,*" the old woman said approvingly in her papery whisper. He knew that meant *finished*. But his dizzy, spinning mind could only concentrate on the literal translation of the Vietnamese words, which was *Dead, already.*

He tried to concentrate on the old parchment, if only to keep from falling out of his chair. From where young Clay was sitting, the papers were upside-down. He saw that the print was old and faded, and handwritten in a variety of inks now faded to a uniform brownish-purple. He remembered his high school college prep courses at Bloom Township High School. He had taken two years of Latin and two of French. He couldn't make out many of the words, but he had the distinct impression that at least part of the contract was in Latin, not French.

Just as he was about to say something to Toomley, an ancient hand covered his. He felt a shock, like strong static electricity, and the young man who would soon have his scar started back a little and quickly pulled his hand away. His face went pale, he had a moment of strange and total fear, as if moths had crawled across his chest while he was tied in a dark and close coffin.

"And what is it that *you* want?" the old woman asked in her soft whispery voice, at the same time placing her hand once more on his. The skin of her palm was soft, but he could feel the bones within and he had the impression his hand had been captured by a velvet claw.

Young Clay Rhett was now thoroughly alarmed and upset, although he couldn't think of a single reason why it should be so. He just hadn't expected that ancient hand, like a—a *monster's* glove—entrapping his own.

"I—I just c-came here with Toomley."

He never stuttered, but he was stuttering now.

"Because of what?" she persisted. "Because you wanted to make a fortune, like him?"

"N-no."

The woman waved her free hand at the wild half party, half-drunken brawl going on around them. "Perhaps you wanted to experience the joy and pleasures that only a beautiful and passionate woman can bring?"

"No. No. Really, not. J-Just, I guess, to see it, you know, this place. Old Toomley here told me about it, and it sounded, you know, colorful and exciting."

"Ahh...allure...romance...adventure..." The words rolled from her ancient lips in a heavy French accent. The lilt of her voice had the pungency of incense, a hidden quality, as if her spoken words contained hints at the ancient secrets of life.

- "A young man's wish. It's not enough...?" the Frenchman asked dubiously.

"He invited me to share, *n'est-ce pas*? And who are you to say? Beggars cannot be choosers."

The Frenchman shrugged and fell silent. Before he knew it, Clay was agreeing with her. This harmless old woman had a sort of wisdom. She could see right through to the heart of things. After all, that was what he had wanted from the get-go: to see the Orient, like Joseph Conrad. To see war, like Hemingway and Mailer. To see life, like Camus, Sartre and Henry Miller.

"I guess so," he agreed, feeling a little calmer and less rattled now. "You know, to experience life to the fullest, to know it like nobody else. To know joy, you've got to know fear. To know passion, you have to experience pain."

She smiled and nodded to the Frenchman, who picked up her pen and handed it to Toomley. In later years, The Man With The Scar would remember distinctly that it had been her pen. She had taken it from a small pouch she wore at her waist and handed it solemnly, almost religiously, to the Frenchman. Her hand shook, and at the time her movements only served to remind the young man who would soon have his scar that she was a very, *very* old woman.

Even as he was about to sign his fate away, rash young Toomley continued to have no problems or second thoughts about any of this. The misgivings and the anguish for everything else that might have been in his life would only come with time. At that moment, he reached easily for the pen that the old lady had handed to the Frenchman. Toomley quickly and carelessly scrawled his name in the space the man indicated and handed the pen back to the Frenchman, who in turn handed it to the ancient woman who handed it to the young man who was about to get his scar.

Clay tried to hand it back.

"No, ahh...*he's* buying the place," he protested. "Toomley here's your buyer. *He's* your man."

"Yes, of course," the old lady said. "But you must witness, *monsieur*. Witness, *thua ong*, or there can be no agreement."

"Oh, for God's sake, Rhett, sign the fuckin' thing," Toomley said.

The pen in his hand was heavier than he would have imagined, one of those fat black pens with a golden tip. He took one last look around the room and reached for Toomley's contract. His head was swimming from the effects of the powerful drink, and he couldn't possibly read the faded script in front of him.

"You will have what you want," she said. "Sign here."

Clay couldn't take her seriously. He weighed the pen in his hand. "So, I'm signing my life away?"

"You will be saving this ungrateful pig of a man's soul."

"Zees Américaines do not believe in souls," the Frenchman scornfully said.

He looked carefully at the ancient woman, "If I do this...?"

"You will never be bored," she shrugged.

"Okay," he said. "What do I have to lose?"

The ancient paper crackled as he signed.

The Frenchman carefully printed in the date. 31 Janvier 1968. He handed the pen to the ancient woman, who replaced the cap and held it in her hands. There was a brief moment when the two of them, the ancient native woman and the Frenchman with the red-veined nose, seemed to be waiting, anticipating something which was about to begin. And then a heavy, crumpling noise sounded somewhere in the distance, followed by the nearer crackle of firearms, semi-automatics and single-shots going off like little volleys of firecrackers. It was the exact moment when the Viet Cong had started their long-threatened Tet Offensive.

There were a few moments of panic during which the G.I.s were sorting out what was happening and what their chances were. The *Coeur Desir* had not been the victim of a terrorist bombing. They were in some jeopardy, but no immediate danger of death. But something was up, and it wouldn't pay to hang around. They came boiling out the front door, disappearing into the night to rejoin their units.

Clay and Toomley were down on the floor under the table at the first sharp sounds, praying it wasn't mortars with delay-time fuses that would crash through the tiles to ignite a few seconds later inside the building and tear them all to shreds. But after a few moments they too realized there was no immediate threat. They crawled out from under the table and looked around. The room was deserted. Not only the G.I.s, but also the old woman and the Frenchman, had vanished. The only sign of their agreement was the slim briefcase, still sitting on the table with a thin sprinkle of plaster across its worn leather top. Toomley pulled it open, took out the parchment and its leather wrappings, and stuffed it in the back of his pants, cinching his belt a notch tighter to secure it.

The pungent night air was full of distant night sounds, the heavy saw of Brownings, the string-of-firecrackers snap of automatic rifles, the *Pow! Pow! Pow!* of single-shot fire, echoing and reechoing across the city. The heavy scent of fertile delta mixed with the rot of urban decay was now laced with the acrid smell of gunpowder.

"Come on, Clay," Toomley yelled. "Our business is finished here."

Moving house to house, it would take the two of them three bloody days and nights to return to the Brinks B.O.Q. The CIA man had several hideout weapons, and they were able to strip AK-47s from the bodies of several young native men who, from the Americans' point of view, shouldn't have been carrying them in the first place. Moving through the turmoil and panic with deadly efficiency, Toomley somehow had managed to come up with a ruby necklace and an emerald ring by the time they made their way back to the Brinks. And the young man named Clay Rhett, somewhere in the middle of all the bloody horror, had become engraved with a fresh, new scar that intermittently ran down his body, engraving his face, chest and thigh with a mark so he would never again forget what he had signed and what his life had become.

6

The lower Baja peninsula is a great and wonderful place. It used to belong to the United States, but we traded it for a sliver of barren worthless land to build a railroad. So you see, there was Alaska, but there was Baja, too. And just when you thought imperialists were invincible. Screws up your world a little bit, doesn't it, things not quite so neat and tidy anymore...or don't you ever think of these things? Is a map a permanent thing in your mind, perhaps something in indelible ink drawn directly over the fruited plains, over high mountains, across rivers and through lakes by man, God's designated master plan of all He surveys?

Castro's Camp was located on the western coast of Baja in the small and foggy cove of San Ysidro, a starkly beautiful and arid strip of land which curved itself into a small crescent moon bay about sixty miles down the road south of Ensenada, and perhaps eighty miles south of the U.S. border itself. After that distance, it was twelve more miles removed by dusty gravel roads from the two-lane blacktop.

Castro's was something more than a poverty-infested fishing village, because of a little sport fishing operation run by the Castro family for the more rugged saltwater fishermen from *Gringoland*. The one-inch ad in the Sport Fisherman's News proclaimed it was fisherman's paradise. In reality it was a tattered Mecca for those hard-core *Americano* fishermen who brought their own beer and dry ice and liked hauling in the big ones while they were roughing it well off the beaten path.

The indefinite lines of the place caused it to look very much like it might be a syrupy beige painting by Salvador Dali or perhaps a surrealistic one-horse town transplanted from one of Sergio Leone's mixed-up and ill-thought-out *spaghetti westerns*. They were little more than a group of leaning, paint-peeled shacks falling in on each other; they seemed to have been misplaced on this forlorn and deserted scrap of shoreline before they had a chance to collapse into the paint pigment or celluloid film from whence they had come.

The tan VW bus with the white top chugged up to the lone gas pump, and as it sputtered and sighed to a halt, Randy pulled the handbrake and wearily eased himself out of the driver's seat. He walked around to the side by the gas cap, flipped open the flap, unscrewed the cap and started up the pump. A whirring noise began, and a slow dribble of gasoline started running into the black hole that led to the tank.

The Man With The Scar slid open the side door and jumped to the sandy ground. *At least Millie-the-troublemaker was still sleeping*, he thought. Her heavy snores had been a complement to the steady roar of the sturdy 4-banger engine for the last twenty miles. By the acrimonious tone of their conversations and the few heavy glances Randy had managed to cast his way, The Man With The Scar had realized the younger man wasn't entirely happy with his draw in the lottery of pulchritude and affection. He had wanted to say something that was both man-to-man and fatherly about *patience pays* and how *time cures all*, but he didn't want to risk Millie overhearing. All they both needed was for her to lurch awake and launch herself headlong into the conversation with her patented stentorian roar.

The Man With The Scar raised his hands over his head until his muscles popped. Without thinking, he started to go through his Military Dozen, first doing the arm twirls, and then the neck crunchers and the body twists. Castro's seemed an exceptionally sleepy place at ten in the morning. The sad collection of shacks looked like they would fall in on themselves even as he watched. What boats may have recently been tied to the now empty posts of the battered and rotten wooden pier had probably left at dawn's first light. The few shacks at water's edge appeared deserted, and the only sign of life was a thin wisp of smoke drifting hesitantly upwards from a tilting tin chimney on one of the buildings.

A teenager wearing cutoff jeans and a heavy scowl came from the nearest building and took over on the gas pump, which continued running at a very slow rate. By now, The Man With The Scar had done his spread eagles and was working on fifty push-ups.

"I like the way you can see the gas in that little glass thing," Randy said.

"Don't look—too close," The Man With The Scar replied between push-ups. "It's got a lot—of dirt—in it."

He finished his fifty and jumped to his feet.

"You're in pretty good shape...for an old guy..." Randy said, chuckling as if he'd said something funny.

"You have to be, in my business."

"Which is?"

"Survival."

Randy laughed like that was funny, too.

A red truck appeared in the distance, coming down the same dusty road they had traveled. The Man With The Scar couldn't help but notice that Randy's expression shifted into sincere interest when he saw the newcomers heading towards Castro's.

"Company's coming," The Man With The Scar said.

Randy's face lit up with a big smile.

"Fisherman's paradise," he said. "The last untamed wilderness." He slapped the teenager on his bare shoulder, "Keep pumping, amigo. Full to the brim." And then he wandered away towards the largest of the shacks.

When the red truck pulled up about a hundred feet away, he was there to meet it. Two scruffy-looking white men got out, and the three of them spent the next few minutes hugging and shaking hands.

The Man With The Scar did a few last stretches, torso twists and arm twirls. He noticed that Millie's blouse buttons

had mostly come open in her sleep, more than enough to
show her ample, braless figure.

"Big melons are the sweetest," he said to no one in
particular.

"*Muy delicioso*," the teen agreed.

"Hey, you're too young for such thoughts. What would
the padre say?"

"You mean, if he were here?" the teenager grinned,
showing a mouthful of cracked and broken teeth.

The front door on the passenger side opened and Millie
sleepily crawled out of the bus.

"P-p-pigs!" she shouted. "Rank and runny porkers!
Filthy boys!" She looked around and spotted Randy in the
distance. "Why didn't Putzer illuminate me his friends were
arrived?"

Without waiting for an answer, she took the M-14,
somewhat covered by a heavy blue blanket, from the car and
walked toward the café.

"She must have meant you when she said 'filthy boys',"
The Man With The Scar said. "My thoughts have always been
pure as the driven snow."

"*Aieee!* Look at that ass," the teen said. "That will melt
your snow."

The Man With The Scar walked away from the VW bus,
making his way the short distance down to the deserted,
sandy beach. Squatting, he dug a finger into the moist sand.
Using one hand to shield his eyes from the sun, he looked
north along the gentle curve to where the shore met a series
of distant cliffs that plunged directly into the sea. The sand
was littered with logs and smaller branches, and strewn with
strands of strange-looking olive-green seaweed that were
heavy with little, pulpy nodules. The air smelled of brine. He
filled his lungs and turned to look to the south, where a similar
horizon greeted his gaze. He decided it was good to be alive
here, enjoying a moment of peace. He was in the
southwestern corner at the western end of the continent he'd
crossed and crossed again so many times over the decades.
He wondered again if he would have the resolve to answer the
summons of Beverly and Gwen and Karen, to trek his way one

last time across the Southwest and the plains states to the shindig at the Contempo. The sun glanced off his bleached hair. The gulls wheeled and cried overhead, disappointed that he had no fish to gut and share with them. The lonely wind whistled, and he knew he would find no answers there. He stood and walked back to the small cluster of buildings.

A cheap chrome plated bell jangled as he tried the door under the faded wooden sign that said Castro's Cafe. These words were printed in hand-painted letters faded with age to a faint and sandy pink shadow of their former selves. A plump, gypsy-looking lady glared at him and went back to the solitaire hand she'd laid out in front of her.

"You wanna beer, get it yourself," she grunted in a distinct New Jersey accent.

"I was just going to suggest that," the man replied. It was still mid-morning; but, from his experiences in rural Mexico, anything with alcohol was better than drinking the water. He went to an ice chest and retrieved a bottle of Coors that had most of its label worn off.

"Two dollars," the woman said.

He took two dollars from his wallet and placed the bills on the counter.

"Pigs," she said.

"Huh?"

"All men are pigs."

"Is it catching?" he asked.

"What stupidity are you talking?" Her glare deepened, twisting her face into a parody of itself.

He noticed her shift several cards before continuing her game.

"Do you always cheat?" he asked.

"You, of all people, should ask." Her voice was heavy with scorn.

"You don't even know me," he replied mildly.

"I know enough." She gestured impatiently toward the red truck outside.

"What does that mean?"

"You men from the North, you come and you take what you want and then you go again. Well, I tell you, the land will endure, and we with it."

"Come on. You have a Brooklyn accent."

"Smart-ass. What difference does that make?"

He stood and edged towards the door, "*Vaya con Dios.*"

"You, of all people," she said, barely able to restrain her disgust. *"Vaya con Diablos."*

By the time he returned to the bus, Randy had pulled it sideways behind the red truck, and the three men were busily transferring red, blue and yellow Igloo ice chests to the compartment in the center of the bus where the missing middle seat once was. By careful stacking, they had packed two layers with eighteen chests in all.

"You going to fit back there, Clay?" Randy asked with a wry little grin.

"I suppose." The Man With The Scar shrugged.

"We buy tuna at a buck a pound. Sell it in L.A. at six bucks a pound."

Randy's friends were eyeing them both with stony gazes.

"Oh, here," Randy said. "Meet my buddies, Pez and Jimmy Ray."

"Is this going to be a *problem,* Randy?" the one called Pez asked.

"No, it isn't a *problem*," Randy answered. He seemed annoyed at the question. "Our friend Clay, here, may be of *great assistance* along the way."

"You're sure of that, Randy?"

"You have to trust my judgment."

There was a long pause, and then Pez spit on the sandy beach.

"It's your fuckin' neck, buddy."

"Where's my fishing poles?" Randy asked.

Jimmy Ray slapped his own forehead. "Ja-hesus H. Christ, ah almost forgot," he twanged in a Tennessee drawl. He jumped up into the back of the red truck and returned with a dozen rods and reels.

"Get those, would you, Clay?" Randy asked.

The Man With The Scar took the loose bundle of fishing poles, which were sticking out of a garbage bag tied at the end with a piece of twine. With Randy's help, he managed to wedge them on top of the ice chests with the tips pointing forward. Randy adjusted them twice, finally insisting the longest poles be arranged so they stuck out of Millie's window. He cranked the window up so it was only open two or three inches.

"'Kay. We are ready to roll," Randy said.

"Uh-uh," Pez said, sticking his hand out. "There is just one other little matter."

Seeing the transaction phase was approaching, The Man With The Scar backed away from the group.

"I'm going to take this beer bottle back," he said.

"Yeah, you do that. Good for the ecosystem, or what the fuck," Pez said.

As The Man With The Scar turned away, he caught a glimpse of a fat wad of U.S. money in Randy's hands. The Man With The Scar hadn't seen Millie since she woke up, and there weren't too many places she could be in that tiny sprawl of a fishing village. *Feets, don't fail me now!*, he was thinking as he plodded steadily in the direction he'd chosen, towards the cafe.

Behind him he could hear the sounds of a beginning argument. Randy seemed to be pleading innocence. The commotion sounded like it might be winding up into a full-blown tropical disturbance, but he kept moving forward, steadily plowing through the soft sand, placing one foot after the other in the general direction of the cafe.

"That bankroll is lookin' a little light there," he heard Pez say in an uptight voice that carried all the way to the cafe.

"What kind of shit you trying to pull here, Randy?" Jimmy Ray said. "You agreed that's what it was going to be!"

"I see we got to learn you a lesson here, Randy-boy." That last sentence from Pez was said with a flat, hard shelf of menace.

The Man With The Scar didn't bother to turn around, not even when a rifle coughed from the half-open door of the ladies' room, an outhouse shack with a skirt painted below a half-moon cut in the door. Once. Twice. Three shots. Four. They were evenly spaced, with time to resight and squeeze down on the trigger. The M-14 could shoot straight, he had to say that for it. And, since none of the bullets were whapping into the ground or the buildings around him, he had to assume that Millie wasn't shooting at him. The Man With The Scar sighed in relief as he reached the sagging screen door and let himself into the cafe. He found a half-full plastic garbage can and deposited his empty beer bottle.

The gypsy lady appeared to be in the exact same spot as before, except now his two dollar bills were no longer on the counter. The tip of one of them was peeping from the black lace of her big bra.

"*Gracias, signora*," he said.

She laid down an ace of spades and, after a moment's hesitation, calmly slid it back in the deck. Her next card was the black queen. She carefully played it and spat on the floor without looking up at him. The next card out was the joker. She looked at him again, this time nodding as she played it.

"It won't be easy for you," she said.

"It never is," he remarked idly as he left, wondering to himself if feminists and guns made up a worse combination than liquor and cars. Or dynamite and idiots, he mused. Or gasoline and pyromaniacs.

7

Poets, philosophers and folks who earn their coin by donning religious robes will all tell you that there's a very thin line between life and death. They will explain with neat arguments and definitions, and speak of misty things like *passing beyond the veil* or even *going to one's reward.* But the truth is, they don't have a clue. Death is a mystery, and so is life, civilization's learned, and wise old farts are just as much in the fog as the rest of us, every one of them.

Not only that, but when it's *your own* life on the line, there's very little learned opinion and advice that can be of much use to you. In those circumstances, the wisdom of the brave warrior and the craven survivor both take trump over idle conjecture. For example, here are a few pieces of wisdom: *A six-foot bullet will absolutely miss a man who is five foot eleven. You never hear the one that gets you. The hole in the barrel looks bigger when it's pointed at you. Dead men tell no tales.*

In this same vein, I assure you there is a certain messiness about violent events that doesn't ever translate into the newspapers or even the Channel 7 Live Action News Reports. And so it is that, while certain events that took place at Castro's Camp can be narrated, it is nearly impossible to convey anything of the sense of maniac fury or the mad panic that ensued.

"Do not procrastinate! Your fate, relate—The money, honey! Snag it! Quick, quick, slick gerbil-dick!" Millie shouted as she jumped into the driver's seat and fired up the van.

"You didn't, for Christ's Sake, have to *shoot* them!" Randy screamed over the seat at Millie.

"Ariba, Ariba! Soy Dora Explora! Come on, Boots! Sling it, fling it, bring it, wing it, vaminos, amigos!"

Randy grabbed the bag and dove into the front seat. The Man With The Scar managed to jump in through the side door, climb over the coolers, and make it to his place on the back seat. The VW van fishtailed as Millie hit the gas and they headed out of Castro's Camp, going as fast as they could go.

Somewhat later, Randy, now driving, was still grumbling, "Really, you didn't have to shoot them."

"Oh, mango-pango pork-pie dipper," she replied, slipping into a loose New Orleans black patois, "Ah saves the man's tootie frootie pitootie, and this be my reward. It's de black-bitch curse, be loved by man."

"You're white, Millie," Randy said.

Time went by. Things happened. They traded places.

Now Randy was riding shotgun, while Clay drove the Volkswagen bus steadily north. Millie had decided on this new arrangement after Randy's nervous driving landed them in a sandy ditch some few miles from Castro's. For a while the position of the bus had seemed hopeless, and the couple had actually started back down the road for the red truck when The Man With The Scar suggested that, if they unloaded the ice chests and the two men pushed from the back while Millie steered, they could probably regain the road.

This accomplished, once they were on the road again, Millie thought it would be a good idea to clean the M-14, and so they had switched their seating arrangements.

The Man With The Scar didn't mind driving. It gave him time to think, to watch the road while he concentrated on other things. At that moment, he was thinking about how one of the ice chests had tipped over and opened when they were moving them. The fish inside, which were frozen stiff as blocks of ice, had tumbled to the dust. He had seen immediately that they were yellowtails, not tuna.

"You want to leave them, Randy?" he'd asked.

"God, no," Randy said, quickly dusting them off as best he could. The Man With The Scar shrugged and helped Randy pack his dirt-grimed fish back in the chest. He noted that they'd been quick-gutted, with the heads still on. He knew that was the way the better fish stores liked to sell them. He didn't say anything to Randy about the fish being yellowtails, which only sold for four dollars a pound, even at the best stores.

He drove for an hour in silence punctuated with Randy's intermittent outbursts of doubt and Millie's gibberish.

"Putzer futzing mungo prick-gobbling backstabbing billy goat hampering gork-screwing donk-wangling...I cannot screw this damn bam-bam shazaam back together..."

"It's not a bam-bam, Millie, "Randy lectured. "It's a rifle."

"And-it's-a-lucky-fucking-thing-for-you-right-now—"

The Man With The Scar let several miles pass in silence before he chose to speak. "I think it's better anyway," he said quietly.

"You-think-*what*-is better, jabby scabby scar-man? What is the meaning behind your perceived illumination, Watson Waterboy, bitch to Sherlock, oh mighty scarred prince of the East?"

"Well..." He spoke calmly, letting time pass before he spoke again, "It's not like you are lacking for firepower. If it was me, I'd sort of wipe my prints off the parts of the possibly incriminating weapon as I threw them, one by one, out the window."

She didn't say anything, but he could tell by the difference the air pressure made on his ears, she'd opened the side window next to her. The road was all but deserted, empty for long stretches in both directions. He caught a glimpse or two of her in the rearview mirror. She had calmed down and was humming to herself, carefully wiping the parts of the rifle as she might dry a plate or a cup or a glass, and then flipping them out the window to clank on the road behind them. She was humming that Janis Joplin ditty from the Pearl album, *Lord, won't you buy me/ a Mercedes-Benz? My friends all love Green Peace/ I must make amends. Work hard for my money/ On Putzer depends. Lord, won't you buy me a Mercedes-Benz?* She even added the half-crazy little laugh at the end.

Miles passed, and the van was driven in turn by Randy, The Man With The Scar and Millie. They did parallel stretches on dusty, bumpy gravel roads, and then went for a while on the asphalt highway.

Millie was driving while The Man With The Scar watched from the front passenger seat and Randy slept in back. They had traveled for nearly an hour without seeing another car heading in either direction.

"Surreal," Millie said suddenly, the word dropping unexpectedly into the silence.

"Yes," The Man With The Scar agreed, "Like a Dali painting."

"We just need a few melted clocks," Millie laughed.

"Look sharp," he advised, pointing to the dead tree branches pulled across the road ahead.

"Ho, ho, ho. Native alert! Honk, honk, honk! Look snappy, you crazy jump of gerbil-humpers!!"

"Looks like three armed men. They're not wearing uniforms."

"W-w-well, too bad they caught me on a b-b-bad day! Mamma comin' out to play!"

One man stood in the middle of the road, in front of the tree branches, waving a red flag. The two others stood on either side, their rifles held at arms ready. Millie grinned at The Man With The Scar. In spite of himself, he couldn't help grinning back. She didn't ask him what she should do; she stepped on the gas.

"Mucho loco-moco, mudder fokko. You peek the wrong gringo, pingo-fingo!"

The armed men dove for the roadside, throwing away their ancient rifles. The man with the flag couldn't get out of the way fast enough, and the corner of the boxy van on the passenger side thumped and spun him in the air. The cloth from his red flag got caught on the windshield wiper.

"Souvenir!" Millie said, spinning the wheel. The van skidded between the road and the ditch at its side, narrowly avoiding the dead tree branches. "Get it for me!"

They were past the roadblock, accelerating down the empty two-lane blacktop. The Man With The Scar wound down his window and pulled in the flapping red flag, which proved to be made of heavy plastic.

"What does it say?" Millie asked.

"Home Depot," he replied.

Randy's sleepy voice called out from the backseat, "Hey, Mil-ster, what's going on?"

She grinned at The Man With The Scar and yelled back over her shoulder, "Noco loco, putzer-fokah. Go snore more, happy hump fuck-boy. Enjoy, enjoy. See ya later, screwivator, we go long time, G.I. Only ten dollar, I give you beautiful brown-eye babee boy..."

The shadows lengthened, and the van drove on steadily across the picturesque desert like a scene from a television commercial for a Las Vegas casino, the part where they drive across miles of empty nothingness before getting to the gaudy bright lights of nothingness.

Perhaps it is time to reflect on the nature of friendship. Hitchhikers, college students and army people particularly are thrown in a people-stew like a pot of carrots, beans, potatoes and meats, and then vigorously stirred around. Some of the oddest combinations become friends, or at least long-term acquaintances. Perhaps they are tied by events more binding than birth. Perhaps they would like to get away, but they can't. Take The Man With The Scar and Dave Toomley, for instance. Their mutual fates were sealed from the moment they scratched their names on that ancient document, that night at the whorehouse in Da Cao. It was the same physical document, but their fates ended up being painted out in different colors...Toomley's being mainly green, which stands for money, which sticks to him in his own variation of the Midas Curse.

Or take the example of the hitchhiker. Our favorite man with the scar, wandering through a foreign and notoriously corrupt land, is thrown in the deep tub with two complete strangers. He doesn't know them; and they certainly don't know him or they would have dumped him faster than a gambling Chinaman with an unlucky number. And don't think for a minute that the two young people from Northern California aren't exploring their options.

Indeed, Randy and Millie had to stop many times along the way for whispered conferences, and these conferences seemed to increase in number and intensity as they drove north. It was nearly ten at night by the time they got to the border. The Man With The Scar had been elected to drive. He shifted the VW bus into neutral and drifted to a stop behind the long line of cars in front of him. The engine puttered lazily and he stretched his shoulders to get the kinks out of his neck muscles.

As the line slowly moved forward, he shifted into first and gave the engine just enough gas to close the gap in front of him. Then he put the bus back in neutral, pulled the hand brake, and sat there, calmly waiting for the line to move forward again.

"It's going to be a while..." he said calmly. "The Mexes are checking tight, tonight."

Millie, in the passenger seat at his side, started fussing with a tube of lipstick.

"Why?" she asked.

"Well, you never know why. Maybe they've been tipped off. Or maybe it's nothing."

"Crap, crap, crap, crap," Randy muttered sleepily from in back.

He gestured in front of them. Thirty cars ahead, they could just make out a small squad of men in olive uniforms scurrying around the lead car in each line.

"Oh God," Millie murmured. She dropped her lipstick to the floor. "Putzer, putzer, doin' whatzer..."

"Silly-Millie. Everything's going to be alright, hon." That was Randy, murmuring bland assurances. He sounded a little scared, but she was white as a sheet.

"Oh, sure," she snapped. "Easy for you to say, Putzer." Then she was whispering, almost to herself, "I won't believe it until I see it with the whites of my own eyeballs..."

"Now, Millie..." Randy comforted in the soothing tone he used when one of his high-fliers went down thirty points before he'd had a chance to bail his clients.

"How bad be bad?" Millie asked The Man With The Scar, her voice dropping into a *faux* baritone. "Tell me straight, Bogie. I can take it."

"I don't know, Millie. We're too far away to see exactly what they're up to."

From where they were, they could make out a squad of brown uniformed men swarming around each car as it entered their brightly lit inspection area.

Millie twisted her hair between nervous fingers, and she was little girl lost. "Ohh. Ohh. Ohh. Do the time to pay the crime." And suddenly little girl lost became Madonna, a fallen angel, bitter and hopeless, "Fail, fail, fail, jail, jail, jail...oh, nail me in the cunt, why don't you?"

The Man With The Scar moved up until the van was fifth or sixth in line. Ahead of them, the Mexican border patrol was swarming around the cars, poking tires, opening luggage and peering under the frames with mirrors mounted on poles. The Man With The Scar slowly drove forward. He was relaxed, his cap halfway down on his eyes.

"Oh, dear God, sweet-tart, baby," Millie prayed, "Oh, Only Oly Oly Ocean free, Omnipotootie, Almighty softly bite-y, Ever-Present Friendly Pheasant, Kindly All-Forgiving Creator...All-Delightful Munis-potator...Oh,Swell, Almighty, Radiantly lovely, Lordificent, Nifty, Kindly, Ever-Ready Heady Teddy, On-The-Go, Handsome Ransome...Maker of all beings including both the huge and the very tiny dicks like Putzer-boy here—"

"Just calm down, sweetie," Randy tried to reassure her.

"Oh sure!" She slipped into something mildly Germanic like a quick-change of verbal clothes, "Easy for you to say, Putzer-boy-vonder. Vas denks du? Eina kleina cuntisika mina...which translates, Oh my sweet little cunt, in case you don't speak low German."

"It's okay, Millie."

"Okay for you, maybe, but me, no thank you, Donald Duck." And now she was speaking some pidgin English, probably imitating a Central American refuge, "I not spend my child-fruit-filled years doing crap in a dirty hole." And again into deep South black patois, "Not me, honey-lapper putz-man. Dis gal not goin' to give out to every gerbil-whackin' dick-dacker who come sniffin' for a quick bite of snatch. Who dat sniffin' roun' my door? No, no, no, dolorosa..."

"Now, Millie, just calm down, sweetie pie face. Fifteen minutes, and it will be all over."

"No-no-no-no-no! Not for me!" And suddenly she was the Lone Ranger's Tonto, "Me jump horse here, kimosabe!" She took a brave swat at opening her door, but the fishing poles stuck through the window wouldn't allow it.

"Fu-Fu-Fuck this!" she said. "Look out, sailor. You got a flailer! Grab the family jewels!"

She reached over and opened the driver-side door.

"Mmmm," she said, kissing the scar on the driver's forehead and rubbing her breasts against his face as she climbed over him.

"Maybe some other time," he said, trying to be gallant with one of her knees in his groin. By then Millie had already crawled out of the bus, and if she heard him she didn't bother to reply.

"Brief, but pleasant," The Man With The Scar said to nobody in particular.

She had her knapsack and was making her way between the cars, back the way they had come. The Man With The Scar wondered how many cars she would have to pass before someone offered her a ride. Probably not very many, he guessed.

"Millie! Come back here!" Randy was shouting now, probably thinking the same things he was. And then Randy also clawed his way across The Man With The Scar's lap, and fell headfirst out of the bus. He didn't seem hurt; he jumped up to run after Millie and then stopped, seeming to remember at the last minute where they were and that they were on an important mission.

"Oh. Clay. Look, as you can see, she's gone a little crazy...Can you just drive it across?"

Randy had lost his composure. His gaze went back and forth between the man sitting behind the steering wheel of his bus and Millie's rapidly retreating figure.

"Look," he said, "I'll get her and walk her through the pedestrian gate. You drive on through and meet us on the other side."

Randy didn't wait for an answer; he was already dogtrotting back between the lines of cars in search of Millie, who had disappeared from view.

The Man With The Scar eased the VW bus forward and braked, eased the bus forward and braked. After thirty minutes, he was second in line, and then the border police were swarming around the little van like busy ants. One scanned the bottom with a mirror on a long pole. Another kicked the tires and a third thumped the panels all around.

"Feeshing—eh, Pops?" the one with the clipboard said.

"Don't call me 'Pops', Sonny-boy," The Man With The Scar said, taking the chance on aggressive, but grinning to show he was really an all right guy and that his words were just a joke.

His quick appraisal proved right. The man with the clipboard showed a quick flash of white teeth under his thick black moustache.

"I want to see theese *fabuloso* feesh."

"You bet," The Man With The Scar said proudly. He got out of the van and came around to the other side, opening the door with a grand gesture. He set the closest three of the ice chests on the pavement and then two more. He made as if he was going to remove even more of them. The chests were heavy, and he worked as if they were more of an exertion than he actually felt.

"Stop! Stop! Ees enough!" the man with the clipboard said.

"More than enough," the man said, panting slightly. "Am I not a magnificent fisherman?"

"Ho-hoo! So many feesh."

The man knew his cue when he heard it.

"Too many, actually. I will have to give them away—to friends, to my mother-in-law, whom I hate in the customary way, to the people at work." He scratched his head, as if coming up with an idea. "Say, you wouldn't like one or two for yourself...?"

"Oh, I could not, señor."

The man knew he had to raise the ante.

"I understand. The fish would spoil before your shift was over. I know—take a whole chest."

"Oh, I could not."

"Look, I have nearly twenty. These chests are free; I work for the Igloo, the company that makes them."

"Oh, well...in that case."

"I insist. Will this one be okay?" He pulled a red chest away from the others.

"Well, you have so many," the man with the clipboard said.

"Oh, here, take these three. Some for your friends. That way I won't have to put them back in the van."

"Señor, you are too kind."

"No, just kind enough," The Man With The Scar said to himself. He raised his voice, "Can you get that door?"

"Certainly, amigo," the Captain said as he slammed the sliding door shut.

The Man With The Scar got back behind the wheel, put the van in gear and drove across the short space to the American side of the border. The Americans liked his looks and waved him on through, just another fisherman back with the spoils from Mexico.

Randy and Millie were looking out of a big plate glass window that viewed the autos going through the checkpoint.

"There he is!" Randy said. They both waved excitedly.

Inside the van, The Man With The Scar drove calmly forward. He checked to make sure he had a Toblerone bar in his shirt pocket. Maybe he imagined it, but he thought he saw Randy and Millie waving from behind a big wall of glass in the reception area. He shifted from first to second and the van moved smoothly forward. He gave a little wave in their general direction. From behind the glass, Randy and Millie's gestures seemed to become more and more frantic.

The Man With The Scar took a bite from the Toblerone bar. He gave another terse little wave and a fleeting false grin; then shifted smoothly into third, the van picking up speed nicely. He didn't see any reason to stop.

The 1974 Volkswagen van disappeared into the night, heading north for San Diego. By then, Randy and Millie were jumping up and down and frantically gesturing from behind the plate glass. Of course, they couldn't ask anybody for help, as that would have taken some serious explaining.

Millie calmed down first, patting her hair and looking around for a washroom to freshen up.

"Are we in tru-tru-trouble, Futzer Putzer?" she asked.

Time went by and The Man With The Scar found himself driving alone on the 405 north through San Diego. He reached into his knapsack and peeled open another of his Toblerone bars, and bit off a triangular chunk. The chocolate was brittle from being melted too many times, but it was dark chocolate and he was glad to have it.

He was remembering a place up ahead just outside Oceanside where a small cutoff road led to a fairly deep cove. The marines liked to take their women out there, to roll around in the dusty sand on a cliff overlooking the sea, but it was the middle of the week and the place would probably be deserted tonight. The fish were probably already spoiled, but he would be sure to stab through the bags of white powder in their stomach cavities before tossing them over the edge and letting the whole mess drift out to sea.

The place was there, just as he'd remembered. But it was colder than he figured and stabbing the frozen fish was more difficult than he'd imagined, even with a big hunting knife he found in Randy and Millie's secret firepower compartment. He worked steadily, the sweat beading on his forehead and making him feel too hot and too cold at the same time. He hoped all this wouldn't make him sick. When you are on the road, little things can easily magnify and become showstoppers.

When he was done with the fish, he threw the weapons over the side, figuring this was Marine Base land, and there was already so much rusty scrap along the beach that a few more pistols and an old shotgun wouldn't make any difference. He was tempted by one small automatic. It looked like a .32, and might be useful. But then he remembered how heavy anything became when you had to carry it around, and he threw it over the cliff as well. He already had an old Borchardt in the bottom of his knapsack, an odd-looking pistol with a hair trigger, a long snout and a bulging back end that looked like the stomach on a pregnant spider. That one already weighed over a pound.

Randy's big bundle of money was in a dusty gym bag, and so The Man With The Scar took that before tossing the gym bag in a long fluttery arc after the weapons and the boxes of ammo. He didn't bother to count the money. He saw it was made up of hundreds, so it had to be a decent chunk of change.

He checked the coded handwritten lists he had scratched over the years in his notebook. He had a safe deposit box in a Bank of America near the pony track at Del Mar, *where the surf met the turf,* as their ads happily tooted. It didn't surprise him to have one located so close to where he was. He had safe deposit boxes all over the United States. The money didn't earn interest, but then, he didn't pay taxes on it, either. Maybe he could find a motel for the night, and then stop by Del Mar in the morning.

He piled the empty ice chests back in the bus, put the fishing poles in on top of them, and drove a few miles to a Chevron station at the northern end of Oceanside. He pulled into a parking space next to the pay phone, and spent a few minutes talking to himself with the phone up against his chin.

"Okay, then, that's what I'll do," he said decisively, hanging up the phone.

He walked over to the attendant, who lazily eyed him over a wrinkled sheaf of green race sheets.

"My bus is overheating," The Man With The Scar said.

"Ahh. However, unfortunately, we have no mechanic until tomorrow," the attendant's voice lilted back at him with an East Indian accent.

"Well, can I leave it where it is until tomorrow morning?"

"Yesss...if you leave the key with me."

The man took the keys from his pocket and placed them in the little sliding tray.

"Don't steal my bus," he warned, grinning to show he wasn't serious.

"Ahh, yes," the attendant smiled back. "I am tempted to the very limit of my virtue by such a valuable machine."

"If I don't come back in three days, it's yours," the man said, waving as he walked away in the direction of a Howard Johnson's he had noticed just a few blocks down the service road. The 24-hour Denny's next door to HoJo's looked inviting, so he had a piece of apple pie with a scoop of vanilla ice cream and a cup of coffee before he walked back to the on-ramp to the 405 south to San Diego. Further study in his little book had revealed he also had a safe deposit box at a Wells Fargo near Point Loma. He selected a hitchhiking spot where he would be seen from a long way off, and where there was ample space so the car could pull off the road and let him in. But traffic was so light that no cars came, and after a while he moved into the tangled nest of acacias and bottlebrush on the side of the road. He lay on a thin bed of dried leaves, using his knapsack for a pillow. He was used to such sparse accommodations, and he soon drifted into the usual troubled nightmares that made up his sleep.

The Man With The Scar dreamed, and for once it wasn't his regular dream of the *Coeur Desir*. In this dream, he was back in Southern New Mexico. It was the early '70's, and after the end of his Horror Tours to the wet green lands of death, he'd finally gotten away from the war. He'd used his savings to buy two thousand dusty desert acres with an old cabin that had no indoor plumbing. His place was located about fifty miles outside Silver City. It included a piece of dry-bed creek, a little scraggy-pine mountain—a 2,300 foot hill, really—and a dozen old glory holes. He'd bought a sturdy, ten-year old pickup truck and loaded it with picks and shovels, pulleys and rope and plenty of dynamite. He'd known about this place because, ten years before, back before the *Coeur Desir* and the endless craziness that had followed, as a college boy he'd done his summer geology field camp in this area. He'd promised himself that someday he was going to come back and, using his knowledge of strata and igneous intrusions that he thought might somehow be special and unique, he was going to do what the desperate miners of the Great Depression had never accomplished. He was going to find the Mother Lode.

The weeks and months which followed had been filled with mindless pick-work as he opened one of the more promising of the old glory holes, shored up the ancient, rotting timbers, cleaned out the owls and rattlers, and started an offshoot side tunnel from the main shaft.

He'd had his fair share of cave-ins, snakes and incidents with the touchy dynamite, but all in all, after Nam, he was finding the experience restful; that is, until one moonless night when he was awakened by the sound of an airplane cutting its engines and pulling a dead-stick landing on the alkali flat at the base of the mountain where his cabin was located.

He took his Borchardt and crept silently into the nearby pines. But he didn't have to worry for his own safety. The plane was a silvery DC-3, and the pilot was Dave Toomley.

"Need a favor, Clay..." Dave had said. They were sitting on the porch of the cabin, watching the crescent moon rise over the distant horizon as they drank Johnny Walker Black straight from a bottle which they passed back and forth between them. The Man With The Scar saw that his old friend had gained a couple of pounds, mostly around the waist. Toomley was wearing a diamond on his index finger that looked big as a walnut, and he had at least a pound of heavy-linked gold in a chain around his neck. *True to his fate,* The Man With The Scar thought.

"Sure. Anything, Dave." Since their adventure at the *Coeur Desir,* The Man With The Scar had the strong but peculiar notion that Toomley's life and his own were forever intertwined, and he was sure that Toomley felt the same, even though the two of them had only met a few times over the years since that fateful evening in *Da Cao* when the Vietnamese had started to celebrate Tet and ended with gunfire raking the land.

"I want to store a few things out here for a couple of weeks."

"How big?"

"Pallet size."

"Sure. I'll get the truck."

The Man With The Scar backed his pickup truck next to the door on the side of the DC-3.

"Remember how we used to throw flares and leaflets out of these?"

Toomley grinned and nodded. "Yeah. And people who wouldn't talk."

"You, maybe. I never did that." The Man With The Scar didn't believe Toomley had, either. But he wasn't sure.

With both of them pushing, the pallet tipped and slid onto the back of the pickup.

"Where you going to put it?" Toomley asked.

The Man With The Scar shrugged. "Closest glory hole okay?"

"How do we get it back out? Ropes an' pulleys?"

"Sure." The Man With The Scar couldn't stop admiring the plane. "By the way, you fly this thing in here yourself?"

"Oh. I almost forgot. That's the other thing." Toomley disappeared in the depths of the DC-3 and returned dragging a body. It was a middle-aged Vietnamese man, dapper-looking except for the small bullet hole through his left temple.

Toomley shrugged. "He tried to do the same to me."

"Dave, that's a body..." The Man With The Scar said.

"You always did belabor the obvious. Clay, this scum was going to put me in the dirt!"

"Anybody I can count on coming to look for him?"

"Nobody. Not ever."

"Any other instructions?"

"If I don't come back in three months, take the stuff from the pallet and put it in a safe place."

"What is it?" The Man With The Scar asked.

"Money," Toomley replied with a happy little smile. "Lots and lots of money."

They stood together for a moment, two men thinking about a broken-down, out of place cottage named *Coeur Desir,* a Frenchman with a lopsided grin and red veins on his nose, and a very old *ba* with stringy hair and bright orange betel nut juice at the corner of her mouth.

"Whose money is it?"

Toomley shrugged again. "Spoils of war. Saigon government was in power almost a decade before we got Diem shot. Funny, I never used to think of money as being so bulky."

"What ever happened to that contract you and I signed? Remember? You were going to buy a whorehouse."

"Oh, I don't know," Toomley said, "It's around somewhere." He was looking out over the tan-gray surface of the hard-packed sandy dry wash that he was going to have to use to lift his plane back into the night. "Three months, Clay. I'll be back before then."

That night after the moon moved a little higher in the sky, Dave Toomley took off for an unknown destination, and the next day The Man With The Scar buried the Vietnamese stranger in a shallow indentation on the back side of his mountain. He covered the slight body with rocks, and then triggered a small avalanche down on the gravesite with several sticks of dynamite. The explosion uncovered a little vein of quartz. Since the vein was made interesting with occasional sprinkle of pink and light green tourmaline and one thin wire of gold that sprayed and regrouped and occasionally plumped into soft little nuggets, the months passed swiftly while he followed it down and back into his mountain, and all the while the talus pile grew and grew over the grave.

Before The Man With The Scar knew it, nearly a year had passed by, and Toomley still hadn't returned. After that, he began to follow Toomley's instructions. He bought a used pop-top for the back of his truck and began taking extended road trips around the country, depositing stiff packets of $20, $50 and $100 bills in safe deposit boxes in places he'd always wanted to visit but had never gotten around to, like Caledonia, Minnesota, Corpus Christi, Texas and Wallingford, Vermont.

8

It's hard to figure people out. The Man With The Scar (that he got the night of Tet, 1968, while crossing Saigon on his return to Tan Son Nhut) decides to hitchhike halfway across America to his 40th class reunion. He's got a quarter of a billion dollars earning absolutely no interest at all in safe deposit boxes around the country, and another quarter billion earning as much in a glory hole in southern New Mexico—yet he stops at the wharf in San Diego to collect what he figures is his rightful compensation from the old sea captain.

Captain Griggs was working late, poring over the piles of invoices scattered about in the pool of yellow light on his distressed antique desk. In spite of the fog, the weather was kicking up and he could hear the slap of waves against the piers. There was a whisper of sound behind him; he looked up in time to see one of his own chairs crashing down on his head. When he regained a semi-woozy consciousness, his head felt like it was clamped in a vice and he found himself tied in the big armchair in which he ordinarily sat when regaling fat and flush businessmen with yarns of the heavy tuna tonnage to be pulled in on one of his long-range trips. There was sticky tape across his eyes and mouth.

"Tis your albatross, come to pick up his pay!"

Griggs grunted and growled, but the tape held.

"I'll pull the tape from your mouth if you promise to be quiet," the man's familiar voice said.

He nodded in the darkness, and the tape was jerked from his lips.

"May a thousand fleas infest your armpits," Griggs muttered. He salted his language with salty sayings like that, playing the role of a lord of the seven seas who drank and brawled in every port around the world.

"Aye, Captain."

"We live in an electronic age, matey-boy. And I know the print of your black thumb," the captain said.

"The what?" The Man With The Scar asked.

"I have your mark. The shape of your face. I know you, Clay Rhett, for the vile bilge-dog you are." The name spilled scornfully from the captain's lips. "Social security. Driver's license. Credit cards. I got them all. From now on, you're a hunted man, and I'll see you hang from a yardarm."

"Your boat doesn't have a yardarm. No sails at all, or did you forget?"

There was a sound of a metal box opening.

When he heard that sound, the captain became infuriated and fought against the tape binding him. "May a camel spit in your face, you dirty blaggard! Why don't you go rob an ATM or a 7-11?"

The Man With The Scar dumped all the money from Griggs' petty cash box in a plastic grocery bag. "This isn't a robbery. You're forgetting, Griggsy; you owe me six months back pay." He paused for a moment. "By the way, just what is a 'blaggard'?"

"I owe you nothing, you scurvy vulture!"

"In a few moments, that will be true."

A long silence developed between them. Finally the captain spoke in a low voice, as if confiding his innermost secrets, "Rhett, you caused me a lot of problems."

"Maybe. But I made one of the better bacon-and-egg sandwiches ever seen on the high seas."

"You blew up the kitchen halfway down Baja."

"Nonsense. It exploded by itself."

"Bluebeard's balls, Rhett, I had nothing but trouble since the moment you came onboard the Southern Seas."

"Adventures, Captain. You had excitement and adventures."

"Horse piss! You think about it. We got caught in two heavy blows, nearly got capsized. Lost our refrigeration, had to throw away a big mess of fish. Clipped off the end of the dock in Cabo; that little *adventure* cost me a small fortune. Three of my clients suffered heart attacks and one even died. The Southern Seas caught fire and we nearly lost her. Crossing shipping lanes, we clip a freighter, lose an engine. And that goddamn fool paddler."

The Man With The Scar nodded, remembering. "We did share some times. Don't forget the waterspout."

"You are a fuckin' albatross, mate."

"You have to pay the albatross, too, Captain. Didn't you ever read your Samuel Taylor Coleridge?"

"You *shoot* the albatross!"

"That's a form of payment," The Man With The Scar agreed, a slight smile lighting his face. "You should have thought of that sooner, Griggsy-boy."

The captain lost all his quaint and gruff sea-lore language and his voice sounded querulous and petty. "You jumped ship, Rhett. There's a law against it."

The man replaced the tape across the captain's mouth. "I don't think so," he said. "Maybe at sea the captain can be a dictator, but on land the worker is allowed to quit."

Blanked by the tape, the captain's reply was a muffled roar.

The Man With The Scar across his right eye tipped his hand in a brief salute.

"I'd like to stay, but I've been invited to an exclusive party at the Contempo. The albatross bids you *Cheerio*."

He turned out the light and carefully pulled the door shut behind him. The pier was all but deserted. One pair of lovers with an arm around each other's waist gazed out to sea. The Man With The Scar pulled back in the shadows and watched them for a moment.

The fog was a ghastly presence as it swept wraithlike past the pale orange streetlights that hung above the pier. The money from the captain's small lockbox had all been in small bills. It made an awkward lump in The Man With The Scar's jacket pocket.

He looked again towards the lovers, who had now walked to the furthest end of the pier. He was in no hurry. His arthritis was acting up in his bad knee, the way it did when the weather changed. He thought about the larger lump of bills that he had placed in his bank safe deposit box in Del Mar that morning. That deposit came to $37,500, exactly. That was an odd sum, he thought, unless you figured that $50,000 minus $12,500 was $37,500. One way of guessing what had happened at Castro's was that Millie had skimmed 25% from the money Pez and Jimmy Ray had been expecting. It was a C.O.D. shipment, and they had certainly been arguing about the amount due. He wondered if Millie had talked it over with Randy beforehand, or if she'd simply lightened his wad without telling him. Millie was an interesting combination of liar, petty thief, gun moll and little-girl-lost. The Man With The Scar, who seemed in his wanderings to pick up a variety of stray alley cats, defrocked ministers and other outcasts, decided he liked her.

He took the frayed spiral notebook from his pocket and carefully studied the coded pages. He never went to the same safe deposit box twice in a row. It looked like the next closest box was a Washington Mutual in Escondido. And it occurred to him that, if he took the inland roads, this bank was on the way he would have to go to visit his dearest old friend. The thought of their ancient, brief but passionate love affair with its shockingly violent ending set his mind to wandering again.

It had taken place a few years after he had temporarily set aside his dig in his New Mexico mine, which had become extremely difficult due to unstable rock formations that had given way and nearly buried him several times. He was working in Phoenix, had talked his way onto the staff as a hotshot reporter for the Sun. They soon learned to love him at the paper; Clay Rhett was always where the action was. She—the girl who was soon to become the love of his life— was just out of college, doing a fling as a society scribbler before settling down to the real life she wanted: the house, the dogs, the kids, the whole front yard. From the moment their eyes first locked, it was romance at a glance, and the two of them fell head over heels, hopelessly, recklessly in love. For his part, he had never felt that way before or since, that wonderful, hopeless and yet hopeful feeling when you throw all your dreary past lives away and go dancing along common sidewalks with your feet never quite touching the ground. After a whirlwind courtship, they had married swiftly and secretly, in the face of her father's furious threats. The old man was a state senator, and he had planned and plotted her marriage to crusty old Carlos Perez, a land baron and one of the wealthiest men in the Southwest. In a wild chase from the chapel to the airport, bullets had shattered the windshield of The Man With The Scar's rented Chevy Nova. The small car had overturned, and the love of his life had been killed. *Adventure and excitement,* he'd thought bitterly as he held her crushed and dying body in his arms. In that moment, he had been forced to recognize and finally admit that which he had long suspected—for reasons he would never fully understand, his innocent remarks and signature on an old scrap of parchment was to be his lifelong curse. *May you live in interesting times!*

Now The Man With The Scar thought of his lost love while he waited quietly in the shadows until the Point Loma security patrol car made its regular sweep through the parking lot. And then, with a last look after the lovers, he limped across the foggy lighted area and disappeared up one of the myriad streets leading away from the sea. After a time, his thoughts drifted away from his one true love, and he found himself wondering what had happened to his old CIA buddy, David Toomley.

It was a lonely and godforsaken spot as far out on the Mojave Desert as Flame Boy's impatient ways would allow Ice Man to drive. Dusty knew the area well, because the landscape was dotted with little depressions where he'd laid to rest six or seven unfortunates who had crossed the two of him over the past dozen years. As he looked around, he was feeling a little confused, like a fusty blue jay, over just where he'd buried this or that walnut, maybe more like the proverbial dog with too many bones who had already used up all the obvious places and now couldn't start digging without the risk of uncovering old treasures. But, being out of the way like this little corner of the Mojave was, he was amazed that Randy, the Seventh Wonder of the Yuppie-boy World, had found it at all. He watched Randy's VW bus as it bumped its dusty way over the back road to where he waited. He lifted a Coke from the Big Boy Styrofoam cooler in his backseat and managed to drain it before Randy pulled up and nervously walked towards him, already waving his hands and yammering his senseless excuses as he came.

Flame Boy was itching to get out and do his work, but Dusty tapped his fingers and drew dirty little bathroom wall drawings in the dust on the hot front fender of his jet-black BMW while Randy explained about the money, which was gone, gone, gone. Ice Man listened to the wild-eyed tale of how Boy-boy had picked up some old guy with a slash across his face like he'd been cut by a saber. How the dope pickup had gotten screwed up because Pez and Jimmy wanted an extra cut of the take. How Randy had managed to get the stuff anyway, but then the Mexicans had gotten wind of something at the border, and he doped his hitchhiker, the old geezer with the deep scar down his face, into driving the van across. But the geezer had panicked and unexpectedly driven off into the San Diego night in Randy's old tan VW bus with the white top and a load of dope with a street value of nearly four million dollars. And how Randy, by sheerest dumb luck, had spotted his bus in a gas station, but with the dope missing and the geezer miles gone to nowhere.

"I think he probably lives in Cabo San Lucas," Randy said, going over the details yet another time. "He has the dope. I-I'm sure of it..."

"You don't sound so sure."

"Well, I am," Randy said, feeling peeved at having to repeat his story so many times. "Why did we have to meet way out here in the desert, anyway?"

"You don't like nature?"

"Nature is hot and nasty. Look at you. You're sweating like a pig."

Dusty tried not to let his anger get away with premature murder. He sighed and patiently began to review the description of the man with the saber scar, "Randy. One thing at a time here. You say he was an *old* man."

"I don't know how old, Dusty. Sixty, maybe. Fifty, maybe. Hell, he was older than me. Over forty, for sure."

"Dark skin and blond hair," Dusty prompted. "Doesn't that seem very strange?"

"I don't know from strange, man. It was like he was out in the sun a lot. A deep tan. Bleached mustachio, you know, like a Hell's Angel?"

"Did he have a potbelly like a biker?"

"No." Randy was sounding irate. "He was skinny. I mean, not skinny. He was *ordinary*."

"What else?"

Randy racked his brain and remembered the man telling stories of cooking on the high seas. He was fairly sure scar face had been a cook on a fishing boat. He relayed everything he could remember that the man had told him, about how the captain of the boat he had worked on was a loser and how the man had jumped ship in Cabo San Lucas.

"What else?" Dusty asked.

"*Nothing* else. Wait—he seemed to limp a little, come to think of it."

"Which leg?"

"His right leg. Same side as the scar."

"Anything else? Anything at all?"

"Nope. That's it."

That was, indeed, *the big it* for Randy. In one smooth motion, Dusty brought up the pistol he had been resting at his side. Flame spat from the silencer, and a small hole appeared in the center of Randy's forehead. Randy's mouth jerked open, but he toppled on his back without saying a word.

"And there you go," Dusty said to nobody in particular.

Having done the dirty work, Flame Boy walked off in a huff, leaving whomever to handle the details. Dusty sighed and looked about helplessly for a moment. He was a slight, well-knit man who didn't like physical labor. He wiped a lock of kinky yellow-brown hair from his eyes and began to drag

Randy's body by means of one of his flashy, high-topped walking shoes. The body offered no special resistance as Dusty dragged it around a big rock and dumped it in a shallow grave. Dusty picked up the square-toed shovel and began spading the sandy gravel back into the hole. It annoyed him that he was going to have to drive Randy's old bus somewhere, and then he was going to have to come back for his own car.

"Now, Mister Randy Boy-Boy, you see why I was sweating like a pig," Mr. Ice Man said in his peculiar, polite but clipped educated black accent. "It's hard, digging a suitable enough hole, which I have done specially for you, out of the goodness of my heart." There was no answer, and Dusty kept on shoveling.

As he worked, Ice Man visualized their next move, just the way the shrinks on the daytime talk shows always said to do it. They were going down to San Diego to talk matters over with a charter sports fishing boat sea captain. Ice Man could see himself handling the whole thing, walking on a big wooden dock past rows of white boats trimmed in reds, greens and blues. He was wearing light blue boat shoes, a pair of tan cotton pants, a light blue polo shirt, and a captain's hat tilted at a rakish angle over his silvery BluBlocker sunglasses. He saw the captain coming towards him, arms extended in greeting. The sea captain in his mind was an amiable, jolly man who was chuck-full of information about The Man With The Scar, knowledge that he was delighted to pass on to Dusty. Ice Man saw himself posing as a boat insurance salesman, or perhaps a private detective whose specialty was tracking down seafaring men with news of inheritances. The two of them would have a pleasant meeting after which Dusty would quietly be on his way with the information he sought, and nobody would get themselves killed.

But it was a very hot day, made worse by the hard work it was to throw dirt around on the desert. Most of Randy's body was still uncovered, but Dusty decided to sit in the shade and contemplate for a while. He couldn't decide which he hated most, the shimmering vile desert or somebody stupid like Randy, who just couldn't follow simple orders and get his job done right.

9

Trouble, they say, is where you find it. Some live their lives in the peaceful shade, in the shallow pond, in the gentle stand of birch trees. Others dare the rapids, dive from moving objects, thrill to the hunt and the chase. Still others have no choice. For these few, it isn't a matter of finding trouble; it is a question of trouble finding you.

The two U.S. Forest Rangers, the middle-aged lifer and his younger female assistant, were parked at the base of the steep cutback grade that led up the eastern face of the High Sierras, mostly killing time until the last shift of the last day of the season was up and they could drive back to town. The assistant, Rene Riniatta, waited in the front seat with her feet up on the dashboard of the old green Blazer while Gus walked back fifty feet or so to pull the metal bar across the road and lock the gate, officially marking an end to the summer camping season in this section of the country. Rene fiddled with her stamped-shell silver earrings from Italy, impatient to be gone. From where she was sitting, she could see in the big rectangular side mirror that Gus was working his ass off trying to free the gate, which had rusted over from last year. His face was red and he was squirting at the metal joints with a slimy can of Liquid Wrench and yanking the heavy swing gate up and down. She wasn't surprised at the effort it was taking. Some of the nights had already been freezing, and there was a scum of blue-gray snow wherever the direct sunlight didn't hit. But locking the gates was his job, and she didn't move to help him. Gus was too lazy, anyway. It served him right; a guy like that needed a good kick in the butt every now and then, just to keep his juices going.

Rene was idly examining the shine on her nails in the dull afternoon light when she saw the solitary hiker coming their way up the long, winding piedmont grade from Lone Pine. It was 15 minutes until the lone walker finally trudged past the Blazer. Gus was still back at the gate, cussing and fuming.

"Where you think you're going, fellah?" she said, frowning out her open window at the hiker. She'd learned the forest ranger's outfit did her little good unless she established command right from the first dog bite. After a summer of bullying stupid weekend campers to douse their fires and showing them how to bury their own shit, the necessary roughness burst automatically from her lips.

The hiker glanced at her briefly, and then continued on without saying anything or even breaking stride. She had a brief glimpse of bleached hair and a deep scar running perpendicular from his hairline through his dark aviator sunglasses and continuing downward in a rending tear that cut through his cheek.

"Hey," she shouted, "what the hell you thinking, Buster-Buddy-Boy?!" She pushed the door open with her foot, hoping to catch him a good one in the chest. The man was more nimble than she would have imagined; he jumped sideways and easily avoided the door.

"I asked you a question," she shouted.

Luckily, Gus chose that moment to return from his task. He was all sweaty and red-faced and in no mood for an argument.

"Mister, mister, mister," he said, waving the can of Liquid Wrench and his other empty palm in the chilly graying air. "Road's closed for the winter."

"Don't worry, I'll walk on the shoulder along the side," the man said without breaking his stride. "I won't be using the road, which, as you say, is closed."

Gus moved to intercept him, and stood, arms akimbo, directly in his path.

"I'm sorry, mister, but I can't let you do that. That's a National Forest Area. You need a permit to hike up there. We stopped issuing them about a month ago. It's just too dangerous, with winter coming on."

The man ground to a reluctant halt, like an old windup phonograph player or a lawn mower that was out of gas. Rene could see the hiker's face working as he thought through what he would say.

"You know the big rock off to the left as you make the last turn into the park?" he finally asked. He took off his sunglasses and carefully placed them in the jacket pocket of his khaki shirt. His eyes were steady, light blue-gray in color, and the skin was wrinkled at the corners of his eyes as if he'd spent years outdoors, squinting into the sun. His blond hair was thinning on top, and his mustachio was bleached nearly white.

Rene studied the neat space, about a quarter-inch wide, where the scar cut through his right eyebrow, dividing it in half, and decided it was probably one of those foolish dueling scars young college boys picked up on their year in Germany or France. Rene knew all about fencing; she'd been on the team three years at Middlebury College, even tried out for the Olympics. *Tough shit*, she thought, *he should have kept his guard up.*

"Mister, we don't have time for a palaver, here," Rene said, imitating the western hard-ass talk she'd heard the entire summer.

"Observation Rock," Gus said, fueling her anger as he effectively undercut her authority. "We know it."

"I don't know its name," the older man said. "But you can see a long way from there, actually all the way clear across Owens Valley to the mountains to the east."

Gus didn't want to hear any more. With the pulling of the steel bar gate across the road, he had officially completed his season. He was eager to get back to Lone Pine. He had a reservation up the road at the Thunderbird Motel in Bishop. A shower, a change of clothes, a good hot meal, and who knows, a man could get lucky with one of those young ladies who thought they were cowgirls, that is, if the music was still thumping by the time he got to Whiskey Creek.

"Mister, I don't really have an extra moment for this," he said.

The man's gaze held steadily on his face, holding his attention.

"I spread my wife's ashes there, some years back," he said.

Rene hopped out of the car to join Gus.

"Whoa, hold on there," she said. "Old man, if I were you, I'd shut my mouth right now!"

"What do you mean?" he asked mildly.

"That is strictly illegal. What do you think this is, a cemetery? You're looking at government land, here!"

"I never thought that it might be against the law," the man said. "*We the people*, you know?"

"Never thought about it?!" she scoffed. "Not even a little bit?"

"No. The notion never came up." The man didn't sound particularly concerned or, to her mind, appropriately contrite.

"It's over fifteen miles up those switchbacks to that rock you're talking about," Gus said, squinting up at the heavy overcast. "It's already four in the afternoon. And it's going to snow tonight."

The Man With The Scar was talking again, almost as if he hadn't heard either of them. "I like to go back there every once in a while, just to say hello, or goodbye, or maybe a little of both."

"Well, it's going to have to be next year," Gus said. "Come on, we'll give you a ride back to town."

"No thanks."

Gus reached to take the man's arm; Gus was big and fast, and, although he'd been concerned about the little half-basketball of a tummy he'd been carrying for the last year or two since he'd turned thirty-five, he was still very confident of his persuasive ability. Rene moved quickly to one side and

116

behind the newcomer, thinking she'd be able to jump on his back if he gave them any trouble.

"Don't give us any shit now, buddy-boy!" she yelled.

In that moment, Gus seemed to overextend his body motion, at least that's the way he remembered it later on. The old man barely brushed his arm, it seemed, but the road was slick and Gus suddenly lost his footing and fell heavily to the pavement. Pain sang shrill notes from his chest, and Gus felt like there were spikes driving into his lungs with each gasping breath he took.

The old man didn't pause to help, or even to study what had happened. He moved away from them more swiftly than either of the rangers would have believed possible from such a geezer. He wasn't running; *loping* was maybe a better word. While Gus was still on his stomach, feeling the pain and trying to roll over, the man had already made his way around the closed steel gate, which was only designed to keep out motor vehicles, and was trotting on up the road.

"Come back here, you bastard!" Rene shouted.

"Get the rifle from the truck!" Gus screamed.

She wasn't familiar with Gus's habits; it turned out he kept his rifle in a blanket behind the front seat, and a box of shells in the glove compartment. By the time he told her where everything was and she found the shells and managed to slip a few rounds in the rifle, the old man had disappeared around the first bend in the road.

"Asshole. He can't get away like that," she muttered to herself. She took off in a dogtrot in the direction he'd gone. But when she rounded the first bend, the road ahead was empty. She picked the most likely hiding places on the broken rocks on the high side cliffs, and emptied the rifle, the shots making a throaty bark and the bullets caroming off the granite rock faces and whining away toward Owens Valley.

She turned back with a vague satisfaction that instantly drained to an empty, hollow feeling. The old geezer stepped out from behind a rock directly behind her, not three feet away. She noticed his knapsack had been placed carefully at his feet, and he was wearing light leather gloves. She reversed the rifle and swung the butt in a short, ugly arc towards his head. Her weapon whistled through thin air without making contact with anything, and in another moment he jerked it from her hands. He tilted his head slightly and held up one gloved hand; she understood the expression on his face as a calm and strangely unsettling command to give him space. She had been about to lunge for him, but that look and his simple hand movement paralyzed her, told her of the futility of such a charge and held her rooted to her distance from him. He smashed the barrel on the hard road pavement three times, quickly and efficiently, until he was certain it was bent enough to be useless, and then tossed the rifle back to her.

During their brief encounter, neither of them had said a word. He gestured with a nod of his head; she was free to go back down the road.

"The passes are already snowed in," she hissed, "so you can't get to the other side. And you don't have the gear or the supplies. You're going to have to come back down this way, and soon."

He gave her another sideways nod of the head, this one a little more impatient.

She backed around him and started down the road back the way she'd come.

"And when you do, we'll get you, you lousy son-of-a-bitch!"

But they never did get The Man With The Scar. In fact, that was the last time Gus saw him. Rene herself had to drive into town, to get Gus checked at MedWard One before the nurse left at six. The foothills at the high northern end of Owens Valley took on eight inches of snow that night, and the weather for the next few days turned bleak gray, with wet, chilly gusts of cold wind pumping down from the sheer eastern walls of the Sierras like Frosty's fists.

It turned out Gus had three separated ribs. He had to be driven on to the hospital in Bishop where he was taped and then laid up for a week. Rene certainly wasn't going to drive back up a slippery, dead-end road by herself to wait for some crazy old fuck-head who was probably already frozen coyote meat lying at the bottom of a godforsaken canyon. At least, that's where she hoped he was.

Rene Riniatta would go back to her mother's apartment in New York City, and then on to the Bahamas where it was always gloriously hot and summery. That ridiculous day, that Thursday when she and Gus closed the Butterfield Creek Meadows Road for the season, was the absolute end of her *western odyssey*. She was going to get out of it as fast as she could; she dumped the injured Gus off in Bishop. She waited around a few more days, lurking around the base of the mountains. Then an entirely unsatisfactory happening occurred, something which left her grim and bitter. She left town to soak some of the summer's grime away in a hot water tub at a friend's condo tucked under the ski runs at Mammoth Village. But the early autumn snow was still thin, being mostly man-made, so she hooked up with another friend's private plane for a direct shot back to L.A. and then caught the first jet she could for the Big Apple.

She couldn't say her mother, who'd had her own foolishly romantic flings in the savage 70's, hadn't warned her. Rene told anyone who cared to listen she'd had enough of the flies-on-horseshit way with the barren, silent pine trees always looking down and presuming to judge her, enough of that to last a lifetime. Leave it all to the beavers and the garbage-picking, fleabag bears. She headed south and hooked on as a scuba instructor on an ultra-lux cruising boat that puttered around the Caribbean like it was one big tropical pond. She concentrated on *mellowing out*, intending to work her way to some semblance of forgetfulness of her *wretched mountain time* with whatever stiffening white, yellow, black and brown penises and softly unfolding labia that sweet Aphrodite sent her way.

On April 16 of the following year, the snow had retreated to where Gus was able to unlock the steel gate across the road and forge his exploratory way on up the still icy switchback road in his old green Blazer. With his tire chains clanking over the bare stretches of asphalt, he made it nearly to the trailhead at Butterfield Meadows before the big drifts across the road told him he could go no further.

But before that, as he came around the last winding turn before the steeply climbing road left the switchbacks to run across the plateau through the first of the high valley meadows, he slowed down and then pulled over onto the wide gravel turnout by Observation Rock.

He sat for a while, and then turned the engine off and hitched himself out of the truck, using the steering wheel for leverage. A week before, the HMO doctor had said he was all the way back, one hundred percent and up and running, but his ribs still ached sometimes, and he wondered if he'd ever really be right. He thought it over again for the millionth time. *Had he simply slipped and fell to bang himself on the ground, or had that old man somehow managed to sneak in a punch as he was on his way down?* What Gus remembered most clearly was the image of a sudden, upside-down world, but lately he'd also seemed to remember, somewhere in there, his chest striking the old man's knee. Couldn't be. It was just an old man, and he, Gus, had fallen wrong, that was all.

Gus stood there for a moment or two, looking from the truck to the rock and back again, not knowing what he was looking for or what he should reasonably expect to find. He didn't even really understand why he'd pulled the Blazer over. Idle curiosity, maybe.

The snow had melted away from all but the northeast corner of the rock. Gus took a deep breath in the crisp air. He turned clockwise in a slow, complete circle, and then walked to the back side of the upturned finger of black-black granite, feeling foolish and hearing the empty crunch of his own footsteps on the gravel as he went.

"Yep. You sure can see a long way," he said to himself, almost as if he was continuing an agreeable conversation.

He saw the wingspread of a golden hawk gliding in the thin, crisp air. It was hanging high above the nearest cliffs, and yet well below his present vantage point. Far and away he could see the first green tint coming to the lowest reaches of the great, empty valley, and beyond that, the dark eastern mountains in the distance where he knew Nevada lay. *It surely was a sacred place, if a body was of a mind to think that way.* Gus shivered and zipped up his down vest. *Too cold to be making a fool of himself for nothing like this. There was nothing here.* And in his hurry to get back to the warmth of the heater, he almost missed the very thing that he was searching for without really knowing what it was. He had turned and was walking back to his faded green Blazer, and there it lay, practically at his feet, frozen in the caked snow which had turned to whitish, semi-clear ice at the base of Observation Rock. One single coral pink rose, looking fresh and pretty as if it had just been cut that morning.

Ice Man lingered by the shallow grave, taking another long rest between his short and furious bouts of shoveling, and wondered why he hadn't thought to bring Bopo along to do the spadework. Bopo was the perfect shovel man; the poor bopster couldn't find his way to the bathroom, much less remember a site in the desert. But Bopo was back in Oakland, probably resolving minor disputes with a tire iron, and Dusty had to amuse himself with Randy's wallet. There were a couple of hundred in twenties, which Dusty put in his own pocket. He flipped the credit cards into the shallow hole, trying to hit the heel of one of Randy's shoes, which was the last of Randy still showing above the sandy soil.

He was about to flip the thin leather wallet after the cards, when his exploring fingers pulled a photograph from behind a flap in a hidden compartment. It was a badly lit amateur photo of a college girl with frizzy blond hair. The shot, from the waist up, revealed a very embarrassed and naked young woman who was trying unsuccessfully to cover her ample breasts with her hands. In spite of the novice nature of the photo, Dusty found himself getting excited. Before he knew it, he'd pulled down his pants and was masturbating into the shallow grave.

"Sorry, Randy," he said, "sometimes I just can't help myself."

He was about to flip the photo after the credit cards when he turned it over. On the back it said, *Millie—How do I love thee? Let me count the ways.* And—*Glory Be!*—there was a San Francisco phone number. Dusty put the photo in his own wallet and sat in the sparse shade at the side of his black BMW. He knew he had to shovel some more, but he didn't really feel like it. Randy hadn't mentioned anything about a girl going along with him. But with a yuppie amateur on a drug run, anything was possible.

10

Lord won't you buy me just one literate friend?
Someone to guide me, my words to defend?
I live here in Hollywood/ On no one depend
Lord won't you buy me/ just one literate friend?

Ah, yes, my friends, give respect and credit where credit is due...but let's get on with it, shall we? What on earth is Drug Lord Dusty doing flying to the southern tip of Baja? One thing is certain: he will run into the ancient One-Eyed Mexican who is the friend of The Man With The Scar (said scar that he received in South Vietnam on that fated night when traveling from the Coeur Desir, a house of ill repute, to Davis Station). And one other thing is certain: though Dusty is a half-crazed killer, he is in for a little unexpected grief...

A few years earlier, a bad early photo of Dusty that was taken from his Eldridge Cleaver Era had been featured on America's Most Wanted. There he was in his dreadlocks, looking wanted as hell for the murder of a CPA in Walnut Creek. But it didn't bother him much because he didn't look like that anymore. Even moving in and out and around the country was no problem for him, thanks to a well-paid friend of his at the DEA who furnished doctored IDs and even passports whenever he needed. Wearing his closely clipped head of hair, a pair of steel wire-rimmed glasses and a standoffish look of superiority, Ice Man passed through airports as a bristly, arrogant gentleman of education and, by the way, color.

This time his Southwest Airlines flight south down the spine of Baja was full of fishermen and honeymooning couples, and since especially nobody on vacation wanted to dick with a militant, light-skinned black, he had an easy time of it.

Once he got to Cabo, he poked around the boats and the bars for a few days until finally one afternoon an old, one-eyed Mexican promised to tell him everything he wanted to know about The Man With The Scar running through his eyebrow in return for a little cash and maybe a knock or two from the bottle with the worm in it. Dusty agreed they would meet that evening.

It turned out to be one of those muggy tropical nights when a warm and heavy fog covered the softly rounded folds of arid land near the tip of Baja like a fuzzy cotton blanket.

Dusty had said he'd like to get together somewhere quiet where they could talk, and the ancient, one-eyed man had suggested the patio beside the swimming pool at the Hotel Mar de Cortez. As the pool was unlit, there would be no night swimming, and they could be alone under one of the big umbrellas and yet could still attract the attention of one of the waiters from the bar should their thirst demand it. He was so old, Dusty joked that he hoped he could manage to stay alive until their meeting.

But the ancient one did not laugh. "Thank you, *señor*, but I have become very skilled in matters of personal survival," he said with a very serious note to his words. Neither Ice Man nor Flame Boy could take the old fart seriously; Christ, the man was so skinny the elastic in his pants made the material bunch up, and the threadbare jeans still looked ready to head south.

That evening, Dusty showed up early for the meeting. He distastefully rubbed the light coating of sandy mist from one of the steel-tube-and-plastic chairs that he would have to sit on. He was wearing a light tan cotton suit he'd purchased from Nordstrom's in San Francisco. Ice Man was very particular about how he looked and what he wore. *Clothes make the man*, Dusty's mamma had always said. This suit wore like iron, but it also picked up smudges like a dirt magnet.

He selected his seat carefully so that the old man would be seated looking into the single light source while he was simply a black shadow, framed in light. *Power play seating.* Ice Man coolly visualized the old man giving him the information he wanted, and the two of them shaking hands and parting amicably.

Dusty sat down and waited, but before his eyes had a chance to adjust to the darkness, the old man's voice reached him from the deepest shadows of another corner of the room. Apparently, he'd gotten there first. *Checkmate on the power play seating.*

"Did you already order for us, señor?"

Dusty indignantly replied that he had not, and heard the flap of plastic sandals shuffling away toward the lighted bar area.

Once the beers and the mandatory bottle of tequila were settled in position on the table, the old man sighed and started to sit in a chair across from Dusty. He was so thin as to be bony, with skin wrinkled like that of an elephant. He, however, proved to be just as concerned about the sheen of dew on the chairs as had been Dusty, and he wouldn't sit until he had wiped his own chair dry. Then he moved the chair so they were both in shadows.

"Are you finally ready?" Dusty asked. "You know, I've come a long way to talk to you." He could feel the impatient tug as Flame Boy flared in indignation.

"Ahh, s*eñor*," the old man said. "I am most complimented. And you do not even know me."

Ice Man held his tongue and counted to five under his breath. He felt so tense, the internal struggle to hold Flame Boy down was almost physical. Back in Oakland, this loose-lipped asshole would already be dead.

"I am seeking information on a friend of mine. An old man with a scar." Ice Man forced a thin smile and made a vertical slicing motion with his hand across his right eye.

"Yes, my nephew tells me this already. I know him quite well, actually. And what is it you wish to know?"

"Anything. Everything. Name. Where he lives. What he does."

"I thought he was a friend of yours, s*eñor*."

"Now that there was just a figure of speech. Come on, man. Do you know him or don't you?" Flame Boy hated the whining quality he heard coming from Dusty's mouth and in that moment he resolved somebody was going to die here.

The old man cocked his head, staring at him but saying nothing. Dusty felt a heavy weight begin to fill his chest until he felt it might explode. He patted his pockets for a Mylanta tab, and finding none, brought out his wallet, extracted a hundred dollar bill and placed it on the table. The fact that the crisp, new bill clung to the wet surface of the tabletop pleased him, and he tapped and smoothed it with his finger until it clung to the surface like a label.

"Clay Rhett," the old man said softly. His lone eye, bright like a sparrow's, concentrated on Dusty's finger smoothing down the single bill.

"What?" Dusty asked.

"That is the name of the old man with the scar. But to me, you see, he was a young man, age being a relative thing."

"Look, don't get philosophical on me. How do you know him?"

"We were on a fishing boat together for some months this past summer. He was the cook and I was the slave."

"What boat?"

"The Southern Seas. It is an American sport fishing boat, stationed out of Point Loma, in San Diego."

"I know of that boat. Is he on it now?"

"No. He has retired from his life at sea."

"And where has he gone?"

"To a meeting at the Contempo."

"And when will it be, this meeting?"

"November 29th," the old man recited proudly. "In the evening. That is, as you yourself can calculate, yet some weeks distant, so you can have a chance to meet him there."

"And where is this Contempo?"

"Somewhere in the land of the suburbs south of Chicago. Perhaps Captain Griggs would know more certainly."

"How's he getting there?"

"He prefers the two-lane blacktop."

Dusty realized Flame Boy was so eager to come popping out that he was actually grinding his own teeth, something he hadn't done since grade school when they made him wear one of those rubber fitters all night long until he stopped. He noticed that, although the old man's hands trembled and he looked often at the drinks on the table, he had yet to sip either beer or tequila.

"Old man. Drink. Now."

The old man reached gratefully for one of the shot glasses.

"No. The other glass."

"*Señor?*"

"Drink from the other glass."

The old man did as he was instructed, tossing the double shot down in one motion and then wiping his mouth with the back of his hand.

"*Gracias*," he said.

Dusty nodded, tapping his fingers on the table.

"And you're sure you do not know the location of the Contempo?"

"I do not know it, s*eñor.*"

"Do you know any more? Anything else at all?" Dusty asked.

"I have told you what I know."

"Then the money is yours."

"Thank you, s*eñor.*" But the old man did not bend forward to peel it from the table. He sat in his chair, arms folded, watching Dusty until the American became tired of waiting.

"How old are you, anyway?" Dusty asked.

"I will be 94 in December, on the Nativity of Our Lord, *Jesu Christi.*"

"You ain't going to make it," Flame Boy said, smiling an evil grin as he took the pistol with the long silencer from under his arm.

But with a move equally as practiced, the old man took a rusty grenade from his jacket pocket and held it over his head, pulling the pin with his other hand in the same moment. The grenade was one of the World War II "pineapple" variety. Most of the original olive paint had flaked away, leaving the dull gray metal. The pin fell to the table with a little clink. There was a moment of silence between them as Dusty's two eyes locked with the old man's single glittering eye.

"It is an old grenade, señor," the old man said softly. "Like me, very, very old." His lone eye glittered in the dim light. "And, also like me, with very little to lose."

"That's a fucking museum piece," Dusty said. He tried to laugh, but his voice had become thick and hesitant.

"There is the chance it will not go off," the old man admitted with a shrug of his thin shoulders that Dusty did not like because the grenade seemed likely to slip from his grasp at any moment.

"All of life is choices," The Man With One Eye continued.

"I said I don't need no more of your fucking philosophy lessons. What do you suggest we do now?"

"No one is hurt this time, señor. You put your little pistola away and walk from the table. After a time, I put the pin back in the grenade. We go our separate ways."

Dusty tried to peel the hundred dollar bill from the table, but it now resisted his efforts.

"No, señor. I gave you what you said you wanted. Now you must leave the money for me."

"Well, fuck you and the big white horse you rode in on!"

The very old man nodded politely. "And your ancestors, chained to the boat."

"Are you calling me a nigger?!" Flame Boy roared, ready to pull the trigger and leap for cover.

"Under the Almighty, we are all, as you say, niggers. Vaya con Dios, señor."

- Dusty was choking with fury, but he saw no choice

other than to stand and back away from the table. He made a big show of putting his gun away, but the old Mexican shook his head.

- "No. Leave the pistola on the table, *señor.*"

Dusty angrily set down the pistol and backed away. The old man was now standing, hand cocked behind his ear and ready to throw the grenade. When Dusty got to the corner, he darted around it.

There was a slight motion from a far corner of the dark courtyard. There was a young man in a Hawaiian shirt and a loincloth.

"Kill, Polly, Kill!" he shouted.

"Killlllllll!" the macaw screeched as it launched itself toward Dusty.

Dusty panicked and dove as the huge attack bird zoomed over his back. As he hit the deck, the pants leg of his expensive suit caught on the thorns of a purple bougainvillea. He pulled away, scratching his leg and ripping his pants.

"Oww! Mamma, what am I doing wrong?" his voice sounded in a little boy's plaint. He rolled on the ground and came up with his ankle hideout gun in his hand, pointed and on the ready. But the parrot, the kid in the Hawaiian shirt and the old one-eyed Mexican were gone.

Ice Man waited outside the hotel for a few hours, hoping the old, one-eyed Mexican would drink to his victory and get careless, but the old man did not exit the hotel, or if he did, Dusty didn't see him. All Dusty got for his time was a damp suit and a runny nose. His Mexican contacts seemed less than sympathetic, or maybe they honestly didn't know who *old one-eye* was, or the parrot boy, for that matter. At any rate, the greasers were of absolutely no help and Dusty wrote the old fart off to experience, figuring that was the last he would ever hear of him. Ice Man headed for the airport, intent on a flight to San Diego and a meeting at Point Loma with a certain Captain Griggs.

11

To be so close to death so many times! Does it numb a person to life's pleasures, or does it make them more desirable? Facing the prospect of cold dirt in one's face, is not a glass of wine that much more refreshing? And if inviting one beautiful woman to your bed is that attractive, then how about two? But enough of idle philosophy. Time to get on with the story, and here we begin not with The Man With The Scar, but with the girl with the extremely foul mouth, even though twitchy-faced and greedy of manner.

Millie wasn't even sure why she expended the effort since Randy's future plans obviously excluded her, but still she had tried and tried to explain to *Mister Big-shot Stockbrokerman* that his chances of convincing Dusty to give him another opportunity in the drug running trade were zero or less. But Randy had brushed her aside and was already on the phone to Oakland before she could open or shut her mouth, making his crazy, gerbil-fucked-up plans to meet with Dusty somewhere out on the desert.

"No, we're in L.A. The valley, actually. The police found my van...Yes, he had a big scar running down his face...no fish, just empty plastic coolers on the beach."

Randy held the phone away from his ear at the outraged squawk. Then he listened and scratched instructions on a hotel notepad. As he wrote, Millie gestured broadly, spasmodically trying to get his attention and disagreeing with everything he said into the phone. Randy did his best to ignore her while she silently mouthed a huge NO three times.

"Yeah. Tomorrow. I can make it, Dusty. Yeah, I've got your cell phone."

"N-O-O-O!" Millie silently pantomimed one last time. But Randy had already hung up the phone and was picking up his suitcase.

A brush with danger does funny things to a man; Millie could see that Randy was now eager to go back and *make good in Mexico*, or even to get the much bigger new assignment that Dusty was hinting at over the phone.

"Oh lover purple gerbil-dick, don't go! We can run away, start a new life in Scherhazabad or Nepal!"

"Silly-Millie," he crooned, stroking her hair affectionately like she was a stupid little dog, "There's no danger. Dusty said I can work it off. He's even got a new assignment for me. Something really big this time."

She knew her Putzer was a successful young man of enterprise and not inclined to take seriously any advice from his plump and curly-haired blond friend, shrill as she could be. Randy often lectured that he had gotten to where he was by knowing the wants, needs and desires of *Joe Average Person*. And when Millie heard him launch into his classic *wants and needs and desires* speech, she put her fingers in her ears and gave up arguing.

They were hiding out from both her father and Dusty at the Aku Aku Motel in Woodland Hills at the west end of the San Fernando Valley. Thinking of the way she wanted to remember him always, she pressed her hips against Randy and kissed his lips.

"Darling, don't go!"

After a moment, he broke away from her clinging embrace and headed out the door, smearing lipstick off his face with one sleeve as he went.

"I'll wait for you forever," she cried, flinging an arm dramatically in his direction.

"You bet you will, sweetheart," he said, giving her a thumbs-up and a last brave wink. Then he pulled the door closed behind him and was gone.

Millie stared at the door, counting with a hitch of her hip, "One—Two—Three—Four..." She stopped, spinning half around and staring at herself in the mirror on the wall. "That's long enough. Oh, Putzer-boy, you are one dead yuppie stockbroker."

She made a beeline for her suitcase and started frantically packing. She pulled a wad of money from under the mattress and stared at it. "People got killed for this," she said, remembering how she'd skimmed it from Dusty's money, part of the load that was supposed to pay Jimmy Ray and Pez in Mexico. She tossed it in the suitcase and threw some jeans and T-shirts on top of it.

A half hour later, she had packed her scant belongings and was waiting for a ride from Ava, a big Scandinavian girl she'd known at UCLA. Ava ran a halfway house for battered women, and so Millie rammed her own head against the motel door, giving herself two black eyes and unlimited sympathy from Ava, who claimed she knew enough about men to want to castrate them all.

After that, Millie spent ten glorious days dutifully collecting $300 each morning from Mumsy's credit card and depositing it in her own account, which was under the name M.A. Bernathy. She also had a driver's license in the same name, and so felt reasonably sure she was safe from the old dragons. After ten days, the ATM ate her mother's credit card, and Ava tried to do much the same to Millie in the big four-poster bed in the guest bedroom, and Millie's Westwood Village sojourn came to a shrill and abrupt end.

It was a clear blue-sky day, one of those days when the High Sierras looked like they were cut out of cardboard and stuck in front of a piece of cerulean blue construction paper. Janie and Frances, two beautiful women in their mid-thirties, were on the lower piedmont, heading towards the mountains and hoping to get up to Butterfield Creek. They were driving a red Jeep with a white canvas top down in the bright sunlight, laughing and singing their liberated version of an old college drinking song:

> He's got a pair of hips
> Just like two battleships
> Say, girls...that's where
> > my money goes!

They pulled up to a green Blazer parked by the side of the road and peeked in at the Forest Ranger snoozing with her hat tipped over her eyes.

"Hey, Ranger-danger!" Frances called. Frances was more of a honey blond, while Janie went for the platinum look.

"Yoo Hoo, Sleeping Beauty!" Janie chimed in.

"Hey, Nature Slut!" Frances roared, "Is this the way to Observation Rock?"

Rene raised her hat, slowly and scornfully flicked the two of them off, and then lowered the flat felt brim over her face again.

"Whooooo! Mother Nature, forgive us!" Frances said.

"Humping Bambi makes you grumpy!" Janie added. And they drove on up the road in gales of their own laughter.

But rounding the next bend, they saw the iron bar pulled across the road. Frances slammed on the brakes and they came to a screeching halt in front of it. There was a man with an old white scar running down the right side of his face sitting on a fallen tree trunk by the side of the road, talking into a cell phone and looking like he was waiting for a ride. He stood and held up one hand, indicating he wanted to finish his conversation.

"Hector," he said into the phone, "your mom isn't going to change, but that doesn't mean you can't be your own man. If you like a girl with a nose ring, that should be your own business...right...and a nipple ring...and a—never mind, I don't want to know."

"Hey there, lonely drifter. Wanna tomato?" Janie, ever the impatient one, called out to him. She held the fat red tomato like she wasn't sure she wanted to give it to him or throw it at him.

"Hang in there, Hector," he said. "I've got to go now. This is the Long Distance Dad, signing off. As ever, don't tell your mother I called."

He put the cell phone in his jacket pocket, picked up his knapsack and walked over to the cherry-red Jeep. He took the tomato from Janie and bit into it. Red juice ran down his face.

"Delicious," he said.

"Last of the season," Janie said, thrown off a little by his friendly approach.

He nodded his head at the metal bar pulled across the road. "Sorry, but the season's over for Observation Rock. Please don't shoot the messenger."

"We shoot everybody we don't like." Frances shrugged. "Wanna ride?"

The Man With The Scar threw his knapsack in back and climbed in after it. Frances turned the ragtop Jeep around and they headed back the other way. Janie teased him with another tomato, holding it between her surgically magnificent breasts.

"*Muy delicioso*, no...?" she asked.

He reached for the tomato and she slapped his hand, but in the next moment she grinned and handed it to him.

"I just can't say no," she said, reaching into the basket full of tomatoes on the floor in front of her. As they approached the green Blazer, Rene started it up and swung in front of them, blocking their path.

"Oh, no you don't, Buster-Buddy-Boy!"

"Is that you?" Frances asked.

"Who?" The Man With The Scar asked.

"Buster-Butty-Boy."

"Not me," he said.

"She must have the wrong perp," Frances said, gunning the jeep onto the gravel edge of the road. They came dangerously close to plunging down a twenty-foot embankment, but there was just enough room and they managed to zoom past. As they went, Janie managed to score a tomato on the Blazer's side window.

Rene, livid with rage, stamped her foot to the floorboards and the Blazer peeled rubber in a long, smoking weave, headed after the red Jeep.

"Oy vey!" Frances shouted, "Nature Slut's got a hard-on. Seat belts!"

"Probably something we said," Janie added, reaching for more tomatoes.

Rene pulled directly behind them, bumping the Jeep to force them off the road.

"That bitch is going to dent us!" Frances yelled, angrily pitching a large plastic coke bottle back at the Blazer. The bottle shattered the glass on the passenger side of Rene's Blazer.

Janie scored again and again with her tomatoes, direct hits on the Blazer windshield. Rene's vision was so impaired that she had to look out the side window—and Janie scored a lucky hit to her forehead!

Completely disoriented, Rene drove off the road, through some willows and into a shallow stream. She sat there steaming, looking like she was going to burst a blood vessel.

"I am going to kill him," she said. "I will personally kill him."

But for the moment, there was nothing she could do. The Blazer wasn't going anywhere. She could hear Frances and Janie hooting and laughing as they drove off.

"Tomato-pasted that bitch!" was the last thing she heard as they drove on down the mountain.

Heading south on 395, Frances swung the Jeep left on the cutoff for Death Valley. They were all singing:
Throw a silver dollar
Down on the ground
And it rolls because it's round...
A feller never knows what
A good girl he's got
Until she slams him down...

Almost immediately, she did a right onto a dusty gravel parking lot and drove up to a Clippy's General Store. The women jumped out and ran on ahead. The Man With The Scar took his time, looking things over as he followed after, wariness having become an old habit.

He wasn't noticed as he quietly entered the small store, which was a rustic, wanna-be 7-11 stocked with expensive Cheetos and Cokes for the tourists. A scruffy manager and equally scruffy hanger-on were behind a small counter near the door. They were leering at the women as they gathered provisions from the narrow aisles.

"Hoo-whee!" the scruffy owner said to nobody in particular, "Things be looking up!"

"Those aren't real," his scruffy friend said, nodding to where Janie was bobbing on by.

"Sure they are," the scruffy owner said, a hurt look on his face.

The girls were doing a fast blitz through the junk food aisles, and soon had a pile of Doritos, miniature apple pies and Fruit Loops piled on the counter.

Janie smiled at The Man With The Scar, holding a bottle of wine between her breasts, "Cheap dago red?" she asked with a witching smile.

The Man With The Scar smiled, nodding approvingly at her. He looked at the scruffy storeowner, "That all the chocolate?"

The storeowner, soured by his interruption, said, "You don't look like a man who could handle his sweets."

The Man With The Scar shrugged, trying not to make anything of it, "I'm pre-diabetic."

"Pathetic city dude." The scruffy hanger-on pushed past him and made towards Janie, "Hey there, sweet baby-cakes."

"Shut up, Puke-face," she said.

In a flash, the scruffy hanger-on turned mean, approaching Janie with a menacing attitude, "Why you—"

Ever proactive, Frances gave him a push that sent him sprawling over stacks of junk food.

The scruffy owner reached behind the counter, pulling out a shotgun and aiming it at Frances. He motioned to Janie with the shotgun, "Over here, sweet-cakes, by your pal." He looked around, realizing everyone wasn't accounted for, "Where's that hippy sweetheart of yours?"

He felt the cold edge of a pistol barrel at the side of his head. It was The Man With The Scar holding his ancient 7.63 mm Borchardt pistol. The antique ancestor to the Luger looked like a pregnant spider.

"Slow down there, Ace...We're just looking to buy a few provisions. Though I should shoot you on principle for your lousy chocolate supply."

The scruffy owner set down his shotgun and slowly raised his hands in the air.

Seeing the pistol, Janie looked at Frances. "Surprise, surprise!"

They stuffed their mouths with gummy bears and tied the two men up with duct tape that they made sure to pay for. No patrons interrupted their business, and in another few minutes they were heading east on 136, a two-lane blacktop leading roughly toward the north end of Death Valley.

It wasn't exactly in the right direction, but The Man With The Scar wasn't going to worry about it. He had six weeks to get to the shindig at the Contempo, that is, if he didn't change his mind about going there.

This could work out to his advantage. Because it was already mid-October, he might avoid a potentially bone-chilling trip through the Rockies by taking the Southern Route through Arizona and New Mexico. Frances stopped a few miles out of town for a pee break. The Man With The Scar wrapped a dramatic red-and-black bandanna Samurai-style around his forehead. With his dark aviator's sunglasses, only a small piece of his scar was apparent on his right cheek.

The long road wound past the dry Owens lake bed. The two women said they were half sisters and that they were both running from their husbands. From the backseat he could see the handle of what looked like a big automatic pistol under the driver's seat.

"What did you think of Thelma and Louise?" the older one asked him.

"That's a movie, right?" he asked.

"Right, Thelma and Louise."

"I never saw it," he lied.

"How could you not see a great movie like that?"

"I worked on a tuna boat. You know, a sport fisher? Out for a week, come in, spend the night doing dirty laundry, turn around, go back out."

"You never got any time off?"

He shook his head. "Captain Queeg was a driven man; it's understandable, he has to pay off his big loan on that boat."

"That wasn't his real name."

"No. It's Griggs. He runs the Southern Seas, a 110-footer out of Point Loma."

Their hiker was a fisherman. That seemed to ease them up. Actually, he corrected them, a *cook* on a tuna boat. They liked that even better.

They drove the hot Wrangler over Townes Pass with Vivaldi's "Four Seasons" blaring from the big add-on boom boxes. They directed him to break out some smoked Gouda cheese from their cooler and pass it around. They all munched on walnuts imbedded in dark chocolate lumps that he found in the cooler in back.

He'd been over this road before, and so he pointed out abandoned mines and distant buttes of interest while the Jeep chugged easily through Mesquite Flat Sand Dunes. They stopped in at Death Valley Scotty's to marvel at the glass house, and pulled into the Furnace Creek campgrounds, where they found time to break open the first of a series of bottles of red wine.

"We have a tent," the younger one bragged.

"A tent, plenty of dark chocolate and a case of good Merlot. You came prepared."

"If you could help us assemble the tent, we might let you sleep with us."

"A most generous offer," he replied politely.

The brand-new tent, which resembled a thin-skinned igloo, was not as easy to put together as the instructions promised, but he had it up in under an hour. He found thick porterhouse steaks in the cooler and cooked them over an open grill, and the three of them huddled together under their single blanket and drank another bottle of fine wine while the sky blackened and filled with stars and the night chilled around them.

"Why aren't all men like you?" the older one said.

"Because they aren't," he replied.

"Where were you when we needed you?" the younger one slurred.

"Safely tucked away on a tuna boat," he answered. They seemed to think that was outrageously funny.

"At the risk of repeating myself, we have a tent," the older one said. "And it's getting chilly out here in the desert."

"You think we'll all fit in there?"

"We like each other."

"Then I suggest we get in with all dispatch."

"I love the way you talk," the younger woman said, brushing his cheek with her lips.

"Share, share," the other said, taking his arm.

It was some hours later, in the middle of the night at a time when they were all a jumble of happy tangled arms and legs, that they settled back and each began reflecting on their lives.

"Tell us about you," the older woman said.

And since he'd had the wine and the fun and was contented in a sleepy way, he began to tell them the story of the *Coeur Desir*, how Toomley had convinced him to take a cab ride that fateful night, how they had met the Frenchman and the ancient woman with orange betel nut juice dripping from one corner of her lips, and how the drunken brawl had swirled around their table while they signed their souls away. They were good listeners, so he continued with a few of the highlight adventures of his life since then: how he'd been in the house next door to the Symbionese Liberation shoot-out in Los Angeles in 1974, and on the plane during the Croatian hijacking at La Guardia in '76, how he'd been fishing nearby when the construction accident happened at the nuclear power plant at Willow Island in '78, his hike down the Gulf Coast in September of '79 just in time for Hurricane Frederick, in Beirut on April 18, 1983, in Libya in '86 for the U.S. air strike, the blizzard in Maine in '87, the earthquake in Los Angeles in '94, a few dozen disasters he could remember off the top of his head, and then he went on to talk about some of the fine things Toomley had collected. He omitted the time Toomley had stopped by his desert acreage with the DC-3, as well as the moment of horror and pain when his own car flipped over and smashed into the pine tree, killing his new bride.

"An old Oriental woman and a Frenchman," Frances mused, "I don't know if they were exactly after your soul."

"Right," Janie said, clearly entranced by the puzzle, "Isn't that the devil's business? Remember that silly Disney movie, "The Devil and Max Devlin"? Elliot Gould plays a schlump who should go to Hell and Bill Cosby has all kinds of trouble signing him up."

"The Frenchman said the word soul," The Man With The Scar said. "I'm sure of it. He was disdainful, as if Americans didn't believe in souls."

"Who knows what a soul is, anyway?" Frances asked, dismissing the notion as a bad idea. "Sounds like it had more to do with your fate or karma."

"Any more of that Merlot?" Janie asked. The Man With The Scar poured her another glass.

"I think you're being tested," Frances said hesitantly.

"Yes," Janie agreed immediately. "Both you and Toomley, dreaded CIA man, are being tested by the gods."

"What gods?" he asked.

"Don't be an atheist," Frances chided lightly.

"All right, then, there are these gods. But why? For what earthly reason?"

"Earthly. Ha, ha, ha." This caused another round of laughter between the two women who had their own inner club and their own shared secrets. If they made The Man With The Scar uneasy, he didn't show it.

Janie reverted to an earlier conversation, "So, the boat actually ran into the dock?"

"Yeah," The Man With The Scar agreed, "Cut it right in half. Brave fishermen scattered like ants. Captain Griggs calls me his albatross."

Frances was running her fingers through his hair, "We never met an albatross we didn't like."

"That's right; it's men we don't like very much."

The two women erupted in tipsy laughter, as if this was very funny. The Man With The Scar knew he was on thin ice, but he was used to skating on the very thinnest.

"Some men are pigs," he added agreeably.

"Ahh, yes they are," Frances said agreeably. "Take them to the slaughterhouse!"

"Lucky you're an albatross," Janie said, lightly touching his nose.

"A scarred one, to boot."

Janie trailed a finger, following the scar down his face, "How far does it go?"

She pulled up his shirt, seeing that it tracked on the lower part of his chest, both up and down, as far as it had been exposed. Suddenly she was semi-serious, "Wo-hoo...? Further?" She trailed her finger down the scar to his belt line.

"Why don't we see...?" Frances suggested.

"We all could see," Janie said. "Could we?" she asked The Man With The Scar.

He shrugged agreeably, "Hard to avoid it. This is a very small tent."

Frances ventured a hand, "And a very big scar..."

The next day they headed south, referring frequently to their AAA California/Nevada road map. They bumped along mostly on gravel roads through long and deserted stretches of desert, but they never lost their good-natured spirits. And when they pulled into Laughlin at sunset, they were red-faced, wind-burned and still laughing.

Frances, still at the wheel of the dusty red Jeep, pulled up to the semi-grand entrance in front of the Pioneer Casino. The women were singing:

He's got a hickory stick
Hotter than my trusty Bic
Hey, girls, that's where my money goes!

The Man With The Scar hopped out of the Jeep and headed for the door. A doorman looked over his shoulder and seemed to recognize them. He had the sadly defeated look of a habitual loser, even dressed in his bellhop's outfit. He glanced at a newspaper in a nearby dispenser, double-checking to make sure of his first impression. There, on the front page was the splashy headline, "AX-WOMEN STILL AT LARGE!" And there were pictures of Janie and Frances, smiling in sedate earlier times.

The doorman, thinking reward money, yelled and ran after them, "No! Wait! Wait, come back!"

Frances gave him a gay little wave and accelerated along a clear path away from the casino. The doorman dove for the back of the jeep, hoping to hang on to the roll bar, and he actually connected for a moment. But he was not used to such violent exercise. After a few moments, he couldn't hang on. But now he'd picked up considerable speed. He rolled off the driveway, down a small bluff and into a bed of cactus. This was, after all, Laughlin, where the casinos are carved out of the desert.

"Owww!" the doorman wailed, "Cactus! Oh, Je-hesus!"

The Man With The Scar walked past the newspapers without giving them a second glance. The two women had confided that they hoped to continue south and cross into Mexico below Yuma before dawn. He'd asked that they leave him off on the main road, and they'd done more than that by driving him up to the Pioneer.

For all the joking and fun they'd shared, they'd given him something to think about, and even a faint new ray of hope. Once one admitted and recognized that something incredible had actually happened to him and Toomley, why limit the possible explanations to the old Christian ethic of guilt, damnation and hellfire? Hadn't the gods once given Prometheus the gift of fire, and hadn't Hercules' soul risen from its funeral pyre as he, himself, was granted godhood status?

As The Man With The Scar walked through the lobby, there was a new spring to his step. He paused in front of a gift shop, looking affectionately at the newspapers with photos of the two women he'd been with for the past few days splashed across the front page of a day-old Phoenix newspaper. Apparently, the parting with their husbands had been somewhat less than instant or amiable, warrants for the two women's arrest having been issued for murder by arson, gunshots, stab wounds and dynamite.

12

You see that girl, the one it seems you've just been thinking about...Was it ten years ago, or was it just last week when the two of you were so close together? Who cares, time doesn't really matter in affairs of the heart. But then, what do you know about such affairs? Hasn't every relationship you've ever chanced ended up in heartbreak and disaster? Or does it just seem that way?

And this whole conversation is a disaster in and of itself, because, although The Man With The Scar has his moments of lustful delight same as any man, he doesn't really want to meet up with Millie. He just would like to be left alone for a while, left to get on with a normal, uneventful life. As if that's going to happen...

Having learned to test the local waters upon his arrival at any new place, The Man With The Scar decided to walk around to a few of the casinos before checking into a hotel. He was making his way through the Edgewater Casino when he spotted the girl with the frizzy blond hair. She was sitting at a five-dollar blackjack table. He invested in five rolls of silver dollars and sat at a corner slot machine where he could watch her play.

He slowly and automatically fed the machine in front of him a dollar at a time and pulled the handle carefully, as if feeling the trigger action that spun the cylinders, but he never watched the combinations that came up and only rarely checked the tray at his knees. He didn't seem to be having Toomley's luck; his pile of silver slugs was slowly diminishing. When the cocktail waitress came by, he asked for a tonic water.

She gave him the one-raised-eyebrow look.

"Tonic Water. Quinine Water," he repeated.

"With nothing in it?"

"Straight. It beats back malaria, which I happen to have, in addition to arthritis, a bad back and gout in my big toe, which I get eating chocolate to keep my sugar levels up."

"Geez," she said, giving him a look of disgust, "I don't want to hear." She brought him the tonic water, but after that, she left him alone, which was what he wanted in the first place. In the next half hour, he lost most of his money and everyone who was playing blackjack at the table he was watching had come and gone twice except for the blond with the frizzy hair. He collected the few remaining coins from the pan in front of him and walked over to take the vacant seat next to her. The dealer, a clean-cut young man with bleached blond hair, frowned at him. The Man With The Scar wondered if it was his desert rat appearance, or the fact that he'd not had a shower since the campgrounds in Death Valley.

The girl with the frizzy hair lost a hand.

"Stinkbug sucking, billy goat pig-fart rocker-fubbing roadie-flaming, fig-ficking...I hate to lose," she said. "Hate, hate, not so great. See you later, lose-ilator."

"Hey, you got lots of chips left," the dealer said.

"So I do, muckeroo." She sat down and pushed another small pile into play.

"You can't seem to get ahead," The Man With The Scar said quietly to Millie.

"Yeah, I know," she answered without looking up, "Nothing greater, cogitator. Win one, lose one." And then she was a tough black madam in a Detroit brothel, "My big black ass been here hours. Right here on this here chair. Here."

A new dealer replaced the old one. The Man With The Scar watched as the new dealer, a wanna-be Tom Cruise with fast hands, shuffled six decks and frowned at him.

"Maybe you wanna try another table," he said. "She's just a beginner."

He pushed the shoe towards Millie and held out a blank yellow plastic card. Millie obviously didn't know what to do. The Man With The Scar took the yellow plastic divider card and stuck it into the fat six-deck shoe.

"Shut up and hit me," he said to the dealer.

The dealer's frown deepened, but with a glance over at his pit boss, he did as he was told. Millie looked up and recognized The Man With The Scar.

"Hello, Millie," he said.

"What?! It's *you!* Curse you, Red Baron! *You—you* purple gerbil-gulping maniac! Where's our goddamn *fish that you stole*?!"

She missed with a roundhouse left and fell on the floor. She came up all red-faced and flailing, and he had to grab both her wrists.

"Control your enthusiasm," he said quietly. "And I don't think this is the place for you to discuss your criminal past."

She struggled to hit him, but he wouldn't let go.

"Calm it," he said, more firmly this time. "You're in deep crap, as it is."

The pit boss gestured to two burly men who started to move in their direction.

He let go of her arms. She stood there, trembling and glaring.

"Wha-What? What? What?"

"Sit down and play, and I'll tell you."

She breathed once heavily and then did as he suggested. The two grim and beefy men who were halfway across the room paused and glanced over at the pit boss; then slowed and began to show an interest in one of the crap tables. The pit boss himself came over to their table.

"Is this man bothering you, ma'am?" he asked.

"Losing my money is bothering me, you gerbil-dick. Who asked you, anyway?" She spoke in a deeper voice, playing to her invisible audience, "I come to play." And then, in even deeper tones tinged with menace, "Stand back, you fools. I don't want to have to kill you. Can't you see I'm radioactive?"

The pit boss's face flared red, but he had no alternative other than to back off.

At a bar near the blackjack tables, Dusty's man Bopo was working his way through a string of Michelobs at the bar when a disgruntled Leon joined him.

"Yo, bro, any luck?" Bopo asked.

"Them cherries are hard to come by."

"I mean the girl."

"No, I never seen her."

Bopo looked past Leon to a curly-headed girl at the blackjack table. It was Millie.

"How 'bout that one over there?"

Millie lost another hand, and the dealer raked in her chips.

She puffed out a breath of air, imitating a soulful Jamaican singer, "You broken d' heart of many a poor gal...but you'll never break dis heart of mine..." She pushed another small pile into play.

Leon took a swig from Bopo's beer without bothering to turn around and look at the girl Bopo indicated.

"Yeah, like it's that easy."

"Well..." Bopo looked uncertainly at the girl.

Leon pointed to the cocktail waitress.

"All white girls look alike to you. Look, 'Po, there go another one."

Bopo shrugged in dejection, thinking he was probably wrong. He was used to being wrong.

The Man With The Scar piled his silver in five neat stacks of five and placed the first stack in play. The dealer's eyes flicked around the room and then his hands moved deftly, the cards flashing onto the green felt. The dealer had a 19, Millie won with a twenty, while he and three others around the table went bust. The Man With The Scar eyed the sloppy pile of chips in front of her.

"Been here long?"

The dealer had pulled in the winnings, paid Millie, and was waiting for their bets. The Man With The Scar shoved another of his little stacks forward. Millie pushed a big stack in without counting.

"Now observe the regurgitation," she said. "I be bound to lose this one." The cards fell, proving her point, "See, see, see, Willie-the-flea."

"Yes, I know. I have been watching. You win the little ones and you lose the big ones. How long have you been playing?"

"All afternoon," she said. "Not bad for starting with a hundred lousy bucks, huh?"

"What did you use to buy your chips?"

"You never ask a lady that, sailor."

"Could it possibly have been some of the drug money you lifted from Randy?"

Millie's eyes widened, but she was still in denial. "I don't get it. What are you talking about?"

"You figure; you're a smart girl. Where do you think Randy got the money that he was going to use to buy the drugs?"

Her eyes widened, "You don't think they could mark it somehow?"

"Sure. Almost certainly."

She looked around wildly, as if she was ready to dash out of the casino.

"No," The Man With The Scar said. "Time's not right yet."

This time, everyone at the table lost but Millie. A fat man got up and left, the disgust plain on his face. Millie shrugged and played a twenty-five dollar chip, and won again while everyone else lost.

"Good guys aren't the only ones who mark their money. They're holding you at this table, Millie," The Man With The Scar said softly.

"Tha-tha-that's refreshingly stu-stu-stupid!"

He pushed another five dollars into play while she played another twenty-five dollar chip. Again, he lost while she won.

"Not so loud. Listen to me: They're waiting for somebody to show up. Somebody who wants to talk to you."

"C-C-Crap-farts! I never heard anything so dumb."

"I'll prove it. Play everything you've got."

"But there's over a thousand dollars here."

"You won't lose. I guarantee it."

He played another five coins, while she uncertainly pushed the entire pile of chips in front of her into the game.

"You don't want to bet so much," the dealer said unhappily.

"Why not?" The Man With The Scar asked.

The dealer looked at the pit boss, but all he did was shrug helplessly. The dealer dealt Millie a 12. The dealer himself had a 4 showing. The Man With The Scar advised her to stay, and the dealer went bust with a 23. So they both won, and Millie doubled her money in one hand.

"Increduble-duble-duble-duble," she babbled. "Toil an' tubble, lots of fubble. Yeah, yeah, yeah for Team Millie. Gooooo—DEFENSE!"

"Okay, let's go," The Man With The Scar said.

Millie reluctantly eyed her big pile of chips.

"So soon? I'm on a roll, sweet potato."

"Alright," The Man With The Scar agreed, "One more time. Play it all."

Wide-eyed, Millie pushed all her chips forward.

"Now you really don't want to..." the dealer started. The Man With The Scar tapped the table limit card, which read $5-5,000 LIMIT.

The dealer reluctantly counted and stacked her money. He took his time about it, and when her bet was ready, he signaled the pit boss.

"Action," he said.

The pit boss came over.

"I'm sorry, sir," he said to The Man With The Scar. "I'm going to have to ask you to leave."

"Deal them, dick-face," Millie said to the dealer, ignoring the pit boss. Her voice dropped, "Or d' mob gonna erase you. Erase yer face rur ya."

The dealer looked at the pit boss, who reluctantly nodded. The dealer was clearly pissed. He laid out a 10 for The Man With The Scar and an ace for Millie. He himself had a 5 showing. Sweat was suddenly beading his forehead.

"Wheel them and deal them, Slick," The Man With The Scar said.

The dealer shoved an ace towards him.

"Blackjack," The Man With The Scar said calmly, staring at the dealer's hands.

The dealer's plan had been to slip Millie a low-numbered card in the moment of enthusiasm over The Man With The Scar's blackjack. But there was no moment of enthusiasm, just a hard-eyed stare from his scar-faced customer. And in his haste, a 10 fell from the dealer's hand, landing on the table halfway to Millie.

"Double blackjack!" The Man With The Scar said quickly. "Hurrah for us!"

"Wait...I..." the dealer started to protest.

"Anything wrong?" The Man With The Scar said to the pit boss. "You were standing right here. We can look at the replay." He gestured to the ornate glass ceiling overhead.

"No, nothing's wrong. Pay her," the pit boss instructed through gritting teeth. "You have to move to a higher limit table, though."

He watched the dealer pay Millie and The Man With The Scar, and then started to walk away.

"Okay," The Man With The Scar said, "Time to leave."

Millie, arms around her pile of chips, was looking longingly at the shoe.

"NOW, Millie," he repeated. "While we still can."

He handed her the cup he'd been using at the slots, and she reluctantly piled her chips in. They stood and made their way to the cashier's booth. From their lookout station at the bar, Bopo saw that Millie was leaving. He tried to get Leon's attention, but Leon was yelling at the horses on the television above the bar. The horses crossed the finish line and Leon sat down, his frustration splayed all over his face.

"What you want, nigger?" he said to Bopo.

Bopo turned around, but Millie had left the blackjack table. He didn't see her anywhere.

"Nothing, Leon," Bopo said. "I was just cheering for your horse."

Things weren't going smoothly at the cashier's booth. The cashier fussed around like he didn't have enough money, and then called for a red-faced man with a pencil-thin moustache who tried to question Millie's age.

"You've already seen her I.D." The Man With The Scar said firmly. "She filled out the tax form. Let's go. Money. Right now."

The cashier glared at him, but started to slowly count out Millie's money in tens and twenties.

"Hundreds," The Man With The Scar insisted. "We don't want to be here all night."

The manager glared at him, but he took back his big stack of small bills and counted out forty-five hundreds, one twenty and a five-dollar bill.

"Thank you, sweet Dick-Face," Millie said sweetly as she tucked the money in her purse.

13

Flame Boy sat at the airport in Oakland, grinding his teeth. He'd sent Leon and Bopo early because they were such fatheads he was sure they would miss the plane. But his meeting with a chubby little mortgage broker who was helping some of the boys bury their income went a little longer than he'd planned. They'd met in a Chinese restaurant, and the mortgage broker had insisted the garlic lobster had a hint of iodine, and hence was probably yesterday's dish warmed-over. The maître d' had agreed, and showed his shame and regret by having one of the waiters reach in a big tank for two new lobsters. The waiter triumphantly held them in the air while water dripped from his long-sleeved white shirt.

The new lobster dish was splendid, and in between bites, the mortgage broker proudly presented certain papers which he had moused to elevate one of Dusty's soldiers in the eyes of the U.S. government—Here was a young soldier who had yet to graduate high school; yet his tax forms showed him to be a computer analyst with a salary that would make it possible for him to move into a $600,000 ocean view home in Santa Cruz.

In spite of his tight schedule, Dusty was genuinely pleased, but then, after the lobster dish, the mortgage broker insisted on a round of fortune cookies and another pot of green tea, and that took still more precious minutes. By the time Ice Man finally pointed his big Beamer towards the freeway, the Oakland, San Francisco and San Jose airports were all socked in by fog and he was visualizing his pudgy little mortgage broker friend in a place where the sun never shone. He tried beeping Leon's pager, but his own cellular phone sulked quietly in his jacket pocket.

Dusty remembered with a sinking heart that Leon had been in the repair shop when the call from Laughlin had come in; in fact Leon had been the one who'd taken down the message about the Betty Boop white girl with the frizzy hair and the $100 bill that lit the lights when they ran it through their machine. It made Dusty nervous thinking of Leon and Bopo catching up to the girl without him.

Dusty fidgeted and ground his teeth while the heavy fog swirled by outside the huge airport windows, making the grounded jets look like giant, shiny-skinned frogs spraddled on the damp tarmac. He remembered his fortune cookie had read: WATCH OUT FOR SURPRISES.

Is there something so symbolic about taking off in a fog that writers like me have to employ it over and over and over again? Or maybe it's just that Oakland does get a lot of fog. At any rate, Drug Lord Dusty seems intent on catching up with The Man With The Scar. He even has some tough busters helping. But anyone who survived Tet '68 with one small scar extending from over his eyebrow down past his chin and then continuing across his chest down past his abdomen, missing vital parts by an inch or so, and then on down his thigh to end in a star on the top of his foot—that is to say, anyone who survived Tet '68 with nothing more than that—is probably more capable than he seems. Dusty would be wise to observe that. But then, Dusty is impulsive and rash, and a psychopath we haven't seen the likes of this side of Harvey Dent in *The Dark Knight Returns*.

Dusty was on the tarmac at the Oakland airport near a weather-beaten and dirty two-engine plane. The pilot-owner of the plane had the unlikely name—or nickname, nobody was really sure—of Pig-Ops. At the moment, Pig-Ops was wiping spark plugs on an oily rag. He squinted at the plug in question, and, still dissatisfied, wiped it on his shirttail.

"Good enough," he said finally. He wore glasses with lenses thick as coke bottles. He gave the plug a last squint and started to screw it back into the engine.

Pig-Ops was a giant of a man, with a gaunt frame hunched at the shoulders, as if he'd tried to shrink himself down to hold normal conversations with people of regular height. When he wasn't loading his stomach with his customary two six-packs a night, he flew his twin-engine Beechcraft on intermittent runs to small stretches of straight dirt roads near out-of-the-way flyspeck Mexican towns like Rumorosa, Pascualitos and Algodones. There he would buy special prefilled knapsacks which he then dumped from his plane at altitudes of below 100 feet onto carefully pre-marked fields near ant's ass burgs like Ocotillo, Mt. Laguna and Glamis, which were rural or undeveloped desert areas on U.S. soil, fifty miles or so north of the border.

Dusty started to count out twenty-dollar bills into his outstretched hand. This should have been a joyful moment, but Pig-Ops was accepting the money with a great deal of reluctance.

"Uhh...Dusty...fog..." he said. "They're closing the airport."

Pig-Ops wanted to explain how he didn't like the idea of losing his license, but Dusty's business paid the bills, and he was well aware of the pistol with the long silencer that was stuck in the specially designed pocket of Dusty's pants.

"Maybe we go tomorrow?" Pig-Ops suggested.

"Tomorrow isn't an option."

Dusty tapped him on the shoulder with the new pistol that appeared magically in his hand. Like his last pistol, it had a long silencer extending from the barrel.

Pig-Ops, a very nervous type for someone in his line of work, jumped when he saw the pistol. His glasses dropped to the floor, and he went down on his knees, fishing for them.

"Right, Dusty," he agreed, finding the glasses and sticking them back on his nose. One of the lenses was now cracked and starred, but it was no time for minor details.

As they climbed into the plane, Dusty's phone rang. Pig-Ops was grateful for the interruption, though the call didn't seem to do anything for his client's grumpy mood.

"Leon?! Where you at, man? I had a page in on you for hours."

"Well, you cain't get no page on a airplane. We called you as soon as—"

Ice Man cut him off, so Flame Boy wouldn't have to kill him. Dusty hated obvious liars. "Leon, *listen* to me."

"Yeah. Go 'head, Dusty."

"We got fog here, but I convinced Pig-Ops, going to fly me direct to Laughlin."

"You going to take off in fog?" Leon sounded as incredulous as Pig-Ops, before Dusty had started feeding his hand.

Ice Man shrugged, "Nobody can take off or land, so we ain't going to hit nobody. All fat-butt here got to do is point it straight and read them little dials on his dashboard. We be up over the soup in two, three minutes."

"If you don't hit nothin' coming in when you're going out."

"Leon—!"

Leon knew that tone.

"You just keep the lookout for that girl."

"Yes, sir, boss."

Leon cringed when he heard Dusty's tone. Dusty could snap so fast that sometimes he almost seemed like another person. But that was *deep thinking* for Leon. All he could figure to say that was safe was, *Yes, Boss.* And he meant it with all his heart.

Pig-Ops took his seat in the captain's chair, while Dusty sat in the copilot's seat. The engines coughed to life, and Pig-Ops clicked his mike on.

"Uhh...tower..." he said, "thanks for giving us clearance..."

He winced at the angry squawking noise from the earphones; then said, "Right-e-o. Here we go. Clear as a bell down here."

He gave a nervous glance at Dusty, who still hadn't put his pistol away. Dusty nodded encouragement, and Pig-Ops pushed the throttles forward. The engines gave off an unhealthy clatter, and the plane moved forward and was swallowed by the fog.

Millie was working her way through a Cobb salad heavily loaded with blue cheese dressing, boiled egg yokes and half-inch squares of greasy bacon. The old man with the scar had escorted her to her room, to pick up her things. But when they came out of the room with her single small suitcase, a security man had been standing at the far end of the hall. He'd let them pass and take the elevator to the lobby. They had walked along the river under the glare of the garish lights from the hotels until Millie had proclaimed she was hungry.

"I'm eating for two, you know."

"I didn't know," the man said.

They were sitting at a small table in a brightly lit cafe onboard the Colorado Belle, a big cement building tricked out to pass for a paddleboat steamer if you weren't paying attention.

"Yes. Randy's baby." She shifted into the voice of an old news narrator from the days when they did the news in cinema houses, "Although he is nowhere to be found, the legend of the mighty Putzer lives on."

"And where is the proud father?" The Man With The Scar had picked out their new watcher, a heavyset young man who had come in a few minutes after them and sat down to a cup of coffee that he wasn't drinking.

"Come to think of it, gerbil-dick wasn't exactly overjoyed at the thought of parenthood. At least not with me." She pouted for a moment, remembering the unpleasant time when she had broken the great wonderful shining lie to Randy, and then sank into her Teutonic persona, "Vell, our new daddy-kins vent to join his force mit his slimoid buddy, Dusty. Zat vas nearly von veeks ago..." She shook her head, her silence finishing the thought for her.

"Where did you learn to shoot a rifle?" he asked.

"Kvestions. You ask so many kvestions. I never shoots a bang-bang gun," she said, eyeing him with a perfect calm stare, "Zat is for soldier-boy."

"And you've never been to Mexico."

And then she was a far Eastern purveyor of fine teas and spices, "Ahh, you so right Meester Chang. Is it nice, these Mex-i-co?"

The Man With The Scar stood and stretched, flexing his weak knee, which tended to stiffen up on him.

"Whu-Whu-Where you going?" she said, her voice normal except it was full of sudden alarm. A burly fellow who had been watching them began fishing in his own pockets for money.

"I am going to the Contempo," he said. "It is far, far from here, and I must be on my way."

"Alright, *alright-i-o! Setten ze*! Jesus, you're touchy. Sit, sit. Mamma Bear will tell the entire fairy tale."

"I don't want to know it," he said.

She jumped to her feet and ran after him. The burly fellow stood to intercept Millie, but she pushed him backwards over a chair.

"Hey, rude boy, la-la-ladies first," she said, running after The Man With The Scar.

"Okay, I fess up. I am not presently—how do I say this delicately?—not with child." She followed him out of the restaurant.

They turned a corner and The Man With The Scar suddenly pulled her with him to the wall, at the same time warning her to be quiet.

After a few seconds, a barrel-chested young man came trotting swiftly around the corner, just in time to accept a perfect flat-handed blow to his throat from The Man With The Scar. The young man fell to the floor, gurgling and grasping at his throat.

"Come on! They'll be after us!" The Man With The Scar said. Millie inched past the man on the floor, and hurried after him.

It surprised Millie that a limping old scar-face like him could have such swift and efficient hands. She found herself wondering what else he could still do.

14

By now, those of you who have been following along recognize The Man With The Scar, if not by his scar, by the string of uncomfortable and even dangerous events that seem to be his lot in life. The scar itself, at least the moment of the inception of the scar, was not very difficult or complicated.

In the madness of their erratic and less-than-hasty retreat across Saigon, Dave Toomley, CIA man, had managed to accumulate a considerable amount of cash and jewelry in an orange webbed plastic shopping bag (one of those bags the ba's use to bring home the day's fresh meat and produce). The Man With The Scar had appropriated an AK47 from what looked like a Vietnamese preteen.

He and Toomley were standing on the street level, underneath a balcony from which the intermittent rap of gunfire could be heard. The shooters—at least, one of them— became aware of the presence of the two Americans below and began trying to drill them from the top down. By reaching far over the ledge and firing straight down, he could just about reach them. Toomley, seeing their position was no longer safe, grabbed the AK47 and dove across the street, attracting a hail of gunfire. Once he was safely behind a large gum tree, he took aim at the VC irregulars on the balcony.

But before he could get off a shot, the man on the balcony returned his attention to The Man With The Scar and managed a short burst, one single bullet of which managed to crease the forehead and in fact the entire body of the American below.

All this, of course, was the prelude to the restless and adventure-filled life that followed. And so, we pick up again with this curious tale of drug lords and foulmouthed pretty girls, of desert rats, thugs and other unprincipled fellows. By the way, have any of you ever seen a Borchardt semi-automatic pistol? Cartridge clip loads through the grip, 7.63 mm ammo. The Man With The Scar has seen one. In fact, he owns one, and it has a hair trigger...but I repeat myself, and you'd kind of expect that in the first place, wouldn't you?

On clear nights like this one, Pig-Ops flew by the seat of his pants, that is, he tossed his flight plan to the wind and followed the roads and the winking lights of the towns, which he had memorized until he had an extensive map of the Southwest in his mind. He flipped the little switch that turned off his night lights and flew at around 1500 feet, low enough to make out points of interest without attracting attention.

"Damn, man! There it go, again," Dusty said. One of the engines had been running rough since their takeoff, and it had him nervous.

"She's always like that," Pig-Ops replied with a high, nervous laugh.

Pig-Ops noticed engine number two was also running hot. He didn't say anything about that. He couldn't see any reason to worry a passenger unnecessarily, particularly someone with excitable genes like Dusty. He slammed one hand against the gauges in front of him. This had the effect of shutting off one of the engines.

Dusty stared at the silent propeller in wide-eyed wonder. "Lord, save us! What we do now?"

"Don't worry, Dusty. We've still got one good engine. We're 50 miles north of Laughlin. We'll be there in no time...Oops...!"

The second engine cut out. Only 250 feet in the air, the plane glided down in silence.

They had looped around Vegas, and Pig-Ops had picked up 95, a two-lane blacktop that ran parallel to the long north-south section of the Lake Mead National Recreation

Area on the west side of the dammed up Colorado River. At this time of night, the road was deserted, a lighter gray line drawn straight south through the desert.

Pig-Ops feathered the props and pushed the plane into a gentle glide.

"Tell me you doing this on purpose," Dusty said. "You getting back on me for being a little rough on you back in Oakland."

Pig-Ops noticed that, the more frightened Dusty became, the more he dropped his quasi-literate manner of speaking for the slurred Oakland street dialect of his youth. He figured now wasn't the time to bring it up, even in polite conversation.

"Calm down, Dusty. I'll just land her on the road. I've done it a million times."

A multiple electric motor whine sharpened as the landing gear came down. A red warning light indicated they hadn't locked in place. Pig-Ops slammed the gauge and the light went out. He lined up the road, frowning to see this stretch of 95 was unimproved, which meant the little hump hills hadn't been bulldozed out to make one level stretch. But, at least at this time of night the road was totally deserted. He would just lift her over the appropriate hump and drop neatly into the little depression beyond.

At the last moment, he had to push Dusty away, as the man was clutching him the way a drowning man grabs a rescuer.

"Dusty, get away! Let me land!"

The plane touched lightly on one wheel and ran for 50 yards before it seemed to realize the others hadn't locked down. Then it sagged over and one wingtip caught in the sand and sagebrush on the side of the road.

"Holy comolians," Pig-Ops said in a moment of true amazement as he felt the world go out from under them.

Dusty grabbed him again in a panic-stricken hug. Pig-Ops struggled to push him away, and this action probably saved Dusty's life, because the rest of the ride was extremely swift and violent.

It would have been better if the remaining wheel had collapsed, but it stubbornly remained locked in place. So, instead of pancaking and sliding on the road, the plane flipped over and spun and skidded upside down through the sandy gravel. It finally came to rest upside down with its crumpled nose tilted into a dry wash at a 45-degree angle.

Alvin Curdle eyed the two black fellers from his vantage point across the bar. Alvin was lean and restless as an old desert coyote. He was wearing his dress-up duds, a Roy Rogers style western shirt, slick sans-a-belt pants and a string tie held at the neck with a big blue lump of turquoise.

Alvin was generally off in the Superstition Mountains, peacefully looking for the Lost Dutchman Mine, but about once a year, usually in the fall, his supplies began to run low. About that time, he would make a few phone calls and then take his last stash of dollar bills and drive his battered old Toyota Land Rover south from Tucson to a little town called Sasabe which was on the U.S. side, snug up close to the border. Nobody but campers went there, and he would slip south into Mexico, walking a few miles to a remote cabin he knew about.

He'd make his deal with the Spanish devils and then walk back north across the border. He'd sleep overnight in his Land Rover and drive back to civilization again with a few small bags of nose candy in the middle of a big duffel bag full of filthy clothing which he hadn't had laundered in over a year. He never went to Vegas, where the streets were too well organized, to make his sales. He didn't have to; all it took was few days of quiet dealing in Laughlin, and he was grubstaked for another go at the mother lode.

Alvin prided himself that he could spot a doper-head— or a *potential* doper-head—a mile away. And here they were, right in front of him. There was the smaller one, black as the ace of spades and weighing in at about 225 pounds. Wearing his silky light yellow-brown jacket with the black stripes and a lavender shirt open at the collar, he looked like some urban hick who'd just knocked over a string of 7-11s and was looking for places to blow his dough. The other one was simply the tubby, dumb one, Alvin thought, somebody like Fat Albert in that old cartoon show. His Raiders jacket over a powder blue t-shirt and his homeboy pants marked him as of the same cut as his buddy. They were too raw to be mob or narcs. Had to be two dorks on the loose, easy pickings for a peaceable old desert rat like himself.

Alvin eased himself off his stool and made his customary approach.

"Hey, boys," he said, his leathery whisper of a voice barely carrying in the room full of the jingle-jangle of the nearby casino.

"Hey, yourself, you old lounge lizard," Leon replied. He wasn't in the best of moods. Being in a casino without a dime in his pocket was a form of torture.

"You fellers use a little nose candy?"

"Get away from us, man," Bopo snarled.

"Wait a minute." Leon placed a hand on Bopo's arm. He nodded to the stringy old fellow, "Let's see the stuff."

"I don't carry it around," Alvin said. "I keep it in my Land Rover."

"Okay, where is it?"

"We got to go a little ways."

Leon shrugged and pushed himself away from the table. "I ain't doing nothing until Moses blows his horn. Show me what you got, old Mister Methuselah."

"Need me to go along?" Bopo asked.

Leon winked conspiratorially at his partner. "Naa, I got it covered." His face got serious, "You keep your eye out for that white girl."

As the leathery old man led him from the casino, Leon felt cold reassurance from the crooked arm of the tire iron he'd lifted from the rented Mustang and shoved in his pants when they'd first parked in Laughlin. He never felt complete without a tire iron, the way, he imagined, Billy the Kid must have felt about his six-shooter, or General Patton about his army issue Colt .45 pistol.

The Man With The Scar told Millie he would park her rented car in one of the outer lots, facing the road for a faster getaway. But once she was out of sight, he drove it onto the highway and across the bridge to the East side of the Colorado River and parked it in the gravel lot in front of a public utilities company. He scribbled a note on a torn french-fries carton and tucked it under the windshield wiper blade on the driver's side. The note said "battery dead—gone for new one." He easily hitched a short ride back across the bridge and made his way to the Colorado Belle. Millie wasn't where they'd agreed to meet, so he backtracked to her old hotel room. He put his ear to the door. After listening to the muffled voices from within for a moment, he took the long-nosed Borchardt from his knapsack. He tried the knob. The door wasn't locked, so he quietly pushed it open.

He'd taken the Borchardt in trade from an antique gun dealer in Guadalajara. People tended not to take it seriously. It was over a hundred years old and looked like an oddly archaic pistol. But it would be a mistake not to realize that an antique can kill you.

Millie was tied to the bed with cords cut from the drapes. Her face was battered and bruised, and she had red welts across her arms and legs. The barrel-chested young man was sitting in a chair across the room, still kneading his bruised throat. The other was a thin man of medium size with tufts of dark brown hair above his ears and heavy eyebrows over dark brown eyes split by a hatchet of a nose. He was going through Millie's suitcase. When he saw The Man With The Scar enter, he crouched as if readying himself for a lunge.

"Don't make me shoot you," The Man With The Scar said. "It's a bitch to find 7.63 millimeter ammunition."

15

To escape the jaws of death yet again is a joy not to be lessened by the fact that you are a drug lord and somewhat the scum of the earth. After all, scum doesn't know itself as such. This then is a constant in the human dilemma. Do you really know that which you are absolutely sure you know, and is it really real? You may research this conundrum further by reading the first chapter of *Lost In the Cosmos, The Last Self-Help Book*, by the late great Walker Percy. However, don't do that now. Now is the time for the further adventures of The Man With The Scar, Dusty the Drug Lord, Big Bad Leon, and Alvin Curdle, the old desert rat who has more lives than a, than a, than a...well, without giving anything away...than a scorpion...

Frightened and shaken from his final flip-over and mind-wrenching impact, Dusty snapped himself free from his seat belts. He brushed the broken glass out of his way and managed to crawl out through the open window in front of him. That accomplished, he slid down the curved nose of the plane to the ground.

The footing was uneven, and he fell backwards into a bush with a smell that oddly reminded him of Thanksgiving and turkey dinners. *Sage! He was in a goddamn sage patch!*

Fearful of spiders, he quickly crawled away from the bush. It was time to take stock. He was stiff and bruised, but his limbs seemed to work okay. He didn't seem to have anything broken.

There was a quarter moon hanging over the horizon with enough light to see that Pig-Ops hadn't been so lucky. With the tall pilot's geeky neck twisted the way it was, it was safe to assume he'd flown his last enterprising flight over the byways of the new Southwest.

Dusty caught a whiff of gasoline, so he limped a dozen yards towards the road to put some distance between himself and the plane. But then he felt around at his waist and realized his pistol was missing. He cursed and made his way back to the plane.

The smell of gasoline was stronger, and he thought he could hear it dripping, but he felt naked without his pistol. Not only that; it was tough beans getting a silencer. That silencer had cost more than the pistol itself, and had certainly been harder to come by. He wasn't just going to leave it to the first moose hunter to come along.

He crawled back inside the upside-down cabin. Pig-Ops looked dead enough, but he gave him a little shove to make certain.

"Always wear your seat belt," he advised.

He felt around in the pile of junk that had collected on the ceiling. Naturally, his pistol was way on the bottom under all the thermos bottles, beat-up old maps and a loose jumble of about two hundred single-pack condoms, and he didn't find it until he'd nearly given up.

Now that his wits were coming back, Dusty thought to extract his pile of hundreds from the zipper-flap pocket of Pig-Ops's soiled flight jacket. Pig-Ops certainly wasn't going to be needing it.

And then, with an instinct at least as old as Robinson Crusoe, he began to scavenge the upside-down passenger compartment. After a time, he was rewarded with a nylon bag containing wads of money, and a knapsack with hotel towels wrapped around two bricks of shrink-wrapped green-green tealeaves.

"Ho, ho, ho. Christmas come early this year. Thank you for your contributions, Pig-Ops. Most generous of you."

He tossed his finds out the window, and crawled out after them. It took him another five minutes to find the trickle of gas leaking from the nose of the plane. One flick of his lighter, and the fire started with a whoosh.

He barely had time to sling the knapsack over his shoulder and hustle the nylon bag away. He was stiff and moving more slowly than usual; by the time he covered the distance back to the road, Pig-Ops and his plane were completely engulfed in flame. The chubby pilot looked a little bit like his name, roasting upside down in the flames. *If only I had an apple for his mouth,* Dusty thought.

The bag-o-money was difficult to calculate, stuffed as it was with loose twenties and hundreds, but the marijuana was good as gold. Finder's keepers, Dusty thought. What had that fortune cookie said about *SURPRISES*?!

Alvin Curdle whistled a happy tune, a little piece of Victor Herbert's "Naughty Marietta", as he led the big black guy to his battered Land Rover, "Naughty Marietta, come be good, say she...*mais Non!* Say me!"

Leon shook his head, muttering under his breath, "Crazy as a loon!" He had no idea what a loon looked like, but it was probably a skinny creature that looked a lot like Alvin.

Under all the dust caked on Alvin's Land Rover, Leon could see the four-wheeler's original color was light blue.

"Hey, old man, don't you ever wash this dumb thing?"

"Only when it rains, sonny. He, he, he!" And he burst into another Herbert favorite, "Tramp, tramp, tramp along the highway, Room, Room, Room, the world is free! We're planters, Canucks, Virginians, Kentucks—Captain Dick's own infantry!"

Alvin had opened the side door and was reaching for the duffel bag filled with his soiled clothing when Leon rapped him neatly across the back of his head with the tire iron. There was a thoroughly satisfying *thunk* after which Alvin flung his arms out and wobbled to the cement floor like a dried spider skin.

"Jesus, old man, you deserve it just for that awful singing!"

Leon stepped over Alvin's body. His nose wrinkled when he opened the duffel bag, which was the old army kind, made of heavy olive canvas and secured by four grommets held tightly closed by a clip attached to one end of the carrying strap.

"Gaah! DIRTY old man..." Leon added, wrinkling his nose.

He was digging through Alvin's foul-smelling clothes and had just found three small baggies with a little dope in each, plus a small, greasy stack of twenties held together with several rubber bands when he felt a sharp sting on the back of his hand. There was a bug with a curled tail sitting on him!

Suddenly wide-eyed and frightened, he smashed the tan scorpion with his other hand, feeling a second, sharper skin-prick as he did so.

"So you found one of my little pets," Alvin chuckled from the cement floor. "You're one dead nigger-boy, you know that, Buster Brown?"

Leon looked over at him with surprise. "Hey, you a *tough* old man!" As he spoke, he connected a backhanded blow with the heavy tire iron across the side of the old man's head. This time there was a crunch that bespoke of breaking bone, and Alvin collapsed as before, without a sound.

Almost as if they were gaining revenge, a second scorpion stung the back of his hand. He whacked it with the wad of money, but it imbedded its stinger deeper.

Near panic at the pain shooting from his hand, Leon remembered a lesson from a YMCA camp that had kept him off the streets of Oakland for one week as a kid. Now he took a gravity knife from his pocket and made two deep X's on his hand. He sucked the blood, but a little sharp thorn came from one of the wounds and before he could spit it out, it had caught on his tongue. He thought he remembered a National Geographic Special saying that scorpion stingers didn't break off, but this seemed to be an exception to the rule, and, after all, he had smashed the stupid thing. He managed to spit the little thorn out. He looked in the mirror and saw his tongue was starting to swell. Okay, he was going to have to cut that, too.

"Oww, Shticker id my tug!" he managed to say.

He stuck out his tongue and moved to get a better angle so he could see to make the cuts with his good hand, but the old man wasn't gone yet. He wrapped both arms around Leon's legs, hugging him and bleeding all over his light brown pants.

"Yaks, sir, Buster Brown...you're one dead feller..." The leathery whisper came from Alvin's bloody lips. He grinned up at Leon, the blood running from between his broken teeth.

Leon lost his balance and toppled over, staining his expensive jacket and ripping it at the shoulder. He sensed that every second was important, yet he had to take the time to reduce the tenacious old man into shuddering silence with a flurry of stabs around the chest and shoulders. Only then could he drag himself back to his feet and get on with his real problems.

The little cross incision on his tongue was harder to make than he would have imagined. His numb tongue seemed to roll away from the point of the knife like a slippery pink fish, and the razor-sharp knife blade didn't seem to do anything at all until the moment he pushed a little harder, and then it cut like it was slicing through butter, making a half-inch gash before he knew what was happening.

"Oh, nooo..." he gurgled.

He stared in the mirror at the stream of blood running down his chin. His hand was now puffing up at an alarming rate. Sucking at the hand made the blood bubble and flow in frighteningly large amounts from the gash in his tongue.

"Hi, I'm Buster Brown," Alvin chanted from somewhere nearby. Leon turned to deliver a deathblow with the tire iron. But he collapsed in mid-swing, crumpling to the ground.

"There's my dog Tide," Alvin continued, "He lives in there too! Hee, hee, hee!" And then the old desert rat's face went blank and he also lay still on the cold cement floor of the parking garage.

16

It is a known thing: The ancient Greeks and the Romans believed in the fates, and everyone from emperors to peasants had their oracles living uncomfortably in caves or the scary old lady cackling next door, both types very useful to stir the entrails of a dead chicken or goat and foretell the future. This apparently did little to prevent the downfall of nations (there is no evidence a single family bundled up the kids and got out of Pompeii the night before the volcano buried it), but who knows, perhaps these fortune-tellers were providing incorrect interpretations or, as one might say more simplistically, reading things wrong.

It is elemental that everyone has a fate. Unfortunately, outcomes only manifest themselves clearly in retrospect. Or is that entirely correct? Can't we sometimes, watching as some young fool with prospects falls like a bleeding star, predict that which will come to pass? We have wise sayings for such circumstances: A fool and his money are soon parted. An apple a day keeps the doctor away. A stitch in time will save you nine. Time waits for no man. Chevy—built like a rock. (Well, maybe not that one.) Too soon old; too late smart. Marry first for love, then for money. Or, marry first for money; then you can afford love. No fool like an old fool. You get the idea.

Still, what if...what if there are these red-eyed demonic (or not) demigods who take a more or less casual interest in the affairs of men, somewhat the way you do with a game of chess or poker? What if they, in our own image, gather at infrequent times like Lent or New Years, collect themselves invisibly around the reality we call humanity, simply because the pathos, fuss and bother interests them? What if they themselves take sides, bore or insult easily, are quick to anger and resentment? And what if they in turn bicker with each other, lay bets, do their own stirring of the entrails?

Why do we even ask these highly theoretical *What ifs?* Isn't there real business here? The truth is, Dusty the drug lord is on his relentless and unstoppable way. He has been wronged, and will now set things right. If ever a black knight were predictable, it would be he. But that's the thing about life; you never know what you're going to run into.

And Dusty, hitchhiking south from his plane crash, is picked up by a hugely powerful and semi-mythical figure with an untrustworthy light in his eye. If the old fart would just slow down below eighty, Dusty would shoot him in the eye and take over the truck. But will the demigods, knowing this, allow the powerfully chested octogenarian to slack up on the gas pedal?

And what of The Man With The Scar (said scar which he received on that long-ago night, retreating across Saigon to Tan Son Nhut Air Base and his waiting bunk at Davis Station, said bunk made up tightly in the prescribed military manner), said Man With The Scar lying there half-dead for lack of a chocolate bar while early morning gamblers walk by and look the other way—but now I'm really getting ahead of the story again, aren't I?

Dusty walked along the road for a half hour before a single car approached. At first, he mistook the oncoming vehicle for some sort of police-ranger 4-wheeler, with the frame set high on knobby wheels and a bar of lights over the cab. But the truck pulled over and a high-pitched voice yelled, "Hey, get in, son!"

The cab was set so high that Dusty had to climb in using a step. It was a huge Ford pickup truck. The back was loaded with logs that had been sawed and split for firewood. The driver slammed the truck back in gear and in no time they were barreling down the two-lane towards Laughlin.

"That your bonfire back there?" the driver asked.

"Huh? Aw, No. I was just...you know, camping in the woods. I woke up and says to myself, 'Time to get on down to Laughlin.'"

"Uh-huh." The driver had a shrunken old man's head with a snow-white haystack of hair stuck on top of a powerful torso. He had huge shoulders and powerful biceps. Dusty could see the old crock didn't believe a word he'd said.

"You believe in the power of the Almighty Jesus?" the fellow asked. He screwed his head around to look at Dusty, taking his eyes completely off the road. Dusty saw a small frosty-haired head sitting on top of a big weight lifter's body looking like old Kirk Douglas on steroids. There they were, flying along in this big, heavy tire pickup, hitting the tops of the humps and bottoming out on the gullies. The pickup truck roared on into the night, and the old man gazed at him like he could wait forever for his answer.

"S-sure I do." It was one of those uncertain times when Flame Boy thought he'd let Ice Man handle it. After all, Ice Man was always running around, shooting off his mouth, letting everybody know how cool he was. "Yes," Dusty repeated for emphasis, "I-I believe I do."

"Me, too." The old man nodded enthusiastically, still looking at him.

"Sh-shouldn't you keep your eyes on the road, sir?" Ice Man asked with as much politeness as he could shovel into his voice.

"All in the hands of the Almighty, young feller. You know, Jesus never asked where the disciples came from, nor what they was up to in their life before he met them."

"Well, that was probably a good idea..." Dusty replied, moving his hand to the pistol at his belt. The old man grinned madly and grabbed his wrist in a grip of steel.

"Damn tooting!" The nod was so emphatic Dusty was worried the guy was out of control. If they'd been moving along at a respectable speed, he would have let Flame Boy jerk out that pistol and pop the old fart over to his pal Jesus right there. But at this speed, he knew it would have been suicide to try wrestling control from a powerful old geezer like this one. The old geezer kept waving his hand in the air, and every time Dusty tried reaching for his gun, he felt that icy grip around his wrist again.

Ice Man decided it would be more prudent to try and talk him down to a decent clip where he could put one in the crazy man's right eye and still control the truck.

"You're kind-of a bible-fearing sort of a guy, aren't you?" Ice Man asked, making conversation.

It was the right question; though he didn't take his foot off the gas, the man lit up like a drunk about to launch into his life's story.

"Thought you'd never ask, Little Black Feller. Sonny-boy, I tried everything when I was your age. I tried drugs. I tried booze. I had me some women. I was married to one of the prettiest and richest and most powerful women in North America. It got me ab-so-lute-ly nothing. I ended up on Mission Street in San Francisco, dead broke, busted spiritually, flat on my ass."

"You seem to be doing okay now," Dusty replied politely. The pickup was going so fast it seemed to want to lift off the little hillocks at the top of each rise, on its way to heaven.

"Sure, now that I found vitamins an' Jesus!" The man nodded emphatically, giving his full attention once again to his passenger as they rocketed along. "How old you think I am? Come on, guess—take a wild shot in the dark!"

The man's eyes seemed to be a light hazel color. Dusty thought they might be light brown; he couldn't tell for sure. But Dusty also thought he saw the flecked golden madness of a true believer staring back at him. And Ice Man was well aware that you had to be careful with people of powerful convictions. As he was jostled on down the road, he wondered if he could shoot straight enough to even hit the guy, much less blow out one of his crazed, God-fearing eyes.

"I don't know how old you are, man—what, 55? 60?" he guessed. Dusty felt like he had to puke. The rocking motion of the truck, swaying sideways and up and down over the low hills, had him feeling sicker than a poisoned dog.

"I'll be 79 this November, praise be the Lord!"

173

"Yeah. Praise be." Ice Man burped uncomfortably, hoping he was showing enough enthusiasm. He wished he had a vita-juice, or whatever the old bastard was on. "Well, I wouldn't have known. You don't look, you know, past 60 at the most."

Dusty was thinking how funny it would be to survive a plane crash and then be taken out by a crazy old coot driving like a bat out of hell on the trail to Nowhere, Nevada. But the road didn't make any zigs into the brushy desert, and they continued straight and true down their narrow lane like a roller coaster on speed. The pickup's bright lights bored into the night ahead and Dusty vowed somebody was truly going to be dead before this one was over. All Ice Man could think was that it was best to keep the old fartburger talking until he could get in a safe shot. "What's your secret, then?"

"I *told* you, sonny. It's Jesus Christ Savior, Our Lord."

"Yeah, but how did you get built up like that? I mean, you got shoulders like a fullback."

"Pumping iron, son. Pumping for Jesus. It's my life, now. And I tell you, it works!"

"I see that it does. I may have to try a bit of that myself..."

That seemed to please the old Jesus-Pumper.

"Amen to that!" he shouted with a high-pitched laugh, slamming his foot on the accelerator.

The Ford pickup shot on through the night like God's Arrow. Dusty could see the lights of Laughlin growing in the distance. He watched in open-mouthed wonder as red-eyed rabbits and even a goddamn deer leapt out of their way.

Ice Man hunched over in the seat and hugged Pig-Ops's bags, the one with the money and the other with the tea, and said a silent prayer for themselves. Maybe, once they got to Laughlin, if he got the chance, he could shoot this guy in the nearest eye just for the principle of the thing. As if he was reading his mind, the old Jesus-Pumper cried out, "I shall not want, for the truth abides in me!"

Dusty gave up on it, convinced there was no way he could take the old man out. At least, they were heading in the right direction. And at their present speed, it wasn't going to take long.

The first light of dawn was competing with the artificial glare of the casino lights by the time Millie and The Man With The Scar made their way from the motel. In spite of the heavy makeup job she'd applied, Millie's cheek was puffed and one eye was closed more than the other.

"Tink d' feds will spot me, Morty?" she asked.

"Probably not until they pull that kinky blond wig of yours out of the toilet."

"You like d' sunners?"

"The sunglasses are a nice touch," he admitted. "You look like any other moll with mouse-brown hair who's just been beaten by her husband."

"Thu-Thanks a lot."

"The truth sucks, doesn't it?"

"You could'a lied, you know. I don't *hafta* know I got the big C."

He felt his energy flagging and knew he had to stop. "Millie. I've got to get a bite of breakfast."

"No way, Jose. They can track me anywhere. They've probably got a hidden mike on me right now!"

"Sure...clipped to the back of your bra...seriously, I've got to get some energy..."

She turned from him with a firm stride, and he followed as best he could. They were making their way along the river towards the lot where she thought her car was parked when The Man With The Scar sat down with a heavy thump on one of the wood-and-iron benches.

"You go on," he said. His eyes were glazed and he was listing to the right.

She shifted to a Jamaican accent, "Come on, come on, old mon. De sun is up and de peoples are beginning to look at you in a funny way."

"Low blood sugar," he said. "Millie...did you take...my last chocolate bar?" As he spoke, his voice lowered, and he sagged more and more until he was lying on the bench.

"Aww, Scareface, honey," she said, reverting to gangster moll talk, "We missed breakfast after that last heist an' I was hungry. I'm eatin' for two, don't cha know? Say, you do look a little under the weather, Slash."

She gave him a shove and he fell over on the bench.

"Even take a Hershey bar," he said as his head came to rest on the wood.

She eyed him sharply, her brown eyes flicking over him like a nervous sparrow. Then her hands quickly moved through all his pockets, taking the few twenties she found in his wallet. There were no credit cards, so she tossed the wallet in the weeds. She wanted to get at his knapsack, but he was lying on it. When she tried to move him, he wouldn't budge, and pulling it out from under him proved a bigger deal than she had intended.

"Hey, you fuckin' whore!"

She turned, frightened by the harsh comment. Her face was ashen under her heavy pancake makeup. Three skinheads stood in front of her, dressed in tattoos, chains, tattered jeans and sleeveless jackets and wearing heavy leather boots.

"Get away from the old geek!"

"Bu-But he's my fa-fa-father," Millie tried to protest.

"Father, my ass, limp-lips!"

They fanned out to surround her, and she barely escaped with her own suitcase, running down the cement sidewalk. They made no move to follow her. Once she darted into the nearest casino, they quickly finished her task, pulling the knapsack out from under him and pawing through it.

The one with the gold ring in his lips found the ancient Borchardt.

"Hey, look, a toy gun!" He pulled it from the knapsack and waved it triumphantly.

The Man With The Scar tried to raise one feeble hand, but the gun went off, pinking a second skinhead in the butt.

"Fuck-pads!" the shooter said in awe, dropping the gun. It was old, and the trigger worn from use, and it fired again on impact, the bullet whizzing past his left ear.

Panicked, he yelled, "Let's go!"

The skinhead who'd been shot in the butt was still in shock. He was uncertain how he should be acting. He grabbed his bloody cheek with one hand, came away with a fist smeared in gore, and let out a low wail.

"Come on, man, it's only an ass wound," one of them encouraged. They took him by the arms and half dragged and half carried him away.

The Man With The Scar closed his eyes. He dreamed he was on a yacht owned by a Greek tycoon. The name of the yacht was the Contempo, and Beverly, Gwen and Karen were there, looking pretty and innocent as they had in their early teens. They held silver wine goblets and were wearing loosely fitting Greek dresses of white silk, each with one pert breast showing and the dresses cinched with a silver clasp in the shape of a 56. 1956, his graduation year. He remembered thinking, *Ahh, forever young!*

He didn't know how long he'd been out, but when he looked up a little boy with dark, innocent eyes and a dirty smear around his mouth was swinging the heavy Borchardt left and right, and making *Pow!, Pow!, Pow!* noises.

"Put it down," the man managed to say before he lapsed back into a semi-coma. The next time he came back to reality, his big sister, a girl of about seven or eight, had joined the little boy. The two of them stood silently in front of him, staring down at him. A miracle—the little girl held out half of an Oreo Double Stuf cookie. The Man With The Scar could see someone had already eaten the white stuff from the center. Still, he opened his mouth, and the girl placed the dark bit of cookie on his tongue like a devil's communion wafer.

17

He's just one desert rat, you say. There is no significance here. What purpose can he possibly have in God's grand plan? Yet Alvin Curdle is as much a man as any other. He likes to hunt for gold in the Superstition Mountains, off there somewhere south of Payson where The Man With The Ice Pick lives. He likes to huddle up to the bar for a cold beer after a hot month or two picking through the dust of Arizona. And he likes revenge. Yes, revenge...vengeance served up cool as vanilla ice cream with scorpions frozen inside. He likes that best of all.

Alvin thought he'd died and gone to heaven. He was in a clean, white, air-conditioned room, surrounded by cloudlike white drapes.

"Wow-wo-wo-wooow...where's my angel wings?" he asked no one in particular.

He felt the bandages around his head and looked down and saw the patchwork of black stitches across his neck and chest. He carefully pulled the long needle from the vein in his arm and taped the rubbery tape back over the small hole in his skin.

He wondered if he could sit up without causing himself too much damage. After a moment he willed his muscles to do it, and with only a minor swimming sensation, was able to push himself into a sitting position. Next, he swung his legs over the edge of the bed. He found he was wearing one of those funny hospital robes, the kind that left his ass swinging in the breeze. At first he thought that was what had awoken him. But then he heard a blood-chilling scream from the bed right next to his.

"Buster Brown..." he said thoughtfully. His ruddy, ancient face lit up like a Norman Rockwell study in amazed delight.

By the time Millie returned, The Man With The Scar was sitting up, eating an Egg McMuffin and sipping his third glass of orange juice. His two young friends sat nearby, quietly munching their own egg sandwiches.

"Orange juice is good for you," he said, saluting her with the plastic carton. "I once met Steve Allen, you know, the famous comedian, and he said—"

"Where's my goddamn car, you ancient fly-sucking lump of bat guano?"

"Millie. I thought you might be back. Meet Donna and Carlos. Their mother makes beds at the Hilton, so they have nothing to do all day but—"

She took a wild swing at him, but with his blood sugar level repaired, he was able to duck and avoid her wild blow.

"Where's my—?!"

He held up one hand.

"Millie. My eighty dollars. You're not going to deny you went through my wallet and threw it in the bushes?"

Her breath was a hiss between her clenched teeth, but she dug in her purse and handed the money across.

"Fine. Now, about your car: I put it in a safe place."

"A safe place. Why?" Her voice was acidic enough to eat through one-inch steel plate.

"So that we could get to it when those guys came after you."

"What guys?!" she shrieked.

He nodded his head. Dusty and Bopo were a block and a half away, but her voice easily carried and the two black men looked in their direction and then broke into a gallop, heading right for them.

"Look, Millie," The Man With The Scar said. "I believe they've spotted us."

"The keys, señor," Donna said. She held up two keys tied to bright day-glow plastic bottles.

"Daddy's going to be really mad," Carlos said.

"It's okay; we've got insurance," his sister said.

Millie looked from the approaching men to The Man With The Scar and back again.

"Oh-oh-oh, screw-pins! Dusty's gonna kill us. You, for sure. Me, ma-ma-maybe I can fu-fu-fuck my way out of it."

"Don't count on it. Come on, I've got a rental."

"Suppose I take my chances?"

"Up to you," he shrugged. He picked up his Borchardt and snapped off a few shots in Dusty's direction.

"Thank you for everything, Donna," he said, handing her the money Millie had given him. He placed his Borchardt in his backpack, carefully making sure the muzzle was pointing away from his back, and then snapped his knapsack shut and hunched into it. He took Millie's arm and shoved her ahead of him down a stairway leading to the river. Two Ski-Doo jet boats were tied up at the river's edge. He handed her one of the day-glow bottles with a key dangling from it.

"Well," she said, playing the huffy heiress, "I just may choose not to accompany you."

He sighed, "Dicey time for attitude."

He turned the key in his own little boat, unwound the rope securing it to the dock, and zoomed ten feet from shore. Millie had to have her moment of indecision, and so he had to unpack the Borchardt and snap off a few wild rounds at the approaching men. The lighter-skinned one was shooting back, the flames spitting silently from the elongated muzzle of a smaller caliber pistol.

By the time Millie made up her mind, tied her suitcase to the loose end of the mooring rope and turned the key on the Ski-Doo, Bopo was lumbering toward her like a galloping stallion. The orange-red Ski-Doo pulled away as he dove with a tremendous splash into the river. For a moment it looked like she was going to get away, but he came up with the suitcase, and the Ski-Doo lumbered away from shore with big Bopo being dragged along behind like a hooked killer.

"Faster, master, flee disaster!" she cried. And, even in their time of extreme urgency, she had time for a track announcer voice, "As they rounded the halfway mark, Hot Flanks, clearly in the lead, was slowed down by Lead Butt, bringing up the rear!"

Welcome to the joyful river of shared assumptions. The sun will rise in the morning. Water runs downhill. Light travels at 186,000 miles per second. Piss, in the wind, will dampen your shoe, and perhaps your pants leg. But suppose for a moment that it didn't. None of it. What would you have then? Well, Alvin Curdle doesn't care. These aren't the sort of bemusements that devil old desert rats. Alvin, having survived his stabbings, has fallen into a smallish pot of gold and will try to make the most of it.

He could see right away that Leon's pants were too wide by half in the waist, but he put them on anyway, tying the thin belt in a little knot to hold them up until he could punch some holes in the leather. The lavender shirt stunk like whore's perfume and hung like a drape on his skinny shoulders, but he decided to keep it anyway because he'd never had a silk shirt and he liked the feel of it.

"When I seen you last, didn't you have a big gold chain?" he asked.

"What?! I'll kill you, you stupid old buzzard!"

Leon's eyes burned, and he shook his head violently, but the rage was muffled in his throat by the tape the old desert rat carefully wrapped again and again around his head, effectively covering his mouth. Gold being anywhere you found it, Alvin slipped the heavy chain off over Leon's head and hung it around his own scrawny neck. Leon's jacket was soiled and ripped, and it was big enough to fit two Alvins, but Alvin put it on anyway, careful to check that the money and dope Leon had taken from him were still in the pockets.

Alvin rummaged around in the cabinet against the wall until he found some vials full of clear yellow liquid, and some needles. He assembled a neat little row of injections, wondering all the time what was in the vials.

"I'll bet I could do this," Alvin advised his patient. "I seen plenty of medical shows on the television set.

Leon's eyes widened as Alvin carefully wiped his arm with a ball of cotton.

"Settle down, Buster Brown. This here is just like a little snip of ER I seen in a bar in Pahrump, or maybe it was Henderson; anyway, it was for sure one of those times. I remember it plenty well. I'd been dreaming about a burger and a beer for weeks until I left the quest in the silent, empty spaces for a night on the town. I know you always rub the arm with a little ball of cotton. I'm not sure why you do that, but I do want to get this right."

Alvin squinted one eye and expertly snapped a finger on one of the vials, letting a bit of the unknown yellow liquid squirt in the air.

Leon struggled manfully, but he was firmly strapped to the bed. He'd been out of his mind when they brought him in, and had punched out an orderly and two nurses before they gang-tackled him and brought him under control. As the first needle punctured the skin on his powerful biceps, he lurched about so violently that Alvin thought he was going to rip the straps that bound him, and perhaps even get away. But the straps held, every single one.

18

Were you actually hoping Millie and The Man With The Scar would get it on, as they say? Not very likely, if you ascribe to cosmic destiny, the right vibes or any of that California light-headedness. Why not, you pout? Well, friend, everybody can't bed everybody all the time. It simply can't be done. Even for a prodigious fellow like The Man With The Scar, there just isn't enough of a good thing to go around.

As it was, he had to run over Bopo three times at full speed before the big man let go of the suitcase and started to dog paddle in dizzy little circles. The second man on shore had stopped shooting, and was running for the Ski-Doo rental place, undoubtedly to acquire his own ride across the river.

"Millie, get rid of that suitcase!"

"No way, you dweeb-humping thimble-dick!" she shouted over the twin whine of the Ski-Doos. "Anyway, you're supposed to rescue me! It's your job, and you're slower than an old dodger's fart! You not de *man,* you de *mule!*"

They were nearly across when The Man With The Scar heard a heavier roar in the distance. Their chasers had acquired a speedboat. With no time to spare, The Man With The Scar leapt from his Ski-Doo and sloshed through the shallow water and up the sandy bank on the eastern side of the river. He found a fallen tree trunk on which he was able to rest the long barrel of the Borchardt. His first shot starred the thin glass windshield on the approaching boat, which then swung in a wide circle and headed back for the other side of the river.

Millie drove her Ski-Doo so violently into the shore that she was flung from it and rolled on the sand. The Man With The Scar helped her up and saw there wasn't any serious damage.

"Come on, let's go!"

"My suitcase!"

"Leave it. We don't have time."

"No, fellow conniver! I tell you, no!"

He was forced to half carry and half drag her waterlogged suitcase. They made their way as fast as they could, going a half mile upstream along the sandy shore and scattering a few hikers as they went, and then they were able to scramble up the riverbank and crawl through a hole cut in the wire fence.

He grumbled as they limped along.

"What say you, gerbil-scar?" she asked. "Cease your mad grumbling at once, or off with your head!"

"Life being unpleasant enough the way it is, and all, would it be too much of an imposition to ask you to go it on your own for a bit?"

"Polite old fart, aren't you? Say that in ordinary, plain English, would you, dimble-dick?"

"You're asking *me* not to speak in tongues?!"

The Man With The Scar sighed, shook his head and turned away from her. Maybe she would just vanish if he ignored her long enough.

Yes, they still serve the Navajoburger at the Amigo Cafe in Kayenta. You can get one there, and sometime before you pass through the eternal veil, I recommend you try one. That should be enough. Just one.

It took some willpower and a boot to her curvaceous butt, but Millie was long gone by the time The Man With The Scar found himself hitching his way through Tuba City.

He threw his backpack over his shoulder and munched a bite from a Toblerone bar, the deep bittersweet kind with the honey sweetening that, as you know, he liked best of all. A

184

pickup truck pulled over and he crawled in back between two warm bales of alfalfa. The sun was pleasant on his face and life was good. That ride took him a ways up the road, until the driver, an old Apache, left him off at the Amigo Café in Kayenta, Arizona.

It was getting on to be two in the afternoon. Inside the café, Johnny Tuesday munched his Navajoburger and felt he was just lucky enough to be alive. The meat was tough and greasy, probably horse, and the two slabs of oil-dipped Navajo bread were even worse. Nobody ordered the Navajoburger but folks passing through who were looking to eat local color, but Johnny had a huge frame, halfway between six-foot and seven, and he felt he needed his share of pure grease to keep the meat on his bones. He washed it all down with Coors, anyway, so it wasn't half bad.

The part about being alive, well, the rest of his crew weren't, and that had something to do with the luck, both bad and good. The week before, Johnny and his crew had been sitting an oil rig in an isolated dry and dusty area out near Grey Mountain, which was on checkerboard land just off the western end of the reservation. Johnny was no geologist, but he'd hunted oil for years in these parts, and he figured he knew the general lay and fold of the checkerboard as good as any book-boy with a parchment on his wall saying he'd graduated from Texas A&M or Colorado School of Mines. In that patch near Grey Mountain, for instance, he knew you were going to strike oil down around 2,100 feet, or you weren't going to strike it at all. He also knew, the way you hear things, that that particular square of empty land was up for buy-back by the tribe.

It didn't bother him that Holden Begay, their spiffy little half-white engineer, had been carting away a pipe here and a pipe there, moving it off to other jobs. That's how they counted depth, by the pipe, and Johnny figured Holden was calculating they were already down around 2,000—counting those misplaced pipes—when they really were only at 1,600 at the most.

Johnny kept his mouth shut. That's how he stayed on as a rigger, and that's what kept his two kids, Johnny, Jr. and

Glorianna, in the good school at St. Michaels, rather than the mind-numbing BIA schools where you learned how to be a second-class citizen in your own country.

Everybody was surprised when they hit the first bubble at 1700 feet. First there was a big, whistling gas blow and then a shot of thick, gunky oil. Everybody was shouting and happy except Holden, who looked like he'd just swallowed a live chicken, feathers and all. Johnny figured the little man should have trucked off more pipe if that was the way he felt, but he didn't say anything.

That night, they had a party; one of the drivers had to go 150 miles round-trip for beers and carryout fried chicken. They all cheered when the battered red truck showed as a dusty speck on the horizon, and they made short work of the meal, too. After everybody had his fill, Holden got up to make a little speech.

"By golly, we all done well," he chuckled.

"Who would have thunk, oil down there at just over 1,600 feet!" one of the men wondered, and there was a round of cheers for that.

Holden's face blanched a little. "Well, we don't know how much oil."

"Shoot, Holden! The way that sucker blew?!"

"Gas pressure don't mean necessarily there's a lot of oil..."

"We SEEN that sucker flow, Holden. Come on, man, she's still running out there. You can see it from here."

"I know, I know. But we're going to leave that to the big boys. Look, we're way late on our schedule. We're just going to cap her off and move over near Farmington." This announcement was met with a chorus of mixed cheers and boos. It was nice to hang around while a well proved out. On the other hand, Farmington was a lot closer to home, to wives and families.

It took a few days to cap the well and clean up the area. Holden was more paranoid than usual about the environment, and so they had to bulldoze local dirt over the oil spot. He even made them pick up the cigarette butts and stray paper and throw all the refuse in a big, blue barrel. Johnny watched thoughtfully, but said nothing, though he knew that was compulsive, even for Holden. By the time they were finished, you'd have to know the local dirt the way Johnny did or refer to their own marks on the company maps to even know a drill rig had been out there.

Johnny, who'd spent two lousy tours in Nam—'70 and '71—was used to taking orders. Cleanup was easy duty, and they were being paid for it. Why should he say anything?

Then they'd all piled into their pickup trucks, eager to be going home to the women and kids they hadn't seen for the better part of a month. Now, barely two days later as Johnny sat munching his Navajoburger, the four other members of his crew were all dead, two in an overturned truck on a deserted back road, one in a knife fight in a bar, and the fourth from food poisoning. *Four in a week.*

Johnny had started home, too, but somewhere along the way he realized he was close to the cemetery where his wife was buried, lost to him when his youngest, Glorianna, was born. When he was a kid, Johnny had gone to St. Michael's boarding school, so he had traded his Indian superstitions for those of the blackrobes. He didn't place too much faith in Navajo beliefs; so, instead of shunning the place where his wife's remains were buried, he made a spiritual pilgrimage to talk with her spirit, to bring her up-to-date on the latest family happenings and to say how much he missed her. Later, he figured the sudden change in his schedule probably saved his life.

He heard about the fiery pickup truck accident on the radio, saw the reports on the knife fight and the poisoning in the paper the next morning after spending a night in a Kayenta motel. After that, he'd phoned Grandma, had her take the kids out of school and quietly drift them into family hogans near Shonto at the remote northern end of the rez. He was quietly turning over these events in his mind when a voice brought him back to the present.

"You recommend the Navajoburger?"

It was an older gentleman, sitting a few stools down.

"Naw. Not really," Johnny drawled with a grin. "I'm eating it, but I can't recommend it."

The man nodded, and ordered an ordinary cheeseburger. Johnny noticed they both were sitting around the shorter elbow-end of the counter where they could look across the room and watch the door. The stranger was wearing a faded army jacket. He had a pleasant enough face, if you ignored the deep gash running straight up and down through the right side of his face, cutting the eyebrow and leaving a crease in the forehead and the cheek below. There was a faded knapsack at his feet, open as if he might want to get a book out to read while eating, or something. Alarm bells went off in Johnny's head.

"Live around here?" Johnny asked.

"Nope. Just passing through."

"You must be out in the sun a lot. Hell, you got a deeper tan than I do."

"Fishing boats," the man said. "Down Baja way."

"What's that like?" Johnny asked, relaxing a little. The hands checked out, rough and hard-looking. It was tough to believe a man who did physical labor for decent wages could be dangerous in the ways that worried him right now.

"You get sicker than a dog the first two days. Seasick. After that, the days, one by one, do have their glory. I mean, not all of it is great. Most sport fishermen are amateurs. Lazy, fat, rich assholes, truth be told. You got to help a lot or they'll excite themselves right into a heart attack."

"That ever happen?"

"Oh, sure. Two, three times."

"What you do then?"

"If you're only a hundred miles or so, you make for the nearest port. Ruins a whole day of fishing. If you're on a two-week run, you bag 'em and put 'em in the freezer with the fish."

"Go on!" Johnny scoffed.

"Naw. They have to sign a paper saying it's okay, and that's how you do it..."

The Man With The Scar broke off his thought as two men entered the cafe together, closely followed by a third man. The first two looked Mexican, dark complexioned with heavy eyebrows and stubby beards. The third was a lean white man, bald and scowling.

All three took seats in different corners of the restaurant, the two swarthy Mexicans at different tables and the angry white man at a stool at the counter.

"Friends of yours?" The Man With The Scar asked.

"I'm afraid so," Johnny said.

"I smell an Injun," the angry-looking white man said, staring at Johnny. The waitress headed for the kitchen.

"I can handle the smeller," The Man With The Scar said, loud enough so that everyone in the cafe could hear. "The problem is the Mex on the left. I believe he's got a shotgun under his coat."

"I think I got him," Johnny said. "Who gets the other Mex?"

"Whoever's fastest."

"Hey, red-skin asshole!" the angry white man yelled, pulling a blunt-nosed .38 from his pants pocket.

In one smooth gesture, The Man With The Scar took the odd-looking, long-barreled pistol from his jacket and shot the white man above his left eye. At the same time, a huge nickel-plated .44 appeared in Johnny's hand. The big, shiny gun barked and the man with the shotgun flew back across the cafe, his sawed-off weapon blowing out a window as he went. Both the .44 and the Borchardt pointed at the remaining man, who showed no iron and only moved to slowly raise his hands in the air.

"Tie," Johnny said.

"Tie," The Man With The Scar agreed.

Local businessman Ridley Hawkins sat in the sheriff's office, waiting for word of the slaying. Ridley was one of those lanky Western men that pulp writer Louis L'Amour would have called *a lean drink of water.* His thin face was adorned with a droopy moustache, and he favored worn jeans and cowboy boots.

When the news finally came, Ridley's face turned sour and mean. "Crazy Bill Parsons shot by some stranger...?"

"Yup," the sheriff said, "An' one of the Tex-Mexes blown away, too also."

"What about the other one?"

"He's still alive."

"Well, Sheriff, let's get to him!"

"Slow down, Ridley." The sheriff sank back into his wooden rocking chair. "He's been captured by Johnny and his friend."

"What friend?"

"Some old guy with a scar on his face. Waitress said that the stranger suggested they call the newspaper."

"Oh, Jesus..." Ridley ran a hand through his thinning hair, mussing it up and then smoothing it back. "What would they want to do that for?"

The sheriff eyed him for a moment and then gave a laconic shrug, "Something about an oil swindle, somebody trying to squeeze the Indians again."

"Jesus!"

"Waitress said they called the Farmington Times and then took the Tex-Mex away with their weapons pointed at him."

Ridley thought about how much that remaining Tex-Mex knew and how much the huge Navajo might have pieced together, and then reminded the sheriff of favors past and future in a way that wasn't exactly friendly. The sheriff unhappily commandeered every patrol car they could lay their hands on, and even threw up a roadblock on the west side of Farmington. But they'd been led down a false trail. They couldn't find Johnny Tuesday's dented white Ford pickup, and it was another three or four days later when the scoop about the big land oil-grab scandal showed up in the Gallup Independent.

A week later, the sheriff had a call from Northern California, from a man who said he was a detective working for the Oakland Police force. The man, who sounded to the sheriff like one of those prissy blacks with not enough real brains and too much education, said he was interested in the specifics of the shootings at the Amigo Cafe, particularly in anything they might be able to tell him about the whereabouts of the stranger who had helped Johnny Tuesday.

"Nobody knows anything about him," the sheriff grumped.

"Didn't one of the waitresses or somebody say he had a big scar on his face?"

"That was in the paper," the sheriff grudgingly admitted.

"You mind if I come out and poke around a bit?"

"Why yes, I do mind," the sheriff replied. "Out of your jurisdiction."

And with that, he slammed down the phone. *Off the hook*, he thought. *Now maybe it will finally dry up and blow away.* But he knew it wasn't going to. The critical search for Johnny Tuesday had been unsuccessful. Johnny had crawled into a hole somewhere and wasn't going to come out until this all blew over...if ever. Their last card, Johnny's two kids, hadn't showed for school. Worse, an owl-eyed geologist named Holden Begay was missing, and Ridley Hawkins was now the subject of a budding investigation into what could develop into a huge land scandal involving local ranchers, a pack of smart-yapping lawyers from Phoenix and two or three top officials in the Navajo tribe. So far, none of the reporters had dug deep enough to spot the money Ridley's dummy corporations had donated to the sheriff's last five or six campaigns. But the sheriff figured it was just a matter of time.

19

Here we are, you and I, cast adrift in this leaky life raft of a novel...somewhat like our own lives, I might add. Or don't you ever have that feeling of being propelled headlong, willy-nilly into the future, come what may, no matter what you say? You argue, *But what of memory*? Yes, I reply, we can go back in reflection, and that can be a joy or a sorrow. But no man can stop the course of a bullet, the gleam in a pretty girl's eye or the drift of a leaky boat.

All right, it's a given then that time itself is a one-way arrow, and the clock cannot and will not be turned back. Still, then, can't The Man With The Scar find any peace? And failing that, is there no one friend, no other body in the known universe who understands what he's feeling and what he's going through? Apparently, there is at least one.

They were in a narrow canyon of thickly layered sandstone, camped on a ten-by-forty foot ledge a stone's throw above a small stream. The Man With The Scar was hunched next to a small pine-knot fire, pushing around six small trout in a blackened pan.

"You use this same pan for gold?" he asked.

"Sure," Johnny said.

"You ever find any?"

"Red Man not tell tribal secrets to white-eyes."

"I guess that means no."

"Yep. Guess so."

The canyon was so narrow that the dancing firelight cast a small glow on the sandstone walls. While The Man With The Scar cooked, Johnny studied a wrinkled piece of paper by the flickering light.

"So you think you want to go to this reunion?"

Time passed. A coyote howled somewhere in the near distance. Both men thought about it for a while. There is something about the vastness of the desert that makes men pause and reflect before speaking.

"I'm not sure," The Man With The Scar finally said. "Did you ever go to a class reunion?"

"Yeah, once. I was in the army at the time, so I showed up wearing my uniform, medals and everything. I thought I'd get myself some easy poon..."

"How'd that work?"

"Just back from Nam. Got spat on by some peace-loving liberals."

"Hmm." The silence lengthened again, both men thinking about wet green places, sudden wild, gurgling screams in the night, and close, blinding explosions and their bloody aftermath.

"Where'd you meet the old woman?" The Man With The Scar asked, trying to keep it casual, like this wasn't the only person other than Toomley who might know what he was talking about.

"What old woman?" Johnny said, just as casually.

"Three Tex-Mexes all hang up their fast draws at the same time..."

"I honestly don't know what you're talking about," Johnny protested.

The Man With The Scar shook his head, "Yeah, you do...You're in a bar or a whorehouse someplace. You're young and maybe lonely. There's this really, really old lady, maybe the oldest woman you've ever seen. And maybe somebody else with her. They invite you to have a drink and give you this paper to sign...and for no goddamn reason at all, except you're young and full of piss and vinegar, you scratch your name...and after that, nothing is ever the same."

As The Man With The Scar laid it out, Johnny's face took on an expression that was more and more serious. He sighed and nodded.

"It was in Venezuela. I was working an offshore oil rig. Had alternate weekends off in Aruba...God, I remember she was the oldest woman I'd ever seen. Ancient lady. Features like a Mayan statue..."

"And what did you ask for?"

Johnny grinned ruefully, "Well, at that time I didn't have any children...and it bothered me, I guess..."

"So you signed this funny-looking document...?"

"I was young. What the hell did I know?"

"I never met anyone else before, who had...you know, this opportunity."

"Me, either." Johnny grinned, thinking about it. "Now I got more kids than beans...and half the husbands in Four Corners paying hit men to take me out. I get tired of it. Sometimes, I'd just love to hear a woman say, 'No'." The moment lengthened, each man thinking about the woman who had changed their lives forever.

"Don't burn the fish," Johnny said finally.

"Yas, sir, boss."

They ate in silence, looking out over the sweep of the canyon. Johnny knew that, from where they were, at the edge of a small Anasazi ruin tucked back in a sandstone cut a few miles behind the more widely known Betatikin ruins, their small fire wouldn't be observed beyond the lip of the canyon shelf.

"I got some good grass," Johnny suggested.

"Why not?" The Man With The Scar said.

"'Born to be wild'," Johnny said. "Born to be wild an' free."

Johnny lit up and they passed around the homemade. They smoked in silence and the sweet blue smoke drifted up through the pines. Johnny was thinking about his Kathleen, gone now seven years come June, and lying under a hilltop stone. And The Man With The Scar was thinking of ashes spread near a dark rock on a pass through the High Sierras where the hawks and an occasional eagle wheeled on silent wings.

Neither man said anything for a long time. The fire burned low until the knots were dull red embers that threw off no light. Overhead, the haphazard scatter of stars blazed in a black sky, just the way they'd always done since that storied first night when Coyote scattered them from his blanket to play another of his goofy tricks on mankind.

Dusty's black BMW would have stood out in Kayenta even without the California plates. And, there being few gentlemen of color residing in or showing more than a pass-through interest in that part of Northern Arizona, he did stick out like an infected thumb. Then too, two hulking black fellows accompanied him, one with a bandage around his head and the other moving stiffly like he'd just played three or four back-to-back football games.

Two days later, one of Johnny's nephews heard about the sheriff's exotic visitors while lounging on the front porch outside the Shonto trading post. There were six or seven older Navajos sitting around on the front porch. Johnny's nephew had wandered down to the trading post to see if Sue Mae, a girl he was sweet on, was working that day. He was all disappointed and set to leave when Bill Jimmy, who worked as a part-time deputy for the Navajo Police, pulled up in his dusty green Ford Explorer. Bill got out of his truck and did his stretch and yawn to get the kinks out of his shoulders. He came over and hunched on the ground near the old men. He found a short stick and drew looping circles in the dusty sand. For about a half hour they talked about the weather, the crops, the price of sheep's wool, all of their talk in slow, intermittent drawls separated by lots of silence. Bill threw away his stick and wandered in to get himself a Dr. Pepper. And then he came back, took a big chug of the Dr. and let it slide about the sheriff's visitors, "They was three black fellers, all slicked out in city duds."

"I'll be," Old Shorty said, leaning back on his favorite barrel and letting go with a lethal brown stream of tobacco juice. He missed the long line of ants he'd been aiming for, so that was only one out of three. Maybe he was losing his aim, he thought. *Old age creeping in, and him not even that old yet.*

Nobody else said anything, and then Bill Jimmy let slide the question that had been on his mind all along.

"Nobody around here seen Johnny Tuesday lately?"

"Nope. Not lately." Old Shorty tried to work up a spit, but it was too soon. Nobody else said anything, though a few of the men shook their heads as they studied their boots.

The nephew didn't say anything either, or seem even mildly interested. He finished his big one-liter Pepsi, and even hung around for an extra half hour before he wandered off to who-knows-where.

The next evening, which was on a Thursday, The Man With The Scar was sitting alone in the Amigo Cafe, surrounded by the cold remains of his cheeseburger and fries when Dusty, Leon and Bopo walked in. Leon and Bopo sat at a nearby table while Dusty pulled up a chair at The Man With The Scar's table. The man from Oakland took out his pistol, set it within easy reach on the checkered red-and-white tablecloth and put the menu on top of it.

"I want to know three things," Dusty said.

The Man With The Scar nodded, but said nothing. He didn't seem surprised, or frightened, or worried. *That's his first mistake,* Flame Boy thought to himself. *He's not dealing with Ice Man the pussy foot, here.*

"One: Where's my fuckin' money? Two: Where's my fuckin' dope? And Three: Where's that fuckin' woman?"

The Man With The Scar nodded and sipped the last of his Coca-Cola.

"Fair enough," he said. "Seeing as you've 'got the drop on me', as they say in these parts. First, most of your money is in my safe deposit box in California. Second, about fifteen percent of your dope is in the hands of some Mexican border guard, and you are never going see it again in this life. The rest is dissolved in seawater, somewhere off Oceanside, where I don't believe I have to add that you're never going to see any of that, either. As for strike three...I don't know. The lovely Millie and I parted ways right after Laughlin."

"Why?"

"We weren't exactly friends, you know. More like casual traveling companions."

"Why would you fucking let her go?"

"You couldn't see she was trouble?"

"No, man, I couldn't. What I saw, she was a nifty piece of ass—Now me, *I'm* trouble." Flame Boy patted the menu at his side.

The Man With The Scar nodded in a noncommittal manner.

"What else?" he asked.

"Old man, we're not communicating, here. For starters, I don't believe a fucking word you've said."

"For instance?"

"For *instance*, why did you steal my dope if you was just going to dump it?"

"I don't like dope."

It came over Flame Boy like a hot wind that he hated this common-looking man with his sun-bleached hair, his mysterious, ever-present scar and calm, unflappable ways. Hated him and was going to have to blow him away.

"That attitude's going to get you killed," he said. "'Died because of attitude', your fuckin' obit is going to read." He reached for his pistol, but in the fraction of a second before he could get it from under the menu he found himself staring into the black muzzle of an ancient, odd-looking pistol that The Man With The Scar took from where it had rested on his lap under the table.

"That's not going to be so easy," The Man With The Scar said.

Leon and Bopo leapt to their feet, but before they could take a step forward to help their boss, a huge Indian stepped from the kitchen with an equally huge and shiny pistol in his hand. The Indian carried Pig-Ops's two bags in his other hand. Dusty knew that wasn't a good sign; those bags had been locked safely in the trunk of his car.

"Those are *my* bags!" he yelled.

"We know," the Indian said. "An' if you insist, that's the story we're going to tell the sheriff."

"Sit down, boys," The Man With The Scar said, waving his aged black pistol at Leon and Bopo. "Sit down and enjoy the bonfire."

"Bonfire? What you talking about?" The words were no sooner out of Bopo's mouth when he heard a hollow *BOP!* noise from the parking lot.

Dusty sagged back in his chair, glaring at the table and wondering if he dared let Flame Boy go for his pistol.

"That machine was my baby," he whispered. "That machine cost me over $80,000." His words were clipped, his voice heavy with contained fury, "And you, mister, are going to die."

"Keep at it, and one of us is," The Man With The Scar quietly agreed. "That's for sure."

"Death comes to us all," Johnny Tuesday chimed in philosophically, "But for now, Oh, Three Wise Black Men from the West, we accept your gracious contribution of the contents of these two bags, for all the inconvenience you've caused in this here remote part of the world."

The fact that piles of money seemed to roll his way lately hadn't gone unnoticed in the mind of The Man With The Scar on his face. Now, it started him thinking once again, after all these years, about Toomley. He wondered if his old CIA friend was still alive, and if so, what he was up to. He remembered they had both signed the old parchment on the same line. *If Toomley was dead, could Toomley's Midas curse somehow have rubbed off and gotten mixed up with his own?* That would make for a life even more unbearable than the one he now possessed; one blessing assuring him so much danger he could never settle down, and the other granting him untold wealth that he could never enjoy. He shook his head, eyeing the bags in the Indian's hand and the angry, dangerous black men in front of him. *In a way, that already was his reality, wasn't it?* On the other hand, if Toomley had wanted to contact him, how would he ever find him?

20

It's a long way from the tonky bars of Hai Ba Trung Street, from the faded glory of the shops on Tu Do, from the rattle and clang of 100 P Alley. That was half a world and thirty years ago. Young men should be allowed to grow old, to sit in the shade of the banana and rubber gum trees and play with their grandchildren, to drink fine spirits at night by the light of the full moon. There is not much of growing old gracefully in the life of The Man With The Scar. But there are the roads and the continual unwinding and when these things are what you have, you can continue in the certainty of a familiar pattern. It becomes your habit, as much as any other life. Still, there are the doubts and concern for the future. Has he lost the vital half step? And, perhaps more important, will the road ever come to an end? If so, what will be there for him? Will there be warnings before, dour hints, signs that the bottle of luck is about to be drained to the last drop? Perhaps these signs are already everywhere. How many tulips do you have to see to know it's spring? How many gray hairs to recognize the winter?

A huge Navajo, two kids that looked like his and a limping man with a scar on his face pulled a big Ford pickup truck into a bank parking lot in Gallup, New Mexico. The man limped into the bank with an empty white sandwich bag with the words "Jack In The Box" printed in red on the outside. In fifteen minutes, he returned with the sandwich bag filled. He handed it to the big Navajo.

"Not enough yet," he said, shaking his head. The Navajo gave his kids a peep. Their eyes widened, but they said nothing.

"You sure?" the Navajo asked.

"Albuquerque," the man answered. "See, we want one of the really big ones, maybe an over-a-hundred-footer, with twin diesels."

But there wasn't enough money in Albuquerque, either, so The Man With The Scar hit his safe deposit boxes in Santa Fe and Taos before he was satisfied.

Once he had the money, he called the bar in Cabo from a dusty pay phone outside a Shell gas station to the north of Taos. It took the bartender five minutes to find Jolita. While he was waiting, Carlos the musician picked up the phone. They talked for a few minutes of matters of consequence to men such as they were, and then Carlos thought they were finished and hung up the phone. It took The Man With The Scar another fifteen minutes to get through again, and this time Jolita was waiting.

"Jolita?" he asked, imagining her soft, dark eyes, her long lovely hair and slight frame as if she were standing there in front of him.

"Clay? Ees that *jou*?"

"Jolita. Listen carefully. You must find the old man with one eye for me."

"He is out on the street, selling his fancy birds to the *turistas*."

"Well, get him. Tell him we're going to buy a boat and put out to sea."

"Will we become pirates?"

"Yes, Jolita. Good pirates."

"We don' get to keep the treasures for ourselves?" She sounded vaguely disappointed.

"Well, maybe a little..."

That seemed to comfort her.

Dusty was sitting in the big swivel chair in the office of Dusty's Car Repair. His new red 8-series BMW was sitting in the drive where the pumps used to be when the place had been a Union 76 station. He was surrounded by four of his young mechanics. It was getting on late in the afternoon, and there wasn't much of anything to do around the shop. Leon and Bopo were there, and Joe-Boy, who was Jimmy Ray's cousin and had come out West from Tennessee at about the same time. Little Petee, a chubby Italian boy with a perpetual scowl and an unruly lock of hair curling down his forehead, was pushing the dirt around with a broom. Georgie-Porgie, of course, was nowhere to be seen.

A dark green Grand Cherokee pulled up next to his BMW. It had Abernathy Industries printed on the side in small neat letters. The dark window on the passenger side rolled down, and a finger beckoned. It was Oakland Police Detective Jack Macy.

"Dusty. Over here."

Dusty sighed and stretched, thinking he would let Ice Man handle it.

Ice Man agreed. He stood and lit a cigar, and then strode over to the Jeep.

"Jack, my man."

"I ain't your man, scuzball."

"No need to get insulting, Detective. What can I do for you?"

"This here's Mister Abernathy. He's looking for his missing daughter." Jack handed across a Xerox of a photo of the girl with the kinky blond hair.

Dusty blinked twice and did a sarcastic little curtsey and then swept his hand in a grand gesture, "Be my guest. Take a look around."

Jack tried to stare him down. "You ain't seen her, huh?"

"No, man. What you take me for, hang around with a classless beaver like that?"

There was a half choked back, angry retort from within the Grand Cherokee, but Jack raised a hand to calm down the driver. He continued his interrogation of Dusty.

"Or her fiancée, Randy, who used to spend five nights a week fixing up his old VW bus in your place right here, and now is also among the missing?"

"Maybe they has e-loped together, Detective." Ice Man raised one finger and gave a sideways Sherlock Holmes expression, as if to say, *A-ha! The mystery is solved!*

"If that's so, maybe you can explain why you and Wide Frick and Fat Frack over there were arrested in Laughlin after creating a public disturbance by chasing a young woman who fits the description?"

Ice Man decided he'd better switch from *smart-ass* to the *poor me* routine.

"Always the black man, ain't it, Jack? You been on my ass since I opened this place. Can't stand to see honest folks of African-American descent get ahead, can you?! Just give me time to call my lawyer, Mister Big Time Detective! We going to straighten this mess out right now!"

"No hurry, Dusty," Detective Jack Macy said calmly. "We've got plenty of time."

The Man With The Scar sat patiently in his rented Mustang convertible. He was parked in an almost deserted supermarket shopping lot on the northern edge of Taos. After fifteen minutes, a pastel yellow Chevy Suburban pulled up next to his Mustang. The window on the Suburban rolled down, and he was looking up at a pale skinned young man with light reddish-blond hair.

"This isn't going to take long, is it?" the young man asked, the impatient whine noticeable in his voice. "I've got a busy schedule today."

"Hello, Hector," The Man With The Scar said, wondering for the hundredth time what had to have been on the woman's mind to saddle a kid with a name like that. "It shouldn't take too long. I want to show you something."

"Shall I follow in the truck?"

"No. Come on, we'll take my car."

The young man was lanky and well over six feet. He seemed uncomfortable as he folded himself into the smaller car. The Man With The Scar showed him how to move the seat all the way back to give his legs more room.

Once they were on the road, the older man's eyes drifted from the highway to his companion. "You're almost thirty now."

"Twenty-eight," Hector said, keeping his eyes straight ahead.

"And how's your mother?"

"Same as ever."

"Does she ever talk about me?"

"What's to talk about?"

He drove in silence for a while, remembering the first time he'd seen Joanie. It was in the middle of the 60's and they were standing in a boarding line at Dulles Airport in Washington D.C. It had been after his first Nam tour, just before returning for his second dose. He was a Spec 5 on his way to Travis Air Force Base in Northern California, and she was a pretty, perky, redheaded Private First Class heading home to Billings, Montana for the Holidays. Before they knew it, they'd spent the weekend together at a Howard Johnson's Motel near the Denver Airport.

They were lying together across the bed, spent but happy, when she pulled apart the little world they'd built.

"I think we should stay like this forever," she said.

"Can't," he muttered sleepily. "They're shipping my butt back to the Orient."

"Lets go to Vegas!"

"What...?"

"No waiting. We could get married overnight there. My girlfriend Marie and her beau did it."

"Joanie...I don't think that's such a good idea. I'm going back into a war zone."

"You just don't *want* to get married."

"We only just met—"

"See!" Furious and red-faced, she started separating their things. Her clothing went into her luggage. She threw his shoes and whatever else she found of his in his general direction. After seeing what she was up to, he retreated to the bathroom and locked the door. Through the door, he heard her calling a cab. Ten minutes after that, she was gone.

She never wrote or called or got word to him, but he'd had a sixth sense about her, a vague notion that it wasn't entirely over between the two of them. Still, she never answered any of his letters, and he'd had to pretty much figure out the rest with the help of a private detective he'd hired when he finally came back from Vietnam for the last time.

The detective, a sad-eyed alcoholic from Montana, named Milo Milodragovitch, met him in the battered lounge of a motel in Colorado Springs.

"You knocked her up," the detective said, downing his whiskey and signaling the bartender in the same gesture. "At least, somebody did. I guess it was you. Timing is about right."

He laid a copy of a birth certificate on the table. The Man With The Scar picked it up with numb fingers and studied it. "I have a son named Hector..."

Milo scratched one wrist restlessly, now openly glaring at the bartender. "I mean, I think so," he said. "The dates you gave me, when the two of you shacked up, it works out."

"Yes. It works out. Is she alright?" Seeing the detective's plight, The Man With The Scar waved and held up two fingers for the bartender.

"That one will always be alright," Milo said, nodding gratefully when he saw his drink was on its way.

"Of course, within a month of your little fling, the lady had known she was pregnant. What's she do? Takes sick leave and runs back to Billings to marry Bill Lutz."

"Who's Bill Lutz?"

"Her high school sweetheart, if we can believe the 1958 high school yearbook."

"How the hell did you find that out?"

"My job," Milo said with a deep, raspy sigh, and downed his drink. He didn't mention it had been as easy as a trip to the Billings public library. The Man With The Scar bought him another round, and paid Milo in cash.

"I may ask you to check up on them, from time to time."

204

"You're the man buying," Milo said with a little shrug of one shoulder.

The army let her go, of course, and she had two more kids, a boy and a girl, with Bill before he decided to head for Tacoma, Washington with a girl he ran into at the telephone company office where he worked. Joanie moved back in with her parents, found a job at a local artist's supply house, and, one by one, the kids started school.

The Man With The Scar had occasionally traveled to Billings, where he would open a new safe deposit box and then, at considerable risk, loiter around grade schools and public parks, and later, football games to witness Hector's fairly undistinguished career as a wide receiver. Joanie had let him pay for Hector's education (at least the money never came back to the post office box return address). He wondered if Joanie would recognize him if they'd accidentally bumped into each other at the hot dog stand at halftime. But then, she never attended the games, so there was little enough chance of that.

The ice age had continued over the years; she had refused to acknowledge his existence, quietly hanging up the phone whenever she heard his voice. By the time Hector was in high school, she had moved her little family to Boulder, Colorado, and was working on a degree in Fine Arts. A year later, Hector himself enrolled at the University, and four years later was awarded a degree in government science, an oxymoron if The Man With The Scar had ever heard one.

It was only by accident that Hector had come to know of the existence of The Man With The Scar. He had picked up the phone once when his mother was out. Hector was then a sophomore in high school.

"Hi," The Man With The Scar said, "I'm your dad."

"You're not Bill," the quavering voice on the other end of the line replied.

"No, I'm not. I'm Clay Rhett. Your mom's been mad at me since before you were born."

"Why?"

"Well...she wanted to get married, and I didn't."

There was a long pause on the other end of the line, and The Man With The Scar was afraid his son was going to hang up. Then the tentative voice spoke again, sounding much older than his years.

"And now, are you sorry you didn't?"

"I don't know, son. Your mom is pretty strong-willed. I don't think we would have gotten along."

There was another long pause, then the words, "No. Probably not."

"I don't think it would be a good thing to tell her I called. It would only make her mad."

Hector said, "Sorry, I got to go." He sounded rushed and flustered.

After that first call, The Man With The Scar had dialed the same number every few months. When Joanie answered, which was most of the time, he'd hang up without saying anything. In all those years while Hector was attending high school and college, he'd managed to speak to him only a handful of times.

Now, as they drove south along the river, The Man With The Scar hardly knew where to begin a conversation.

"How's your brother and sister?"

"Married. Not to each other."

The Man With The Scar smiled. Maybe there was something to this stuffy, pretentious kid after all.

"Where we going?" Hector asked.

"Silver City."

"Oh, Lord, no! No, no, no! Look, I agreed to see you, but this is different. I really have to get back. Mom's expecting me at the gallery."

"I own property down there. I once shot a deer right from the front porch of my cabin." He didn't mention some of the other things that had been shot on his property. "I thought you might like to see it. Don't worry. I'll have you back before sunset." Under his breath, he added the word *tomorrow*.

By this time, they'd cleared Taos and were traveling toward Santa Fe on 68, a major divided highway that hugged the Rio Grande. The Man With The Scar had been keeping his eye on a big semi-truck two cars in front of them. The truck was weaving and wobbling, as if it was overloaded and there was some malfunction, something to do with the wheels.

"Hang on!" he said suddenly, breaking as hard as he dared.

The back axle on the trailer in front of them suddenly disconnected. There was a metallic screech and a cloud of dust blew around them. The individual truck wheels went bounding down the highway, bouncing incredibly high in the air and rolling with the traffic flow while the trailer tipped and split open, spewing scrap metal across the highway. Cars and light trucks wove everywhere as they tried to avoid piling into one another. The Mustang spun around once, and then they were on the wide road shoulder. The Man With The Scar fought for control and brought the car to a shuddering halt a few feet from a steep incline. He found himself looking down at the boulder-strewn bank of the river. He unsnapped his seat belt, shoved the door open and jumped from the car.

"Come on, Hector," he yelled. "People need our help!"

"Us? But we can't...what can we do...?

"We can help. Come on."

The two of them ran back to a clustered and smoking pile of five cars that had been less fortunate than they had. From somewhere inside that tangled wreckage, a baby cried. An anguished female voice cried out, "My GOD, My GOD, why me, why meeeee...?"

The cars had started to smolder, thin wisps of smoke rising from crumpled hoods. Even as The Man With The Scar watched, flames started from the underside of an overturned Chevy Blazer. He and Hector and three or four other motorists worked like madmen, and managed to pull an old woman, a heavily bleeding young man, and a baby who looked absolutely unharmed from the vehicles before the first ambulance arrived.

"We'd better back off," The Man With The Scar warned.

"No," Hector shouted. His eyes were lit with an unholy gleam.

"But, it's going to go up any second."

Hector was on the ground, squirming under an aged pickup truck to get at an overturned Volkswagen Jetta convertible. The Man With The Scar heard his son's voice from under the pile of wreckage, "You're going to have to pull me out by my legs."

"You can't—?"

"By my legs, I said. Now! Getting hot in here!"

The Man With The Scar did as he was instructed. But Hector seemed stuck. He wasn't moving, and he wasn't coming out by himself. The acrid smoke was in their faces and the flames were dancing from one car to another over their heads.

"Get your feet on the truck and get some leverage!" Hector yelled. "My hair's going to catch on fire if you don't hurry!"

With his feet propped against the pickup truck, The Man with The Scar was able to pry Hector inch by inch from under the car. But he was only halfway out, showing only the lower half of his body, when he obstinately refused to budge any further.

"Hector! What are you doing?"

"Dad! Give it some butt! I'm roasting under here!"

The Man With The Scar gave one final pull, and Hector's body reluctantly came out from under the carriage of the pickup truck. He wasn't alone. He was pulling the blood-soaked form of a young girl.

"Couldn't leave her," he gasped as men came running with a stretcher. He was overtaken by a coughing fit.

"Too—much—smoke," he gasped.

"Come on, son," The Man With The Scar said, leading Hector away from the now blazing pile of cars. By then, there were several police cars and a big square orange-and-white ambulance on the scene. While they watched, a fire truck sprayed foam on the flames, snuffing it out almost as quickly as it had started.

Several wrecking trucks moved in like dark beetles, already intent on clearing the road.

A half hour later, The Man With The Scar and his son sat together in the Mustang. They were blood-smeared and exhausted.

"We're smudging the white leather..." Hector said.

The Man With The Scar nodded numbly. "Those people would have died. That girl, for sure. You saved her, no doubt in my mind."

The Man With The Scar had never been less sure of anything than what he was now doing, and the accident hadn't added anything to his peace of mind. He started the engine, but made no move to leave. *What should he do? What would be best for Hector?* He was full of remorse for the past and of fear for the future. It seemed to him that, beginning back in the early days when he was just an empty-headed kid himself, every time he'd dipped his hand into the stream of life and made an important decision, he had been wrong. Choosing English over something practical like Engineering at college. Volunteering for Vietnam. And then, life after his night at the *Coeur Desir* had been a total mess: no stability, nothing solid, no family gathered around him, just the swirling whirlpool and endless whip of dangerous events running in front of his bewildered gaze. Of course, he'd gotten better at survival, after a while. But still, was he about to launch Hector on a similar course? How could he be certain? On the one hand, Hector hadn't signed the damn paper. But damn it, neither had he, not really. Well, maybe he had signed, but absolutely under false pretenses.

He leaned back on his leather seat and stared at the blank canvas over their heads. He saw no answers there. *There were no real answers, anyway; there was only life, and living it the best way you knew how.*

"How did you feel about it?" he warily asked. "I mean, all that back there, and you in it, as a part of it?"

He found he couldn't come straight out and tell the boy about the *Coeur Desir*. Hector may have come a ways, but he absolutely wasn't ready for that. The Man With The Scar resigned himself to turning the car around. At that point, he was willing to give up whatever crazy, half-baked plan had been in his mind. He would take the boy back to his mother, and that would be the end of it.

"I—I don't know..." Hector frowned, thinking about it.

The Man With The Scar was telling himself he would give his son a better chance than he'd had. If he couldn't be open about everything that had happened, he'd at least try to be kind.

"Well, do you want to go back?"

"Back where?"

"To your mother."

It wouldn't be so bad. Perhaps, in time, Hector would even find some mousy little girl that she would approve of, and then he would marry and have a family of his own. But Hector surprised him again with what he said next.

"No. You were going to show me your desert cabin. I'd like to see it."

"So I was." The Man With The Scar nodded, slipping the transmission into drive. "And the accident didn't change your mind?"

Hector shook his head, staring back to where the tow trucks were pulling the last cars off the paved road, "I—I've never done anything like that before. Never."

"And how do you feel now? Are you feeling anything?"

"I feel...I don't know—*alive!*"

That gave the older man pause. Maybe he was giving up too soon, out of a dread which even he couldn't define. Maybe they could try it a little more, move on down the road a bit with it. The kid had everything to learn, but who knew, there were no rules written for this sort of thing. There had to be at least a chance that it would be okay.

"Do you mind if I call you 'Heck'?"

"No. That would be okay. I mean, I think I'd like it." The kid was jazzed, still on the incredible high that comes from saving a human life, and in so doing, escaping the jaws of death, yourself. The Man With The Scar knew that, at that moment, life with his mother in her high-price art gallery must have seemed faint and very far away, and Hector would have agreed to nearly anything.

They traveled down the road in silence for quite some time.

"Welcome to my world," the older man finally said.

21

There are times of coalescence. Have you noticed them? You, of all people, should have, aware the way you are. Sunlight dancing off dust motes, the slightest breeze. A sudden formation, spirit-like, dancing on the edge of perception. Is it?...No...It can't be. It is just a memory, the ghost of a suggestion, or perhaps the suggestion of a ghost. Is a vampire, then, the imagined reflection of life, light bouncing off the moon, dew on a spider's web? Is this notion we call a zombie only the fear—rather than the hope—that we actually may not die after all? Vampire, zombie, the living dead. Who among us has not gone to see an ancient friend wired and tubed in his hospital bed, and thought somewhere in there of a death by bullet in a distant green wetland of long ago to be a cleaner, quicker, braver and infinitely more preferable ending to this frighteningly prolonged half-life? Your favorite uncle blathering with joy, sadness and half memories all mixed in his stroke-muddled brain. Your own mother in her 90's, shocked alive, the look of stark, sheer horror on her face, whipped back to life for the 200th time by the dogged pacemaker, once her closest friend, now her tormentor barking her away from the gates of heaven...

Ahh, yes, heavy stuff, my friends...but what did you expect when you found yourself lured into the first happy chapters of The Man With The Scar? After all, this isn't The Man With The Golden Dong. Still and again, I assure you, relief is as near as the delete tab on your keyboard. That said, you will perhaps be interested to note that Toomley, CIA man of old and money magnet by fate, is still alive. Further, all that blithering nonsense at the beginning of this brief monologue about forces coming together probably refers to the fact that characters you have grown to loathe and love earlier in this script now return more loathsome and loving than ever before. Or so it seems.

Dave Toomley raised himself on his elbows and stared across the sterile room. His attention wandered out the window to where the tired sea lapped the shores of Aruba, and then followed the azure blue of the bay to the distant line where it met the deeper blue of the sky. He wasn't really interested in the view, though it was one of the best in the hotel. His entire body was racked with pain. Even his bones ached, and he longed for the ten thousandth time for his old army issue .45 so that he could trigger down on himself and end it all.

His private, heavily guarded suite—more of a hospital suite than a hotel, really—was on a small island just off the main island that was entirely owned and operated by his guardians. From the bed where he was resting, Toomley could see the waves breaking off the shoreline of Aruba proper. The maid had brought his pills, which he couldn't swallow, and his meal, which he couldn't eat. Now they would have to bring the nurse and the needle, and feed him intravenously. That accomplished, they would prop him in bed and bring in the Wall Street Journal. The cable channel would be switched to the continuous stock market update. Then they would swivel his computer keyboard into position over his bed, and his day would begin.

Anna, the Swiss secretary, would be constantly by his side. Anna, whose sweet Doris Day smile hid a sharp brain, hard professional hands, and an agenda that was cold as steel, would await his instructions, and be ready to call the nurse for the slightest hint of a medical hiccup. So far this year, Toomley had earned just over two billion dollars for the quiet international corporation that was keeping him alive. With any effort, he would earn them an additional half-billion before the end of the year. He was big business, bigger than all the casinos and tourist hotels on Aruba.

He saw a speedboat go by, pulling a tourist strapped to one of those multicolored parachutes on a brief, frivolous journey parallel to the shore. That made him think of the *Coeur Desir*, and the man whose name was written on the ancient parchment paper next to his own.

"Clay Rhett. Where the hell is Rhett?" he muttered to himself for the ten thousand and first time. "Where the hell is that fuckin' clown, Rhett?"

"What is that, dear?" Anna came immediately to his side.

"We all get what we desire, don't we dear, sweet Anna?"

"Now, David," she said with a reproving tone in her voice. Anna truly didn't understand why he always went in this direction. They had argued this abstract subject on many occasions, argued to the point where her charge became violently, spitting ill. But this time, he seemed to relax with the question. Just when she was certain he was drifting off to sleep, he whispered, "Or is it that we all get what we deserve?...And if that is so, God help you, Anna."

It was that slow time between breakfast and lunch at Earl's family restaurant in Gallup. Lorrie, one of the waitresses, was resting her feet by sitting sideways on one of the maroon vinyl booths. She looked up from the front page of the Albuquerque newspaper.

"Geez, kiddo, look at this."

She handed the well-worn paper across the table to the girl with the short, henna-amplified red-brown hair. There was a picture of a tangled pile of cars, stretchers, ambulances, police cars, and an Air Med helicopter hovering overhead.

"Man," the girl with the henna hair said softly. "Man o' man."

She wasn't all that impressed with the mangled mess of cars, or even the shot of the dangling helicopter which would win several prizes for the intrepid photographer who had managed to capture the action. What caught her interest was a man in the background who was helping one of the injured into a waiting ambulance. From the poor quality of the newsprint, she couldn't tell if he had a scar on his face or not, but it didn't matter. She knew those surprisingly strong shoulders and that blond-white hair with its flaring mustachio.

"Where was this?" she asked.

"Route 68. Says so right there in the paper."

"No, I mean, where does it go?"

"This is north of Santa Fe, I think."

"Could you get to Silver City from there?"

"Well, that's the road you'd go on if you wanted to get to Silver City from anywhere north."

"I'm out of here!"

"Babes, we don't get off for another four hours."

"No, I mean, I'm burrito history! I've flung my last hash!"

Lorrie knew her friend always showed up for work with a small suitcase. The girl waved as she lugged it from the back room, and Lorrie realized it probably contained everything she owned.

She stuck her thumb out, raised her skirt a little, and her henna hair glinted in the sunlight. It wasn't five minutes before a big old Cadillac loaded with cowboys did a U-turn and picked her up. She was probably fifty miles down the highway before the shift boss even knew she was gone.

As she rode along east towards Albuquerque with the cowboys, Millie was remembering the last night she'd spent with *Old Scarface.* They had shared a motel room in Kingman, a town that Millie remembered as scorchingly hot and annoyingly dusty. She'd gotten a little tipsy on wine. She was sitting on her bed—she had insisted on separate beds— wearing her lacy bra and panties. The bottle of Beringer Haut-Medoc was nearly empty, and she was at that stage where she couldn't quite say what she wanted without slurring the words. She thought she was inviting Old Scarface to a courtly waltz.

"Hey, whaddaya say, le-le-le's do the two-step," was what she actually said.

"I don't like country dancing," he said politely, looking up from a map he'd been studying.

"I don't mean *dancing,* you runt-brain. I mean, like the two of us, you know, the *hokey pokey*?"

That started him off. He finally stopped, wiping his eyes as if he'd been crying. "The *hokey pokey!* I haven't heard that one in years! Is that what you kids call it now?"

"No, a-a-asshole, w-we usually say, *Let's fu-fu-fuck.*"

"That's probably not a good idea," he said, sobering up just enough to shake his head.

"You thump-humping old nip-dinger!"

She poured the last of the wine into her plastic cup and threw the bottle at him. He never saw it, never bothered to turn around, but it didn't matter. The bottle grazed his shoulder and smashed into the wall.

"Why, Rhett," she drawled through a pouting face, "why do you ruin everything with which you come in contact?"

"I don't know, Scarlett, why do you think that is?"

Randy had been gone for weeks, and *Scarface* was the only stiff dick around. Semi-stiff, anyway. No man could resist her. She moved over onto his bed and ran her tongue over his ear. And that's when he had simply picked her up and dumped her, half-naked as she was, back on her own bed.

In the next minute, he'd folded his precious map, donned his knapsack and walked out like some self-righteous Don Quixote. Furious that any man would give her the boot, much less an obviously worn-out old bastard like him, she had yelled and screamed and thrown anything that wasn't bolted down. But it was all for show. After all, he was already gone.

It was nearly a week later that she found the envelope he had placed in the bottom of her purse. There was almost three thousand dollars in hundreds, and a small, hand-drawn map. The brief note said, "My place near Silver City. <u>Use only in serious emergency</u>. Key under obvious rock. Be discreet. That means, among other things, no gerbil fucking." He had signed it, "CR". *Clay Rhett.* That old fart! Where'd he get all those hundreds, adding up to three big slams, anyway?

The war session took place in an elegant dining room at the Abernathy mansion. The room had been converted into a command headquarters of sorts, with maps pinned to the fancy fleur-de-lis patterned wallpaper, and telephones ringing everywhere. Even Dusty thought it was an odd meeting of fellows. Everywhere he went, his burly Asian guards flanked Old Man Abernathy, and he had Abernathy Industries researchers busily flicking at computers while secretaries and executive assistants efficiently fluttered and buzzed about on missions of great importance. Dusty had arrived with his troops, who were lounging around in various stages of disinterest, gaping in slack-jawed wonder at the huge oil paintings on the walls and staring with open lust at the various women in the room, who were all young, white and pretty. Only crusty Jack Macy had come alone. He scrunched in a chair, still wearing a dirty trench coat and puffing a steady string of unfiltered Camel cigarettes, the stench of which was instantly whisked up and away by the air conditioning which moved through the room like an icy wind.

While Dusty was impressed by Abernathy's obvious wealth, he was anything but amused to be dragged over to his mansion at the drop of a hat. He addressed the hulking police detective in his uppity-nigger voice, "You got to be ashamed, Jack. What you want with us here, anyway, man? Need a few more hands to work the plantation?"

"Dusty..." Jack Macy's voice was heavy with quiet warning. "We don't want to have to ask the IRS to try and figure out how you support your lifestyle, do you?"

"The IRS got no business fuckin' with an innocent black man who—"

"*DO* you?"

Dusty gave out an angry sigh and settled back in his chair. He would pass the next five minutes visualizing all the ways he knew to take out Jack Macy. Slow and torturous, he decided. Something with pinchers, a cattle prod, or maybe target practice from twenty yards with gravity knives.

Abernathy called order by rapping his knuckles sharply on the table, not unlike a spinster schoolmarm.

"Gentlemen, here's what we know."

He tapped a clerk at his side. The young man hit a key on a console in front of him, and one wall lit up with the enlarged image of a sports fishing boat tied to a dock. Abernathy tapped again. The image clicked tighter and tighter on the crew lined up along the rail with a catch of tuna, most of which were nearly as large as the men. The machine clicked three times more. Each time the image jumped closer until it centered on one man. The fuzzy definition cleared electronically until they had a fair shot of a middle-aged man with receding hair bleached almost white by the sun and a flaring blond mustachio.

"Clay Rhett," Jack Macy said. "Age 58. Five-foot-eleven or ten. Weight: 190 pounds. Army veteran. Three tours in Vietnam. Bunches of medals. Honorable discharge."

Various shots of The Man With The Scar joined the one on the screen. These were all earlier shots showing a much younger man. Military I.D. A Top Secret Clearance badge photo. An old passport.

"There was a ranger's report that someone bearing an uncanny resemblance to this man created a disturbance in Owens Valley not long ago. We checked the area. No sign of Rhett or Mr. Abernathy's daughter."

Dusty eyed the photos for some time with a sour expression on his face.

"He got any money?"

"Some independent source of wealth, for sure. We haven't been able to track it."

"Not even those IRS buddies of yours? All over my legitimate tax-paying ass and they can't even track one scarred an' mustachioed white bum?"

"He pays cash for everything."

"Ain't any law against that," Dusty grumbled.

"Dusty, for God's sake, would you shut up and listen?"

Dusty glowered at Jack, sure now that the police detective's days were numbered. Dusty had lost his small caliber pistol with the silencer—he'd had to throw it in the river when he saw the local cracker bully-boy police were moving in on him and Leon and Bopo—but he now sported a long-barreled .38 made even longer with its new silencer. He knew as sure as crack was the devil that Jack was going to feel the wrath, and soon.

Abernathy cleared his throat.

"We have uncovered three new things. First, a woman in Colorado named Joan Clark lists Clay Rhett as a source of income on her tax returns. We have reason to believe he has fathered at least one child by this woman. Second, tax records indicate he owns a piece of arid, semi-useless land in southern New Mexico. And third, he has some connection with an old army associate, a David Toomley, whom for the time being we also have been unable to locate."

"What's this Toomley guy do?" Dusty asked.

"We don't know," Abernathy answered.

"Where is he?"

"The CIA won't tell us."

"Hmm. The fricking CI and A." Dusty took off his small, scholarly-looking glasses and wiped them with a napkin he took from the silver tray with the tea and English biscuits on it. He gave Jack Macy the full benefit of his sour stare. "And what's *his* fracking source of income?"

"We don't know."

The laugh came unbidden to Dusty's lips, a short, scornful outburst. It was bad timing, he knew. He just couldn't help himself.

22

There's always something about returning to the homestead after an absence of some months or years. Black widow spiders, perhaps, to clean from the doorsill. Ants or rats in the kitchen. Freebooters or squatters in the bedroom. Life loves a vacuum, and will rush in wherever it sees fit.

The Man With The Scar is, for now, traveling with his son. And in short order, Hector is to learn more about life than he has in all his years. For one thing, he's about to meet the Girl With The Very Foul Mouth.

They'd spent a day wandering around the thick adobe walls of Santa Fe, and another day stopping at turquoise mines as they drove towards the southern end of New Mexico. Once they got to Silver City, The Man With The Scar went into a Big Bear Supermarket while Hector called Joanie from a pay phone. The man returned, pushing a cart loaded with groceries and chocolate bars. Hector was sitting on the hood of the Mustang. He looked ready to cry.

"What did she say?"

"She disowned me." Hector noticed the contents of the cart for the first time, "Whoa, that's a lot of chocolate."

The Man With The Scar tossed him a bittersweet Toblerone bar. "Don't worry, mothers always disown their oldest sons when they run away from home for the first time."

"I think I should get back. She says she has no one to take care of her."

"Did you tell her where you left the Suburban?"

"Yes, I did." Hector had peeled back the foil and was trying to bite off a chunk. The Man With The Scar took it and broke off a piece for him.

"Then don't worry about the rest. She can make do for a couple of days. After all, she's had you her whole life."

"But what will she do?"

"She's only 45. Still time enough to find Mister Perfect."

"Is that how you see her? Just out to snag some guy?"

The man thought about it; then shrugged. "Not really. I don't actually know much about your mother."

"You had to know something about her."

"Well, not necessarily. Just because I'm old and stupid doesn't mean I wasn't once young and stupid."

"Do you want to explain that?"

"No," The Man With The Scar said. "If genes count for anything, you'll find out for yourself." He tossed the keys to the younger man, "Here, you drive."

A few hours later, they pulled off the two-lane blacktop onto a gravel road that paralleled a dry wash. They were fifty miles outside of Silver City. The skies were partly cloudy. A storm front had boiled through a few hours earlier, and at a spot where the gravel road they were following dipped into the normally dry wash, they had to wait for a half hour until the water level went down.

"Where's the road?" Hector asked, nervously eyeing six inches of water that was still rushing through the flat, sandy streambed.

"There," The Man With The Scar said, pointing.

"Kidding, right?"

"No. Right there. Go for it."

But Hector went tentatively, and didn't get five feet before the back wheels were spinning helplessly in the mud. The older man remembered a time long ago when he'd stuck *his* old man's car in a muddy field. He got out and stretched his back, staring at the thunderheads, which had retreated to form a golden crown over a distant patch of mountains. As he watched, a fork of lightning lashed from the dark underbelly of the clouds.

"Did you see that, Hector? This streambed drains off of those mountains way off there."

"Seems to me, our problem is *here,* not *there,*" Hector replied.

"Well, I'd say we got fifteen minutes and then it's going to be here."

"What is?" Hector gave him a sudden, uncertain look.

"Flash flood," he said.

The right size stream-rolled rocks were everywhere. He showed Hector how to place them under the back wheels and they were soon on their way.

Encouraged by the thought of a wall of water roaring down on them, Hector quickly got the hang of driving upstream through the wet streambed, the trick of it being to build up enough speed to slide and spin through the bad spots. They'd gone nearly a mile when he spotted the fresh tire tracks.

"Somebody's been here before us."

"Yes," The Man With The Scar said. "Good spotting."

They did get stuck twice more, and it was nearly a half hour before Hector drove up out of the streambed. The cabin was a basic Kentucky two-room with a sloped roof and a front porch that extended across the front of the frame. The unpainted planking was weathered and worn, but the structure looked square and like it still sat solid on its foundation.

Hector drove the car toward the cabin, following the fresh tracks across the bumpy terrain. He pulled to a stop behind a white Plymouth Neon in front of the cabin. They could see a white plume of smoke pouring furiously from the chimney. The door popped open and there was Millie, hands on her hips and looking mad as hell. Her still damp dress was clinging to the delicious curves of her frame.

"Gerbil-fucker!" she screamed. "And you sa-sa-said the key would be under an *obvious* rock!"

The Man With The Scar didn't bother to point out that she might have waited in the car or on the porch until the rain was over.

"Come on, let's get inside," he said with a hint of exasperation in his voice. He didn't want to get into an extended conversation with her at that moment. He knew he was going to have enough trouble trying to explain her to Hector.

Dusty was tired and thoroughly disgusted by the time the war party finally started to break up at the Abernathy mansion. They were leaving in one big group when he found himself cut out of the herd by three evil-looking Orientals. He would have pulled his .38 and started popping, but he'd left it under the seat of his new BMW, thinking nothing could happen to him in the home of a rich white-collar crook who wouldn't want to be sued for ruffling a bristly black man.

"What the fuck are you up to, man?!" he said as he found himself alone in a room with Mr. King Capitalist, the rich old dude himself.

Abernathy waved his three Asiatic heavies out of the room.

"Sit down, Dusty," he said. "I have a special offer for you."

Dusty bit his lip and accepted a fine Cuban cigar, thinking to himself, *Well, this is some deal better.* Maybe he wasn't going to have to blow anybody's head off after all. The two men went through the ritual of snipping and rolling the cigars, and then wetting the ends and lighting up and having a fine bonding moment.

"We haven't talked about payment," Abernathy said, once his smoke was adequately fuming.

"Two grand a day for each of my boys," Dusty responded automatically. "Chump change."

"I prefer to call it soldier's pay. And for you?"

"Two hundred thousand now. A half million when we find her."

"Okay," Abernathy said calmly, blowing a blue ring in the air. "But alive. She has to be alive."

"Why?"

The old man eyed Dusty for a moment. "Because someone in our family died recently, leaving my dear, sweet, innocent daughter Millie a small but rather important share of voting stock. I want her to sign that stock over to me, which, obviously, she can't do if she's dead."

"Live costs you a million."

"One million dollars." The old man nodded and stuck out his hand, and Dusty shook it. If he had any questions about the strength of Abernathy's resolve, they weren't answered by the feeble handshake. But there was no doubting the undying hatred in the old man's flinty eyes. Dusty wondered how long Millie would stay alive after she signed over the stock. But he didn't care. It was none of his business.

What father has not brought his son down to the office for the first time, and with mixed feelings of sheepish anxiety and perhaps a faint hopefulness explained how this or that works, why the boss is the way he is, how to get coffee from the balky machine and why the donuts in the cafeteria are always stale and dry? The Man With The Scar never thought he'd have such a situation. After all, Joanie had the kid, and wasn't likely to let go. But then things changed, a new roll of the cosmic dice and he found himself in altered circumstances. Of course, TMWTS doesn't really have an office. He hangs his hat wherever he is, and events come up to meet him with a rush. And so Hector's introduction to his old man's way of life was bound to be...dare we say...somewhat hectic?

Hector, Millie and The Man With The Scar gathered around the stove, which Millie had fired red-hot with generous portions of coal from the nearby bin. Millie handed The Man With The Scar a weather-faded postcard.

"This was stuck in your door," she said.

The postcard was from an island resort complex off the coast of Venezuela. On the back was written in Toomley's sad military scrawl:

Ngoui My,
Xin loi, di vay nha.
David

223

The Man With The Scar studied the postcard briefly and handed it to Hector.

Hector frowned. "What's it say?"

"It's in Vietnamese. It says, 'Mister American, Please come home.'"

"To Vietnam?!"

"No, I don't think so."

The Man With The Scar was hurrying around the house, dumping old clothes out of his knapsack and gathering a few new items.

Hector tossed the postcard on the hot black cooking plate on top of the stove, where it immediately began to smoke and blacken. There was a moment of panic.

"Don't worry about it," The Man With The Scar said. "It can't do any damage. Come on, we've got to go. Last one out, pull the door shut."

"We're going already?" Hector asked.

"Who is this geek, anyway?" Millie asked, jerking a thumb at Hector.

The Man With The Scar turned in the doorway. "You can stay here, but if you're coming, it's *now*. We've got to get out before the wash is flooded." Without waiting for an answer, he was out the door and loping toward the Mustang.

Millie looked helplessly at Hector.

"He's kidding about the flood, right?" Hector asked.

"Wh-Who *are* you, weak-dick?!"

"He's my father," Hector said.

"How could a distractible and totally un-centered feller like that find time to father a child?!!" She threw her hands in the air, but realized there was nobody left to see her grand gesture.

"Shista gevalt! Eina klina cuntsika minah!" she said to herself as the Mustang's engine barked to life outside the front door. She grabbed her half-unpacked suitcase and was running for the car when she realized the door was still open. Hector ran back and slammed it while she pitched her suitcase into the backseat and crawled in after it. As Hector scrambled into the front seat, The Man With The Scar popped

the clutch and the Mustang took off in a shower of spinning gravel.

Seen through Hector's eyes, the trip back down the wash was speeded-up scenes of near misses and close calls, like a scratchy old black-and-white Keystone Kops movie. By now it was deep dusk, and the Mustang was flashing past boulders and tree stumps at high speed, humping through the few standing pools of water and throwing up a constant spray of sandy mud.

"Really, do we have to go like this?" Hector asked.

The man behind the wheel didn't answer. He drove on with maniac-like intensity. It was impossible to tell how far they'd come or how much further they had to go. All Hector remembered was that, somewhere in the wash, he'd heard a throaty rumble from behind them. And he remembered an impossibly tall and violent wall of water chasing after them as their car came careening around the last corner and made a short dash through the sandy stretch where he'd gotten them stuck a few hours before. The Mustang fishtailed and was through, shooting up the side of the wash and onto the gravel road as the wall of water rushed past not ten yards behind them and then thundered on down the narrow canyon from which they had exited.

"Welcome to my world, son," The Man With The Scar said again. Only this time he was whispering so quietly that he must have been speaking to himself.

The unimproved gravel road was sandy and uncertain, but he kept the Mustang sloughing through the ruts at high speed, as if they were still chased by watery demons. They were back on asphalt and had been heading southeast on 180 for almost five minutes when Dusty and his troops, traveling in a caravan of three rented Jeep Cherokees led by a local sheriff in a black-and-white Bronco, turned onto the gravel road and headed for the wash.

Once they saw the raging torrent, the sheriff convinced Dusty there would be no getting through the wash until morning. Even Dusty could see that it was true, and so they retreated to Silver City for the night. When they finally did get through, it was close to noon the next day. Since they were looking at a suspected kidnapping, the sheriff had his deputy break a window in the cabin and crawl through to open the door. Whoever had been here had left in a hurry; there was no way they could be sure the things were Millie's, but there was plenty of lady's stuff lying around.

"I think they're coming back," the sheriff said, giving the grocery bags a quick run-through. He selected a delicious apple and gave it a healthy munch.

"I don't know," Dusty said doubtfully. He was looking at the thin remains of a postcard that had burned on the stove. All that was left was an outline of the dried ink particles. Aruba Sonata, it said in big red letters over an azure shore. Dusty blew once, and the dried ink particles lifted into the air and became nothing.

23

You know how it is when you go looking for an old friend. You don't know if he's going to be fat and bald and maybe a little greasy, or if she is going to look matronly, a wrinkled imitation of her mother, jokes played on you by the gods of space and time. Did you ever suspect, when Einstein spoke of relativity, he was thinking of the warp between memory and years passed by? Probably not, but in a way it certainly applies; creatures of flesh and blood age at light speed, but in memory, not at all. Things are relative, after all.

All that said, this isn't anything about that. Although The Man With The Scar started out for his fortieth reunion, he's now headed on a mission to find missing ex-CIA man Dave Toomley. Dave, you may remember, signed the same nefarious scrap of parchment that seems to have interfered in the normal flow of events in the life of The Man With The Scar. And, of course, wherever our scarred friend goes, can split-personality drug lord Dusty be far behind?

The Man With The Scar was standing in front of an outdoor pay phone at the outskirts of El Paso, chewing a triangular bite from a bittersweet Toblerone bar as he dialed his favorite bar in Cabo San Lucas. When he got through to the bartender, he asked for The Man With One Eye. As usual, there was a considerable wait. He listened to the hiss of the empty phone line while Millie commandeered a few triangular

227

sections from his candy bar and Hector eyed him impatiently from his seat in the Mustang.

"Heck," he called over to his son, "what's going on between you and Millie?"

"What do you mean, Clay?"

"You didn't come back to the motel last night. Remember that talk we had about being young and stupid?"

Hector's face flushed beet red.

"I'm going to have his baby," Millie said proudly, ripping another hunk from the Toblerone bar. "That's why I'm eating for two."

"I thought you were having Randy's baby."

"Wait—who's Randy?" Hector asked.

Millie gave him the arch look of a master criminal. "What a stupid thought, you idiot peasant! This Randy you speak of is a nobody! A savage! Far beneath one who might attract my attention. As are you, yourself, I might add." She shot The Man With The Scar a look of scalding outrage.

Clay didn't know what to reply, but the old man with one eye saved him by coming on the line, "*Amigo! Amigo!!* We bought the boat!"

"What did you get?"

"The boat of our dreams, *El Capitan*! The Southern Seas!!"

The Man With The Scar frowned. "Captain Griggs swore he would never sell that boat."

"You do not know it then, *amigo*? Captain Griggs was shot to death in his office by the pier at Point Loma. The Southern Seas was put up for auction."

"I bet I know who did it."

"*Si. La cucaracha negrito,* ze black cockroach. Undoubtedly, looking for you."

"Should I be worried?"

"Not necessarily; however, at this rate, *señor*, you will be late for your grand dinner at the Contempo."

"Old friend, I've changed my mind about setting out for the South Pacific. What do you know about the Panama Canal?"

"I know of it. Ees a little ditch through the jungle."

"Find out more. I want you and Johnny to bring the Southern Seas over to the Caribbean."

"They have the big tuna there?"

"Never mind the tuna for right now, my *amigo*. We're going after bigger fish this time."

The mid-morning sun was baking the gingerbread houses of Key West as Dusty's party drove their cream colored Cadillac rented from the Budget booth at the Miami airport across the last bridge. Franklin Jacobs saw them coming; hard to miss five big black dudes dressed like refugees from NFL Sportswear and wearing scowls on their faces. William Jacobs and his twin brother Franklin owned identical long range boats which they housed in slips next to each other on the docks off Riviera Drive. William's boat was a little faster, but Franklin's boat had better fish finding radar. When Dusty and his boys showed up, The Man With The Scar and his party were gone, as was William's boat. Business was slow, and Franklin was sitting on deck, talking trade with a dozen other skippers who had gathered on his boat.

"Man look like he ran into a meat cleaver," Dusty said, demonstrating with his right hand like a salute chopping vertically against his own face.

"Yep, I seen 'em. William took 'em out just about a half hour ago," Franklin said, squinting at his watch. The truth was, his brother's boat had left hours before dawn, but as an island boat skipper, Franklin wasn't very much into telling the exact truth about any business matters. He was about forty-five years old, a lean, bald black man, with an affection for captain's caps, boater tennis shoes, white shorts, and shirts with broad navy blue and white stripes. His brother William dressed exactly the same, except his shirts were striped fire engine red and white.

"And where are they headed?" Dusty asked impatiently. One of the pudgy skippers whistled an off-key little tune as he looked at his bare feet. Nobody else said anything and the time started to stretch like warm taffy. But Franklin, who grew up on the keys and could gauge trouble in a man better than most, held up an appeasing hand to Dusty and nodded his head.

"Let's call 'em an' find out. That's the best way. Ain't going to be no guessing, we going to know for sure."

"Damn straight!" Dusty said, taking his hand off the .38 in his pocket and making a show of wiping his brow with a Starbucks napkin he also had in there.

Franklin swiveled on the single chrome leg of his captain's chair, flipped a few switches on the console, and took the mike in his hand. "Zulu Bravo Daphne. Zulu Bravo Daphne. This is Adonis, calling Adonis II. Come in Adonis II."

It was a sun-washed morning, with a gathering of puffy white clouds that suggested afternoon squalls. There was a moment of intense audio crackle and then William's voice came in strong and clear, the mirror image of his brother's, "Hallo, bro."

"Willum's, my sweet laddy. You still headed over to St. Kitts?"

"Who wants to know?"

Since a percentage of their traffic consisted of well-dressed fishermen with suitcases of money bound for offshore banks, the brothers had devised a simple code. People described as nice were suspicious. And destinations mentioned were places they might, but in reality never would, head for.

"Come now, you old scofflaw, it's a nice gentleman and several truly decent looking friends," Franklin said.

"Looking to go fishing, is they?"

"Didn't say, bro. Didn't say. But you know the marlin's been hot the last week or three."

"Humph. I know that be so, Sweet Franklin, just so long as you gots you the right bait."

"Lord, we got nothing but bait."

Dusty found himself getting more and more impatient. As the two brothers chatted on about exactly nothing, he could feel the slow burn working steadily up the cords of his neck towards his *Somebody's Going to Die* level.

"For fuck's sake—ask him where he's headed, man!" Dusty almost screamed.

William's voice came crackling over the radio, "I heard that way out here on the water, bro, scarcely needed radio transmission. Tell the nice gentleman we should be making for St. Kitts to refuel. You want us to wait for you?"

Franklin held the microphone out and Dusty yelled into it, "Yeah, wait for us!"

Franklin clicked off the radio and studied the five prospects in front of him.

"Cost you two thousand for the day, plus fuel. That's cash money."

"I got cash money," Dusty said.

"Excellent. When you want to leave?"

Dusty studied the circle of heavily tanned old salts who were staring back at him from the boat. Too many witnesses to even think of popping natty Franklin and taking off in his boat. Then too, who would drive the damn thing? Bopo?!

"Ahh...we need a half hour to pack an' check out of the hotel. Okay?" Dusty saw the man had his hand out. "What's that for?"

"It'll take a $200 deposit to hold the boat."

For a moment, Dusty looked mean enough to gut a cat. But he'd been tricked by his own duplicity. He peeled four fifties off a thick wad of cash and half threw them at Franklin. "You be ready to go in twenty minutes," he threatened in a low voice.

"Sure, bro. We be ready and waiting."

Key West wasn't so big that five surly black thugs could keep any secrets. Franklin waited five minutes and then started calling around the island. After his third call, he knew that Dusty and his men were standing in front of a desk on next-door Stock Island, chartering a seaplane for the island of Curacao just off the Venezuelan coast. By this time, William would have refueled at Kingston and been thundering southeast across the Caribbean. Franklin walked to the pay phone that was hung from a piling a short way up the docks and called over to Stock Island. He convinced the pilot, an old friend of his, to delay his takeoff for another forty minutes. Just a little extra, to give his brother something of an edge.

Their trip through the air over the Caribbean had been full of bumps and sudden lurches, and to the five passengers it seemed to go on forever. Finally, Dusty figured by the sound of the engines and the way the plane dipped that they were coming in for a landing. For the last thirty minutes in particular their little green-and-white seaplane had been thrown around by turbulence on a continually increasing scale, and Dusty's guys were taking turns throwing up in a dirty yellow plastic bucket. Little Petee and Joe-boy were having a particularly rough time of it. Bopo was hunched in a corner of the plane, and Leon was groaning uncontrollably. Dusty himself was queasy but would probably hold his own. He moved forward in the cramped cabin and knocked on the door to the cockpit. There was no answer, and the door did not open.

"Hey, open this door!"

"Can't," a muffled, gravelly voice came from the other side. "FAA regulations."

"Screw that shit! You want me to blow a hole right through this fuckin' door?"

"It's steel plate," the grumpy voice said, "But suit yourself."

"Okay, man, I was just kidding."

There was no further response from the cockpit. After a few minutes, Dusty raised his voice again, "How come we're landing? We can't be there yet."

"We're landing in Port-au-Prince."

"And why is that?" Dusty's voice was clipped and terse. He was again examining the door.

"Tropical disturbance moving in faster than we had anticipated."

"What's that?"

"Look out your window."

Dusty could see the morning's innocent, puffy clouds had now lined themselves into an angry dark gray wall. The nearer sky had shifted in color from deep blue to a peculiar silvery blue-gray. Dusty felt out of his element. He got the weather from a weatherman.

"Can't we go no further?"

232

"We can go west to Jamaica."

"I'm going to kill somebody."

As if in response, the plane banked into a steep, downward spiral. Dusty hung on to the overhead strap with one hand and snatched the vomit pail from Leon with the other.

"Someone going to die for this," he muttered again, but this time so low that they wouldn't hear him through the steel door. It didn't matter; he was beyond simple trigger-pulling. Dusty knew blowing away a few evil-minded pilots wasn't going to satisfy him anymore. The source of all his discomfort and anger was one very lucky man with a scar across his face. And that luck was going to change real soon from impossibly good to very, very bad.

24

What is it about you people, demanding your adrenaline fix, your touch of violence, your spatter of blood and rat-tat-tat of automatic rifle fire? Don't you get enough of this in the movies? Or is it just the gods again? Everything, it seems, we blame on the gods. Where is your sense of personal responsibility? You can't blame everything on the chocolate bars...or, perhaps you think you can. After all, you point out (keen on motivation), doesn't our hero The Man With The Scar have an uncommon lust for Toblerone, the bittersweet kind in the black wrapper with the red-and-gold label? I tell you, if I hear that Twinkie Defense one more time, every confection in the house is straight in the dumper. Please don't do that to me; I'll only have to go out for more.

Regardless, there are moments when it does come down to the bloodletting, doesn't it? Nothing else will seem to do. Oh, you descendents from the monkey cultures, swung down from the trees and let loose behind the wheel of your zaggy Jags and hepped up BMWs! Now there's another of life's freeways jammed with wretched excess! But on the other digit, who's to say, Lord knows, perhaps the elephants and the whales wouldn't have it any other way, either...except they can't get their flippers or their trunks around the trigger.

And so it came to pass that a largish sport fisher boat hove to (as they say in nauticalese) in front of a swank casino on an island off the coast of Venezuela...

Dave Toomley took it as a good sign that he was able to swallow his evening meal of bland fish and warm milk. After dining, he had Anna and one of the guards transfer him to his motorized wheelchair for his nightly trip to the casino, which involved a pleasant ten-minute roll along curving cement sidewalks past a lagoon, a small park, and even a brief stretch that bordered the sea. As usual, the guards boxed him off from the ordinary tourists. At the entrance to the gaming room, casino guards moved him quickly to his game of choice as soon as he arrived. This being a Thursday, he was wheeled to the roped-off Baccarat table.

Dave Toomley was a living legend at the Aruba Sonata, the quiet, sickly-unto-death man in the wheelchair who almost always won. No one taking their vacation on the island ever stayed long enough to wonder how any casino could or would support the constant drain of his winnings. And yet, Toomley himself was being squeezed dry; the Swiss conglomerate had found a way to turn even this small vice of his into a business advantage. Since the money went into Toomley's offshore accounts, the arrangement provided a neat solution to some of the conglomerate's serious money laundering problems. And since the Swiss were listed as sole heir on those accounts, and it was five to one that Toomley wouldn't last until New Year's (four to one he'd go before Christmas Eve), it was really a matter of the left hand paying the right. Beyond that, it certainly was good for business at the casino, to see someone raking in the chips the way he did.

The house did their best to provide special guests with seating at the tables where Toomley played, and if they were fast and knowledgeable enough and not too timid, they too could share in the spill of wealth. However, tonight as Toomley moved his electric chair to the vacant number 7 slot next to the dealer, an elderly fellow with bleached hair and a horrible scar down his face slid onto the chair occupying slot number 6, which was directly to Toomley's left. The new arrival was wearing purple and black hiking shoes and a many-pocketed photographer's vest over an olive t-shirt that looked many sizes too big for him. The shirt had the shield emblem of the Army Security Agency, an eagle claw grasping a handful of lightning bolts. The headline printed over the shield read: "COVERT DOES IT DEEPER."

From their table, the players could see out the plate glass windows to where the setting sun was a red gold coin above the horizon. Small yachts and sleek speedboats were pulling up to the pier, which was dominated by a huge 110-foot sports fishing yacht.

"Beautiful night, isn't it?" the new arrival gushed to no one in particular. He scratched his faded blond hair and began methodically stacking a handful of fifty-dollar chips in piles of ten on the green felt in front of him. "Look at that big boat out there. God, I wish it was mine!"

Toomley smiled and nodded graciously, but he didn't say anything. A lean Chinese man in a dark suit looked up from the chicken scratching he was making in his small notebook, closed his cellular phone and then saw that the newcomer had taken the seat he assumed was his.

"I'm sorry, sir, but I'm afraid you have my seat." His chilly tone said the newcomer was anything but a "sir", and he expected the seat to be vacated immediately.

"Doesn't seem to have your name on it," was the nonchalant reply.

The dapper little Chinese man sniffed once, sharply, and snapped his fingers.

One of the laddermen at the baccarat table quickly moved to intervene, but the old, bleached-out fellow stared at them both, clearly refusing to give up his seat. There was something to the intense look in his light blue eyes, something bordering on madness, that kept them from touching him. If it came to that, the bouncers could earn their pay. The two laddermen, well aware their duty was to protect the game, were soon engaged in a furious argument with each other.

"Why aren't we beginning?" Toomley whispered. "I don't really have a lot of energy tonight."

Everyone knew it wasn't good to keep Toomley waiting. The laddermen looked over to the pit boss, who looked to the shift boss, who in turn looked to the casino boss. The casino boss, a trim black man in a dark blue pinstripe banker's suit accented with a crisp white shirt and a bold patterned Italian silk tie, gave the slightest of nods and walked away. The boss's decision bumped smoothly down the ranks, and one of the laddermen drew the unpleasant job of escorting away the ruffled Chinaman.

The game of Baccarat is pronounced with a silent 't' and is not nearly as simple as it seems when you first cut the deck. In fact, the house needs a team of employees just to keep the game going. In addition to the laddermen, who try to settle arguments and keep track of the mundane side of play, two dealers and a caller also help run the game. The dealer's main job is to collect losing wagers and pay winning bets. The caller encourages players to bet on ties, which happen in Baccarat about 10% of the time. Although ties pay eight to one, as opposed to the ordinary win which pays only one to one, through the rules of play, ties are stacked in favor of the house.

"Nice T-shirt," Toomley said softly. "Design it yourself?"

"Not the emblem," The Man With The Scar replied.

"How's my billion?" He spoke more softly, because Anna, his ever-suspicious angel, was edging closer.

"About half spread around, half still in the hole."

"Troi, dut, nuoc, oi! You had years to do that." His Vietnamese curse, which meant *Sky, earth, water, everything!* seemed to say it all.

The Man With The Scar shrugged.

"It *was* a lot of money..."

"Was...?!"

"Is. Is a lot of money."

Anna tried to push between them.

"Darlink, is this man bothering you?"

Toomley batted her with one weak hand, like he was backhanding a fly.

"Get away, Anna. Hey, we going to start here? I'm going to die before I get my first hand."

As if on signal, the dealers broke out eight new decks and began shuffling, lacing and salting them in swift and intricate variations.

Everything seemed in order. The casino boss turned his attention back to the general tone of the evening. As he walked to the long, curved bar, he noticed a dithering old man with one eye who eased up to the polished ebony and took a seat on one of the stools. The casino boss, whose name was Guy La Fleur, could barely contain the frown which pushed the ends of his lips down. Although the old man was wearing a florid red-and-white sports shirt, his cheap plastic go-aheads and scarred and knobby knees sticking out from stained Bermuda shorts clearly bespoke of a man who had no business being in the casino. As Guy was about to have him removed, the old fellow made a big flourish of pulling out a crisp one hundred dollar bill, which he set on the bar.

"A marguerita, *por favor*," he said.

Guy gave a swift hand signal, and one of the bartenders immediately brought his drink in a huge, frosted glass.

"On me, old man," Guy said. "One drink, and then you hit the road."

"*Ahh, gracias, patrone!*" The old man smiled and put his hundred dollar bill back in his shirt pocket.

Toomley twisted his neck with some obvious pain, surveying the room.

"I recognize the one-eyed greaseball, " he whispered to The Man With The Scar. "How old is he now, about a hundred and ten?"

"Mexican, Toomley," The Man With The Scar chided. "They don't like to be called greaseballs."

"Zips. Gooks. Dagos. Lugans. Greaseballs. It makes no difference. In God's eye, everybody's a nigger, Clay."

"Philosophical, Tooms. But oh so bitter."

"You came all this way to give me a lesson in social correctness. How grateful should I be?"

"Pay attention, Dave. The big Navajo is ours. The young geek by the door leading to the pier is my son. And the girl with the purple-red hair is his new lover."

"Nasty friends," Toomley whispered.

"You should talk."

"At least you've got a son. Congratulations. What makes you so sure he's yours?"

"And they say old age makes you sweeter."

The caller announced, "Gentlemen and ladies, place your bets. Baccarat is about to begin."

Toomley pushed two $100 chips onto the "players" slot in front of him and The Man With The Scar duplicated his move. They were betting two hundred each that the player's cards would beat the bank.

The first player was an excitable blond girl seated at position number one. She dealt four cards, in sequence, the first and third card for herself, and two and four for the bank. Their face value was a four and five for herself, and a one and a two for the Bank. In Baccarat, a total of nine is the highest possible number, all combinations of ten or over dropping the first numeral.

The caller intoned calmly, "Player has a natural nine, Player wins nine over three."

Seven of the players at the table lost; five, including Toomley and The Man With The Scar, had won. Toomley let his $400 ride, and so did The Man With The Scar. Baccarat is a simple game for the players, if you've got the money. But it is also a "streaky" game, that is, one of its characteristics is for streaks, that is, for runs or patterns with a certain similarity. Figuring a possible streak in the making, three of the players who had bet on the bank now switched over to bet on the player.

"How fast can this thing go?" The Man With The Scar asked.

"My chair? Not fast enough."

"Can you disengage the gears?"

"Sure."

"Do it."

The blond dealt four more cards, a five and a three for herself and two ones for the bank.

"Player has a natural eight, Player wins eight over two," the caller intoned. The blond whooped and the dealer handling their side added $400 in chips to the accumulated wealth of Toomley and The Man With The Scar.

Anna, who had been straining to overhear the quiet conversation between the two men, came between them, "I must insist, is this beach bum bothering you, *cher*?"

"Beat it, Anna," Toomley said in a hoarse whisper.

She tossed her platinum locks angrily, but The Man With The Scar put his arm around her waist before she could stalk away.

"This your squeeze?" he asked Toomley.

"I am the squeeze of no man," she answered savagely, trying to pull away from him.

"Alright, you don't have to take my head off. Hang around, for luck."

"Right, for luck." Toomley's sardonic whisper was at his ear.

"Here, for you, Anna." The Man With The Scar took four chips and added a separate little pile to his play. He put one hand inside his vest, as if fishing for a pack of cigarettes.

Toomley pushed his winnings up to the Bank slot, indicating he would wager on the bank on the next round of play. The Man With The Scar followed Toomley's lead, taking his arm from Anna's waist and pushing his and Anna's chips up to his own Bank position. Toomley hesitated for the briefest of moments and then pushed his chips into "Tie". The Man With The Scar quickly imitated his motion.

"Hey, this is good, Anna," he said. "We're going to make a pile."

"The old habits die hard, no?" Toomley whispered. His wasted face was lit with a faint grin.

The cards flashed. "Bank has seven and two," the caller droned. "A natural nine. Player has four and five...a tie."

The Man With The Scar scooped Anna's winnings and handed them to her.

"I go now," Anna said, obviously flustered.

"No, not just yet."

"What do you want of me?" Anna hissed at The Man With The Scar.

He took the Borchardt from his waistband. It was wrapped in a small beige towel. The dark, ugly barrel stuck out of one end. He shoved it quickly in her side.

"Put those chips in your pocket. Get behind the wheelchair, or I'll blow a big hole in you. Calmly, now. Look happy, if that's possible."

Toomley had gathered his winnings on his lap. The moment Anna got behind the wheelchair, The Man With One Eye climbed stiffly up on the bar. He was a very old man, and the casino owner almost pulled him down before he made it. But, once he was up and tottering on the bar, he triumphantly pulled open his flowered Hawaiian shirt, revealing a skinny chest made bulky with dozens of dark red sticks of dynamite. He dramatically waved something that looked like a television remote in the air.

"*Attention, Amigos*! This is very old dynamite, very touchy, and it may go off at a moment's notice!"

By now, Anna, accompanied by The Man With The Scar, had Toomley halfway to the door. It looked like they might make it without trouble when Millie pulled a stubby Walther MPL from under her skirt. She slammed the wire stock efficiently into position and with a grand, dramatic gesture, started shooting at the ornate cut glass chandeliers hanging from the ceiling.

The casino guards quickly pulled their weapons, for that was their job, and returning gunfire slammed into the plate glass windows from a half dozen positions around the room.

"Damn! Hector, get your woman out of here!" The Man With The Scar yelled. By that time, Millie was changing clips. He had a brief glimpse of his son dragging her out the door while she attempted to get off a last few bursts.

Anna chose that moment to regroup and run away with Toomley. The Man With The Scar left his feet in a flying tackle, and the wheelchair went spinning in a little semicircle while he and Anna rolled on the floor with the cross fire flying above them. Through it all, Toomley sat calmly watching.

"Come on, Clay," he whispered merrily. "Can't you even take out a lady? We got a boat to catch."

"Some lady," The Man With The Scar grunted as she kneed him in the groin.

He backhanded her across the mouth, and managed to get Toomley's wheelchair rolling in the right direction. Anna was wiry and strong, and she came after him without a moment's hesitation. She leapt on his back, and they made their way out the door with her kicking and scratching and biting. Johnny Tuesday was waiting and unceremoniously dumped Toomley—wheelchair, chips and all—into the boat. Then the big Navajo threw The Man With The Scar and Anna onboard and leapt in after them.

Millie had already set up her position, merrily firing from an open window in the galley, with Hector looking around in open-eyed wonder. Last to board was The Man With One Eye, who came shuffling out the door, blood running from one arm while he tried to rip the packs of red sticks from his body with the other. Johnny Tuesday ran to help him, and managed to pull him back over the rail.

The old man with one eye glared at him.

"I could have made it myself, *amigo*."

"You Spanish. Always so fucking proud."

The old man smiled happily at him. "*Amigo*, do you have any idea how many times I have been shot? It is truth itself that I was in the revolution..."

Johnny Tuesday took a closer look at the wound. The bullet had gone between two sticks of dynamite into the old man's chest.

"You are one lucky fellah," Johnny agreed.

"Roadside flares do not explode, *señor*."

"Yeah, but they ignite. This blood loss is going to make you real sick."

"I know, *señor*." The old man suddenly seemed deflated and shriveled.

"We'll take good care of you," Johnny said softly.

The sailor behind the wheel hadn't had any experience at getaways, and Millie had plenty of time to shoot out more plate glass windows. The Southern Seas pulled slowly and gracefully away from the Aruba Sonata casino dock with bullets whacking into the sides of the old PT boat and pinging off the superstructure.

"*Viva los guapas,*" the old man muttered weakly. "*Viva El Mexico...*"

25

Some things simply have to be said straight up. There's nothing quite so vindictive as a...well, err, a vindictive woman. But you, being up on the dictates of karmic fate, recognize that vengeance is the loosest of cannons.

As for The Man With The Scar, he is too busy for such philosophic concerns. Does he recognize Rene, who only wants to kill him, as the forest ranger girl he met on the piedmont at the base of the eastern slopes of the High Sierras? Would it matter if he did? And yet, this is the second time they've met. Nothing in his life, since he signed that damned parchment, has been coincidental. So it is a sign...but of what? And, once more, isn't that the human condition in spades? We are enormously perceptive individuals—we can READ the signs. And yet, and yet, we just can't seem to figure out what they mean.

As they cruised toward the string of postage stamp sized sandbars and uninhabited little islands that flank the long Southwestern shoreline of Aruba, Rene Riniatta had the warm sun on her perfectly shaped breasts and the wind in her hair. Aruba was south of the general hurricane track, but there was a larger than usual swell to the deep blue-green waves, the aftereffect of the tropical disturbance which was now west of Cuba and building steam for a run north through the Gulf in the general direction of New Orleans.

Rene was sitting topless with her firm buttocks loosely bound in a neon green string bikini, idly watching as they cruised past De Palm Reef Island and The Aruba Nautical Club. She was sunbathing on the uppermost deck of the fifty-nine-foot Scuba-Dooba, a posh craft that had pioneered a profitable business the owners called Naked Encounters, dropping pairs of yuppies-in-the-buff onto deserted islands around the Caribbean for a rarified and well catered Swiss Family Robinson meets Adam and Eve experience. Rene was examining the way the bright afternoon sunlight glanced off her nails as the Scuba-Dooba cut towards the main island. After a moment or two, she became aware of an unusual commotion erupting on the wooden boat dock next to the Aruba Sonata casino.

"Jeff, hey, Jeff!" She yelled down to the muscle-bound kid who was handling the wheel.

"Yo, Rene," he yelled back, happily ogling the elegant uplift of her bare breasts.

"You pig," she shouted. "Look what's going on!"

"Hey, baby, I see what's going on."

"No, over *there*, idiot! Looks like they're shooting a movie!"

"Yee, haw! Let's go see!" With that, he heeled the boat over, nearly launching Rene over the side in the process, and made a beeline directly for the casino.

As the Scuba-Dooba approached, a much larger boat was slowly pulling away from the dock. With the course Jeff was taking, it would pass within a stone's throw of them.

"I got the whole plot," Jeff yelled happily. "There's these young Italian wanna-be bank robbers, see? Only New York is too tight with cops, so they decide to come to the Caribbean where they steal a big fishing boat and pull off a casino job!"

"Everybody's got a movie script, Jeff!"

But she didn't have any better ideas and was inclined to agree with him, until—impossibly!—she saw someone she recognized from her ill-fated *western odyssey*! It was The Man With The Scar, the old fart who had managed to dump her and Gus, her forest ranger partner, and then slip past them on the road up to Butterfield Meadows and into the High Sierras! *So he hadn't been transformed into frozen coyote meat after all!*

Without thinking, Rene climbed down to the main deck and ran for the scuba gun rack that was bolted near the back of the cabin. *That boat was going to pass within a few feet of the Scuba-Dooba, and she was going to skive that scar-faced buster right in his liver!*

Dusty stretched his cramped neck muscles and tried to exercise by walking back and forth in their damp little communal cell. For some reason he could not begin to figure out, their pilot had called ahead, and the Haitian police were waiting for them on arrival. After shaking them down for their various weapons, and extracting the U.S. dollars from their wallets, they unceremoniously led them deep into a far and isolated corner of the city jail.

Dusty felt a nasty head cold coming on from the constant chill, and his brain hurt from trying to make sense of the Hispanic pornography scratched into the moldering concrete walls. He could only take three paces and then he had to spin in a half circle and walk back the other way. Leon and Bopo, who were sharing the same cell, knew better than to climb down from their stacked bunks when he was in the walking mood. Leon could see from the pained look on Bopo's face that he needed to take his turn pissing in the hole in the floor; Leon shook his head *no, no, no, no,* just to be sure Bopo didn't make that fatal mistake.

Dusty had used his one call to contact Millie's father back in Oakland. Some of the things Mr. Abernathy had said didn't set well with him, and he'd added the old bastard to the lengthening list of people he was going to pop off at the first opportunity. The call hadn't gone the way Dusty had visualized it, but after negotiating the rates on Dusty's troopers to half price for the duration of their jail term (as they couldn't very well be chasing Millie if they were behind bars), Mr. Abernathy had said he would see about getting them released. Since then, entire days and nights had gone by.

245

Meanwhile, tropical storm Judith had been roaring back and forth over Port-au-Prince and, as their jail cell didn't have any glass panes over the barred windows, they'd been soaked since the first blow. At the height of the storm, the sewer system had backed up, shooting a steady gusher of foul water out of the hole in the floor. By this time, Dusty was living in a dull red fury. He just wished he had his gun back so he could kill anybody and everybody who crossed in front of his sights.

Night was falling when Oakland Police Detective Jack Macy wheeled his Dodge Intrepid smoothly around the curves of the splendidly paved private road that wound for a quarter mile through the carefully cultivated new growth redwoods and the auburn hills of Northern California to Abernathy's mansion. At first, when the rich old coot had sketched out Dusty's problems, Jack couldn't see going anywhere fast to help a crook like Dusty out of his troubles, but as he watched the growing pile of hundreds Old Abernathy stacked in front of him, he started to think, What the hell, maybe he did need to use up some of that back vacation he'd logged on the books. He managed to keep a straight face when he heard Dusty and his boys were in a ratty little jail that was upchucking from the toilet, which was a hole in the floor.

"Oh, yes, sir," he told Mr. Abernathy, waving the stack of bills he picked up from the table. "I'll get him out, right away!"

Jack jumped up like he was going to rush right home, pack his jockstrap and his snub-nose police .38 and get on the next plane to Florida, but he slowed down considerably once he was off the Abernathy property. In fact, he stopped completely for a few rounds of refreshments at the Green Lantern, a cops' bar on the more common fringes of Palo Alto. He didn't bother to tell Old Abernathy that, with all the history between him and Dusty, it might take a few days, more or less, to get around to the actual details of any sort of rescue.

Jeff throttled forward and the twin diesels of the Scuba-Dooba thrummed under Rene's bare feet with an excited pitch. She ran along the deck, eager to get to the spear rack in time to get off a clean shot before the Southern Seas pulled out of range. Rene was a speargun enthusiast, with a great, newfound confidence in her abilities. She had been spearing a wide variety of pretty, rainbow-colored fish constantly for several weeks, even nailing several species she was later informed were undersized or protected as endangered species. While it was true all of her fish hunting had of necessity been underwater, firing a speargun is fundamentally simple and in her mind she couldn't see how the experience was any different in air than in water. *No question, she was going to nail this guy!*

Meanwhile the Southern Seas seemed to shudder and pause directly in front of their own boat in an odd and unusual way. *Luck of luck!* Rene saw the problem—the larger boat was still tethered to the pier by a long mooring rope that, in their obvious haste to depart, some slacker had failed to cast off! The pitch of the Southern Sea's big twin diesels rose to a frightening howl as a big American Indian-looking guy behind the wheel threw on full power. The thick rope pulled taut as a bowstring, but Rene could see they weren't going anywhere. Suddenly, a girl with henna-red hair burst on deck, and, oblivious to the storm of bullets flying in her direction from the casino, began firing at the rope. Strands started to pop one by one, but she hadn't done nearly enough damage to sever the thick, many-stranded line before she ran out of ammunition. She angrily shook the hair out of her eyes and fumbled to extract the old clip and jam a new one into her weapon.

By this time, Rene had passed by several Cressi Sub SL's which she felt were inferior in favor of her favorite speargun, a Russian-made Seabear pneumatic. "Reliable and extremely powerful," her instructor had told her shortly before they combined her first kill with a bout of making frantic love underwater before the needles on their tanks went into the red. She pulled at the Seabear and the weapon came smoothly from the rack into her hands at the exact moment the larger boat seemed to swing even closer. What excellent timing! It looked to have a hundred feet of line, more than enough for her purpose. Working as if on automatic pilot, she quickly secured the end of the light filament around her wrist and lined up her shot. She could make out the blue-and-orange bird of paradise pattern and count the big white buttons on The Man With The Scar's short-sleeved Hawaiian shirt.

He had to see her; he was staring directly at her. For a moment she thought he was frozen in fear. But he didn't look afraid. He was staring at her as if she were from another planet, as if he couldn't be taken out by a nearly naked Amazon. *If so, he was suffering a terminal case of overconfidence!*

Two-handed, she held the Seabear out in front of her, aiming for the third button down on his shirt. She took a deep breath and held it, squinted one eye while she aimed and finally squeezed the trigger. Shooting from the lurching deck was difficult, and her aim was a little high. Still, the titanium spear whizzed from the stainless steel barrel, straight and true towards the neck of The Man With The Scar, with the thin nylon retrieval cord smoothly uncoiling in its wake. But at the last impossible second, just when Rene was sure he was skewered under his chin like a big fat grouper, the entire dock behind his boat sagged and came apart. The Southern Seas lurched forward, and the heavy barbed spearhead from the Seabear lodged in the varnished wooden cabin frame less than an inch from the neck of her intended victim. And, because Rene had wrapped the end of the line around her left arm to assure his capture, when the entire 110 feet of the Southern Seas took the line, it yanked her overboard like a flea in a hurricane. The last thing she saw as she tumbled into the water was the girl with the henna hair, renewing her getaway efforts by firing a new clip at the thick rope, which was now towing a hundred yards of planking out to sea.

Before Rene could unwrap the cord from her wrist, the line from her own spear gun had dragged her through the water to the side of the Southern Seas. She untangled herself from the line, but now she was in the powerful grasp of the undertow and in the next blink of an eye she was sucked down under the hull of the big boat. For fifteen horrible seconds her nearly naked body was rudely bumped and bounced along the rough bottom of the hull. Through no effort of her own, she narrowly missed being chopped into shark bait by the huge twin screws at the back end of the Southern Seas, before finally being spun free in the boat's heavy wake.

Rene came up to the surface sputtering and bewildered, bitterly aware of the salt water stinging the many cuts and scrapes on her body. She treaded water, looking around for Jeff, but the miserable putz was gaping at the last of the gunfire and hadn't even noticed she'd been rudely jerked from the boat. He was going to pay big time for being such a meat-brains, she would see to that. But what infuriated her more than anything was the look she saw on the face of The Man With The Scar; there was something cold and inhuman about him. She wished he'd shouted at her in anger or triumph, wished he'd showed any emotion at all. When she came up after her hellish moments under the hull, she saw he'd moved to the back of the boat where he could watch as she bobbed back to the surface. As the Southern Seas pulled away, he raised one hand in a salute or a farewell. He continued to stare back at her, and she had a sudden crazy notion, an indescribable feeling of loss and sadness from him. She knew it was a stupid and impossible thought, and yet he looked almost...lonely.

Jeff finally spotted her in the water and spun the Scuba-Dooba around at an enthusiastic pace to come back for her. She dog-paddled fearfully, wondering what the odds were that she could avoid being run over for the second time in a few minutes. As The Man With The Scar's boat receded into the distance, it was still towing a few planks in its wake, and the girl with the henna hair was trying to get another clip into her automatic rifle. The Man With The Scar was receding into the distance and into her past at one and the same time. Rene felt relieved that their lives had touched for the final time. She was glad she was alive, but she was even happier that she would never see him again. She was going to have to get away from this Caribbean jaunt. Things were just getting too weird. Maybe she would go bother her father in Italy, or see if the snow was ready in Aspen.

26

Can anyone after so many years actually right an outrage, right a great wrong, sew up an enormous rent in the fabric of space and time (as Captain Kirk might say on an early episode of Star Trek)? Well, ex-CIA man Dave Toomley and The Man With The Scar are certainly motivated to try...

Jack, Dusty, Leon and Bopo sat at a table cluttered with half-empty glasses. They were in the café near the deserted Aruba Sonata casino, watching as the excitable little casino owner directed his workmen to secure plywood over the windows that had been blown out by the gunfire. They weren't really interested in a bunch of scruffy Dutchmen pounding a few nails, but it was the only action around.

"Did you know Aruba is under control of the Dutch Empire?" Jack asked as he listened to the guttural chatter of the workmen.

"The Dutch Empire. And what the hell does that consist of? This one dinky island a couple of miles off the coast of Venezuela?"

"Now Dusty. Don't get your blinking balls in an uproar."

"I'm asking you a question, man."

"Here. Read the goddamn brochure yourself."

"I don't have to know what it says. I know what it means."

"What does it mean, Dusty?" Jack sighed, sorry he'd asked practically before the words were out of his mouth.

"It means, you about as far out of your jurisdiction as a man can get, you sorry excuse for a law enforcement officer."

"You forget we're on the same team here, Dusty, my man."

"Teamwork?! You let us rot in that jail, back there on Haiti."

Leon and Bopo looked at each other and then glared at Jack, as if the idea that Jack might have intentionally extended their unpleasant stay had just occurred to them. He threw his hands out wide, and gave them his innocent cop look. "Dusty...guys! I'm the man who got you out. I got you out! Cost me a fortune, too."

Dusty ticked the indignities off on his fingers. "Nasty voodoo muckheaps kept my .38, too. Kept all our iron. And my bread. And my solid gold Cartier. And my dope. You going to get me my money back, Jack?"

"Aww, that's a shame, taking you out of the action like that."

"FedExing me another one, Jack. And it's going to be here in plenty time to pop your sorry ass."

"No way to talk, partner. No way to talk." Jack leaned back in his barrel chair and put his feet up on another chair. "You did right to send the rest of your troopers back, though. Nothing we can't handle by ourselves, and I know they must have been costing you a fortune."

"Yeah, right. Like you give a crap about my money." Dusty figured from the way Jack was talking that Old Abernathy must have cut him in on the reward. *Oh well,* he thought to himself, *Add Jack to the hit list.* One body, more or less, floating in a sea of blood, wasn't going to make that much difference.

"How much he say to bring back the daughter?" Dusty asked idly, yawning and looking at his cheap new Casio G-Shock sports watch. It had more dials and readouts than he would ever know what to do with.

"Same as you're going to get."

"Same money, or in addition to?"

"I get two million; you get two million."

Dusty nodded as if in agreement. He didn't bother to mention he'd only been offered one million. It was just another case of the white man tricking the black man, getting him to eat off the sorry-ass back end of the pig again. He was trying to remember if Old Man Abernathy was already on his kill list.

"Two million. Zat is nothing," a voice behind them said. They turned to see a short, bald man with a shaved head that looked like a little egg sitting on top of a body shaped like a bigger egg. The man's cream white suit and matching vest added to the resemblance, and the twin toes of round eggshell-colored leather shoes peeping from under the perfect line of his pants completed the effect.

"Two million bucks is a lot of semolians, Mister Egg," Jack sneered, giving the newcomers a spadeful of his typical contemptuous cop attitude.

"Shut up, Jack." Dusty was eyeing the funny little man and the two lean blond snuffmeisters who flanked him. Dusty couldn't quite place the European accent, but he could smell big money a mile away.

The egg-shaped man tapped their table with an ornately carved antique cane that was crafted of solid ivory. "You bring me zee man in zee wheelchair, and I will give you $40 millions USA, in tax-free dollars, in your own offshore accounts."

"Is that $40 million, or $40 million *each?*" Jack asked.

"Shut *up*, Jack," Dusty said.

The Southern Seas had to camp out two days in the Atlantic outside the port of Cristobal, waiting their turn at the Panama Canal. The canal gave preference to freighters and large cruise ships, which steamed past them with regularity while they fretted and wondered what the Swiss were up to and how soon they would be following after them.

The Southern Seas was finally allowed through the first lock and onto the wide and irregular Gatun Lake loosely tied together with a small flotilla of sailboats.

As the Southern Seas was the largest by half of any of the boats in their group, the canal pilot came on board their boat. He was a scruffy little man with a chronic look of deep suspicion, but he knew where the trench lay and to stay far enough back from the steamer in front of them. The weather was hot and sticky. The air was windless and thickly humid, and tempers started to get short.

The feud between Anna and Millie had been simmering for some time, but the Southern Seas was across the lake and beginning its cautious run through the confined waters of the narrow Gaillard Cut when Anna complained to The Man With The Scar about Millie.

"Just what is it that bothers you about Millie?"

"She is too trigger-happy."

"W-w-wait a stick-stackin' minute!" Millie called from halfway across the deck. "Is that slappy slut talking about me?"

Millie handed Hector her stubby little Walther MPL and waded right in with her fists flying. Toomley cheered for Anna, apologizing to The Man With The Scar that, after all, she'd taken care of his every bodily need for a matter of some years. A crowd of onlookers from the nearest yachts were cheered by this interruption in the boring tedium of the endless jungle greenery sliding by.

"Nobody bets with Toomley," The Man With The Scar ordered, realizing it would amount to an automatic win for Anna. He allowed the two women to roll and scratch around for a while before having Hector and Johnny Tuesday pull them apart.

The Man With The Scar looked at Johnny.

"Who's steering the boat?"

"Jesus Philipe. The pilot. He gave me ten dollars to put down on the blond woman."

"He's going to be disappointed. I think it was a tie."

Once they had the two women separated, The Man With The Scar gathered everyone on the back deck for a palaver intended to clear the air.

"I don't know why you don't j-j-just dump the bitch overboard," Millie complained. "She's going to give us away the first chance she gets, anyway."

"Double-bitch, yourself," Anna remarked haughtily, borrowing a handkerchief from Toomley to daub at a trickle of blood running from her nose.

"It wouldn't do any good, anyway," The Man With The Scar spoke up. "They're probably tracking us by satellite. I'll bet they know where we are right now."

"Yes, they do. To within a few meters," Toomley nodded in sad agreement.

The Man With The Scar studied his old friend, thinking how far science had come since their days together in Saigon, when a simple covert radio fix depended on primitive equipment, luck and the weather.

"Where is it? In the wheelchair?"

"I wish," Toomley replied. "I had stomach cancer. It was too convenient; as long as they had me opened up, they sewed it right in here." He lifted his shirt to reveal a long reddish scar running across the pale skin of his stomach.

Since there was nothing they could do to remove Toomley's locator device, the meeting dwindled as the various parties drifted away to sleep in the bunks or grill themselves something in the same kitchen where The Man With The Scar had once toiled. Finally, Toomley, Anna and The Man With The Scar were the only ones left on the deck.

"*Anh, oi....*" Toomley started in halting Vietnamese with a little French thrown in. "*Toi muon noi tieng Viet avec vous.*" I want to speak Vietnamese with you.

"'Avec vous'?!"

"Come on, Clay, I haven't spoken Zip in over 20 years."

"For ze sake of Christ Almighty!" Anna hissed angrily. "If you want to speak alone, *say so.*"

She retreated to one corner of the stern where she stared moodily at their muddy wake.

"She's not a bad woman," Toomley said. "A little spiky, but what the hell..."

"What do you want to tell me, Dave?"

"It's funny, really. The Swiss are desperate to get me back. They think I'm going to die and that they're the ones who are keeping me alive. Stupid, greedy people."

"If they're not, who is?"

"Actually, *it's* keeping me alive; you know, our little bargain. I should have been dead months ago. I'm a medical miracle."

"Consider yourself lucky."

Again the sardonic laugh dropped from Toomley's wasted lips. "You have no idea of the endless, endless pain...I'm a living dead guy, Clay. I just want out, and there's only one way that I know of."

"What's that, Dave?"

Toomley and The Man With The Scar stared at the green walls steadily retreating from them on either side of the canal.

"Where's our contract?" Toomley asked.

"Contract?"

"For the whorehouse we bought in Nam."

"You bought, Dave. Not me."

"You know your name's on that paper."

"Well, think back. You said you had the contract, that time you dropped your cool billion off at my place. I never saw it again after that first night in Saigon when I...witnessed—"

"After you *signed.*"

"Okay. After I signed."

"I was very religious about it. I always kept it with me, at least until I dropped by your place in New Mexico."

"In your own shiny DC-3 with no running lights, insignia or identifying numbers and the dead guy in the co-pilot's seat."

"It was him or me, old buddy. Anyway, the contract was under all the money, on the bottom of that pallet we dumped in your old mine."

"So you couldn't even be honest with me about that?"

"Come on, you had to have found it."

"Dave, there was *hundreds of millions* of dollars. I tried to do what you told me, but I don't think I even got halfway through. If it was there, it's still there."

"Well, the only hope for us is to get that contract."

"Hey, it should still be there...down there in that glory hole with the owls and the desert rattlers."

"My only chance, Clay."

"Okay, Dave. If that's what you want, we'll go get it."

The two men eyed each other, thinking about what they had to do and wordlessly assessing their chances of pulling it off. The Man With The Scar pulled at his blond mustachio.

"Just one problem. Once we do get it," he asked, "you think they're going to just let us erase our names?"

"No, I haven't lost my brains along with my ability to screw, Clay. I don't think it'll be that simple."

"Maybe there's some spell, or we could bless it with holy water."

"Yeah, or you could shoot it with a silver bullet." Toomley shrugged and gave him a wan smile. "I know you'll think of something."

The Man With The Scar shrugged. "I'd like my name off the page as much as you."

After another hour, the pilot sent word they were nearing the Pedro Miguel Locks. The Southern Seas had to thread through Pedro Miguel and then the locks at Miraflores, and then they could slide by the Panamanian port of Balboa and put out into the Pacific Ocean.

27

So let's pretend, just for a moment. Each of us has his or her special demon, a private demigod, as it were. The rules are probably vastly more complicated, but since we don't know them, for the sake of this conversation, we might as well ignore them.

Okay, we don't know the rules; what do we know? Well, let's say we're agreed that your fate is ruled by this semi-bored omnipotent creature who from the looks of things isn't really paying attention half the time. At least, it seems that way. So, you ask, what am I pretending to ask here? Well, here it is: suppose you had one shot, one chance to ask your favorite deity just what the hell is going on. Actually just what would you ask? Would it be any more than a long, horrible scream? Or would you just be too scared to say anything at all, blood run cold by this scaly black thing with flaring red eyes...oops, that's my own private fright; who knows, yours might be green and fishlike, with lizard eyes and suckers for fingers.

Still, put all that descriptive nonsense aside. Suppose (and it will never happen this way) but just suppose for a moment that your personal demonic presence decided to come a little more than halfway, that is, agreed to show up perhaps smoking or glowing a little, but otherwise not really very upsetting. What would you ask him, her or it? What? What? What?

Alright, that's enough about you. Obviously, you're not going to answer. I'm not even upset; after all, I don't have any right to know. But how about The Man With The Scar? Hey, he's my man; he lives because I drew him out of air (as perhaps your own demigod did you). Has our friend TMWTS already met his demon in the form of the wizened old Ba he first gazed on in the Coeur Desir that long-ago night in Saigon, in January of 1968, if I remember correctly? Or is that old, old lady simply another messenger to the demons, encouraged to do their bidding for perhaps one more drop of the divine intoxication that means life to us all?

Shouldn't I be able to answer these questions? After all, am I not the writer of this incredible adventure? And yet, perhaps I can't. What do you want from me?—I'm just the scribe. Perhaps, like the rest of you, I only know what I see. Sure, there are hints and scraps everywhere, but would you have me stir the entrails for you? Wouldn't you rather gaze at the leaves in the bottom of the teacup for yourselves? It is, after all, your very own personal teacup. Nothing too scary in there, just tea leaves, you know, just tea leaves...

"Where the hell they going now?"

Dusty and his men were still in the casino on Aruba. Dusty himself looked uncomfortable and out of place in his wild tropical shirt and fawn-colored shorts. They were sitting in plastic poolside chairs outside the impromptu satellite tracking room the Swiss team had up and running like a fine watch. The Europeans had wasted no time bringing in a planeload of tracking gear and setting up shop in a small side room of the casino that was normally used for counting and sorting money. Mister Egg—they openly dubbed him that after he refused to tell them his real name—had stayed most the night, but now he was replaced by his two silent blond snuffmeisters, who sat at attention on a broken-down sofa that had once been made for love. Bopo and Leon had lifted the back pillows from the sofa and were snoring on the floor. Jack paced back and forth, looking like a crusty lizard who never needed sleep. He rolled a cold stogy around in his mouth and blinked into the tracking room.

A balding blond man with wire-rimmed glasses sat at a knockdown banquet table that was cluttered with electronic gear. He looked like a retired army computer nerd. He tapped the nail of his index finger on a computer color monitor, "They have left their ship." This called for the return of Mister Egg, who showed up in fifteen minutes wearing a fresh light beige suit that resembled the last one down to the last detail.

"Anything else?" Mister Egg yapped in his shrill accent.

"I think," the balding blond man with the wire-rimmed glasses said, "they have boarded a plane from Acapulco. Their position now moves very rapidly almost due north."

Dusty studied the blip on the screen as it crawled up the superimposed map of Mexico. He took a ruler from the table and placed the bottom tip on Acapulco. The blip was at the six inch mark. And the twelve inch mark hovered just below Albuquerque.

"Yeah, I know where they're going," he said.

Hector had wanted the window seat, but as the plane flew above an endless blanket of puffy white clouds, he had quickly fallen asleep.

Millie slid her hand out from his and placed his limp hand on his lap, patting it once as she did so. She was still wearing her white wedding dress. She smiled at The Man With The Scar.

"Wh-what about Old One-eye?" she asked. "I like him."

"He's going to make it. He'll be out of the hospital in a few weeks. Johnny Tuesday will wait for him and they'll take the Southern Seas back to Cabo."

"Wasn't it a lovely joining of our families in wedded bliss?" she said for the tenth time.

"I enjoyed it," he replied. "I never had one of my own."

"That sweet old padre with his fuzzy white chops," she sighed. "That funny little mission church."

"It really was very nice."

"Y-you don't think Heck-the-peck and I will last, do you?"

"The odds aren't in your favor. Just don't hurt the boy. He hasn't had much...life experience."

"My first virgin," she smiled. "But you'd be surprised. My Heck-love can take it. He's tougher than you think."

"Wait until you meet his mother."

"Will she be touchy that I stole her little baby boy?"

"Words cannot describe it."

"We did send her a wedding announcement," she pouted.

"I doubt a postcard from Acapulco was what she had in mind."

"And we are going to make her a grandmother."

"I don't know that she's going to take that very well, either."

"Well, gerbil—"

"Shhhh," he said, holding a finger to her lips. "A touch of decorum is in order. You're a married woman now."

"Yes, I am." A wan and hopeful smile turned up the corners of her lips. "I fi-fi-finally did something right, didn't I?"

"Yes, you did," he agreed.

She was half-crazy, excitable as a new colt and a natural born liar, but The Man With The Scar decided he liked his new daughter-in-law. For her wedding present, he was going to give her as much money as she could carry. Maybe he would even let her borrow the wheelbarrow from the old mine so she could haul away a bigger load. He was sure she'd like that a lot.

28

You'll believe me when I say there's a pattern to the known universe. Oh, sure, you'll say, agreeing more or less immediately. You'd probably be thinking about the endless repetition of day to night to day, the phases of the moon, the four seasons... Known universe, I repeat. And then, after I say that a second time, you still agree, but perhaps more hesitantly. You've gotten this far; you've already been along for the ride, as it were...I've hinted at things less transparent, hidden motives, games of chance, swings of fortune good or bad, and perhaps even the rise and fall of nations, migrations, birth and death of races, colonization, evolution...the patterns become less obvious and certainly less patently predictable...Einstein and Hawking's known universe, I say, refining my definition still more—and you throw your hands up in despair. Knowing something of E&H, you are aware of the uncertainty principle, and that your once unshaken faith in science must now be tempered with the unsavory thought that, though our heads may be in the clouds of light, we may never quite get our feet out of the muck of ignorance. Humbling and disgusting. Why go there? And yet we must. At least some of us. The rest of you have already hit delete, and I'm afraid you are a non-issue, like complaining about the government and then not voting.

I speak of real things and they cannot, will not and should not be ignored. You and I are the same; our lives move forward as arrows. We all have this in common. And the best of us try our best to pierce the gloom, to correct for air currents and to adjust for the force of gravity so that we may strike our targets, whatever they may be. The very best of the best even correct for curved space-time and apparent bends in the path of light beams. I don't kid myself; I am not one of the best of the best, or even of the best of us. I only hint at outside forces whether they be beneficent, uncaring or malevolent...I raise the possibility of their presence, a simple grazing cow somehow aware of the miraculous floating vision of the Blessed Virgin Mary. The spring grass is fresh and sweet; I turn my attention back to another mouthful. Or better, I turn over the edge of the slipcover, see what is there and then run bleating for the safety of distant trees. Hopefully, even my timid gesture, taking that little peep under the cover, is not a huge mistake. You know the old story, *Those who go looking for evil will certainly find it.* But how about the reverse, *Better to find the unknown before it finds you?* Eve, Eve, why did you point out that damned apple in the first place?

But now, what of The Man With The Scar? What of Toomley, ex-CIA man turned solid gold financial prognosticator? Apparently, you can live with your demons an entire lifetime and never grow accustomed to the pace. Or do you think Clay and Dave like what they have become? Would you? Or would you feel somehow cheated out of that other life, the one that might have been, that would have been, if it had not been for the rash actions of a single night in long-ago and faraway Saigon?

Another question might be, Does in some way the demon-spawn of your life's forecast become so inextricably twined with your awareness, your existence, your very being that *you become your fate?* That other could have, would have, should have existence now totally and forever gone, lost in space-time beyond recall. If this is so, both men are hopelessly damned, trapped like Howard The Duck in a world they never made...and, perhaps, so too we are also...

It had been almost ten years since The Man With The Scar had lowered himself into the glory hole into which he and Dave Toomley had dumped the pallet of money. In the first year after Toomley's visit, he'd gone at his assignment with a passion, webbing the country like a crazy spider to open safe deposit boxes in every state and stuff them full of wads of money. He paid five years in advance for the boxes and he kept carefully coded notebooks, and duplicate notebooks in one of the glory hole shafts on his property.

In the second year, he concentrated on offshore bank accounts. He'd drive down to Key West and chartered a fishing boat. Eventually, there were seven island accounts, and he'd committed the numbers to memory. But there was so much money that the enormous volume of it, the sheer logistics of moving it around, gradually got to him, and he'd eventually walked away with the job about half done. After all, a man can spend only so much in a lifetime, and he wasn't going to waste his days squirreling away nuts for old Toomley, who didn't need it in the first place because Toomley attracted money like ticks to a longhaired retriever.

The Man With The Scar was sweeping away cobwebs on his jerky way down the glory hole when the beam through which the pulley was looped at the top of the hole broke, and he bumped and banged his way the remaining twenty feet to land with a cloud of dust on top of the tarp of heavy blue plastic that he'd tied over the remaining stacks of money. The old wooden pallet cracked and gave under his weight; that and the thick piles of money saved him from breaking his back.

"You okay, Dad?" Millie's voice drifted down from the small, bright opening above him. He couldn't speak. He found himself staring at a huge diamondback, coiled and ready to strike. He was thinking how odd it was that Millie called him "Dad" while Hector still struggled to call him anything at all. He threw up one arm, and the snake buried its teeth in his jacket. He whipped his arm around to the rocky floor of the hole and managed to get a foot on its head.

"No problem down here," he said. "Just a snake I've got to kill."

He extracted the Borchardt from his jacket. It took three carefully aimed shots to sever the snake's head from its body.

Ears ringing, and coughing from the dust he'd stirred up, he kicked the head and still-twitching body into a corner and then untied the tarp and began stacking money around the sides of the pallet at the bottom of the glory hole. There wasn't enough room, and soon he was scooping through a waist-high pile of loose hundreds as he worked his way deeper and deeper toward the last layer.

The parchment was there, just as Toomley had said. He opened the old oilskin paper and scanned it briefly. Yes, his signature was still right after Toomley's, bright and clear as if he'd penned it yesterday. He looked around for something sharp, and his gaze rested on the severed snake's head. It was slippery and bloody, but he thought maybe he might try to scrape the letters off with one of the sharp teeth. He started on the second "t" in Rhett, and it *was* coming off; at least, it seemed like it was, when the snake head, slippery with blood, turned in his fingers and one fang punctured him on the right thumb. There he was, at the bottom of a dry well with his contract in one hand and a rattler's head dangling by one fang from his thumb. He shook it off easily enough, but he didn't have a knife, so he had to content himself with squeezing blood from the wound and then sucking on his thumb.

He'd read somewhere that snakes pumped the venom into their victims through hollow fangs. Since the rattler had been dead, he doubted he'd taken in much poison, unless the reaction was some sort of automatic response. It seemed all right, so he decided to ignore it. There was work to be done.

"Hello, down there." It was Millie's voice from above. "We've rigged a new beam!" He felt the slap of the rope they tossed down to him. Before he tied it around his waist, he took a last look at the parchment. A single drop of his blood had landed on the parchment, near the "t" he'd been trying to scrape off. He rubbed at the blood, but it only made things worse, ending with a big russet smear across his name.

He shrugged helplessly. There was nothing more he could do about it. He carefully folded the oilskin around the parchment and placed it in his knapsack, packing it with decks of hundred dollar bills. Then he tied the rope around his waist and yelled to Hector and Millie that they could start hauling him back out.

Toomley seemed unconscious when they returned to the cabin, but his eyes opened and he smiled as he accepted the oilskin bundle. He didn't bother to open it, simply clutched it to his chest and folded both arms over it.

"Where do we go now?" Hector asked.

"Please, darling, Heck-love, I'm c-c-counting," Millie said from the kitchen table where she was arranging stacks of hundred dollar bills.

"I don't know," The Man With The Scar said. "I think we wait."

"No," Toomley whispered. "There's a place up the road. I saw it last night on our way in."

"Where?"

"Near a town called San Lorenzo. Just before we crossed the creek."

"You're sure?" Hector asked.

Toomley was too exhausted to say anything more, but the smile on his face hinted at a new hopefulness that hadn't been there in all the time since they'd spirited him from the casino on Aruba.

"He's sure," The Man With The Scar said for him.

Night had fallen by the time the DC-10 carrying Dusty, Bopo, Leon, Jack, the strange bald fellow they called Mr. Egg and his two silent Swiss snuffmeisters taxied to the end of the runway and disgorged its passengers into the Albuquerque airport. Dusty went straight to the FedEx desk and retrieved a package he'd had forwarded, unopened, from Aruba. Old Man Abernathy was already there with a big Dodge Caravan he'd rented, and by midnight they'd driven south past Polvadero, Elephant Butte Lake and Truth or Consequences, and turned off onto the two-lane blacktop which would take them to Silver City. Dusty was driving, pushing the Caravan as fast as it would go through the winding mountains. The wind was gusty, and the slab-sided van moved around a little bit. Annoying, but nothing Dusty couldn't handle. He'd topped

Emory Pass and was gunning it through a long, flat stretch of road towards San Lorenzo when a big puff of night desert air pushed them to the right. Dusty tried to compensate, but he was on gravel and the steering wasn't responding. Both front tires inexplicably blew and the van flipped over on its side and whipped about like a top, spinning nose over tail through five or six complete circles and ending up in a dusty ditch next to the road.

They crawled out of the crumpled van and examined their various bruises, bumps and nicks. Everyone was only slightly the worse for wear. Bopo was holding one arm like he might have re-broken that old football collarbone, and one of the snuffmeisters was bleeding from a cut over his eye. Mr. Egg, who had taken full advantage of the driver's side airbag, was none the worse for the wear. Jack, who had instinctively curled into a ball, had a swollen eye where one of his knees had banged his head.

"What we going to do now?" Leon said to no one in particular.

"Go over there, fool," Dusty said. He was pointing to a big, ramshackle building set off from the road by a potholed gravel parking lot that was half-filled with cars and pickup trucks. In the distance they could make out the twang of a country western band, and two eager and newly arrived pickups sent up plumes of dust as they spun into parking positions.

Dusty's little group formed an irregular line and shuffled along the gravel path at the side of the road. As they crossed the road, the music grew louder. They could hear the plaintive wail of a full-throated country western singer, a woman who'd obviously been wronged, and they could make out the shouts and distant laughter of the assembled crowd.

"What is this place?" Leon asked.

"Boy, don't you ever get out of the city?" Jack growled.

"Don't call me 'boy'."

They saw a huge blue heart fixed to the roof of the building. It was outlined in blue neon, and scrawled in brazen red-orange letters across the heart were the words, "*My Desire.*"

"For fuck's sake, quit your bitching," Dusty yelled over his shoulder. "It's a country western bar. Come on, let's see how the shit-kickers do it."

29

You've waited thirty years to talk to the girl of your dreams. The moment comes, and she doesn't look any different. She hasn't aged at all. She looks exactly as she did three decades ago when you first met her at the Coeur Desir...the oldest woman you had ever met.

Aside from that, everything else goes exactly as planned. But it's someone else's plan, not your own. So what do you do? You hang on, and you do your best. You wouldn't want anybody you care for to get hurt, would you, not because of your own youthful stupidity one night in January of 1968...

It is an understatement to observe that The Man With The Scar wasn't feeling well. Once he saw the big blue neon heart over the swinging doors and heard the jumbled riot of music and laughter, he knew Toomley was right. He looked over at Johnny Tuesday, who was going in and out of focus.

"What was the name of the bar—in Venezuela...?"

"I honestly don't remember." Johnny scratched his head, looking around as they entered the dance hall, "Something Italian...*Adorato Me Cora*, or something like that...why?"

"You know why. Mine was *Coeur Desir*. They mean the same thing...Heart's Desire."

For over thirty years he'd planned and plotted what he would do when he returned to the *Coeur Desir*. After all, it had been a simple mistake, his signing on as a witness, and should be easily resolved.

But as he entered the crowded country western dance hall, his swollen thumb hurt and he could feel the blood throbbing in his temples. He automatically reached in one of the big pockets of his vest for a sugar fix, but his backup chocolate was gone, probably pilfered by Millie who had acquired a ravenous taste for his bittersweet Toblerone bars.

Toomley rolled his wheelchair to a table near the wide polished sweep of the wooden bar, and the rest of them followed. The Man With The Scar walked calmly through the boisterous crowd, seemingly oblivious to the music, the jostling and the fights breaking out here and there.

"Come wiz me, Hector, m-m-my man. Bam-bam shazaam. Time to show me what you got." Millie soon had him Texas Two-Stepping on the dance floor, which was packed with frenzied boot-kicking couples.

Johnny looked like he was in a trance of his own. "It doesn't necessarily have to be..." he started, but then his voice trailed off in disbelief. He took The Man With The Scar's shoulder and pointed across the room. At a table, sitting all alone, was the oldest woman either of them had ever seen. Except that they had both seen her before. Now she was dressed in traditional Navajo ceremonial garb, and seemed almost too frail for the wide silver belt around her waist and the heavy silver blossom necklace hanging loosely around her thin and wrinkled neck.

The Man With The Scar walked up to the table and gave her a slight bow, "Chao, ba..." he said, speaking in Vietnamese for the first time in many years. He noticed that, though the crowd swirled around them, she seemed to exist in her own separate dimension, aloof to any thought that harm or accident might come to her.

The Ancient Woman gave him a slight nod of recognition. There were two bottles on the table in front of her. One was half full while the other was almost empty. There were three empty shot glasses on the table.

"Ya-ta-hay," the woman said, indicating that Johnny and The Man With The Scar were to sit.

"Ya-ta-hay, Ancient Mother," Johnny said. He started to reach for the nearly empty bottle, but the old woman shook her head, brushing his hand towards the half full one. Johnny poured himself a full glass and knocked it down.

The old woman nodded her approval and turned to The Man With The Scar, "And you?...You still have some little left..."

"Will you share with me?" he asked.

Johnny took his arm and shook his head in warning. "Maybe you don't understand the full meaning of the bottles..."

The Man With The Scar pulled out of Johnny's grasp and reached for his nearly empty bottle. He poured out equal portions for himself and the old woman. But there wasn't enough, and so each glass was only half full.

"Oh, what the hell," Johnny said, reaching for his own bottle. He filled The Man With The Scar's glass, and then did the same to the other. "Here you go, Revered Mother."

The Ancient Woman took the glass in her clawed hand and drank greedily. For a moment her cracked and withered features seemed to ripple and dissolve, and The Man With The Scar thought he almost saw someone—or something—else, but then the vision faded and he was simply looking at the oldest person on the face of the earth. He took his first sip from his glass.

"Like nothing else, is it?" He smiled.

"Drink. Drink," the ancient woman encouraged, smiling enigmatically at him.

He did so and, water-eyed, shook his head. The drink was every bit as powerful as he remembered.

The ancient one had turned her attention to Johnny, "And did you have your many sons and daughters...?"

"Oh, yes," Johnny replied. "All the blessings of fatherhood."

By now Millie and Hector returned to the table, flushed and glowing from their time on the dance floor. Millie sat next to The Man With The Scar and whispered in his ear, "Your son is sooo nice. I'm sure I'm going to have his baby. M-maybe twins."

The Man With The Scar gave her an indulgent smile and patted her arm. "He could do a lot worse," he said, "Particularly now that you're trying to clean up your language."

"You noticed," she grinned.

The ancient woman was now looking at him. He unsteadily took the parchment wrapped in oilskin from the knapsack that had been resting on Toomley's lap.

"Did you bring the pen?" he asked her.

Her yellow eyes held firm on him. "Have you gotten what you wanted?" she asked.

"I never asked anything of you."

She shrugged as if he was stating a minor and irrelevant point. "Has your life given you what you had hoped?"

"So many adventures...unbelievable..."

"What do you want now, having lived such a life?"

"Give me the pen. You really got me on a trick, you know you did."

She shook her head sadly. "You already signed one time. You don't need the pen."

"I only signed as a witness. I think it makes a difference. I should be able to cross my name out."

She took the pen from a pouch on her lap and held it, just out of his reach.

"Is that what you really want?" she asked.

He reached for the pen, actually grasping it. It was just as heavy as he remembered. His hand had gone numb and the pen was almost impossible to hold with his thumb swollen over twice its normal size. He somehow got the cap off, but as he reached over to scratch out his name, his head fell to the table and he found himself staring sideways at the ancient woman.

"It's so lonely, you know," he said as the pen rolled from his limp fingers. "No one to tell my troubles to."

"You meet new people all the time."

"You're toying with me. You know what I mean."

The old woman said nothing further. Her face was blank and expressionless, as if she'd seen everything in the world and so his strange behavior didn't surprise her. For a moment he thought perhaps he saw a flicker of agreement, or at least cognition cross her face, an understanding of what he was saying. But he couldn't be sure, and he could do nothing as the precious writing instrument slowly rolled further and further from his outstretched fingers.

A hand rescued the pen and picked it up just before it fell off the end of the table. The hand belonged to Dusty, though whether Ice Man or Flame Boy was in control wasn't obvious at the moment. The Man With The Scar wasn't surprised. He'd seen Dusty burst in the front door clear across the room, followed by his two henchmen, a white guy in a porkpie hat and an old geek he figured was Millie's father.

"Oh, my, my, my," Dusty said. "I haven't seen one of these since my schoolteacher Sister Cedilia signed my 5th grade report card, way back at St. Mary's when I was just a little pickaninny at my mammy's knee."

Dusty placed his pistol next to the parchment and sat at the table. He turned the pen over and over in his hands as he spoke, "Look what I got here now; I got The Man With The Scar, I got the man with the golden touch, and I got Randy's old girlfriend, all together in one place. I'd say I just hit the jackpot."

"We hit the jackpot," the man wearing the porkpie hat said. "And I'm Jack, I ought to know."

"Some day you're going to interrupt once too often when I'm speaking, Jack."

Without hesitation, Dusty reached in the open FedEx package at his side and took out his pistol. Flame spat once from the silencer at the end of the barrel and Jack Macy slid to the floor with blood and clear fluids leaking from the collapsed place where his right eye had been.

"And I guess this was the day." Dusty cleared his throat and looked around the table. "Now, ladies and gents," he said, "we going to have ourselves a talk."

"Is that what you want?" the old woman said, "A talk?"

Dusty sighed, "Who let this old squeeze in here?"

"Humor her," The Man With The Scar said, talking from his sideways position on the table.

"And why should I do that?"

"You're the man with the gun and the pen. How could it hurt? And you might learn something you'll need later on."

"Ain't likely, scar-face."

"What do you want?" the ancient woman repeated.

Toomley ordered a round of beers from a short-skirted cowgirl. The Man With The Scar, without lifting his head from the table, insisted on a Manhattan and a candy bar. His drink came in a Margarita glass, and the candy bar turned out to be a pack of sugar-free Certs, useless under the circumstances. He munched the maraschino cherry, which gave him enough of a boost so he could raise his head and sip the drink. It helped a little, but he still felt dizzy and sick to his stomach. The room spun and twisted around him and he found himself on the table again with his head leaning against one arm.

Dusty placed his long-barreled pistol on the table and glared at The Man With The Scar.

"Now I've just got three questions," he said.

The Man With The Scar nodded calmly, waiting.

"Haven't we gone through this before?"

He even tried sitting up a little straighter, though he knew the train was on its course and much was now firmly in the hands of the gods.

"First, where's my money?" Dusty yelled. "Second, where's my dope? And third, why would an old fart like you mess with a badass mudder like me in the first place?"

"Okay. Let me see if I can get these numbers right," The Man With The Scar said. "The marked money that was in Randy's duffel bag is currently in a safe deposit box in Los Angeles. At least, 75% of it is. Most of Millie's 25% skim is in a bus depot locker somewhere in Arizona."

Millie shrugged and pouted, once again little-girl-lost, "A poor female child has gots to make her way somehow in a world of strife and danger."

Dusty looked like he wanted to hit her, but she was across the table.

"Approximately 15% of your dope," The Man With The Scar continued, "is in the hands of the Mexican border guards. *La Mordida*, you know? I dumped the remainder in the ocean, off a bluff near Oceanside."

"Way to go, Dad!" Hector said, giving him an approving thumbs-up sign.

"Why did you do that?" Dusty asked through clenched teeth.

"Actually, that's four questions," The Man With The Scar said, "but it's your gun...I did it because I don't like dope."

Dusty's face twisted in anger, "You-don't-like-dope."

He raised his gun and was surprised when the ancient woman calmly reached over and stuck her index finger in the barrel to get his attention.

"What do you want?" she asked him.

"I don't want interruptions!" Dusty shouted. "Bopo, drag this old bitch out of here."

"I wouldn't try that," The Man With The Scar said mildly.

"Bopo..." Dusty repeated, his voice rising sharply. Bopo stood and moved toward the ancient woman, but before he could touch her, a heavy wagon wheel chandelier fell on his head, knocking him to the ground.

"What do you want?" the Ancient Navajo Woman asked Dusty again, no sign of impatience in her voice.

"Cain't you do nothing right?" Dusty screamed at Bopo. He looked over at Leon and indicated the old woman with a jerk of his thumb. Leon rose to his feet, but as he moved toward her, a beer bottle sailed through the air and connected with the center of his forehead. Leon went down without a sound.

"What do you want?" she asked again.

Dusty beamed his most charming smile, trying to visualize just where he was going to shoot her.

"It's about time somebody asked me that, old woman. Here I been chasing these folks halfway around the world, it seems, and nobody ever asks what good old Dusty wants. Well, I'll tell you. I want everything this lucky man's got."

He pointed with the pen across the table at Toomley. "I hear he's the fellow with the Midas touch."

Dave Toomley nodded, the faint ray of hope showing in his eyes. "Yes, I am that man."

"Excepting, I want better luck with women than him," Dusty continued. "Man with the Midas luck ought to be able to do better for himself than this scrawny bitch, here."

Dusty aimed his pistol in Anna's direction, but she had the presence of mind to duck behind Toomley, and Dusty's shot flew off and punctured a Coors Light mirror hanging behind the bar.

"Then sign," the ancient woman replied, indicating the parchment.

"And what be this, bitch?"

The old woman's expressionless gaze took him in. "It is the deed to everything Mr. Toomley owns."

"Right. And he's just going to give it to me."

"In return for my life," Toomley said.

"Shit, you look like you should have died and gone to hell weeks ago. You want to stay alive?"

"No," Dave Toomley said, fixing him with a stare. "Sign it. It's a valid contract."

Dusty shrugged. "Alright, then. I'm going to take everything anyway, it might as well be legal." He scrawled his signature on the line indicated by the old woman. Then he raised his pistol and fired three times across the table directly into Toomley's chest.

He turned his pistol on The Man With The Scar, but the dying Toomley took the Borchardt from the knapsack on his lap. Seeing the familiar antique Luger-like weapon pointed at him, Dusty jumped back from the table, and the bullet intended for his chest caught him squarely in the groin.

Dusty screamed in pain, doubling over and clutching the dark red bloodstain spreading between his legs.

"Oh, God, no, no, no! I don't want to die!"

"Oh, you won't die," Toomley whispered.

"We won't let you die," a strangely egg-shaped man said. "I'm already sending for an ambulance."

Toomley smiled and raised one blood-soaked hand to point across the table at Dusty. "Yes, there's your new man," he said. Toomley could feel himself drifting away, like a dry leaf in a chill autumn wind.

"Well, I had my run here, old friend," he whispered to The Man With The Scar. His gaze moved to take in the old woman, who had retrieved her pen and parchment and was dispassionately watching him.

"*Thua ba, oi*," he whispered, "Is there anything more?"

"*Mot lan nua*," she replied. "One time more, you'll see..." Perhaps it was because he wanted to believe so badly, but he thought he detected a hint of compassion in her cracked and aged voice.

The Ancient Woman's quiet gaze left him and traveled around the table to settle on Hector.

"What do you want?" she asked.

"No!" The Man With The Scar shouted, "Not my son!"

The Ancient Woman gave The Man With The Scar a long stare. "You have just used up your second wish." She started to say more; then changed her mind. The moment of silent communion between them lengthened.

"Fine," she agreed finally. "Then...who did you bring?"

"No one. I wouldn't wish the things that come with your bargain on my worst enemy." He looked at Hector. "Not even your mother."

The old woman pulled an ancient golden timepiece from the folds of her dress. "My time is very short. I have other appointments to keep."

"Not my son," The Man With The Scar repeated.

The Ancient Woman nodded. She took Johnny Tuesday's bottle and shook it, measuring just less than half remained.

"He is out of it now. Because you shared with me...twice...you can have what remains of his."

Johnny, who had been taking in all the chaos and bloodletting in wide-eyed amazement, looked as if he didn't believe his good fortune. "I—I can go?!"

The old woman nodded, "I would go far...and fast."

Johnny jumped up from the table and started for the door.

"And leave your pickup truck in the parking lot," she called after him.

Johnny threw his keys on the crowded dance floor. "Free Dodge Ram pickup truck! Under 50,000 miles!"

In no time, a fight broke out over the keys. Johnny winked at The Man With The Scar, ran out the door and was gone.

"Well, I'd like a shot at it," Millie said, glorious as Elizabeth Taylor when she laid her earrings down in the White Diamonds commercial.

The ancient woman looked at The Man With The Scar.

"No, you wouldn't," he said. He nodded at Dusty, doubled over, still holding his genitals.

"That's the way it works," The Man With The Scar explained to Millie. "Women will lust for him, but he won't be able to do anything about it."

Millie looked at the widening patch of blood and urine staining Dusty's trousers.

"I-is that what happened to you?"

"No, I asked for something else."

"Well, I'd still like a shot at it—" Millie looked around for the old woman, but she was gone.

The game was over, at least for the moment. Three decades had gone by, and the old woman had come again, and he was still bound by his contract. He took Hector by one arm and Millie by the other. "Come on, you two. You've got real lives to live."

30

Nothing ever ends, you know. Read your Einstein and your Hawking if you doubt me even for a moment. But there are pauses, completions to be followed by continuations, periods after which at some point and in some place and some way it may be that one may find new sentences. And so it is that we are about to come to one of those.

The Man With The Scar sat in the Silver Café in Silver City, in a booth covered in maroon vinyl. He was sipping decaf coffee and eating a chocolate donut with chocolate chips sprinkled on top of a thick layer of chocolate frosting. He felt oddly alive, at least fifteen years younger than he had the day before. On inspecting himself in the mirror that morning, he'd found that most of the gray was missing from his hair.

"I tried to give her everything." Millie's father, who was seated across from him, was whining about his life with his daughter.

"I never knew my own son," The Man With The Scar replied. "I never even saw him for years and years. Just a phone call here and there. Still, he turned out okay."

"You're lucky. Millie was the most obstinate, willful, unresponsive child."

"Maybe you didn't understand her."

"She's sick. Crazy. I understand her alright."

"I don't know. I'm guessing she'll be able to take care of Hector. Just the kind of woman he needs. Keep him on his toes. Maybe we'll be grandparents soon."

Old Man Abernathy eyed The Man With The Scar with obvious dislike. "Oh, sure, that's just what I need."

"What do you mean?"

"Every time there's a new member added to the family, it dissipates my control of Abernathy Industries."

"That must be very hard on you."

"Hell, that company's been my entire life. You sure you don't know where they're headed?"

The Man With The Scar shrugged. "Honeymooners. Made me promise not to tell."

"Look, I'm a persistent man. I'll find out. I'm going to hang out on your heels until I *make* you tell."

"I've already warned you, that isn't a good idea."

"And I told you, I don't know what the hell you're talking about, buddy."

The Man With The Scar took a bite of his chocolate donut and sipped his coffee. It was good decaf, and he regretted that he wouldn't be able to finish the cup. From his position in the booth, he could see far down Main Street to where a point of dust was boiling in their direction. It had already roared through two distant red lights before he saw that it was a huge double-hitched gravel truck. He saw it had four more stoplights to go before it reached the café. He was guessing it would probably make it through all four without a hitch.

"Got to go," The Man With The Scar said. He tossed money on the table and was out of the booth and on his way before Abernathy could think of anything more to say.

Abernathy wasn't concerned. He knew the guy, who was little more than a wandering bum, wouldn't get far. He'd have the Silver City sheriff pick him up before he could get out of town. He checked and—*glory be*—the fellow had left way too much money to cover the few bucks they'd spent on coffee and rolls. The habits of a lifetime took over and Abernathy switched bills; he felt happy dropping the fiver—food and tip included—and pocketing The Man With The Scar's twenty.

He was a little surprised, though, at how fast Millie's new father-in-law had gotten up and made his exit. He didn't really *bolt from his seat* or anything like that; it was just that he had moved with a simple quickness, almost graceful like an animal, maybe like an old wolf or something. One moment they were discussing grandkids, and the next moment he was up and gone. He was going to have to stay sharp to make sure the old guy didn't slip away.

A few more seconds ticked off before Abernathy noticed the huge gravel truck bearing down on the café, but by that time it was way too late.

Rene Riniatta was studying the way the Kansas sun, ghosted behind the thickening clouds of an approaching cold front, glinted off her nails as she drove west at over a hundred miles an hour in her racing green Jaguar convertible. She'd been kicking back for a couple of weeks, healing the scrapes and bumps from being rolled around naked under that big boat in the waters near Aruba, when the boringly endless *islands thing* had started to get to her. The snow, she'd heard, was fantastic in Vail. So much snow that there was danger of slides. Something about that appealed to her, and she'd cut her easy ties and taken the first flight to Miami, and then on back to New York City to pick up the Jag. She'd decided she wanted to drive across. Driving helped her think, and she felt she had some heavy thinking to do about where everything was going in her life and what the hell was the meaning of it all, anyway.

She was glad she'd decided to motor it instead of just flying to Denver. The weather had been cold but decent. The roads past the Missouri were straight and clear, except for a few icy patches to keep it interesting. Patches of tan corn stubble interrupted the empty gray-brown fields, and it all flew by in such a mesmerizing blur that she almost didn't see the distant hitchhiker out of the corner of her eye. He was on the other side of the divided road, obviously heading east, the way she'd come. She was surprised she'd seen him at all.

She whipped along for another mile before it registered that she actually recognized him. She slowed and then bumped through the dry center grass in a skidding U-turn. She drove back slowly, craning her neck to make sure it actually was him while she passed by at a crawl. Once she was sure, she slowed down even more, and then pulled to a stop.

"I'll kill the son-of-a-bitch!" she muttered to herself.

The road was absolutely deserted in both directions. Her Jag rested in the outside lane, purring softly and waiting for her next command. She didn't bother to move onto the shoulder of the road. Rene was trying to make up her mind whether to put the car in reverse and run him over or wait and then shoot him once he got in. She didn't have to check; she knew the big 9 mm Browning was sliding around under her seat, within easy reach.

Before she could make up her mind, he opened the door, flung his knapsack in back and slid into the seat next to her. Now she was going to have to clean blood off the seats of the Jag and probably spray the floor, too.

"Hello," he said. "Rene, right? I had a feeling we might meet again."

He didn't seem surprised to see her, though she figured the odds on that had to be about a ka-billion to one.

"I am going to kill you, you know," she said.

"Sure," he replied easily, "but not here. Why get blood on the seats?"

Rene accelerated quickly, steering with her knee while adjusting the radio. There was nothing but twangy music. She slammed the dashboard in disgust and managed to grab the wheel just in time to correct her steering and swerve around a slow-moving tractor.

"I hate Country-Western," she fumed.

"Who doesn't?" he agreed. "May I?"

He reached for the radio tuner.

"I told you there's nothing but—" she snapped. But before she could finish her sentence, Mozart flooded the compartment.

"The 17th," he said. "One of my favorites."

Rene shot him an incredulous look. Her hand loosened on the automatic pistol and she let it slide to the floor next to the door.

"You like Mozart?"

"What civilized human being would not?"

She eyed him uncertainly. He leaned back against the seat with his hat pulled low over his eyes.

After a time, he spoke again.

"Can you tango?"

"The tango happens to be my favorite dance," she replied.

"I am a master of the tango," he said.

She eyed him again, not knowing what to say. They drove along in silence at somewhat over 120 miles an hour, Rene steering with the fingertips of one hand.

"Look," he said, "I know this is a little sudden, but I need somebody to go to a dance with me. How about you?"

"You'd have to be a *grand* master of the tango. How old are you, anyway?"

The Man With The Scar smiled at her, a quick, boyish smile, and she found she liked him, at least a little bit, for that smile if nothing else.

"Not as old as I was yesterday," he said. "Why does it matter? I am alive."

They drove on while glorious Mozart flooded the passenger compartment. If you were a demigod, hovering along invisibly, drifting along with the Jag in a bored sort of way, you would have heard them talking as they drove on.

"I can't believe you want me to go to a dance with you," Rene was saying.

"Why not?" The Man With The Scar replied. "You can always kill me later."

"Like, if you do a bad tango."

"Right," he agreed.

Rene was starting to be in a better mood. She didn't know it yet, but she was starting to feel happier than she had since she was a little girl. It was as if numbers had clicked together, combinations had formed, and a lock had clicked open on her feelings.

But then you, dear reader, traveling along with the eavesdropping semi-deity (who was simply traveling along for the ride, or the game, as it were), you, I repeat, would have noticed a shift in Rene's mood, from pure joy to the beginnings of uncertainty.

"What's that?" you would have overheard her say.

- And, "I promise you one thing, Rene," you would have heard The Man With The Scar respond, "You'll never, ever be bored."

"You don't know me very well. I've got a very low threshold of boredom." A momentary silence, and then she spoke again, "Do you hear something? Maybe a jet engine?"

And knowing what you do about the life and destiny of The Man With The Scar, at this point you wisely decide it is safer to ride along with the semi-deity. You smoothly pull up and away with the aloof creature, and as you go, you see far below the dark green Jaguar receding down the distant silvery band of the highway.

And one thing more; entering from off-camera left and moving left to right across your radio dial (as the sportscasters sometimes say), you see an airline cargo plane with one flaming wing. It is a huge plane that appears to be descending on a direct course that will make contact with the green sports car. The flagging jet aircraft with a big FEDEX painted on its tail is still a good distance away, perhaps 10 or 12 seconds. It appears that it may try to land on the highway.

And because you are with the demigod, you are actually able to hear Rene's voice over the sound of the airplane.

"Where is that noise coming from?" she asks, suddenly more alarmed. "My God, it's getting closer!"
And The Man With The Scar, trying to calm her and at the same time warn her a little bit about what her life has become, replies in a calm yet firm voice, "Look sharp now, love. I think we can get through...but this is where it starts to get interesting."

ABOUT THE AUTHOR

Like The Man With The Scar, the author traded away his ordinary life for one of adventure. He should have ended up with a mail route in Steger, Illinois or blown a faulty heart valve on the fiery hot beds at Inland Steel in Chicago Heights. But he traded that away for something more uncharted and uncertain. You can read the explanation (excuses) for the way he turned out in his family and biographical works: The Devildogs of Old Sauk Trail, and Tinsel Wilderness. Today he lives on the bad side of the San Andreas fault, and one can only speculate how that might turn out.
More about him, his books, his life, and his so-called adventures at www.johnklawitter.com

John Klawitter